W9-CZH-538

NO ONE BELIEVED A FATHER WOULD ABUSE HIS OWN DAUGHTER. NO ONE— EXCEPT HER MOTHER.

The nightmares would end for her precious four-year-old daughter, Stephanie. Allison Warren would see to that. She had tried once before—in the courts—but her twisted ex-husband's legal connections and standing in the tight-knit community had robbed her of justice.

Now she would seek that justice *outside* the law.

For Allison and her daughter were seeking sanctuary in a labyrinthine world of underground "safehouses," middle-of-the-night escapes, and constant terror in a cross-country flight for freedom—from the flawed system that would imprison her and from the ruthless man who would not stop until he had them both . . . For Stephanie, the bad dreams were fading; but for her mother, the nightmare was just beginning. . . .

SEE MOMMY RUN

Ⓞ SIGNET

PAGE-TURNERS!

(0451)

☐ **STRANGE FITS OF PASSION by Anita Shreve.** Mary chose the small Maine town because it was far away from New York City. And everyone in town knew right away that she was running.... "A finely written literary thriller."—*The New Yorker*
(403002—$5.99)

☐ **EDEN CLOSE by Anita Shreve.** This novel of love, terror and mystery weaves a tale of obsessive passions, and of the shadows cast over life by dark deeds. "Tantalizing!"—*New York Times Book Review*.
(167856—$4.99)

☐ **BAD DESIRE by Gary Devon.** "A *very* good psychological thriller!" —Mary Higgins Clark. "More than a superb novel of suspense ... a deep and compelling story of the truly dark sides of love, and ferocity of passion."—Gerald A. Browne.
(170989—$5.99)

☐ **WELL AND TRULY by Evelyn Wilde Mayerson.** Loss, redemption—and falling in love again ... "A fine novel that makes for compelling reading."—James Michener
(169883—$5.50)

Prices slightly higher in Canada

Buy them at your local bookstore or use this convenient coupon for ordering.

NEW AMERICAN LIBRARY
P.O. Box 999, Bergenfield, New Jersey 07621

Please send me the books I have checked above.
I am enclosing $_____ (please add $2.00 to cover postage and handling).
Send check or money order (no cash or C.O.D.'s) or charge by Mastercard or VISA (with a $15.00 minimum). Prices and numbers are subject to change without notice.

Card #_____ Exp. Date _____
Signature_____
Name_____
Address_____
City _____ State _____ Zip Code _____

For faster service when ordering by credit card call **1-800-253-8476**
Allow a minimum of 4-6 weeks for delivery. This offer is subject to change without notice.

SEE MOMMY RUN

Nancy Baker Jacobs

A SIGNET BOOK

SIGNET
Published by the Penguin Group
Penguin Books USA Inc., 375 Hudson Street,
New York, New York 10014, U.S.A.
Penguin Books Ltd, 27 Wrights Lane,
London W8 5TZ, England
Penguin Books Australia Ltd, Ringwood,
Victoria, Australia
Penguin Books Canada Ltd, 10 Alcorn Avenue,
Toronto, Ontario, Canada M4V 3B2
Penguin Books (N.Z.) Ltd, 182–190 Wairau Road,
Auckland 10, New Zealand

Penguin Books Ltd, Registered Offices:
Harmondsworth, Middlesex, England

First published by Signet,
an imprint of New American Library,
a division of Penguin Books USA Inc.

First Printing, May, 1992
10 9 8 7 6 5 4 3 2 1

To my son, Bradley Baker, with love.

1

Allison loaded the last of the suitcases into the Buick's trunk, shifting it into place beside the two larger bags. She pushed the trunk lid down firmly until she heard the latch catch, then wiped her damp brow with the back of her hand. Lord, it was hot, even at two in the morning. Or was it just that she'd worked up such a sweat doing the packing? She'd spent the hours since tucking Stephanie into bed hurriedly putting clothes into suitcases, filling boxes with canned and dry foods, picking and choosing among the material possessions of her life. Now the backseat of the car was piled high. The metal box with the legal documents rested on the floor behind the driver's seat, and the red and white picnic cooler that held the last of the milk and orange juice sat behind the passenger's seat.

In the kitchen, Allison thirstily gulped down a glass of water. For an instant, it helped cool her; then her stomach lurched dangerously. No, she told herself; she couldn't be sick again, she wouldn't. She'd spent half of the last week in the bathroom tending to her touchy digestive tract; between that and the heat, she'd dropped seven pounds. But now there was no time left for nerves. She took a deep breath and willed herself to calm down. Everything depended on her. She held her wrists under the stream of cold water, then splashed her reddened

7

face. A shower would be better, but she didn't dare risk the delay.

She quickly washed and dried the glass she'd used and put it back on the cupboard shelf with its mates. The house must be left clean and tidy. She'd make one last check before waking Stephanie. The red brick rambler was the only house Allison had ever owned and the first place where she hadn't had to worry about rent increases or eviction notices. She'd spent five years here, ever since she'd quit the airline and moved here to marry Karl Warren. In some ways, it seemed a lifetime; in others, it felt as though she'd arrived just yesterday.

Wistfully, Allison ran a finger over the built-in oak china cabinet in the dining room. It was dust free and its glowing finish was as smooth as the day she'd applied the final coat of varnish. This house seemed almost a part of her. She'd painted and papered its walls. She'd weeded its gardens and shoveled the snow from its driveway. Now she would miss it . . . but she couldn't start thinking about that. She would focus on how good it would feel to see the last of Wood Lake, Wisconsin, and its mistrust of outsiders. And, especially, how good it would feel to see the last of Karl . . .

Her thoughts darted back to the early days, when she'd come here as a new bride, full of hope for the future. She'd believed she was in love with Karl. Now she wasn't so sure. Truth was, she'd been staring her thirtieth birthday in the face, hearing her biological clock tick. Suddenly the pressures of her life, the constant travel, the forced smiles for the passengers, had begun to feel unbearably oppressive. And then Karl appeared on the scene—a few years older and a bit stodgy, perhaps, but solid, dependable, obviously a good breadwinner. He was a well-established insurance attorney who had investments in real estate. Maybe not too exciting, but definitely grade-A husband material. When Karl proposed, it had seemed right and Allison had been a happy bride. She'd left her so-called glamorous life behind, anxious to feel settled once and for all.

The first few months had been happy enough. Allison had spent them fixing up the house, planning intimate parties for Karl's friends, trying to find her place in the town. She became pregnant quickly and three months of severe morning sickness kept her housebound. Karl was not sympathetic. Instead of being solicitous, he became more and more critical of Allison's ailments. Hurt and disillusioned, Allison retreated emotionally. Little by little, their marriage began to deteriorate into little more than mutual tolerance.

With Stephanie's birth, the chill between Allison and Karl increased. Finally, Allison filed for divorce. Karl strongly resisted the split, more because he didn't want the neighbors to brand him a failure, Allison felt, than because of any love he felt for her. Still, despite their bitter battles over the divorce, she never had had occasion to fear her husband. Karl was a big man, a powerful man, given to occasional childish temper tantrums, but she'd never been afraid of him . . . until now.

Allison circled back to the kitchen, where her eye fell on the wastebasket. It wouldn't do to leave garbage behind in this heat, yet setting the trash can at the curb three days early would draw attention. She filled a black plastic trash bag, carried it to the garage, and wedged it into the Buick.

What was she forgetting? For the dozenth time, Allison counted the money in her purse—three hundred twelve dollars and forty-seven cents in cash. She had her checkbook and, most important of all, the toll-free telephone number. Not that she really needed it written down; the number was branded in her memory. She mentally checked off the remainder of her preparations list. The car was in good shape, the gas tank full, and the new road atlas on the front seat. The family photographs and her grandmother's few pieces of jewelry were in the big suitcase. Everything else—the furniture, books, dishes and kitchen equipment, most of their clothes—would have to stay behind, but that couldn't be helped. Someday, she promised herself as she looked around with moist eyes, she would replace all this.

In the front bedroom, four-year-old Stephanie lay curled up in the center of her bed, her small fingers gripping the tattered ear of her beloved stuffed rabbit, Flopsy. Her right thumb was planted firmly in her mouth. The thumbsucking habit would mean orthodontia someday, but Allison didn't have the heart for Karl's harsh remedies; there were far worse things for a child than having an overbite.

Allison gazed a moment at her sleeping child, her coal-black eyelashes on ivory cheeks, her coils of chestnut-brown hair against the pale yellow pillowcase. Stephanie had inherited features of striking contrast—Karl's dark hair and her mother's fair skin and blue eyes. Allison reached out and gently brushed a lock of hair from the child's forehead; it was lighter than air, softer than down on a baby duck. Any mother who wouldn't fight to protect such perfection, such innocence, didn't deserve a child.

It seemed almost cruel to wake her; she had so few peaceful nights, free of terrifying dreams. But it had to be done. Tentatively, Allison shook one small shoulder. "Steph. Stephanie, honey. Wake up."

Stephanie moaned slightly, then jolted awake, her eyes wide but uncomprehending. "Mommy! Mommy!"

"Mommy's right here, sweetie. It's okay." Allison stroked the little girl's head and folded her into her protective arms. "Everything's all right. You only have to wake up for a few minutes."

Stephanie rubbed her eyes with one fist. "Is it morning?"

"Not yet, angel. It's still night, but we're going for a ride. You can go back to sleep when we get in the car." Allison lifted the child to her feet. "Use the potty and then we'll go."

"Where, Mommy?"

"First to visit Auntie Ruth on the farm. Then we'll see."

Stephanie tightened her grip on Flopsy. "Where's Daddy?"

"Daddy's not coming."

"I don't hafta go to his house in the morning?"

"No, sweets."

Stephanie dropped the rabbit. "Okay." She slid off the bed and padded toward the bathroom. Allison quickly pulled the yellow quilted spread over the bed, smoothed it, and picked up the ragged stuffed animal with its ridiculous gingham dress. When the bunny was new, it had worn a straw hat with holes cut out for its ears as well, but that had long ago disappeared. Now one of the ears hung loose, nearly severed from the worn gray head. Allison added a small pink robe and matching slippers from the closet to her armload.

The phone's ring shattered the silence. Allison's breath caught. Damn. She made a dash for her bedroom across the hall and reached for the bedside phone. "Hello."

"Allison," a low voice answered. "Sorry to wake you."

"Who is this?"

"Marlys, across the backyard. Got up to use the bathroom and saw a light in your garage. Somebody was movin' around out there a few minutes ago. Want me to call the police?"

The neighborhood busybody. Allison took a breath and forced frustration from her voice. "Thanks, Marlys, but nothing's wrong. I couldn't sleep, so I've been cleaning out the garage."

"At this hour?"

"Mommy." Stephanie crawled up on the bed.

Allison silenced the child with a finger placed over her lips. "There's nothing to worry about," she said into the phone. "Just go back to bed."

"Can't expect neighbors not to be concerned. Ain't safe for a woman livin' alone these—"

"Marlys, *please*. I'm fine. Go back to bed before you wake up Joe."

"I was just tryin' to help—"

"Good-night, Marlys." Shakily, Allison replaced the receiver and stared at her curtained back windows. Damn! Marlys Crowley's snooping was exactly what she didn't need, tonight of all nights. Would the nosy old bitch really go back to bed or would she sit up, watching the house to catch Allison's next move, hungry for gossip to trade on the open market of the town's social scene? She'd have to take that chance; tomorrow would be too late.

"Mommy."

"Come on, angel." Allison took the child's hand. "Put your robe on over your J's and we'll go."

She strapped Stephanie into her carseat, shut off the garage light, and climbed into the driver's seat. Backing the car slowly into the street, she hit the remote control that closed the garage door.

They were two blocks from the house before she switched on the Buick's headlights.

The eastern sky was growing light as Allison reached the dirt road leading to her sister's Central Wisconsin farm. Stephanie had slept for most of the trip. Only once did she wake herself, shrieking,

"Snakes! Mommy, Mommy, help! Owie. Don't hurt me. Snakes!"

Allison had pulled the car off the road to hold and comfort the child until she calmed down. "Mommy's here, punkin. It's just a dream. Mommy wouldn't let any bad old snakes get her baby. There, there, sweetheart . . ."

Eventually, Stephanie had dozed off again. Now, as the Buick bounced along the rutted road toward the Perskys' house, she awoke quietly. "We there yet, Mommy?"

"Almost. This is the road to Aunt Ruth and Uncle Vern's farm. It's just a few more minutes."

"I gotta go potty."

"Me, too."

The fields on either side of the road were parched, the crops stunted. Although it was mid-August, Allison saw that the corn was no taller than normal for early July, a result of the drought that had Ruth and Vern near desperation. No wonder they were worried about defaulting on their farm loan.

Allison steered the Buick into the side yard near the kitchen door and turned off the engine. A brown and black mongrel dog, yelping his welcome, trotted toward the car. Allison opened the door. "Hi there, Heinz. How ya doin', boy?" The dog leaped at her legs as she tried to climb out. "Down, boy." She scratched the mutt's ears, then firmly pushed him out of the way.

The kitchen door opened. "Allie!" A middle-aged, sunburned woman tying a faded green chenille bathrobe around her body stood in the doorway. "What're you doing here?"

"Oh, Ruthie," Allison said, holding back a sob. "Ruthie, we've run away."

2

The Perskys' kitchen smelled of coffee, bacon grease, and barnyard odors that drifted in through the open window. After breakfast, Stephanie's cousin Lucy had taken her to see the baby pigs. Vern and the three boys had embarked on their morning chores. Sitting at one end of the large pine table, the sisters had the house to themselves. Allison's face was streaked but her eyes were dry.

Ruth leaned forward, her elbows against the worn red and white checked oilcloth table cover. "Finally. I never thought they'd leave so we could talk in private." Her pale lips twitched. "Start at the beginning, Allie. I want all the details."

Allison took a long sip from her chipped blue china cup and swallowed. The coffee was hot, but stronger than she liked it; the little breakfast she'd eaten was churning in her stomach. "I lost in court, Ruth. The judge wouldn't listen to a damn thing I said and he wouldn't even let Stephanie talk."

"But why?"

"You tell me. What he *said* was that Stephie's too young to testify, that she wouldn't be a reliable witness, and that I'm a troublemaker who's trying to use her daughter to trash her ex-husband."

Ruth's jaw dropped. "What gives him the right to say a thing like that?"

"He's the judge . . . got a license to play God in that court. Truth is, Ruthie, I think I lost because

14

Judge Winston doesn't want to believe one of Wood Lake's good ol' boys could really be molesting his own little girl. So he tells himself I must've invented the whole story, either because I'm a vindictive bitch or because I'm crazy."

"But what about those expert witnesses you told me about?"

"My lawyer said the pediatrician's examination wasn't conclusive enough, that we couldn't use her testimony. All that really means is that Stephanie hasn't suffered any permanent physical damage . . . yet. It was the child psychologist's testimony I really thought would make a difference."

"And?"

Allison rested her throbbing head in her hands and sighed. "That son-of-a-bitch judge wouldn't even listen to her. Said psychology isn't an exact science or some bullshit like that."

"So how come shrinks testify in so many trials?"

"Shit, Ruth, the whole damn thing was a setup, had to be. I didn't even get a real trial. It was just a closed hearing, in the judge's chambers, with Karl sitting there the whole time, this self-satisfied look on his face. Does the judge talk to Stephanie, ask her what that son of a bitch has been doing to her for God knows how long? Hell, no! The kid's only four years old, he says. Everybody knows little kids make things up. Well, they sure as hell don't make up *this* kind of thing!" Allison slammed her fist down on the table; her cup bounced in its saucer and tipped. A stream of dark liquid snaked toward the floor. "Damn!" She grabbed the cup and righted it.

"Don't worry about it." Ruth grabbed a dingy dishrag from the sink full of dishes, squeezed the dishwater from it, and wiped up the spill.

"I'm sorry, Ruthie. It's just that I get so upset." Allison's fists were clenched, her nails biting into her palms. "I can't eat and I can't sleep and I swear too much." She closed her eyes and sighed. "How can they do this to a little kid? I just don't understand how people like that asshole of a judge can sleep at night."

"If a person doesn't want to see something, Allie, he finds a way not to see it." She tossed the cloth into the sink; it landed with a splash. "Anybody understands that kind of thinkin', you and I oughta."

"But I just don't see how the bastard could completely ignore everything Dr. Gunderson had to say," Allison said bitterly. Dr. Elizabeth Gunderson was a recognized expert in child psychology. She held a Ph.D. in psychology from the University of Minnesota and taught courses at the University's Duluth campus. Specially trained to work with sexually abused children, she had a private practice in Duluth. Still, her background and experience had not impressed the court.

Allison pushed a toast crumb back and forth across the tablecloth, following the checkered pattern. "Instead of letting her talk about all those therapy sessions she had with Stephie, or about the night terrors the poor kid has, Judge Winston just gives Dr. Gunderson a hard time about how can she *prove* a four-year-old's telling the truth. Then he lets Karl's lawyer rip into her on the same subject. Jesus, Ruth, they made it sound like Dr. Gunderson and I took turns putting these ideas into Stephie's mind, like we brainwashed her."

"What about your lawyer? Didn't he object to all this?"

"Sure, sort of. But every time he opened his mouth, the judge overruled him. He finally just gave up."

"Sounds like they ganged up on you."

"No lie."

"So now what?"

"The new court order says Karl gets to keep his

visitation rights; he gets Stephie every weekend. If I try to interfere, the judge'll charge me with contempt, throw me in jail, and give Karl permanent custody of Stephie."

"He wouldn't actually do that."

"The hell he wouldn't. Ruthie, these guys play hardball. I made a big mistake when I took on one of them—a lawyer, a hometown boy. I see that now. They're out to teach me a lesson, even if it destroys Stephanie."

"It's just so hard to believe they'd do that, Allie."

"Well, believe it. Hell, I'm not even sure my own lawyer was really on my side. Maybe I'm paranoid, but he's part of their club, too. How hard is he gonna try to prove that some other attorney—a guy he's gotta work with—is a child molester?" Allison pushed back her chair, rose, and poured more coffee for herself and her sister. "I'm so tired I'm running on adrenaline and caffeine. No wonder my stomach hurts all the time."

Ruth stirred sugar and milk into her coffee. "Allie," she said slowly, "let me make sure I understand this. Are you tellin' me the cops're after you?"

"Not yet, but they will be, soon as Karl figures out we're gone."

Ruth shook her head. "I don't know, Sis. Maybe you should go back to Wood Lake before you get yourself in worse trouble."

Allison's head jerked around and her eyes met Ruth's. "Go back? Go back and let that man force my daughter to do those filthy things?"

"Maybe he won't even try to see Stephie anymore, Allie. After all, Karl hardly came near the kid for the first couple of years after the divorce. And he hardly paid any attention to her at all when she was born. I still remember how you used to complain about what a lousy father he was."

"Rub it in, why don't you?"

"Hey, don't be so touchy. All I'm tryin' to say is maybe what Karl wants now is just to beat you in court, you know, save face in his hometown. If he wins, maybe he'll back off again and leave Stephie alone."

"Yeah? Well, listen to this. Last week, I told Mr. father-of-the-year that he'd see Stephanie over my dead body. So, when he came to pick her up for the weekend, I said no, she couldn't go with him. Guess what he did."

"What?"

"Showed up an hour later with Sergeant Buck Linn, from the Wood Lake police. They're old buddies." Buck and Karl had played high school football together; they still played poker Tuesday nights. "So there they are at the front door, the two of 'em. Buck's got the court order and he starts explaining to me, real patronizing, like I'm too dumb to understand, that the law says Karl gets Stephanie on Saturdays and Sundays. He tells me if I don't turn her over, he'll arrest me and Karl'll take Stephanie anyway." Allison shooed a fly buzzing near her coffee cup. "So the question, the way he puts it, is, do I want to spend the weekend in jail or do I want to stay home? Either way, Stephie goes with Karl."

"Where's Stephie while this is goin' on?"

Allison swallowed. "She's hangin' onto my legs, Ruth. She's screaming, 'Don't make me go, Mommy! Don't make me go!' "

"My God!"

Allison pulled a tissue from the pocket of her jeans and blew her nose. "Karl starts pullin' Stephie off me and, when I try to push him away, Buck grabs my arms and holds me. They took my little girl, Ruthie." Allison had been sick to her stomach all weekend, terrorized by thoughts of what her daughter might be suffering and guilt ridden by her inability to protect her. "The only way I managed to make it 'til Sunday night was by telling myself over and over that the court hearing was this week. I was so *sure* the judge would listen to the evidence and that Karl would never, ever be allowed near Stephie again."

"But you can appeal. There must be a way to get some other judge to listen, one who doesn't start out on Karl's side."

"Maybe . . . eventually. But I talked to Dr. Gunderson after the hearing. She says she's seen this sorta thing happen a dozen times. The fathers have the money and the power and people don't want to believe these things happen to little kids. So the mothers and the children end up the losers."

"Still, it's hard to believe . . ."

"You're forgetting, Ruth, I'm the outsider there. Karl grew up in that town. People remember him playing high school ball, for God's sake. Plus he's a lawyer, he knows those courts inside out. Me . . . I'm just a crazy lady accusing one of the local boys of unspeakable acts. Ha! I might as well have accused the governor or the local priest of molesting my daughter. People in Wood Lake would just as likely believe that." A tear slowly slid down Allison's cheek. She wiped at it angrily, then wadded her tissue into a ball.

"Maybe I could appeal, Ruth. Maybe I'd even win someday. But in the meantime, Karl'd get Stephie every weekend, doin' God knows what to her. If I did anything to stop him, I'd end up in jail. He's the child molester and *I'm* the one who goes to jail!" Allison's jaw was rigid. "It's never gonna happen again, not to my daughter. I swear I'll kill the bastard before I ever let him near her again."

3

It was noon and Karl Warren was precisely on time, but his ex-wife wasn't answering the doorbell. For the third time, he jabbed a manicured finger against the button and heard the chimes ringing inside. Still there was no response. He swore under his breath. If Allison thought she could keep him away from his daughter by not answering the door, she had a surprise coming.

He stepped off the porch into the bright sunlight and surveyed the front of the house. The windows in the living room and Stephanie's bedroom were closed and draped. The house didn't have air conditioning; it had to be over ninety in there. As he walked around the side of the house, Karl pulled a monogrammed handkerchief from the pocket of his pearl-gray linen slacks and wiped his brow. The dry grass crackled beneath his leather-soled shoes. Allison wasn't keeping the lawn adequately watered in this heat wave. He'd have to speak to her about it. The bed of zinnias at the rear of the house looked just as dry. And, here, too, all the windows were tightly closed.

"Karl! Yoo-hoo, Karl!"

Karl turned and saw a short woman with pink curlers in her dyed black hair calling to him across the back fence, a bare, flabby arm waving in his direction. Fuck. Nosy Crowley. " 'Lo, Marlys." He tried to keep his voice civil.

"If you're lookin' for Allie, don't think she's home."

"Looks that way."

"Your day to take Stephanie?"

Marlys Crowley probably knew his visitation schedule as well as he did. Maybe he should just tell her it was none of her bloody business why he was here, tell her to fuck off. He'd always wanted to. Instead, he asked, "Know where they went?"

She put down the garden hose she'd been using on her rosebushes, opened the gate between the properties, and crossed the yard. "Actually," she told him, a conspiratorial look on her face, "I haven't seen Allison this morning. Stephie, either. But . . ." She paused for effect.

Karl raised an eyebrow.

"Last night, Allison was cleanin' out the garage . . . at two in the mornin'. Leastways, that's what she *said* she was doin'."

"You actually talked with her at that hour?"

Marlys considered whether Karl's question was meant to be critical. Something about this big man in his dandyish clothes always made her feel a little defensive. "Saw lights on and thought there might be an intruder. Neighbors gotta look out for each other these days. Ya never know, with serial murderers runnin' loose all over the country, rapists, burglars."

Karl nodded. What the hell had Allison been doing, and where was she now?

Marlys continued her tale. "So I called and asked her, should I get the police. Between you 'n' me, she got a tiny bit snippy with me." She wagged a finger in Karl's direction. "Now, if it was me livin' alone like that, no man to protect me, I'd be downright grateful I had a neighbor keepin' an eye out. 'Specially with a little girl in the house."

"I'm sure Allison didn't mean to offend you, Marlys." If only the woman would get to the point.

Marlys shrugged. A caring person like she was could afford to be gracious. "Could be poor Allie's just havin' a hard time lately. Hear you two been back in court." Her round face was eager for details.

"That was nothing but an unfortunate mistake," Karl snapped. "It's been resolved."

She edged closer. "Hear Allison's been tryin' to keep you away from your little girl. Did she really accuse you of bein' some sorta child abuser?"

Karl wrinkled his nose. Body odor on women nauseated him and, at this proximity, Marlys smelled; the heat was no excuse. Suddenly this intrusive mountain of lard was suffocating him. He stepped back abruptly. Marlys Crowley probably knew every detail of the accusations Allison had made against him; she'd probably gossiped to anybody who'd listen. Now, instead of telling him where Allison and Stephanie were, she'd managed to manipulate him into giving her his side of the court fiasco. He'd like to rip that vicious tongue right out of her. Instead he wiped his face with the handkerchief and swallowed the bile that rose in his throat. "My wi—er, Allison—hasn't been herself lately, Marlys. She—she's gotten sort of, well . . . I hate to say it, but Allison's been acting a bit unbalanced. Mentally, I mean. Imagining all sorts of things about innocent people. Unbelievable things. I just hope, now this court thing's out of the way, she'll get psychiatric help."

"You don't say."

"She's not a well woman. I—I've been worried for some time about her mental stability, but you know how hard it is to have any real influence when you're no longer married to a person."

"Well, not firsthand. Joe and I been married thirty-two years now." She paused for congratulations; they were not forthcoming. "But I can imagine. Must be hard not havin' your little girl with you—"

Karl had no patience for this. "So," he said. "You don't know where Allison took my daughter and you don't know when they'll be back."

Marlys shook her head; her curlers bounced.

"If you see them, tell them I'll be back." He turned abruptly and hurried back to the front of the house.

Marlys Crowley stared after him, convinced the entire Warren family was strange.

At the front door, Karl pulled a ring of keys from his pocket and used one on the single lock. He quickly slipped inside and pulled the door shut behind him. Despite the noontime sun outside, the closed-up house was nearly dark. Although the temperature inside was stifling, Karl shuddered with growing apprehension as he wandered from room to room. The house was far too neat. Allison had never been the sort of housekeeper who kept things clean and in their proper places; that was one of the things they'd fought about. There were always Stephanie's toys strewn on the floor, furniture sloppily dusted, magazines left open on the coffee table. But now the house was immaculate.

He opened the pine toy chest in Stephanie's room. Inside were three or four dolls, a set of building blocks, a plastic guitar with a broken string, a pair of strap-on roller skates. The miniature cooking set he'd given her for her fourth birthday sat on top of the white chest of drawers, still in the factory carton. Some of Stephanie's clothes were folded in the drawers, but Karl was certain she owned more than these. Were they in the laundry? He picked up a pair of pink panties trimmed with lace, held them a moment, then dropped them back into the drawer.

He moved on to the room he and Allison had

shared. She'd changed the bedspread. The tailored beige quilt he favored was gone; in its place was a hideous flowered affair—purple irises on a pale yellow background. The woman never had had taste, didn't even know how to dress. Funny how he hadn't noticed when they first met. Of course, she'd been wearing her stewardess uniform then.

Some of Allison's drawers held sweaters, scarves, socks, but Karl found the one where she always kept her underwear completely empty. Half the hangers in the closet were unused, too. When they lived together, Karl had to keep his clothes in the guest room closet because Allison kept this one overflowing, particularly after she became pregnant. She had clothes in three or four different sizes to accommodate her expanding figure. Then, after Stephanie was born, she'd bought even more outfits, in a larger size, that were supposed to be slimming. She'd never really regained her girlish figure, another point of friction between them.

The kitchen bore the final evidence. Karl opened the refrigerator door. It was turned off and the only thing inside was an open box of baking soda. Allison and Stephanie were gone, and not for the weekend. It was obvious his ex-wife had taken his daughter and cleared out. The question now was where. Where would Allison go, knowing he would hunt them down? Knowing when she was caught, that she would go to jail and lose Stephanie to him forever?

4

Allison lay upstairs on her sister's bed, eyes closed, listening to the sounds of children bickering outside the bedroom window.

"Get off that, Dennis!"

"Gonna make me, fart face?"

"Yeah, I'm gonna make ya, ya stupid jerk."

A childish shriek pierced the air, accented by Heinz's sharp barks. "Mom! Mom! Tony's hitting me."

"He's stealin' my bike."

"Stop it, both o' you. This instant. Your Aunt Allie's tryin' to sleep."

Fat chance, Allison thought.

"Ouch! He did it again, Mom."

"Shut up or you're both gettin' a lickin'. That means you, too, Anthony. Twelve ain't too old to get your hide tanned."

"Me! He started it. All I was doin'—"

"Well, I'm ending it. Now!"

Allison heard the phone ringing, followed by the kitchen door banging shut. The boys' voices grew faint as they moved their squabble away from the house. She rolled onto her back and covered her eyes with an arm, shutting out the midday brightness. Every bone in her body ached, yet she was so hot and tense she couldn't seem to fall asleep.

There was a soft knock on the bedroom door. "Allie. Allie, you awake?" Ruth, her hand shaking slightly, turned the doorknob, opened the door, and peered inside.

"What is it?" Allison uncovered her eyes and squinted against the light.

Ruth entered, closing the door behind her. "That was Karl."

Allison bolted upright. "What was Karl?"

"On the phone. Lookin' for you and Stephie."

"Jesus. He didn't waste any time. What'd you tell him?"

"Said I hadn't heard from you ... but I don't think he believed me. Said I should tell you to get his daughter back home right now or he'd send the cops after you. Said Vern and I can go to jail for hidin' you."

"He's just trying to intimidate you, Ruth."

Ruth sat down on the corner of the bed, her fingers nervously pleating the hem of her loose plaid overblouse. "But what if they catch you? If you went back now—"

"No! I told you, Ruth, I'm not going back and neither is Stephanie. Not ever." She swung her legs over the side of the sagging bed, stood up, and pulled on her denim skirt. "We'd better get out of here. You said your bank was open 'til three, right?"

"Yeah ... but you know we haven't got two dimes to rub together, Allie. We can't ...."

Allison sighed. "I'm not asking you for money, Ruth. I already explained that. All I need is for you to help me cash my check and get the quitclaim deed notarized so you can take care of selling the house. You must understand why I couldn't do that in Wood Lake—it would've attracted too much attention."

"How much cash did you say?"

"Fifteen hundred. It's pretty much all I've got left in my account. I only hope I can make it last 'til the money from the house comes in."

"I—I don't understand why you're so strapped, Allie. I thought you were . . . well off, even rich."

"Me?" Allison's eyebrows rose. "Karl's the one who's rich, Ruth. Relatively speaking, anyway. I'm nothing but an ex-wife who works part-time in a bookstore. Or did, 'til yesterday."

"But what about alimony? You were married to a wealthy man."

"I never asked for alimony, Ruth. I told you that when I got the divorce." Allison had been too proud, too determined to make it on her own, with as few ties to Karl as possible. Settling for title to the house had seemed so much cleaner than monthly alimony checks. Now she felt like a fool for not demanding both. If she had, maybe she'd have some savings now.

"You must've had child support."

"Yeah, but it never covered anything extra, and it's gone now. Look, Sis, all I've really got is the equity in that house. It's worth maybe thirty thousand. If you can sell the place for me, it'll be enough to give us a start somewhere new." Allison pulled on a red cotton knit tank top and tucked it into the waistband of her skirt.

"This check you want me to cash . . ."

"What about it?"

"What if it bounces, Allie? The bank'll take it out of our account and we can't af—"

"For God's sake, Ruth, the check isn't going to bounce. I know how much is in that account, to the penny." Allison flopped back onto the bed and pulled sandals onto her bare feet.

"But what if Karl can put some kinda hold on your money? For goin' off with his kid or somethin'. You can't be sure what might happen."

Allison stared at her sister. "Am I hearing you say you're not going to help us?"

Ruth chewed her lip and averted her eyes. "You've

never been poor, Allison. You don't know what it's like not to—"

"The hell I—"

"No! You don't *really* know." Ruth stood up, her eyes narrow, the creases radiating from them deepening. "You don't know the first thing about scraping by. You always had everything you wanted." Her words tumbled out. "You were the pretty one, the one Daddy sent to college. You had that fancy career, travelin' all over the world. All the nice clothes you wanted. Married yourself a rich lawyer—"

Suddenly Allison saw Ruth with new eyes and she was stunned. "You're jealous. You're actually jealous of me, Ruth."

Ruth reddened and stared at her thick, workworn hands. "I—it's just I don't understand why you're comin' to *us*, Allie. We're barely hangin' on. Vern's family bought this place in 1910, farmed it ever since. Now the bank's threatenin' to take it away from us, everything we've got, everything we've worked for. Vern and me—we've just about had it. I don't see how you figure we can help you."

"I'm not asking Vern for a damn thing, Ruth. I'm asking *you*—my big sister, the only one I've got. Who else can I turn to?"

Ruth's jaw hardened. "What about Daddy? He always gave you everything you wanted. Why not ask him to get you the money?"

"Is that what this is about, Ruth? Some stupid childhood grudge, some harebrained idea that Dad loved me more than you? Well, you sure picked a great time to hit me with it." Allison pulled a hairbrush from her handbag and began stroking her hair furiously. "You know as well as I do, all Dad ever cared about was the United States Navy and his bottle of gin, not necessarily in that order."

"Not always."

"Long as I can remember."

"He—he always loved the Navy. But the drinking didn't get bad 'til after Mama died."

"You were fifteen then, Ruth. I was only three. I can hardly even remember Mom . . . or what things were like when she was alive." Allison pulled her hair back into a ponytail at the nape of her neck and fastened it with a tortoiseshell barrette.

"Mama looked a lot like you. She was thin, had the same shade of blue eyes, light hair. Maybe that's why Daddy—"

"Daddy what, Ruth? Favored me over you? Loved me more? That's a crock and you know it." Allison's dominant childhood memories were of an absent father who dumped her on her reluctant grandmother until the old woman died. Then a series of underpaid housekeepers had been hired to care for Tim Mitchell's younger daughter. Ruth, on the other hand, had been sent to boarding school when their mother died, a place Allison had envisioned as a cross between summer camp and Disneyland.

Ruth's eyes narrowed. "You were the one he sent to live with Gram."

"Sure, I got a sick old lady who didn't want me and you got fresh country air and horses. I feel real sorry for you, Ruth. It's all I can do to keep from bawling."

"What the hell do you know about it? That school was like being in prison. It was nothing but a warehouse for girls nobody wanted. And, soon as I graduated, I got thrown out on my own."

"I really do not believe this." Allison threw the hairbrush back into her purse; it landed with a thud. "Here I am, leaving everything I've got behind so maybe, just *maybe* my four-year-old daughter can live a normal life someday. A life where her own father doesn't abuse her. And you're telling me how rough *you* had it when you were a kid."

Ruth kicked at the rag rug beneath her feet. "Why

the hell not? Your problems aren't the center of everybody's world, you know."

"Ruth, you're talking about something that happened thirty years ago!"

"But it wasn't fair. My whole damn life hasn't been fair."

"Nobody's life is fair, Sis. Haven't you learned that yet?"

"You never get over being sent away from your family, Allie, no matter how long ago it was."

Allison sighed. "Gram was old and sick, Ruth. You knew she couldn't take both of us."

"But you were the one Dad picked."

Allison felt her eyes fill, partly from frustration with her sister and partly from the memory of the frightened, lost little girl she herself had been. "You're talkin' like I had a soft life, Ruth. I don't get it. You must've forgotten what Dad was really like." She wiped away a tear. "Whenever he came home on shore leave, I was scared stiff. Was he going to be drunk? Was he going to be hung over? Was I going to get a kiss or a slap across the face? I never knew. If that was caring, if that was love, you sure could've fooled me."

Ruth was silent for a moment. The angry lines around her mouth began to soften. "I—I didn't know, Allie. I thought it was just me Daddy treated that way. I thought he blamed me that Mom died. I used to lie in bed at night at that awful school, thinkin' you and he were—" Ruth choked on the years of bitterness she'd stored up.

"Anybody should be jealous, Ruth, it's me. You're the one who got the good years, even if they didn't last." Allison smoothed the bed cover where she'd lain, as if to erase her presence from the room. "But it's all in the past. It just doesn't matter anymore. All that matters to me now is Stephanie."

Ruth walked to the window and looked across the

parched fields. Her shoulders sagged and her shirt was dark along her spine. "I'm sorry, Allie." She sighed. "I really am. I don't mean to be a selfish old bitch. It's just that sometimes I get to feelin' so overwhelmed." She ran her fingers through her short sweat-dampened hair, pushing it off her forehead. "How the hell'd I end up here, anyway? I was so miserable back then, so alone. I married Vern to get away from all that, thought that'd be the end of my troubles. Truth is, I'm still miserable and alone." She shook her head. "Now I see my own daughter startin' out the same way and sometimes it's more than I can take."

"You can't tell what'll happen to Lucy. She's still young and—"

"I—I always hoped Lucy'd be like you, Allie— pretty, educated, married to somebody'd take good care of her."

"Ha! Some role model I turned out to be." As Ruth turned away from the window, Allison noticed that her eyes were wet. For the first time, she realized how much her sister had aged. It was more than the streaks of gray in her brown hair and the lines in her face; Ruth's spirit had grown old. At forty-six, she was beaten and scared. Allison might be in trouble, but she was a long way from finished. Despite her own fears, she felt a sudden surge of pity for her sister. "I'll get Stephie and we'll get out of your way," she said.

Ruth pulled a tissue from the box on the night table and blew her nose loudly. "Just get your things together, Allie," she said, heading for the door. "You can follow me to the bank."

Allison reached out her arms to hug her sister. But Ruth had already left the room.

5

Allison stopped at a public phone an hour's drive west of Ruth's bank, at the back of a Dairy Queen parking lot. She settled Stephanie, holding a melting chocolate-dipped cone in one hand and four crumpled paper napkins in the other, into her carseat. The car door open for ventilation in the late-afternoon heat, Allison dialed the number of her father's house outside San Diego, then deposited the specified number of coins to cover the long-distance toll.

He answered on the fourth ring. " 'Lo."

"Hi, Dad. It's Allie."

" 'Lo. Allishun, that you?" His voice was vague, distant.

"Yeah, it's me, Dad, Allison. Look, I've got something to tell you."

"I . . . I got some . . . something tell you, Al . . . Allishun."

Allison closed her eyes and started over, speaking slowly. "It's important, Dad. Please listen to me. Something bad's happened."

There was a pause. Over the line, Allison heard what sounded like the tinkle of ice cubes in a glass.

"Dad. Are you listening?"

"Whosis?"

"It's Allison, Dad. Your daughter, Allison. I'm in trouble and I need your help."

"Bad news, Allie. Got bad news."

32

"God damn it. What the hell happened to your promise, Dad? You said you were going to AA. You said you hadn't had a drink in almost a year." She'd known it was a dumb idea to call her father; why had she set herself up like this? Why had she kidded herself that this time—just because she needed him so badly—things would be different?

"Aw . . . Allie. Don' be like . . . don' be . . . Bad . . . bad news."

"Yeah, sure. I've got bad news, Dad, but you're in no shape to hear it. Maybe I'll call you again someday. Cheers!" She slammed down the receiver. "And maybe I won't," she muttered to herself. "Have another drink, you old bastard!"

Tears of anger and disappointment stung her eyes, but she forced herself to calm down. At least Ruth had come through . . . this far. She had the fifteen hundred in her purse. With the cash she'd brought from Wood Lake, they could get by for a few weeks. Once Ruth got the house sold and they had that money, they'd be able to start a new life somewhere. She'd just have to pray it didn't take too long.

"Stephie, watch that chocolate," Allison snapped. "It's about to land in your lap."

The child bobbed her head toward the confection, smearing it across her chin. A trickle of ice milk slithered down the cone and onto her hand.

"Here." Allison grabbed a paper napkin and briskly wiped Stephanie's face and hands.

"Ow, Mommy. That hurts."

"Sorry, puss. This thing is melting too fast. Here, try to eat it over the napkins. I've gotta make another phone call." She pulled the toll-free number from her bag and dialed.

"Helpline. This is Mona."

"Uh, hi. My name is Allison."

"How can I help you, Allison?"

Allison took a breath of hot, dusty air. Her words spilled out. "My—my ex-husband has been molesting our four-year-old daughter. I—I went to court, but I couldn't get his visitation rights cut off."

"I understand." Mona's voice was unsurprised, businesslike. "Where was this?"

"Wood Lake. Wood Lake, Wisconsin. It's in the northwestern part of the state, near Lake Superior."

"Yes. Go on."

"The—the psychologist who testified at the hearing, her name's Beth Gunderson. She gave me this number. Told me you could help us get away, that there were places we could stay, where people would help us hide . . ."

"What's the status now?"

"Of what?"

"The court case."

"Oh. It's over. I lost. The judge ruled for my ex." Allison related the story of her demoralizing day in court.

"Have you got a pencil and paper, Allison?"

Allison searched in her bag. "Yeah. Right here."

"Good. I want you to write down this address. It's a post office box in Kansas City. Send a copy of your court documents and any medical records you have for your child by Federal Express. Give us about two days to go over them, then call—"

"But I need help *now*."

"Sorry, that's not the way we work. We have to check out your story before we can let you into the network."

Allison gripped the telephone receiver more tightly in her sweating palm. "But this is the first chance I've had to call. We had to grab whatever we could and run. Where are we supposed to go? Karl—that's my ex-husband—Karl's already looking for us." Allison felt panic rising. "I'll go to jail if they find us, and Stephie—"

Mona's voice remained calm. "You've got to see our point of view, Allison. We don't know you. You could be FBI or somebody working for a father whose kids we're protecting. We pull you into the underground and a lot of people could be hurt, people just as frightened and desperate as you are."

Allison watched Stephanie's Dairy Queen drip down the front of her grass-green sunsuit, but it no longer seemed important. Her head began to throb. "Mona, please. It's after four on Saturday. We're in some backwater town in Wisconsin with the car all loaded up. I don't even know where to find Federal Express here and the post office won't be open 'til Monday. There isn't anybody else who can help us. Please . . ."

There was no answer.

"Look, maybe you don't understand. My ex-husband . . . Karl's an attorney. He's got friends in the police. My daughter and I've gotta have somewhere to hide, at least 'til we can get a good thousand miles behind us. I—" Allison heard her voice break. "I haven't slept in two days."

Mona sighed. "What's your full name?"

"Allison Mitchell Warren."

"And your daughter's?"

"Stephanie. Stephanie Warren."

"There's just the one child?"

"Yes."

"Which way are you headed?"

"West. I figure we can make the Twin Cities before dark."

"What's the name of the psychologist who gave you this number?"

Hope began to resurface. "Beth Gunderson. Dr. Elizabeth Gunderson. She's in private practice in Duluth and she teaches at U.M.D.—the University of Minnesota's Duluth campus." She gave Mona Dr. Gunderson's phone number.

"All right, Allison. I'll do this much. I'll see if anyone here knows this Beth Gunderson. If so, I'll try to reach her, see if she backs up your story. I'm not making any promises. Call me back in an hour and I'll let you know whether there's anything we can do for you."

Precisely an hour later, Allison called the helpline from a Mobil Oil station in Eau Claire and spoke to Mona, who had managed to locate Dr. Elizabeth Gunderson.

"One of our volunteers will meet you at the west end of the Mr. Steak parking lot," Mona explained. She gave Allison the address of a restaurant in St. Paul's Midway district. "The volunteer's name is Phyllis. She'll want to examine your court papers. If they're in order, she'll take you and Stephanie with her temporarily."

"They're in order. I've got them right here."

"Be there at eight o'clock sharp. Don't go inside the restaurant. If you want to eat, find a drive-in before you get there."

"Okay. Whatever you say. And . . . thanks."

The line went dead.

6

"I'll be damned if she's gonna get away with this, the goddamn bitch! I'll track her down if it's the last fuckin' thing I do."

"Cool down, Karl, you'll have a stroke in this heat. Chances are, coupla days, Allison'll get scared and come home. She'll be beggin' ya not to press charges—"

"You don't know her, Buck. Hell, a woman who'd tell that kind of lie about the father of her child . . ." Karl accepted a cool bottle of Hamm's from Sergeant Percy "Buck" Linn. The two big men, one dark and the other sandy-haired, sat on Buck's front porch, an Igloo cooler filled with beer at their feet. A Sear's power lawnmower sat abandoned on the front lawn. Karl took a sip of beer, letting it cool his tongue for a moment before he swallowed. "Allison's a sore loser, Buck, and as stubborn as they come. And don't forget she used to work for the airlines. She's used to traveling around, living out of a suitcase."

"Not with a little kid, she ain't. Not lookin' over her shoulder for the cops or the FBI." Linn belched loudly. "Can't exactly check into the Holiday Inn on this trip."

"You gotta get on this for me, Buck. Get the State Patrol lookin' out for her car, before she gets too far."

"You know I can't do that. You gotta get Judge

Winston to hold Allison in contempt and issue a warrant before I can do anything official. And you're not gonna convince Winston she's really split 'til she's been gone at least a coupla days."

"She's got my kid, Buck. You don't know what that's doin' to me."

"That may be, pal, but you got no hard proof they've left town. Least nothin' you can talk about. You can't tell Winston you broke into her house; screwed yourself with that move. Without proof their stuff is gone, all you can say for sure is Allison and Stephanie weren't home when you showed up for your weekend visitation."

"Shit." Karl tossed the empty bottle at the green plastic wastebasket on the corner of the porch. He made a perfect basket. "So what do you suggest I do, Buck? Just let the bitch take my kid away from me? I know my rights! I want my kid back. I want the cops on this now. The FBI, too."

"You're no virgin, Karl. You know how slow these things move. By the time you get the Feds involved, Allison and your kid could be in Brazil."

"You saying I should sit here and take it 'til the goddamn system gets around to me?"

Buck looked at his old friend. Just past forty, Karl Warren still had the broad shoulders he'd had when the two played football back at Wood Lake High. But he was beginning to develop a paunch, his hair was thinning, and he looked every year of his age. The pains he took with his grooming, his fancy clothes, couldn't hide that. Buck knew Karl had taken his divorce hard; it had aged him. But in the three years since he and Allison had split up, the two men had never had a gut-level conversation about why it had happened. Karl didn't volunteer much, other than to complain that Allison was a bitch. And Buck wasn't one to pry. He figured it had something to do with a man waiting 'til he was pushing forty to tie the knot. People could get pretty set in their ways. Allison'd been no kid, either. She'd been near thirty, though you'd never know it to look at her. She was used to a far more glamorous life than she got here in Wood Lake, too. Still, she hadn't left town when they had broken up. Allison Warren was a puzzle, had to be a helluva vindictive broad, the way she went after Karl. Buck never for a moment believed those lies she told. Saying those things about Karl, setting her little girl up like that . . . well, some women you never could figure. And now she'd stolen the kid right out from under Karl's nose. Buck wanted to help but, for now, his hands were legally tied. "You want my best advice," he said. "You really don't think Allie'll be back in a day or two, then don't wait. Get one o' them private dicks you use."

Karl nodded. "Looks like I'll have to. I've been using Pete Peterson and his wife, Louise, lately." The Petersons did a variety of casework for Karl, mostly detail work. But occasionally they got their teeth into something big. Last spring, they'd investigated a phony life insurance claim, found the "deceased" alive and well in Miami Beach, and saved United Mutual a half-million-dollar claim.

"Met Louise once or twice. Went to school with my wife over in Pineville." Buck opened a second beer and offered it to Karl, who waved it away. He shrugged and took a slug himself. "Might be a good idea to have a woman trackin' Allie down. Situation like this, lotsa people're more willin' to talk to a woman."

Karl jerked to his feet. "I'll go see them now. And I'll see Judge Winston on Monday."

"Sorry I couldn't do more, Karl. You know I'd like to."

Karl briefly clapped a hand on Buck's shoulder, turned, and stalked across the newly cut lawn.

7

"Mommy, I wanna go home. I'm sleepy." Stephanie squirmed in her carseat, straining against the belt that held her in position.

"I already told you, Stephie. We can't go home. We have to find a new home."

They waited impatiently in the Buick in the Mr. Steak parking lot while Phyllis, the woman the helpline had sent to meet them, sat in the Ford parked in the next stall. Under a flashlight's illumination, the volunteer was carefully reading the court papers Allison had given her.

"I wanna play with my friends. I want Iris." Tears rolled down Stephanie's sticky cheeks as she spoke of her babysitter. "I get to make choca-chip cookies at Iris's. We can live with Iris, Mommy."

"No, we can't live with Iris. You've got to try to understand, Stephie. We can't go back to Wood Lake. Not ever. If we do, the judge will send Mommy away and you'll have to live with Daddy. That's why we're going far away, so Daddy can't hurt you anymore. So you'll always be with me. Now do you understand?"

Stephanie stared straight ahead, stuck out her lower lip, and began to kick the seat.

Allison sighed, barely holding her temper. "Steph, I want you to stop that. Right now."

The kicking continued. Allison reached over and, with a rigid arm, held the child's feet still. Stephanie began to whine, then to sob. Allison felt like joining her. A good cry would help release the tension they both were feeling. "Here. Here's Flopsy." Stephanie grabbed the old bunny from her mother, holding it against one of her wet red cheeks. Her right thumb found its way into her mouth and the crying ceased. In a few minutes, she had dozed off.

Phyllis emerged from the Ford and handed the papers through the open car window. She was a tall, well-groomed, gray-haired woman in her middle fifties. Helping abused women and children was her passion; she'd lived with a battering husband for fifteen years, terrified of staying with him and even more terrified of leaving. After he died, Phyllis had vowed to do whatever she could to prevent other women from living the same nightmare. Gradually, she'd learned to fight back for other women in a way she'd never been able to do for herself.

"How well do you know St. Paul?" she asked Allison.

"I was based in the Twin Cities when I flew for Northwest."

"I'm going to lead the way to the shelter we run. It's for battered women, but we get a few moms and kids like you. I'll lead the way. If you lose me, here's where it is." She handed Allison a slip of paper with an address near the Mississippi River written on it. "Think you can find it?"

"Sure."

"When we get there, drive directly around the back and pull into the garage. The door's open. We want to get your car out of sight as fast as possible."

The shelter was a three-story Georgian brick structure just off Summit Avenue. In an earlier era, Allison thought, it probably housed a wealthy family and its servants. Now three women with bruised faces and bodies, one of them with a soiled cast on her arm, sat in the parlor watching a rerun of "The

Golden Girls" on a portable television set. "Hi," Allison said, as she passed them, carrying a suitcase. Stephanie lagged behind her mother, her tired eyes taking in her new surroundings.

The women murmured a response and turned their attention back to the TV.

"I'm going to put you two on the third floor," Phyllis said, leading the way up the polished oak staircase. The dark red runner was frayed at the edge of each riser. "It gets a bit warm up there, but Saturday nights can be pretty hectic around here, especially hot ones like tonight. You know how it is. People are irritable in the heat. The husbands drink too much beer, they get tanked up, they get nasty, and next thing you know, we've got wives knocking on our door and we're out of beds. At least it's a little quieter on the third floor." She opened the door of a small room with a slanting ceiling that held three single beds. "With luck, we won't need the third bed and you'll have some privacy." She opened the window in the dormer and a faint breeze crept through to the hall.

"This is very nice. Thank you," Allison said. The room was wallpapered in a yellow and green floral print and the bare oak floor gleamed in the lamplight. Two mismatched wooden chairs and a high chest of drawers stood along one wall.

Stephanie belly-flopped onto the bed nearest the window. Its springs creaked. "Can I have this one, Mommy?"

"Soon as you're cleaned up, sweetie."

"Bathroom's across the hall," Phyllis said. "Try not to take too long in case others are waiting."

Allison set the suitcase on one of the chairs.

"Breakfast is between eight and ten in the dining room at the back of the house. If you're hungry now, there might be some supper left in the refrigerator."

"Thanks, but we stopped at McDonald's. Right now, we just want to get cleaned up and get a good night's sleep."

"Right." Phyllis turned back the sheets on the bed next to Stephanie's. "One thing you should know."

"Uh huh?"

"Sometimes the cops bring women here when it isn't safe for them to stay in their homes. So it'd be best if you and your little girl kept out of sight. At least keep away from the living room and the front hall. The rest of the house should be all right. You hear the doorbell ring, make yourself scarce."

"Sure. Whatever you say."

"In the morning, after you've had some breakfast, there'll be time enough to get started."

"On what?"

"The new you."

8

"You must become a totally new person. When you leave here, Allison Mitchell Warren will no longer exist. That means a new name, a new appearance, different clothes, a different car, different interests, a different occupation. Every detail from your old life that could possibly be used to locate you has got to change. Do you understand?"

Allison nodded, feeling more than a little overwhelmed. She sat on a blue cotton-covered patio chair in the second-floor screened porch. Phyllis sat across the small glass table, looking rested, cool, and competent in a lime-green sleeveless dress.

Allison, however, was exhausted after a difficult night. Stephanie had wakened, screaming in terror, three times. Allison had determined that it was the same dream the child had been having for the past few weeks that had wakened her—the one about the snakes. But this time the terrorized child sobbed that the snakes were killing Flopsy by ripping the bunny's ears off. Allison had managed to comfort Stephie and coax her back to sleep, but she couldn't do the same for herself. She'd lain awake, listening for the next outburst, until dawn broke.

Mother and daughter had bathed and breakfasted on corn flakes and milk and orange juice. Now one of the shelter volunteers had taken the little girl to the playroom with two other children who were spending the day at the shelter while Allison learned what escaping Karl and Wood Lake would require.

"This is going to be the hardest thing you've ever done, and you've got no room for mistakes," Phyllis said. "If you get caught, Stephanie will end up living with her father and you'll probably never be alone with your child again." She sipped her glass of iced tea. At ten o'clock, the day was already becoming uncomfortably warm. "Does this frighten you, Allison?"

"It terrifies me. You make it sound like I have to die and be reincarnated."

"That's exactly right. And it's a good thing you're scared. If you weren't, I'd know you weren't taking this seriously enough." Phyllis handed Allison two paperback books.

She read the titles: *How to Create a New Identity* and *How to Get Lost and Start All Over Again*.

"You'll have time to read these later. I want you to pay particular attention to the sections that show how you can be found, so you'll know what to avoid. It could be something as simple as an interest in French movies or belonging to a particular kind of health club that could trip you up. Of course, your friends and relatives are completely off limits. Don't even *think* about contacting them. Ever."

"But—"

"I'm dead serious, Allison. If Karl hires detectives, and from everything you've said about him, he will, the first thing they'll do is watch your family and your friends for the tiniest sign of contact from you. If they find it, you and Stephanie are finished. And if Karl can get the FBI on your tail, it'll be even harder to escape."

A vision of grinding poverty flashed through Allison's mind. "My sister is trying to sell my house for me. I have to have the equity to live on."

Phyllis's eyes moved skyward. "Investigators will be all over that money like ants on honey. You might as well send Karl a 'wish you were here' card, complete with your return address."

"Jesus. What are we going to live on?"

"The network will give you some help, temporary housing while you create your new identity and come up with a workable plan. There are certain kinds of jobs you can get without much of a resumé. They're not very highly paid, but you'll be able to get by if you're willing to work." Phyllis wagged a finger at her student. "Truth is, you'll have to figure on starting all over, from the bottom. If you're not willing to do that, your best bet is to go back to Wood Lake right now and try to negotiate keeping yourself out of jail."

Allison felt weak with fear. If it were just herself she had to worry about, this would be bad enough, but she had Stephanie to feed and house. Yet the alternative was worse. "I'm not going back," she said with quiet determination. "Please, just tell me what I have to do."

"This is Rita," Phyllis said some two hours later. "She's a trained beautician and she's one of our best volunteers." Rita was in her early thirties, a buxom brunette wearing too much makeup. She set down the black case she was carrying and extended her hand. Allison shook it.

Rita took the chair next to Allison's and reached over and lifted a lock of her hair. She rubbed it expertly between her fingers. "You've got good hair, nice and healthy. Pretty shade of blond. Is it natural?"

Allison nodded.

"Good. It's a lot easier when I don't have to fight with an old color job. We'll change it to a shade that flatters your complexion, looks natural. But it'll have to be different, of course. You always wear your hair long and straight like this?"

"Usually. Sometimes I tie it up in a knot or pull it back in a ponytail."

Rita opened her case, pulled out a color card and held it next to Allison's face. "Your skin's got distinct golden tones in it, and you're very fair. If we dye your hair too dark, it's gonna look fake. Something in the red family's my suggestion." She took another card from the case, one with a variety of colored hair samples attached. "Here, this one would be good on you." She pointed to one labeled Copper Penny. "And you can buy this brand in any good drugstore when you need a touchup."

"You don't think it's too bright?" Allison was skeptical; the color Rita had chosen reminded her of Lucille Ball's. "I thought the idea was not to be noticed."

"If people focus on your hair, they're less likely to remember your face. We'll dye your eyebrows to match. And don't use that heavy foundation on your nose; let your freckles show." She made a frame for Allison's face with her hands, leaned back in her chair and contemplated the picture. "A perm, too, if your hair and scalp can stand it after the color. Otherwise, a short haircut. Trust me, when I'm done with you, you'll look like a regular Irish colleen."

Allison's smile was apprehensive. "What do you think, Phyllis?" she asked.

"Rita's the best. You won't recognize yourself."

Allison peered at her image in the bathroom mirror. The mass of rust-colored curls falling to her shoulders seemed alien. She'd never thought of herself as a redhead, or as a curly top, but she'd have to start. Like Phyllis said, she should imagine herself as an actress playing a role, until the role gradually became reality.

She ran a finger gingerly around an ear. Her scalp was sore, but it would recover. Rita and Phyllis had been right. The hairdo looked natural enough on her. And she hardly recognized herself.

"You look 'way diff'rent, Mommy." Stephanie sat on the closed toilet lid, her bare legs dangling. She held Flopsy close against her chest.

"So do you, angel." Allison patted the child's newly shorn head. She'd drawn the line at dying Stephanie's hair; there was no way she'd subject the delicate baby scalp to the upkeep that kind of change would require. Reluctantly, Rita had compromised on a short, boyish haircut with bangs swept away from the little round face. And Stephie looked significantly changed. Allison squatted down to her eye level. "So what do you think? Do we look pretty?"

Stephanie made a face. "I liked my long hair best. Flopsy liked it, too. Huh, Flopsy?" She pushed the rabbit's head up and down.

Me, too, Allison thought. She planted a wet kiss on her daughter's cheek. "Well, I think you're the most beautiful little girl I've seen all day. All year, even."

Phyllis appeared in the doorway. "If you're finished in there, Allison, we have some forms we need your help on."

The blank forms were laid out on a table in Phyllis's office: an Iowa birth certificate; a California driver's license form; a Social Security card. "Stand over there and face me," Phyllis ordered, gesturing toward a bare white wall. She snapped a Polaroid closeup of Allison's face, framed by the new hairdo. "Now, as I told you, all these are temporary. They should get you by until you can get genuine documents. If you forget how to do that, the books I gave you review everything."

Allison was astonished. "Where do you get these papers? They look so official."

"There are printers who supply them, and they

do look very real. But the point is, if anyone checks back with the state that supposedly issued one of them, your cover's going to be blown. So get yourself a real set as soon as you can." When the Polaroid was developed, Phyllis trimmed it to fit the space provided for a photo on the driver's license. "Now, your new name. Something easy for you to remember but not too close to your real one. You have a nickname?"

"Sometimes I'm called Allie."

"Hmmm. That's close to Ellie, which would give you a different initial. How about Eleanor, Ellen, Ella, Elsa—"

"I always liked Elyse. Is that too close to Allison?"

"I don't think so. Elyse it is, then." Phyllis wrote the name on a clean piece of paper. "Now the last name. Maybe something close to your maiden name, Mitchell. Let's see . . . Mitt, Mott, Miles, Mills, Miller . . ."

"Michaels would be good. I read somewhere that Mitchell is a variation of Michael. It'll be easy to remember."

Phyllis wrote "Michaels" after "Elyse" and scooped up the official-looking forms and the stamp-sized photo. "Wait here." She was back in two minutes, announcing, "She'll have those documents ready in an hour."

"She?"

Phyllis's smile was sly. "Another of our volunteers. She has a true gift for forgery. We keep her anonymous. That way, if you get caught with one of her masterpieces, you won't be able to turn her in."

"But what about you? And Rita? Aren't you afraid I, or someone like me, could turn you in?"

Phyllis shrugged. "Last I heard, it wasn't illegal to give people advice, or a room for the night. Or to give somebody a new hairdo."

"How about Stephie? Won't I need new documents for her, too?" The child was engrossed in a storybook.

"That can wait until you get yourself some genuine ID. We'll give you a couple of extra blank birth certificates. You can type in a name and birthdate for her later. A birth certificate's all you're likely to need for a four-year-old. Lucky she's not in school yet, so you won't need school records. For now, it's best to get used to calling her by a nickname. Both of you have to forget her name was ever Stephanie."

"What kind of nickname?"

"Anything that doesn't sound like her real name. Cookie, Sis, Honey, something like that. Get her accustomed to answering to it. Then, when you pick a permanent name for her later, whatever it is, you can keep on using the nickname. She won't have to learn a new name at every stop along the road."

Nostalgically, Allison recalled the nights she'd spent with the dog-eared book of baby names, making lists, picking and choosing, finally settling on Stephanie Suzannah—the second name in honor of her dead mother. Oddly, it felt far less traumatic to pick a new name for herself—she'd never chosen Allison in the first place—than to pick one for her daughter. "I—I don't know. It's hard to come up with something new just like that."

"I heard you call her angel a few minutes ago. How about Angel? She might like that and it's a cute name for a little girl."

Allison turned and softly called, "Angel."

The dark-lashed blue eyes rose from the book. "What, Mommy?"

"I guess it's gonna be Angel."

Phyllis nodded. "As far as your daughter's concerned, from now on, she's Angel and you're Mommy."

9

Tim Mitchell lay on rumpled, sweat-soaked sheets, trying to work up the courage to open his eyes and face the new day. His temples throbbed, his mouth tasted like a toilet, and his stomach belched acid. The feeling was not unfamiliar, but it was one Tim had promised himself he'd never have to endure again. Now he'd blown his promise; nearly a year in AA straight down the crapper.

A hair o' the dog was what he needed. That'd put a brighter glow on the morning. Just a wee nip to take the edge off the hangover, nothing more. He could almost taste it, feel the burning liquid begin to relieve his pain. But Tim had learned a few things in the past year, the most important of which was that he was incapable of stopping with one wee nip. He'd have a taste, then a drink. Next, the bottle would be empty and he'd be off to buy a case. He'd drink until he passed out, and tomorrow he'd wake up feeling every bit as shitty as he did now. Or maybe that'd be the day he just wouldn't wake up.

Tim forced one eyelid open, then the other, bracing himself against the glaring San Diego sunshine streaming through the bedroom window. It threw the room into vivid perspective. One shoe carefully placed on the night table next to the overflowing ashtray and the empty bottle of Gilbey's, its mate tossed in a corner. Pants in a heap on the floor. Shirt flecked with vomit thrown over the back of a bentwood chair. He'd really tied one on this time. Suddenly filled with self-loathing, Tim closed his eyes and pressed his knuckles against his eye sockets. What the hell difference did it make what he did? Whether he drank or didn't drink, who really gave a shit? Former Master Chief Petty Officer Timothy Mitchell indulged in his share of self-pity, but in his heart he knew he had only himself to blame, that he alone was responsible. The way he'd abused his body all these years—close to seventy now—he deserved to die, and he would. Very soon.

That had started this latest trouble. His idea—his certainty—that he was dying. The doc had given him the news—what was it?—two days ago now, maybe three, and he'd been on a bender ever since. The melanoma that had forced him out of the Navy more than a decade ago had come back; now there were inoperable tumors in both of his lungs. Or maybe this was just plain garden variety lung cancer. The doc wasn't sure. Tim had smoked enough cancer sticks in his day to make that a good enough bet, and he'd ignored the black phlegm he'd been coughing up until he could barely draw breath. By the time he'd hauled his ass in to see the doc, there wasn't a helluva lot that could be done. Just wait it out, take the drugs they'd give him for pain at the end.

He had three months, if he was lucky. That was the verdict. Three short months, *if* he took care of himself. That meant no drinking, no smoking. But what was the point? He knew he'd fucked up his whole life, and three months wasn't enough time to put it right. Tim figured he might as well check out of this world feeling no pain.

He threw his legs over the side of the bed and pulled himself slowly to his feet. The room spun, then settled as he gained his balance. He reached for the gin bottle, put it to his lips and tilted his head back. Shit! It was empty. He tossed it onto the floor. If he was going to have a drink, he'd have to go out. Unless he could get the liquor store to deliver.

The bedside clock radio said 7:58. Too damn early. Nothing would be open for at least another hour. Tim staggered to the bathroom and choked down half a dozen aspirin. Maybe coffee would help. Strong, black coffee. Just to hold him 'til he could get another bottle.

The coffee burned Tim's tongue as he drank, but it stayed down. He tapped a cigarette out of the Marlboro pack, lit it, took half a drag, began to cough. Stubbed it out. Damn thing tasted like used shit. Maybe a saltine or a piece of toast would make him feel better.

As Tim placed two slices of stale bread into the toaster oven and pushed down the lever, his eye fell on the framed Serenity Prayer on the kitchen wall. Allie had needlepointed it for him, a gift when he'd reached his first full month of sobriety. She'd sounded so pleased, so happy for him back then.

Allison. Something played around the edges of Tim's mind, something important about his younger daughter. Had she called? Had he talked to her? He couldn't quite grasp it, but he had a feeling he'd let her down. Again. Lord knew he'd never been much of a father. He'd had to face that fact this past year in AA and it hadn't been easy. The guilt almost put him back on the bottle.

Of course. Allison was in the middle of that court thing. She'd been trying to keep that shithead Karl away from little Stephie. Had she called about that? Was there a verdict? Had Allie found out he'd hit the bottle and fallen flat on his face again? He couldn't quite bring it clear, but the niggling thought was there, the idea that Allie had called, that she had asked him for something, that he hadn't been sober enough to give it to her.

Tim took the toast slices from the oven, tossed them on a plate, and carried it to the table. As he chewed off a corner of dry toast and washed it down with a slug of coffee, the first worm of optimism began to slither into his mind. So he had only three months left. That was still enough time to do something important, to make his mark. Maybe he'd undertake a suicide mission. He fantasized going to Iraq, taking out Saddam Hussein. Or maybe heading over to Africa and eliminating Idi Amin—where was old Idi these days, anyway? Hell, a dying man had nothing to lose. Why not check out in a blaze of glory, doing something that would leave the world a better place?

Or if he didn't have enough starch left for anything that ambitious, maybe at least he could try to make amends with Allie and Ruth and their kids— his family, what was left of it. Sometimes he thought the trouble was that he'd always thought too big— the U.S. Navy, political brinksmanship, war—so he'd missed the important little stuff, the people in his own home.

He'd call her right now. Find out. Tim pulled himself out of his chair and lurched over to the kitchen wall phone. Squinting at the list of phone numbers pinned to the bulletin board beside it, he punched in the digits of Allison's number. The phone rang seven times before he hung up.

Maybe she was at the bookstore. What day was it—Sunday, Monday? It'd be later in Wisconsin, nearly eleven o'clock. The store would be open. He punched in eleven more digits.

A woman's voice answered. "Wood Lake Books."

"Allison Warren, please."

"She's not here."

"You expectin' her?"

"Can't say. Who's this?"

"Her dad. Callin' from California. She wasn't at home, so I thought she might be workin' today."

"Supposed to be, but she didn't show up. Didn't show up yesterday, either."

"She ain't sick?"

"You tell me. Tried to call 'er, but didn't get any answer. You find 'er, tell 'er to get in here quick or I'll have to give the job to somebody else. Store's more'n I can handle by myself, 'specially on a weekend."

"Sure. Thanks. And, lady?"

"Yeah?"

"Allison does show up, tell her her old man's lookin' for her, willya? It's important."

"You bet."

Tim replaced the receiver with a sense of foreboding. It wasn't like Allie just not to show up for work that way. Not his super-responsible Allie. There had to be a damned good reason. But it made his head hurt more to think about it; he'd consider it later.

Lord, he could use a drink! The kitchen clock showed it was after nine. The liquor store three blocks over would be opening for the day . . . but then he'd never find out about Allie.

Tim swallowed hard, searched the list of phone numbers and dialed a local number with a shaky finger.

"Hello."

"Roy?"

"Yeah."

"It's me, Tim."

There was a pause. "Missed you at last night's meeting, man. Where were ya?"

Tim took a shallow breath, coughed, and answered. "I—I fell off the wagon, buddy. And I'm dyin' for a drink. I want a drink so bad, Roy, I dunno if I can—"

"Hold on, pal. You're not alone. You made the right call. Be there in five minutes." Tim heard a click on the line. Slowly he replaced the receiver and sat down to wait.

10

"I can't stand this oven much longer," Louise said, lifting her damp brown hair off her neck. "Must be a hundred and ten in here." She took a swig of tepid water from the plastic bottle, wiped off the top, and handed it to her husband, Pete. He drank, screwed the cap back on, and shoved the bottle back under the front seat of the Oldsmobile.

"Don't seem to be doin' much good anyhow," he said. "Hard to believe Allison'd be dumb enough to hang around here long. She'd have to know this'd be the first place anybody'd look for her and the kid."

Louise and Pete Peterson had wasted no time after Karl Warren hired them to find his fleeing ex-wife and child. They'd left Wood Lake at five the next morning and driven straight through to central Wisconsin, where Karl guessed Allison had headed. Now the two private investigators had been parked for almost two hours near the entrance to the Persky farm, sweltering in the midday heat. No one had entered or left by the farm road and the house and barn were too far away to observe, even with the high-powered binoculars. For all they knew, the place was deserted.

"I say we just drive straight up to the house and see if they're there," Louise said. "Worst thing can happen is they've already left and the sister tips Allison off that Karl's got PI's on her tail. She had to figure that was gonna happen anyway."

"Might as well." Pete turned the key in the ignition and headed the car up the dirt road toward the grove of oaks that sheltered the farm buildings. A cloud of dust followed in the car's wake and heat waves shimmered above the fields of stunted corn flanking the road.

Pete stopped the car at the end of the road, just short of the deserted gravel parking area by the house. "I'll keep the road blocked here, Lou. You go ahead and see what you can find out."

Louise opened the passenger door quietly, unstuck the skirt of her pale blue cotton dress from the vinyl seat cover, and climbed out. It felt good to stretch her legs after being cramped in the car for so long. She wiped her brow and looked around. A speckled hen pecked in the dust near the open barn door. Inside, she could see a brown and white cow, its tail lazily swishing flies off its back. Allison Warren's car was nowhere in sight. Louise ventured closer to the house, gravel squeaking beneath her rubber-soled shoes. The smell of fresh-baked bread wafting through the screen door reminded her that she was not only hot, she was famished.

As she approached the house, Louise saw a young boy, dressed only in shorts and a pair of tattered Nikes, sitting under a tree in the side yard. His eyes rose from the row of baseball cards spread out before him on the parched grass and he watched her silently. "Hi," she said, flashing him a smile. "Are you Tony?" she asked, hoping she remembered the names of Ruth Persky's kids correctly.

The boy shook his head. "Nah, Tony's gone swimmin', up at the pond." His voice was heavy with resentment. "I'm Dennis."

Louise nodded. "How come you didn't go swimming, too, Dennis? Sure is hot enough."

He screwed up his face in disgust. "Ma won't let me. Says I'll just get another ear 'fection."

"Say, that's really rough. I used to get ear infections when I was a kid, too. They sure hurt, don't they?"

The boy nodded solemnly. His eyes wandered back to the baseball cards. "I got three Kirby Pucketts," he told her proudly.

"Hey, all right!" Louise moved into the shade of the tree, where it was a fraction of a degree cooler. "Your cousin Stephanie and her mom go swimming, too?"

"Nah, they left already."

"Know where they went?"

Dennis shrugged. "Prob'ly home."

"When did they—" Louise flinched as the crack of the screen door slamming shut pierced the air.

"What do you want here?" A woman in a yellow housedress and pink gingham apron, her hair pulled back into a low ponytail, strode across the yard toward Louise. She wiped flour-covered hands on her apron as she walked, her face stiff and disapproving. This had to be Ruth Persky, Allison's older sister.

Louise forced a smile. "Hello, Mrs. Persky. I'm Louise Peterson. Just hoping I'd catch your sister—"

"She's not here and she's not gonna be here. Now please, go away and leave us alone." The woman's voice was shrill, on the edge of panic.

"Maybe you can tell me where I can find her, Mrs. Persky. It'd save everybody a lot of trouble if we can just—"

"You mean might save *you* some trouble! Look, lady—"

"Louise."

"Whatever your name is. You tell that no good son of a—" Ruth stopped herself. "Dennis, take that stuff inside while I'm talking to the lady."

"I don't see why—"

"Just do it!" she snapped. Reluctantly, Dennis picked up his cards and shuffled slowly toward the house, the toes of his sneakers kicking up clouds of dust as he walked. He turned and glared at his mother, but he kept walking. Ruth waited until the screen door had closed behind him. "You tell that no good son of a bitch Allie was married to to call off his dogs. He's never gonna get that little girl back. Allie says she'll die before Karl Warren ever lays another hand on her kid."

Louise shook her head. "Listen, Mrs. Persky, Allison's got herself into something she really isn't going to be able to handle here. I know she's your sister, but you need to understand that sometimes when they're getting divorced, people get carried away. They imagine things, or they make things up to put the other party in a bad light. But they just don't realize how much trouble they're getting themselves into. Later on, they can be real sorry."

"My sister wouldn't lie, not about something like this." The line of Ruth's mouth was hard.

"I've known Karl Warren and I've worked for him for a long, long time. He'd never—"

"You have any kids, lady?"

"No—no, I don't."

"Well, maybe a career woman like you just can't understand how a mother feels, how she's gotta protect her kids, no matter what it costs her. Maybe that's why you can work for a piece of filth like Karl Warren. But I got kids and I couldn't do what you're doin', not for a million bucks. I could never do that to another mother."

Ruth's words stung. Louise might not have children of her own, but that certainly wasn't because she hadn't wanted them. And she'd grown up with plenty of brothers and sisters, four of the eight younger than she was. She'd changed her share of diapers, warmed her share of baby bottles. Ruth's accusation was just plain ignorant. Louise could hear the defensiveness in her own voice as she replied.

"That's not fair, Mrs. Persky. I love children. I'd never do anything to hurt a child. Look, I know you're upset, but you're dead wrong here. You've got to understand that your sister is way off base. Maybe she's just honestly mistaken, but she made some horrible, completely unbelievable charges against as good a man as—"

"Ha! What that creep's been doin' to his own daughter is what's horrible. He oughta be hung, you ask me."

"The court found absolutely no grounds for those charges, Mrs. Persky. The court says he never touched that child. Think about him for a minute, having to worry about where his little girl is, about whether she's all right. Think about poor little Stephanie, stolen away from the daddy who loves her."

"I'm not gonna debate with you. Allison and Stephie aren't here and they're not gonna be here. Now get off my property."

Louise held up her hand. "Okay, okay. I'm going. But I want to leave you with one thought. Allison Warren has become a fugitive, and the longer she keeps Stephanie away from her father, the harder the court's going to come down on her when they're found. And they will be found, you can count on that. The longer it takes, the harder it's going to be on anybody who's helped Allison hide, too, and that includes you and your entire family, Mrs. Persky. It's real simple—you help her get away, help her hide, you're breaking the law. So, if you know what's best for all of you, you'll tell me where to find her."

"If I wanted to tell you where she is, I couldn't. I don't know. Allie didn't tell me where she was goin' and I don't want to know."

Louise shrugged. "If that's the way you want it.

Just don't say I never warned you." She pulled a business card from her pocket and shoved it at Ruth. "In case you change your mind, here's where you can reach me."

Ruth took the card and pushed it deep into her apron pocket. "I got one last thought for you, too," she said.

"Yeah?"

"Suppose Karl Warren really did what Allison says he did, and you force that poor child to go back. You make her go live with a father who molests her—how in the hell you gonna live with yourself?"

Louise did not reply. Silently, she turned and walked back to the car.

"So?" Pete asked as she slid onto the burning passenger seat.

"Missed them. The boy says Allison and Stephanie were here all right, but they've left. Both he and his mother claim they don't know where they are now."

"Well, it was a long shot." Pete turned the Olds around on the dusty road. "Back to the drawing board. But first I'm gonna find us an air-conditioned bar and a couple of tall, cold beers."

"Some lunch, too. I'm starving."

As they drove toward town, Louise couldn't stop thinking about Ruth Persky's parting remark. What if . . . what if Karl Warren really was a child molester? But no, not Karl. He couldn't be. The whole idea was impossible . . . wasn't it? Slowly, Louise's appetite began to disappear.

11

"Forty-five hundred's the best I can do for you," said Stan Grann, the Used-Car Man. "She's a nice little car, but she's got more'n forty thousand miles on her." A portly man with a salesman's swagger, he circled the Buick for a final look. "Tell you the truth, little lady, I'd like to give you three, four hundred less, 'cept Sis here would skin me alive."

"Damn right I would," said Stella, grinning. A women's shelter volunteer, Stella had accompanied Allison to the used-car lot across the Mississippi River in Minneapolis. "Not much use having a brother with a used-car lot if he's not gonna give your friends a deal."

Allison forced a smile, but her heart wasn't in it. She was tired and it was beastly hot out here in the sun, especially with the heavy plaid scarf she wore to hide her new curly red hairdo. Even in this oddball getup—the confining scarf, jeans, and an oversized shirt that made her look pregnant—she was terrified that somebody she knew from her stewardess days would happen by and recognize her. She'd flown in and out of MSP International Airport for years and she knew a lot of people in this town. She was worried about Stephanie, too, back at the battered women's shelter under Phyllis's watchful eye. Was the poor kid frightened with Mommy away? Standing in a parking lot in the midday sun was definitely not where Allison wanted to be right now and, besides, she didn't really want to part with her car. She sighed deeply. "Forty-five hundred. All right. I guess I better take it." Despite her reluctance to sell, Allison knew she didn't have much choice. She had to dump the Buick fast, before Karl got the cops on her trail. At least she had Stella to help her.

"Good girl," Stella said. "Now, Stan, she's gonna need the full price in cash, and I want you to hold off on the change of registration as long as you can."

"Thursday's the best I can do. Can't afford to hold the car off the lot any longer than that."

"Thursday'll help," Stella said.

"I'll go draw up the transfer documents." Stan took the car's registration slip from Allison and headed back to his converted gas station office.

"Don't feel too bad," Stella said, smoothing the front of her peach-colored shorts. She was as trim as her brother was overweight, with a slender waist and long brown legs. "Stan's giving you a good price and you'll feel a lot safer once you're driving another car, one that's registered in a different name."

Allison shifted her sunglasses higher on her nose. They began to slide back down. "I know. It's just that—well, I only got this one paid off a few months ago. I know it runs and I—I guess I'm just used to it."

"I understand. You're in a tough spot."

"I—I haven't got enough money to buy a new car to replace this one, either." A drop of sweat trickled down Allison's brow. She wiped it away. Lord, this damn scarf was hot. "I've never bought a used car before. What if I get gypped and it breaks down halfway across the country?"

"That's the chance you take when you buy used, but I know a few things about cars. I'll help you buy something reliable."

"Couldn't I buy another car here?" Allison pointed to a dark blue Oldsmobile station wagon parked in the corner of the lot. "Maybe like that one over there. I'd feel a lot better if I could buy a car from your brother, from somebody I can trust."

Stella shook her head. "Too risky."

"Why?"

"To sell your old car, you've gotta be Allison Warren. That's the name the registration's in. If you buy another car off the same lot on the same day, even under a different name, it's gonna be too easy for the cops, or whoever, to figure out what you're driving. And to find you. Besides, Stan may be my brother, but he's running a business here. Cops come around asking questions, he's gonna have to tell them something. This way, all he knows is he made a legitimate buy of a used car from a woman named Allison Warren, he paid her in cash, and he never saw her again. There's nothing else he could tell them even if he wanted to. And, with that babushka on your head, Sam couldn't even testify about your changed appearance."

Allison scratched her scalp through the rough fabric. "Okay. Listen, Stella, I'm sorry. I don't mean to be a whiner. I'm just feeling a little overwhelmed lately."

"Hey, girl, I understand. No need to apologize."

When the two women drove Stella's car into Bargain Used Auto's lot half an hour later, Allison had removed her scarf. She kept a tight grip on her purse, which now held nearly six thousand dollars—the cash from the sale of the Buick, plus what was left of the money she'd gotten from Ruth's bank. "I think a station wagon would be best," she said, "but I can't pay one cent more than the forty-five hundred I got for the Buick."

Stella quickly vetoed the first three cars the salesman showed them. "Let's get real," she said sarcastically. "You got a station wagon that runs on this lot or don't you?"

The salesman refused to be insulted. A wiry, heavily tanned man in his late forties, he wore navy slacks and a blue shirt with "Al" on a nametag above the pocket. He sauntered over to a three-year-old silver Ford Taurus wagon. "This beauty here's your basic suburban workhorse. Perfect vehicle for the family. Plenty of room for the kids, the groceries. Even carry a good load of lumber in the back, you ever have the need to. Give you a good deal on this one."

"What's the mileage?" Allison asked, groping for a way to participate in the transaction. After all, she, not Stella, was the buyer.

"Forty-five thousand, give or take," Al said, lighting his third cigarette. "She's got a lot of good miles left in her."

Stella walked around the car. "It needs close to a thousand dollars' worth of body work back here." She pointed to a dent that ran from the right rear door well into the fender behind it.

"Cosmetic. Nothin' but a little cosmetic damage," Al said. "Like I said, give you a good deal on her. Fifty-two ninety-five, as is."

"Hmmm." Stella checked the alignment of the door, opening and closing it several times. She climbed inside and started the engine.

Allison stood and watched as the other woman poked, prodded, and inspected. Stella got out of the car and peered under the hood, magically revving the engine by pushing a half-hidden lever. Allison felt both stupid and superfluous, yet grateful for the help.

An hour later, Allison drove the Ford off the lot and headed back to the women's shelter. Stella had checked out and approved more things than Allison knew the car even possessed, then she'd bargained the price down to forty-four hundred cash, assuring

Allison that the dented door and fender were meaningless in terms of the car's performance. The temporary registration slip in Allison's bag showed that the wagon was now owned by one Elyse Michaels. The phony ID had passed its first test.

"This new car's got a big owie, Mommy," Stephanie observed. Her brow creased with concern, she ran a pudgy finger along the Ford's damaged side. She patted the fender gently. "Poor, poor car. Don't be sad, car."

Allison smiled. "The car just bumped into something a little too hard, Angel. But you know cars don't feel hurt like people do." Except maybe on television. "Cars don't bleed or cry. Want to help me load up these things so we'll be all ready to go first thing in the morning?" She indicated a pile of belongings she'd removed from the Buick that morning and stored temporarily here in the women's shelter garage.

"Okay." With her constant companion, Flopsy, gripped firmly in her left hand, the child picked up her own few possessions with her right hand and carried them, one at a time, to the car. First a bed pillow, then a small pink blanket, a coloring book and a box of Crayolas, and a couple of picture books. It was a meager collection compared with the mass of toys and books they'd left behind in Wood Lake. Last, Stephanie grabbed her bulky car safety seat and began to drag it across the concrete floor, creating an ear-shattering scraping sound.

"Here, Angel, let me help you." Allison reached for the carseat.

"No, Mommy, *I* can do it!"

Allison backed off.

When Stephanie reached the open passenger door of the car, she carefully set the tattered rabbit on the carpeted floor of the car and patted it reassuringly. Then, using both hands, she hoisted the safety seat into place. "See? I *said* I could do it."

"What a big girl you are, Angel! You did do it all by yourself." Allison's arms circled her daughter and she planted a kiss on the child's beaming face. It was so good to see her smile again.

Phyllis entered the garage, wearing jeans and a T-shirt. "How're you girls comin' along out here?"

"Almost finished. Truth is, we really haven't got all that much stuff left to take with us."

"I'd be happy to lend you a hand if—"

"You've already done so much for us, Phyllis. I'll never be able to thank you."

"Just take care of your little one here and stay safe. That's all the thanks I'll ever need."

Suddenly Allison's eyes filled and she bit down on her quivering lip. She didn't trust herself to speak. Her feelings were so close to the surface these days, and there was such a variety of them. One day, people she'd known and trusted were threatening her and her child, and she'd never known such disillusionment and terror. The next, complete strangers were risking their own safety to protect hers and Stephie's, and her heart wanted to burst with gratitude and joy. It was impossible to remain calm in such an emotional tornado. Allison turned her face away, not wanting the tears that spilled onto her cheeks to upset Stephanie—the four-year-old didn't yet understand that sometimes grownups' tears have nothing to do with sadness or pain.

"The station wagon was a good choice," Phyllis said. "The two of you can camp out in the back if you ever need to. What do you think about that, Angel? Would you like to sleep back here?"

"With my mommy?" Stephanie's expression was wary. She grabbed Flopsy and hugged the bunny to her chest.

"Sure. It might be fun."

"T'night?"

Phyllis smiled. "No, not tonight, hon. Tonight you sleep upstairs, in your bed by the window, like last night. You'll need a good night's sleep because tomorrow you and your mom are going to start on a long, long trip." She kneeled and spoke at the child's eye level. "And know what? When you're gone, I'm really gonna miss you."

Suddenly shy, Stephanie darted behind her mother and hid, peeking around her legs at the other woman.

Phyllis stood up. "Supper'll be ready in about an hour, but I think it's best if I bring a tray up to your room. We've got a couple of new women tonight and a slew of kids with them. No sense borrowing trouble."

After dinner, Allison showered and shampooed her hair. Dressed only in a cool nightgown and sitting upstairs near the open window, she felt bone-tired, but cool and relatively calm for the first time in weeks. Stephanie lay sprawled facedown across the bed, clad only in white panties, sound asleep. Poor kid was just as exhausted as her mother. Allison pulled a thin sheet over the sleeping child.

Now there was only one task left to do before morning. Allison opened her wallet and removed every form of identification that bore the name Allison Mitchell Warren—driver's license, Social Security card, charge and credit cards, various club membership cards, union card. She'd given her MasterCard to Phyllis earlier in the evening. One of the women in the shelter was headed east and had agreed to leave the card in a public women's rest room as soon as she reached Chicago. With luck, someone would find and use it, creating a false paper trail that would lead Allison's pursuers to believe she was traveling east.

Allison picked up a pair of scissors and methodically snipped each ID into tiny pieces, then tiptoed across the hall and flushed them all down the toilet. There. Now Allison Mitchell Warren no longer existed. For now, she had become Elyse Michaels.

12

Tim Mitchell finally was beginning to feel human again. He was well into his second dry day and the shakes were almost gone. Surprisingly, staying off the cigarettes was bothering him more than climbing back on the wagon. He'd lit up three or four times, but after one or two drags, he'd be doubled over, coughing up black phlegm until his ribs throbbed with pain. One day at a time, he told himself. Just take it one day at a time. Surely the nicotine craving wouldn't last forever. Of course, he realized, neither would he.

He reached for the phone and dialed Allison's number for the dozenth time. Still no answer. He was haunted by that foggy memory of a phone call, a plea for help, from his younger daughter. He felt a compulsion to find her, to make sure she was all right. But where the hell was she? She wasn't at home and she wasn't at work. That bookstore woman had been testy when he'd called there earlier today, too. "No, she's still not here. And if you find her, tell her not to bother coming back. The last thing I need around here is an employee who can't show up on schedule."

Maybe Ruth knew where Allie was. She answered on the third ring. "Saw her a couple of days ago, Dad, but I don't know where she's at by now. Didn't she call you?"

Reluctantly, Tim confessed his fall from grace. "It

ain't gonna happen again," he promised. "I just have this terrible feeling that Allie called, that she needed somethin', but I can't for the life of me remember what she said."

"She lost her court case against Karl. That judge refused to change his custody order, said Allie'd have to keep on lettin' Karl have Stephanie on weekends, so Allie decided to take her and disappear."

"Whadya mean, disappear?"

Ruth explained.

"But why would she do that? Can't she and Karl come to some kinda agreement? Divorce ain't no picnic, but people don't just—"

"Dad, this isn't exactly an ordinary divorce. Allie must've told you what Karl's been doing to Stephanie all this time. She says there's no way she can stop him now that the court—"

"What do you mean, what Karl's been doin' to Stephie?" Tim suddenly felt cold, despite the morning sunshine on his back. "I thought this court thing was about child support or alimony payments or—"

"It's got nothing to do with money, Dad. I figured Allison'd told you about it." Damn, Ruth thought, why should she be stuck with telling Dad? It was Allison's problem, her responsibility. She blurted it out: "Karl's been molesting Stephanie."

"Molesting?" Tim's knuckles turned white on the telephone receiver. "You mean—you mean sex—like—" He couldn't get the words out.

"That's exactly what I mean, Dad."

"With a four-year-old? His own kid?"

"Right." She explained a bit about what Stephanie said her daddy had done to her, and about the corroborating statements of the pediatrician and the child psychologist.

"Jesus Christ. That fuckin' bastard—pardon my French, Ruthie, but I'll kill the son of a bitch! I'll blow that pea-brained bastard from here to hell and back again! I'll—"

"Calm down, Dad. You'll do nothing of the sort. This has nothing to do with you. It's between Allison and Karl and she's handling it the best she knows how."

"By spendin' the rest of her life runnin' away? Draggin' that poor little kid along with her? What kinda answer is that? I swear, Ruthie, I'm gonna come up there and I'm gonna get that guy. I'm gonna make him pay for this. Nobody pulls that kinda crap on Tim Mitchell's family and lives to tell about it. Not as long as I'm still drawin' breath. That goddamn fuckin' pervert!"

"Daddy, please! Don't talk like that. You know you're not gonna do anything like that. Now just calm down."

"Don't tell me what I'm not gonna do, young lady. I'm still your father and I don't have to put up with any lip from—" A strangled sound emerged from Tim's throat and he began to cough, hacking from deep in his ravaged lungs. The hideous noise seemed to last forever.

When he had recovered, Ruth asked, "You okay?"

"Got a—got a cough."

"Well, you don't sound good at all. You should take better care of yourself, see a doctor. Wouldn't hurt if you gave up those stinkin' weeds you're always smokin', either."

"Christ, you can be a nag sometimes, Ruth. I dunno how Vern puts up with you."

"Okay, okay, I'm sorry. Go ahead, smoke yourself to death, if you want to. It's your body. It's just that—hell, what's the use. On this other thing—look, Dad, I know you're upset. We all are. But all I ask is that you be sensible. Your shooting Karl Warren wouldn't do anybody one bit of good. Civilized people don't handle things with guns."

"Civilized people don't have sex with little kids, for Christ's sake."

Ruth sighed. "That doesn't mean it's up to you to do anything about it, Dad. You're not in the Navy anymore. It's time you let somebody else fight the wars. Besides, Stephanie's safe now; Allie's making sure of that. You think it'd help anybody for you to spend the rest of your life in jail?"

"Wouldn't much matter. Ain't got that long, anyway."

Ruth was losing patience. It was obvious her father was in one of those moods, the kind that irritated her most. She heard herself begin to lecture. "For Pete's sake, Dad, you're not even seventy yet. You've got plenty of good years left. If you'd just take care of yourself and quit indulging in all this self-pity, you—"

"Ruth, shut up."

"What?"

"I said shut your mouth and listen for once."

Ruth exhaled. "I'm listening."

"I—this ain't just a cough, Ruthie. I've got—"

"What?"

"The doc says I've got cancer. Both lungs."

"God! Oh, Daddy. There—there must be something—"

"No, there ain't. There ain't a damn thing they can do. My lungs look like the black hole o' Calcutta. I got three months, tops."

"I—I don't know what to say."

"Nothin' *to* say, 'cept you were right. Shoulda quit them cancer sticks years ago, like you kept tellin' me."

"Oh, Daddy, I didn't want to be *right*. What I wanted was for you to live a good long life, to . . . to enjoy your children and your grandchildren . . . to—" *To love me, to be a real father—finally,* Ruth thought, but she didn't say it. It was too late now ever to say it. Tears streamed down her cheeks and fell onto her lavender-checked shirt.

"You cryin', Ruth? Hey, don't cry. Please. Listen, Ruthie, you cry, I'm gonna cry, too. This ain't the end of the world. Not for you, anyway. And I ain't worth cryin' about. I got a lot o' good years out of this life."

Ruth pulled a Kleenex from her apron pocket and blew her nose. "Listen, Dad. You can still travel, can't you? If the doctor'll let you fly, I'd really like you to come and live here, with us. You're gonna need somebody to take care of you."

Christ, Tim thought. What a way to check out— cooped up on that depressing farm in the middle of nowhere. Ruth literally nagging him to death—eat this, put on your sweater, wipe your nose, wipe your ass. No, thanks. "I'll be all right here," he told her. "I ain't an invalid yet."

"At least come for a visit—"

"Sure, sure. A visit. I'll do that. There's time left."

"I'll come visit you, if you'd rather. It's just that the kids—"

"No, don't worry about it, Ruth. We'll work it out. Thing that worries me is, how'm I gonna let Allie know? How'm I gonna get to see her and little Stephie before I—well, before."

Ruth's spine stiffened. It was the same old story. Allison came first; Ruth could wait. "I don't have the slightest idea, Dad." She could hear the edge in her own voice. "If Allison calls here, I'll tell her to get in touch with you."

"Yeah, guess that's all we can do, the way things are."

Ruth felt empty and sad, but her tears had stopped. "Guess it is."

"So. I'll check back with you in a day or two, see if you've heard anything."

"Sure, that'll be good. You take care of yourself now. Promise?"

"Yeah, I promise. You, too. 'Bye."

" 'Bye, Daddy. I— I love you, Daddy."

"Huh? Uh, sure. Love you, too, Ruthie. 'Bye now."

The line went dead.

13

Louise Peterson fingered the delicate lace on the pale pink layette gown. The clothes in this last carton were so incredibly tiny. She was always amazed at how small newborns really were; they grew so quickly. She rewrapped the gown in tissue paper, put it back on top of the collection of infant-size sleepers, sweaters, and caps, and closed the lid of the box. She had taken her time searching Stephanie Warren's room, feeling increasingly wistful as she examined the clothes and toys Allison had left behind. Things collected since the day the little girl was born. Things Louise would love to have for her own child . . . if she ever had one. Her period was three days late again, but she'd learned long ago not to get her hopes up. The monthly letdown was too hard to take.

She lifted the box back onto the closet shelf and closed the door. There. The room appeared to be untouched despite her close inspection. If Allison came back today, she'd never know the Petersons had spent the afternoon searching every corner of the place. Louise crossed the hall to the bathroom.

"Sure didn't take much with her," Pete said, as he poked through the drawers in the bathroom vanity. "Enough cosmetics, Alka-Seltzer, cough medicine, Tylenol in here to open a drugstore." He picked up a bottle of Coral Delight nail polish, then dropped it back into the drawer. "Left behind a couple of empty suitcases in her bedroom closet, too."

"The little girl's room is the same way. Lots of toys and clothes. Looks like Allison got the court decision, threw a few things in the car, and ran. Not much advance planning."

"All the better. The less planning she did, the easier time we'll have trackin' her down. You check that desk in the kitchen?"

"Yeah." Louise perched on the edge of the bathtub and watched her husband work. He was beginning to show his age—a slight spare tire around the middle, the dark blond crewcut beginning to thin at the dome—but she still thought he was the most attractive man she'd ever known. "Found a few interesting things." She pulled a small spiral notebook from the pocket of her khaki skirt. "Made some notes." She flipped over a page. "There's a file folder with receipts from bills she paid. So we have her credit card and gas card numbers the easy way."

"That's a bit of luck."

"Last few phone bills were in there, too. I took down the long distance numbers she called. I'll compare 'em with the friends' and relatives' numbers Karl gave us when we get back to the office."

"May be worth something, but my bet's on the next phone bill. See who she called right before she took off. Gotta check the post office and see if she's having her mail forwarded."

"If she is, the paperwork hasn't kicked in yet. There was mail delivered this morning. Comes in through the slot by the front door and dumps onto the floor of the coat closet. There's an electric bill, this month's *Glamour*, and a sales flyer from Sears."

Pete closed the last bathroom drawer and led the way into the kitchen. The built-in oak desk Louise had inspected was neat, with only a memo pad, a blue Bic pen, and a beige Princess telephone sharing the desktop. "Nothin' else in there?"

"The usual stuff—stationery, stamps, envelopes, a bunch of cents-off grocery coupons, warranties for the kitchen appliances. There's some canceled checks, but nothing looks important. Last month's bank statement from Wood Lake Federal showed less than two thousand bucks in her checking account. No unusually large deposits. No evidence of any other bank accounts."

"From what Karl tells us, how flush can she be? She didn't get alimony, and she had all those lawyer's bills to pay in the last few months."

"Yeah, well, she won't get far without money." Louise tried to picture herself suddenly getting in her car and driving until she ran low on money, then looking for work in a strange place. Constantly looking over her shoulder, worrying about being followed or recognized. It was hard enough to visualize being alone under those circumstances, never mind having a four-year-old in tow. She forced her thoughts back to Allison Warren's desk. "There're a few things I *didn't* find that might mean something. No address book, no personal letters, none of the legal papers from the divorce or the custody case. No legal papers of any kind, in fact—birth certificates, passports, Stephanie's immunization records. Unless she's got it stashed somewhere outside the house—a safe-deposit box, maybe—Allison took the time to clean out all that stuff. Probably took it with her."

"Wouldn't you?"

Louise nodded. "Karl say whether Allison kept her passport up to date? Or if Stephanie had one? They leave the country, Lord knows how long it'll take to find 'em."

Pete shook his head. "We'll have to check. But don't forget, unless she's got someone feeding her cash regular, Allison's gonna have to find some sorta work. Her chances of that wouldn't be too hot overseas and I don't see how she's gonna make it without income from somewhere. The sister doesn't look like she's got ten cents to call her own, and the father's retired Navy. He won't have much. My gut says we'll find Mrs. Warren in the good old U.S. of A.—probably waitin' tables in some truck stop." He walked to the kitchen sink, turned on the cold-water faucet, ducked his head underneath, and drank, then wiped his mouth on his sleeve. "Tell ya what else she took with her. Pictures. There isn't so much as one snapshot in the whole place—of anybody. Found three empty frames in the bedroom, but there's no photo albums. Nobody has a little kid without havin' at least one of them baby brag books around. Kid as pretty as the Warren girl, you'd probably have two or three."

I would, Louise thought. *I'd photograph every smile, document every stage she went through, if I had a daughter*. She sighed. "This might give us something." She held out a slip of paper. "It's the top sheet from that memo pad on the desk." Louise had rubbed a pencil lightly across the surface of the paper to reveal what had been written on the last sheet Allison had used and removed. Now the writing showed in reverse, white against the graphite background, revealing the words "Beth Gunderson" and two phone numbers, one with a Duluth area code and the other a toll-free 800 number. "Isn't Gunderson that kiddie shrink Allison hired?"

"Yup. Good work, Lou." Pete gave Louise a playful swat on the fanny, took the slip of paper and placed it inside his notebook. "So tell me, gorgeous, what's your woman's intuition say about where we're gonna find 'em?"

"Not a helluva lot, I'm afraid. Allison might head

for her father's place in San Diego, but Karl says he's a drunk. Not the kind of protector I'd choose."

"Looks like she tried the sister's place already."

"Just a stopgap, you ask me. She couldn't have figured on staying there unless she's a lot dumber than I think she is." Louise pushed her bangs off her forehead; she was overdue for a haircut. "Only thing my intuition tells me is to look for water."

"Water?"

"Yeah. Look around here. Just about every piece of art she's got in this place has somethin' to do with water." A needlepoint harbor scene hung on the kitchen wall. The living room had an oil of a tall ship tossing in a stormy sea. On the bedroom wall hung two delicate watercolors of northern lakes surrounded by pines and birches. "I remember seeing her wheel a stroller down by Lakeside Park when Stephanie was smaller, too. She used to sit and stare out across Lake Superior like most people stare at TV. Just watching the waves, I guess."

"With her old man career Navy, maybe it's in the blood."

"Anyway, I'll be real surprised if we find 'em stashed on some Kansas prairie." Louise checked her watch. Four-ten. "So, what's left here, chief?"

"Third bedroom. Looks like it was only used for guests, but there's a bookcase in there. Might find something in her choice of reading material."

In the guest room, Pete pulled three volumes from the top shelf of the bookcase while Louise inspected the closet. "Here's the blueprint she used to smear poor old Karl," he said, holding up academic treatises on incest and child molestation. "Bet she got those bullshit charges straight out of these."

Louise took the top book and opened the cover. The table of contents listed chapters on the personality traits of molesters, typical signs of abuse in child victims, and psychological treatment options. She couldn't imagine how a woman like Allison, or any mother, could read a book like this, then calmly accuse her husband—whether he was her ex or not—of unthinkable atrocities against their only child. Yet neither could she imagine Karl Warren committing the acts described in this book with his own daughter. Still, one possibility or the other had to be true. Didn't it? Unless . . . unless Allison were somehow honestly mistaken. Unless, truly believing her child had been attacked, she'd bought the books to learn how to help her recover. Louise shut the cover and handed the book back to Pete. Simply thinking about a world in which adults could do things like this to children made her skin crawl. "The whole thing is just so hard to believe," she said.

"Yeah, well, believe it, sweetheart. Allison Warren has to be one vindictive bitch. Listen, Lou, I'll finish up here. How about you go talk to that day-care woman and meet me back at the car? Name's Iris Brinker, lives four doors west, number twelve-eighteen."

Iris Brinker answered the door. A very small boy had his arms wrapped tightly around one of her legs. A petite woman in her late twenties, her dark hair cut pixie-fashion, she wore navy shorts and a hot pink tent top. Louise figured her to be about seven months pregnant.

Louise explained that she was seeking information about the Warren child custody case.

"You from the child welfare?"

"No, I work for the attorneys. I'm an investigator. My questions won't take long."

"Well, I s'pose." Iris lifted the toddler into her arms and opened the door. "Come on in." She led the way through the living room, where two little girls played contentedly with Barbie dolls, toward the kitchen. "Watch out for them toys. You don't want to trip on 'em. We'll have to talk in the kitchen, if you don't mind. Got cookies in the oven."

The house smelled of baking chocolate. Louise's mouth began to water.

"Pull up a chair," Iris said, gesturing toward a beige Formica-topped table surrounded by six chrome and plastic chairs. She plopped the child down on the kitchen floor, where he sat, chubby legs extended at right angles. "Toby want a cookie?" He grabbed the freshly baked round she offered him and greedily stuffed it into his mouth, making happy cooing sounds as he sucked on the treat. Iris pulled a sheet of hot cookies from the oven, put another in to bake and set the timer for twelve minutes. "There." Her hand pressed against the small of her back, she lowered herself carefully onto a chair. "Feels good to get off my feet for a few minutes. Now, what do you want from me?"

Iris Brinker said she had cared for Stephanie Warren for more than a year, on weekdays when her mother worked at the bookstore. In her opinion, Allison Warren was an excellent mother, always concerned with her daughter's welfare. "I'm the one told her there was somethin' wrong with that little girl," she volunteered.

"What do you mean, wrong with her?"

"Well, Stephie just started actin' funny. You know, sexy like. Not the way a four-year-old kid should act."

"Could you be a little more explicit?"

Iris glanced at the baby, who had smeared the gooey cookie from ear to ear. She spoke in a low voice. "First it was takin' off her clothes and touchin' herself in her privates—right in front of the other kids. At first, I figured maybe she's got an itch, maybe she got irritated by bubble bath or somethin' like that, but when I ask her, she says no, she don't have no itch. Then it was the dolls."

"Dolls?"

Iris lowered her voice further. "She'd undress the dolls, the little girl dolls this was. Then she'd take and poke 'em between their legs with crayons. Hard, like she was tryin' to hurt 'em. When I ask her what she thinks she's doin', she just acts scared and starts to cry, won't give me no reason." Iris turned to Toby. "My, you are a picture, aren't you, sweet boy?" She rose and wet a paper towel at the sink, then gently washed the sticky mess from his hands and face.

Louise felt her appetite subside. The cookies no longer looked so appealing. "What did you think was going on, Mrs. Brinker?"

"Lord, I had no idea. I never had a child act like that before, 'specially not a little girl. Final straw was when I caught her with poor little Toby here."

Louise felt a chill. "What do you mean you caught her?"

Iris filled a training cup with milk, put on the cap, and handed it to Toby. He grabbed it with both hands and lifted it to his mouth. "I know all kids are curious about the opposite sex, but this was somethin' way more'n that. What happened was I'm in the kitchen here and all of a sudden I hear this blood-curdlin' shriek. I come runnin' and there's the two of 'em, middle of the living room floor. Stephanie's got Toby's pants down and she's yankin' on his poor little weenie. Hard. She's got the same look on her face like she did with the dolls. I tell you, I swooped down on her and walloped her a good one. Never swatted her before that—never had reason to—but I just couldn't help myself when I saw what she was doin' to this poor little guy."

"Good Lord."

"I just had to tell Mrs. Warren after that. Told her something's wrong with this child, that I can't have her around the other kids unless it stops. I can't take that kinda chance, can I?"

Louise shook her head. "Did—did Mrs. Warren tell you anything about the court case she filed?"

"You bet she did." The timer bell rang and Iris removed another sheet of baked cookies from the oven. "Told me she took Stephie to a doctor and to one of them child psychologists. Found out—" She cupped her mouth with her hand and whispered, "Found out her own daddy'd been doin' nasty things to her." She slid a spatula under two cookies and transferred them to a cooling rack. "Guess maybe those things Stephie was doin' with the dolls and with this little fellow was nothin' more than her tryin' to tell us what was happenin' to her, poor baby. I tell you, my heart just bleeds for that little girl. Said to Mrs. Warren I'm ready to go to court, tell the judge what I seen, if it'll help. Maybe you know if they'll be needin' me? I have to arrange for somebody else to take care of these kids if I'm goin' to court."

"You won't be called to testify, Mrs. Brinker. The hearing was completed on Friday."

"You sure?" A puzzled look stole over her gamin features. "Then why—it's just that I figured Mrs. Warren would bring Stephie back here after this was all straightened out. She usually works Mondays."

"Mrs. Warren and Stephanie seem to have gone away somewhere, on a trip, Mrs. Brinker. I was hoping you might know where they are."

"No. Nobody said nothin' to me."

"Did—did Mrs. Warren ever mention any friends or relatives, anyone she might turn to if—"

"If what?"

"Well, if the court decision didn't go the way she hoped."

Iris tossed the hot cookie sheet into the sink. It landed with a clatter. "You tellin' me they *lost*?"

Louise couldn't meet the other woman's eyes; she stared at her lap. "The judge found that there was no merit to Mrs. Warren's charges against her ex-husband."

"Holy Mother of God." Iris slid back into her chair and folded her hands over her bulging belly as if to protect her unborn child. The kitchen was quiet except for the sucking sounds Toby made with his milk. Iris swallowed and broke the silence. "So what's gonna happen to poor little Stephie now?"

"The important thing is to bring everybody back together, so this thing can be worked out rationally, Mrs. Brinker. Nobody wants to see Allison Warren get herself in any more trouble than she already has. That's why anything you can tell me about where she might have gone, where she might have taken Stephanie . . ."

Iris chewed her lip. "What kinda trouble do you mean?"

"Mrs. Warren defied a court order when she left town. She could go to jail. If she comes back right away, I think that can be avoided, but the longer she stays away, the rougher things are going to be for her."

Iris's expression was grim. "You work for *him*, don't you?"

Louise fidgeted in her chair. Why did she feel she should apologize? Karl Warren had been cleared. He was no child molester. It was Allison who was in the wrong here. "I'm working on behalf of Mr. Warren," she admitted. "He's very worried about his daughter and—"

"I really don't believe this!" Iris struggled to her feet. "Look, I don't have the slightest idea where to find 'em, but I wouldn't tell you if I did." As the volume of her voice rose, Toby looked up anxiously. He dropped his cup with a thud and began to fuss. "I don't mind sayin' you have a nerve comin' into my house like this, lettin' me think you were here to help that poor child."

She's right, Louise thought. She did have a nerve, plenty of nerve; it was an important qualification for the job she did. Usually she enjoyed investigative work, feeling not the smallest pang of guilt when she collared an insurance cheater or helped her side win an accident case. But tracking down Allison and Stephanie Warren somehow made her feel unclean, sleazy. She opened her purse and pulled out a business card. "I'm sorry, Mrs. Brinker, I really didn't mean to offend you. I'm just trying to help a man get his daughter back, a daughter he loves very dearly."

"Ha! He's got a pretty weird way of showin' love." Toby began to cry. Iris bent down, picked him up, and balanced him on one hip. She gently wiped away his tears.

"The judge decided that Karl Warren had done absolutely nothing to harm his daughter," Louise said. "Fact is, it's Allison Warren who's doing the harm." Louise placed her card in the center of the table. "Think about what it must be like for Stephanie to be yanked out of her home in the middle of the night, to be hidden away from her daddy, just for spite."

Iris shot the investigator a stony look.

"If—if you change your mind, if you want to help Stephanie, there's my card. You can call me any time, day or night." Louise headed toward the front door.

"Don't hold your breath."

The little girls in the living room looked up from their dolls and stared as Louise marched through the living room, Iris at her heels. The front door slammed behind her.

Iris Brinker pulled on the door handle to make sure it was latched, then locked the deadbolt.

14

Allison drove the silver station wagon south on I-35, through the Minneapolis suburbs and into the farmlands beyond. The day was young, the air still cool, and, for the first time since they had left Wood Lake, her terror of being caught was seasoned with a sense of adventure. For the first time, she felt they really were going to make it, they were going to have a new life. She even dared to believe she and Stephanie could be happy and carefree again, and that Wood Lake and its nightmares soon would be put far behind them.

Her excitement was not unlike the way she'd felt the time, a year before she married Karl, when she'd embarked on a two-week tour of Japan. As a Northwest Orient flight attendant, she got her ticket to Tokyo practically free, travel industry discounts made hotels affordable. Her problem had been finding a travel companion. Most of her women friends were married and couldn't leave their families; the single ones either couldn't afford the trip or had already used their vacation time. Faced with the choice of staying home or making the trip by herself, Allison had decided to go it alone.

Throughout her journey, she'd felt something missing, she'd had a yearning for someone to share her adventure—a major reason why she became so anxious to find a husband once she returned. Still, the trip was the experience of a lifetime. She was a stranger in a strange land, one where she could not speak the language, where she stood out like coal on snow. A particularly vivid memory from the trip was of emerging from the bullet train in Fukishima, a town in northern Japan, and encountering a group of young schoolchildren assembled on the platform. Not much older than Stephanie was now, the youngsters stared openly at Allison, pointed fingers at her, then chatted excitedly amongst themselves. She smiled and waved and the children giggled shyly in response. A few of the braver ones approached her tentatively. When she stooped down to their height, three or four reached out and gently touched her long flaxen hair.

A young woman teacher hurried over, scolded the children, and shooed them away. "No, it's all right, really," Allison said, wishing she knew the words in Japanese. "I honestly don't mind."

"Gold," the teacher explained in slow, careful English. "Child-len never see hair like gold." She nodded and scurried back to her young charges.

Because the children's curiosity was so open, so innocent, Allison had not felt like a freak; indeed, she had felt special, valuable, adventurous so far away from home. Despite her basic loneliness, taking that trip had made her feel brave, invincible, capable of handling nearly anything.

She had mislaid that sense of her own competence in the years since she'd married Karl. Now it had begun to return. Allison knew she and Stephanie were far from safe, but at least they had made a good start. They had escaped from Wood Lake; they had new, if temporary, identities; they were traveling in a different car, one with Minnesota, not Wisconsin, license plates. With every mile they drove, Allison breathed more easily.

"How many cows did you count, Angel?"

Stephanie dropped Flopsy on the seat and held up both her hands. "Twenny-twelve."

"Hmmm. We've got some work to do on your numbers. Count along with me. One . . . two . . . three . . . four . . ." They reached thirty-two before Stephanie grew bored and began to whine. Allison handed her the bag of grapes from the lunchbox the women at the shelter had packed for them."

They picnicked on tuna sandwiches, carrot sticks, and potato chips at a rest stop past Fairmount, then turned onto I-90 and headed west. They had no set destination, but Allison had always felt drawn to the open spaces of the West Coast. She knew other mothers in her situation had blended into the vast numbers of people living in metropolises like Chicago, New York, and Los Angeles, but she'd never been a big-city girl and she couldn't see bringing her child into that kind of environment. Surely there was a place for them somewhere that could offer anonymity without sacrificing the elbow room she craved. She thought she'd be most likely to find it in the West.

By the end of the day, they had passed into South Dakota. Here the landscape was drastically different from the forest and lake environment of Wood Lake, and from the croplands of southern Minnesota. Now they saw miles of prairie, empty except for occasional herds of grazing cattle.

While they rode, Allison and Stephanie counted cows, dogs, and farmhouses. They played guessing games—whoever guessed the color of the next car they met on the road or the distance to the next farmhouse was rewarded with one of the remaining grapes. They stopped at every rest area and every McDonald's with playground equipment so Stephanie could work off some of her excess energy and Allison could stretch her cramped legs. With all the stops and her strict adherence to the speed limits, the drive went far slower than Allison would have liked, but she dared not risk a speeding ticket.

Shortly after passing the Missouri River, Allison pulled up to a public phone to call the network. She and her daughter had been on the road for more than eleven hours and both were thoroughly exhausted. She dialed the toll-free number and gave her code name, location, and routing, only to learn that she was on her own until she reached Montana; the network had no safe houses in this sparsely populated area.

Luckily, motels were cheap. Allison found a clean, if spartan, one for twenty-seven dollars. Tucking Stephanie into one of the twin beds, she set her travel alarm for six and fell into a deep sleep.

The second day of driving was a repeat of the first, except that the terrain was hillier and the novelty of travel had begun to wear off. They had passed the Badlands and the Black Hills and crossed the Wyoming border when Allison first realized the red car—a Dodge or Plymouth sedan—had been following several hundred feet behind them for a long time. Or maybe the car was simply driving the same route to . . . wherever. She tried to remember when she first had noticed it, whether it had been behind the Taurus after they stopped for lunch, or possibly even since they'd left the motel this morning. *You're being paranoid,* she told herself. Still, when she speeded up, the red car kept pace; when she slowed down, it didn't pass.

Allison's breath came faster and her palms grew damp on the steering wheel. Could Karl's people have found her so quickly, so easily? Had the motel somehow notified him where she was? *Of course not,* she told herself. That was ridiculous. Karl had no way of knowing what kind of car she was driving or that she was using the name Elyse Michaels. Still, that red car made her nervous. She pulled off the highway at the next town and quickly turned off the main street onto a deeply rutted side street, then circled the block several times.

"We there yet, Mommy?"

"Not yet, hon. I—I'm just looking for something."

"I'm *tired* of riding. I wanna get out."

"Just a little longer, sweetheart. Mommy will find us a nice place to stay, real soon."

When Allison pulled back onto the highway, the red car was nowhere in sight. *Idiot,* she scolded herself, *it was just your imagination.* But somehow she knew this wouldn't be the last time she would see demons in pursuit where none existed.

By the time they found an inexpensive motel about a hundred miles past the South Dakota border, Allison's nerves were frayed. Stephanie had whined and complained for the past hour, and Allison was certain she would explode if she had to hear "How much farther, Mommy?" one more time.

Allison quickly filled out the registration card, signing the name Elyse Michaels and giving a phony Minneapolis address and her car's license plate number with two of the digits transposed. She carried the luggage into the motel room.

After a dip in the motel's postage stamp-size swimming pool, both mother and daughter felt their moods lift. "Time to get out and get dried off now, Angel," Allison called. "Let's go have some dinner. I'm starving."

"Me, too." Stephanie climbed up the steps of the pool and Allison wrapped her in a towel, briskly rubbing her dripping hair. "Ow, that hurts!"

"Sorry, puss. Here, how's this?" She draped the towel over the child's head and gave her a quick hug. "Let's go get dressed." The child grabbed Flopsy and headed for the room, dripping a trail of water as she walked.

Gillespie's Golden Steer—Best Beef 'n' Brew in

Town—was directly across the street from the motel and a definite temptation. The thought of another fast-food meal was more than Allison could take. *What the hell*, she decided, *we'll splurge, eat some real food.*

Her hand holding Stephanie's, she led the way into the restaurant's darkened interior. Only two tables were occupied, one by an elderly couple engaged in a heated argument and the other by a man dining alone. Three men in jeans and cowboy boots were seated at the bar off the dining room. Allison chose a booth as far from the other patrons as possible; she took one of the menus wedged between the sugar bowl and the wall and opened it.

The waitress, a buxom middle-aged woman with graying brown hair caught in a hairnet at the nape of her neck, had a friendly, open face. She wore a gold uniform with maroon piping around the collar and sleeves that matched both the flocked wallpaper and the carpeting. "What'll it be tonight, ladies?" she asked, pulling a pad of checks and a pencil from the pocket of her apron and winking at Stephanie. The child buried her face in Flopsy's dress.

Allison ordered the full-pound sirloin with a baked potato and a salad, and asked for an extra plate. "We'll share. I'll have a glass of burgundy, too, please, and she'll have milk."

"Ain't your bunny there hungry?" the waitress asked, glancing at Stephanie. "Want me to bring another plate for her?"

The child raised her eyes and ventured a tentative smile.

"Got a granddaughter just 'bout that age. How old are you, honey, 'bout five?"

Stephanie looked up, but remained silent.

"Four," Allison said.

"Jenny, my son's youngest. Little towhead, full of spunk. Turned five the fifth of July. Actually thought all the fireworks were for her birthday, the little dickens. Couldn't figure out why they got there a day early." The woman laughed. "What's your name, sweetheart?"

"She's shy with strangers," Allison said quickly. "She's called Angel."

"That's pretty. Short for Angela?"

"Uh, no, just Angel." Stephanie's eyes darted in her mother's direction. Keep quiet, Allison silently willed her; don't volunteer that your name is Stephanie.

"That's a nice name. She looks just like a little angel. Where you folks from?"

"Uh, Min—Minneapolis."

" 'Sposed to be real nice up there, from what I've heard. Lots o' lakes and rivers, right? Never been there myself, but I was up at the Mayo Clinic once, 'bout ten years ago. Ever been to Rochester?"

"No. Could we have some bread, please? Right away if you don't mind. We're famished." Allison heard the sharp note in her voice and felt a rush of guilt. It was obvious the woman was only trying to be friendly. It wasn't her fault her curiosity was making Allison nervous.

The waitress's shoulders stiffened. "Of course, ma'am. I'll bring your wine right on out, too." She hurried toward the kitchen.

"Mommy, what's Min— Min— Min apples?"

"Min-ne-a-po-lis. It's . . . it's where we bought our new car."

"Oh. But—but didn't the lady wanna know where we *live*?" The child's brow furrowed above her deep blue eyes.

Allison looked away, ashamed. "Here comes our bread, Angel." The waitress arrived with a basket of warm rolls, a small dish of individually wrapped pats of butter, and a glass of dark red wine. She placed them squarely in front of Allison. "Thanks," Allison called after her. She split a roll, buttered it, and handed it to Stephanie.

She took a sip of the wine and held its acid taste on her tongue for a moment before swallowing. Damn it anyway. So this was how it was going to be—hiding, evading, lying, being terrified of an innocuous chat with a well-meaning stranger. She had always taught Stephie to tell the truth, no matter what. Now she would have to teach her to lie. And Stephie would have to get used to seeing her mother lie, too. How would the poor kid know what was real and what was not? Allison felt a heavy weight had been laid on her chest; she had trouble breathing. How could a child feel safe, protected, if she didn't know what or who to believe? Yet, Allison knew, if she were truthful, her child would soon be back in Wood Lake with Karl. Her fingers clutched the stem of her wineglass. It jiggled and a splash of the dark liquid landed on the white tablecloth. Suddenly filled with an overwhelming sense of loss, she put down the glass and covered her face with her hands.

"What's the matter, Mommy?"

"Nothing, sweetheart," she said, raising her eyes to meet Stephanie's concerned glance with a forced smile. "Nothing's wrong. Mommy's just fine."

15

"What about surveillance on the sister's farm?" Karl Warren leaned forward in the leather swivel chair, placing his elbows squarely on his large teak desk. The desktop was empty except for a clean yellow legal pad placed precisely parallel to the edge of the desk and a gold-filled ballpoint pen nestled next to it. He picked up the pen and absently clicked the point in and out as he spoke. "We know Allison went there once. She may go back."

"Not likely, in my opinion," Pete said. "She's gotta know we'd be lookin' for her there. My money says she's left the state by now. Besides, the layout of that place makes surveillance near impossible. All you can do is sit out on the road, right in the open, see who drives in and out. It's a couple of blocks in on private land to the farmhouse. Can't see a thing from there. Complete waste of time."

Karl scowled. "How hard did you squeeze Ruth Persky for information?"

"Louise talked with her."

"Louise?"

Louise felt Karl's eyes shift to her. She had been silent until now, letting Pete do the talking, as usual in their case reports to Karl Warren. The attorney had a habit of directing his questions and comments to Pete, virtually ignoring Louise's presence. Hearing him say her name startled her. "I—yes, I talked with Mrs. Persky. My strong impression is that she

96

honestly doesn't know where your wife and daughter are now, although one of the boys told me they'd been at the farm earlier and they'd left. The woman seems to believe every word Allison told her about you, too . . . so even if she did know where they were headed, she's not about to tell us."

"Not even if she's threatened with jail time?"

"I tried telling her she could be prosecuted for harboring a fugitive. Not exactly true at this point, but I figured she had no way to know that."

"And?"

"Her response was to launch into a tirade against you." Louise did not add that Ruth Persky's tongue-lashing included her, because she worked for Karl Warren.

Karl muttered something under his breath that Louise could not quite make out. It was just as well. His attention shifted back to Pete, who launched into a report on their inspection of Allison's house.

Louise watched the two men as they conversed— her husband looking slightly rumpled in an old brown tweed sport jacket that was wearing thin at the elbows, slacks that were losing their crease, and a yellow shirt without a tie. His hands gestured wildly with every statement he made. Pete Peterson was full of life, a man whose emotions were readily visible. One of the things that had attracted Louise to Pete was that she always knew where she stood with him. Pete got his fill of game playing in his work; he had no need to do it with her.

In contrast, Karl Warren was fastidiously dressed in a hand-tailored military blue suit, an oyster-white shirt with the perfect length of cuff showing beneath his jacket sleeves, and a burgundy and blue–striped tie. He sat stiffly, his spine erect, his facial expression unreadable. The only clue to his state of mind was his incessant clicking of the ballpoint pen. His office was like him, Louise thought—tidy, organized, lacking in personality. She wondered how he managed to get any work done here, with everything kept so precisely in its place. On the wall behind Karl's desk was a teak table, bare except for a telephone intercom system and a computer. Lining the wall to his left were half a dozen glass-front bookcases filled with matching leatherbound sets of law books, all of them looking new, unused. The wall to his right had a bank of windows offering a distant view of Lake Superior, and the Petersons sat with their backs to the fourth wall, on which were located three locked teak file cabinets, and the door to the receptionist's office. Where, Louise wondered, were the files Karl was currently working on, his telephone memos, his coffee cup, his family photos? She found the place disconcertingly sterile.

"We're waitin' for a report on her credit card charges," Pete reported. "We got her card number and I've got a contact at MasterCard who'll let me know if anything's come through since the day she left here. We're on top of the phone company, too. By tomorrow we should have a report on any numbers she called the last few days before she split— long distance calls, anyhow. And we're checking the DMVs in Wisconsin, Minnesota, Illinois. Nothin' has turned up yet, but if she sold that Buick anywhere close by, we'll find out about it soon as the change of ownership comes through. I'd sure get rid o' that car quick, if I were her."

"How about you, Louise? You're a woman. You should know how Allison thinks. What do you think she'll do?"

Karl Warren turning to her twice in one meeting—had to be a record, Louise thought. "I agree that she'll dump the car, then get as far away from here as she can on the money she's got. Maybe buy another car. Maybe just leave the car at some airport and fly somewhere. She might use her credit card, but I wouldn't count on it. She's not stupid and she has to know we can trace her charge records. Still, she can't have much cash and she may get desperate. We could get lucky."

"Have you checked out her old man in San Diego?" Karl's eyes directed his question back to Pete. Louise's usefulness as a woman apparently was over.

Pete consulted his notes. "Tim Mitchell. Wanted to talk to you about him. The father looks like a good lead, the only family she's got left, 'cept for the sister. I can fly out to California, have a little chat with him, see if I can learn anything. But we might do better by holdin' off, waitin' to see if she and the kid turn up out there. Not let him know we got an eye on him. Trouble is, you put much of a stakeout on Mitchell or his place, you're gonna start gettin' into spendin' real money."

"Do it." Karl's jaw was firm. "I want a twenty-four-hour-a-day surveillance on Mitchell, and I want a tap on his phone. If Allison so much as calls him, I want to know when, I want to know where she's calling from, I want to know what she has to say. And I want to know fast."

"I can get you the shadow, Karl, you want to pay for it, but I don't know about the tap."

"Come on, Pete. Don't tell me you can't find me a California PI who's not queasy about bending the law a little."

Pete pulled on his chin. "Maybe Russ Quinn'd be game . . . but seems like the hard way to me, Karl. You oughta be able to get Judge Winston to issue a bench warrant. Allison's clearly in contempt of his court order. Once you've got that, you oughta be able to get the cops or the FBI to do your surveillance for you, all legal and above board."

"Maybe in a month or two, if they're not too busy. By then she could have my kid stashed in Brazil. One thing I'm learning from this thing is that snatched kids are not exactly top priority with our great American law-enforcement agencies—not when they're snatched by their mothers, anyway. Christ, I've got connections and I can hardly get those guys to return my phone calls. I'll keep after them, Pete, but I want you to talk to this Quinn fellow, get him on this quick."

"Quinn'll cost you, Karl. Twenty-four-hour watch like that, he'll need two, three men minimum on per diem, plus expenses. He'll want a bonus for the tap and—"

"I don't give a damn what it costs! I want my kid back and I want her back now." Karl slammed the gold pen down on the desktop; it hit with a cracking sound. Louise flinched. "That bitch I married isn't going to get away with making me out to be some kind of pervert and then snatching my kid from right under my nose."

"I won't argue with you if you really know what you're gettin' into here, buddy, but this kinda thing can take time," Pete said. "You know that. Remember that Farmville Savings embezzlement case we worked on? Took four months of that kind of work before we even got a lead on that Sadowski fellow, another week before we found him holed up in that backwater town in Maine. But Farmville stood to recover half a mil on that deal. They could afford to spend forty grand to get it. You ready to spend that kind of money?"

"I have no intention of using my own money," Karl said, his voice icy.

"I don't get you."

"Allison is going to get this bill and I'm going to enjoy watching her pay it."

"How you gonna manage that?"

"It's not complicated. She ripped me off for the house in the divorce settlement. The equity's thirty,

thirty-five thousand easy. She's got another five or so in furnishings. Then there's the Buick. Let's say she's worth forty, forty-five grand, minimum. You find her, haul her ass back here, and I'll file suit against her for the costs of finding her and bringing my child back. I'll win, too. Just watch me."

The hair on the back of Louise's neck stood on end. She had no idea whether Allison's allegations about Karl and their daughter were valid, but she did know one thing about this man—he was ruthless. She would not want to cross him.

"Okay," Pete said. "I'll call Quinn. Lou, you got that list of lost and stolen kid organizations?" Louise pulled a typed sheet from her purse. "These people here send out kids' pictures on flyers, put 'em on milk cartons and grocery sacks, that sort of thing. Might as well use 'em. You got a recent photo of Stephanie?"

Karl pulled a photo of a serious-faced, dark-haired little girl from the top drawer of his desk and handed it to Pete. "That was taken three or four months ago. It's the latest one I've got."

"What about a shot of Allison? Sometimes these people will use both the kid's picture and one of the person that took her. We didn't find any photos at the house."

"I've just got this one. Allison kept the rest." Karl handed over a second snapshot.

Pete examined the picture. "Pretty girl. Doesn't look much more'n about sixteen here."

Louise glanced at the photo. The young woman pictured was smiling. She had long, pale blond hair and was wearing a lime-green bikini. She was reed thin, small breasted, and almost hipless. She could have been a child.

Karl snorted. "She was twenty-nine then. This was taken before we were married. Used to take care of herself in those days. Just cut out the face and have it blown up; it'll serve the purpose. The *face* still looks like her." Pete handed the photos to Louise, who stashed them in her bag. "One more thought," Karl said.

"What's that?"

"Feel out those groups. See if a nice little donation to the cause would grease the wheels any, get these photos circulated faster. Whatever it takes, just do it."

"Allison's money?" Louise asked.

"Why not?" Karl's face twisted into a mirthless smile. "That bitch doesn't need any money. Where she's going to end up, the state will pay her keep."

16

Allison turned the knob again, advancing the microfilm to the back page of the next issue of the *Wyoming Weekly Gazette*. She'd spent most of the morning in the local library, carefully checking the obituary notices for 1956 and into 1957, without much luck.

"Mommy, what's this smell like?"

Stephanie, sitting on the floor near the microfilm reader, shoved a scratch-and-sniff picture book under her mother's nose. Allison shifted her eyes away from the screen. "Lemons, hon." She pointed to the picture of yellow fruit. "See the lemons there and the pitcher of lemonade?"

"Uh-huh." Stephanie turned a page. Her tiny fingernails scratched at another picture to release the smell chemically embedded in it. When they first reached the library, Allison had chosen half a dozen picture books from the children's section to keep Stephanie occupied while she checked back issues of the newspapers. It was surprisingly hard to find the right kind of books for her. Dr. Gunderson had warned against exposing Stephie to books, movies, or television shows that might scare her or worsen her nightmares, at least not until the terrifying events of her real life could be dealt with in therapy. Never before had Allison realized how many of the classics could frighten children. She vetoed *Bambi* because of the fawn's loss of its mother. Fairy tales were out, too. They were full of terror: Hansel and

Gretel faced being cooked and eaten by the witch; Little Red Riding Hood's grandmother became a wolf's lunch; Sleeping Beauty fell into a coma; Snow White was poisoned by an apple. Even *The Tales of Peter Rabbit* portrayed Peter being chased by a farmer with a gun. She finally settled on some alphabet and counting books, a Disney version of *Winnie the Pooh*, and *Detective Arthur on the Scent*, a scratch-and-sniff book featuring a basset hound detective in a deerstalker hat. It was this last book that now occupied Stephanie's attention. "Mommy, what's this smell like?" Again, the book blocked the screen from Allison's view.

"Angel, if I don't get this work done, we'll be here all day. You know how to figure it out all by yourself."

"But *Mommy* . . ." The child's voice took on a whining tone that demanded attention rather than information.

Allison sighed. "What is that picture?"

"A pie."

"What kind of pie?"

"I dunno."

"Sure you do. Take a guess."

"Apple?"

"Right! See the apples sitting next to it?" Stephanie nodded. "Now, here's the deal, punkin. You look at the books. That's your work. And let me do mine. Then we can get some lunch and get back on the road. Okay?" Stephanie stuck out her lower lip. "Okay, Angel?"

"I—I s'pose." She sat back down on the floor, crossed her legs, and turned another page of the book.

So far Allison had made notes on three children who had died young, but none was quite right for her purposes. It seemed so macabre, to be sitting here in a small Wyoming library, scanning old newspapers for death notices. To be searching for news of some other unfortunate child's death in an attempt to save her own child's life. Still, it had to be done. If it existed, Allison had to find news of a small girl's death, preferably one too young to have been in school and who had died without any particular notoriety. None of the ones she'd located were quite right. One little girl was five when she died, quite possibly already enrolled in school, which would mean academic records existed. A second had died at three, but she was the youngest of nine; running across one of her living siblings someday was a little too risky. The third tot, another three-year-old, had been kidnapped and found dead three days later; people might well remember the case and her name. Allison finished reading the last entry for 1957, then rewound the microfilm. Her eyes stung.

She inserted the reel for 1958 and fast forwarded to the back page of the January seventh issue. She found it. She read the obituary notice twice to be certain. Katherine Mary Andrews, born in Helena, Montana, on September 10, 1955, had died of spinal meningitis in Buffalo, Wyoming, on January 4, 1958. She would have been just three months more than two years old when she died. She was noted as the "beloved only child of Michael and Mary Andrews of Buffalo." Allison felt a pang of guilt over her own relief in finding the Andrews family's tragedy. Yet, she told herself, her feeling guilty couldn't bring the little girl back to her parents. Truth was, this was perfect for Allison's purposes. Katherine Mary Andrews had died far too young to have left school records. She'd had no siblings. And, best of all, she had been born in another state. It was highly unlikely that the Montana birth records would cross-reference the fact that the child had died in Wyoming a couple of years later, and since Montana was only one state away, she and Stephie could be in the state capital in a day or two. If little Katherine Andrews had lived, Allison calculated, she now would be approaching her thirty-fifth birthday—not far from her own age. Yes, this would work perfectly. Allison had taken the first step in creating a new, documentable identity for herself.

The last paragraph of the notice announced the funeral and burial arrangements, but Allison forced her thoughts away from the long-lost child's misfortune. She reached for her wallet. "Want to put this money in the machine, Angel?"

"Uh-huh." Stephanie quickly abandoned her book, eager for a new activity.

Allison handed her two quarters and showed her where to insert them into the microfilm reader. The child's small fingers plopped them in one at a time. "That's a big girl." She gave her daughter a hug and kissed the crown of her dark hair, feeling infinitely grateful that she hadn't suffered the Andrews family's fate. "Thanks, sweetie."

They listened to the whirring sound as the machine made a photocopy of the page with the obituary notice. When it stopped, Allison retrieved the copy, rewound the film, and put it back in its box. At the librarian's desk, she turned in the reels of microfilm and the children's books and asked for a Buffalo telephone directory. It showed no listing for either Michael or Mary Andrews. Wistfully, Allison wondered whether poor little Katherine Mary's parents had simply moved away or if they, too, had died. "Where can I find a pay phone?" she asked.

"There's a phone booth next to the rest rooms," the librarian told her.

Allison dialed the toll-free number of the helpline and gave her code word. "I'm in Wyoming and we'll be heading into Montana in a couple of hours. Have you got a place we can stay tonight?"

The voice on the other end named a town west of

Billings and told Allison to call again when she'd reached it. Arrangements would be made for someone to meet them and lead them to a farm where sanctuary would be provided.

As she hung up the receiver, Allison felt her spirits lift. She knelt down to Stephanie's eye level. "Well, Angel, what do you want for lunch today? Hamburgers or pizza?"

"I want apple pie and lem'nade," she said with a giggle. "Just like 'Tective Arffer."

17

Exhausted and hot from driving all morning, Ruth parked her pickup in the driveway, fished Allison's keys from her purse, and let herself into the house. It was stifling inside in the noontime heat. She quickly went through the rooms, opening drapes and windows to let in air. The real estate saleswoman would be here in half an hour and it wouldn't help sell the place if the temperature inside was hot enough to roast a turkey.

There, that was a little better. A whisper of breeze coming in the back windows on the north side of the house began to cool it. Ruth pulled a glass from the cupboard, filled it with water at the kitchen sink, and drank deeply. Lord, she'd worked up a thirst, and an appetite to go with it. She checked the refrigerator, but found it turned off, harboring nothing more than a box of baking soda. There were a few boxed and canned goods left in the cupboards— three cans of Campbell's soup, some vegetarian baked beans, cans of tomato sauce, corn, and tuna. Nothing looked particularly appetizing in this heat. She grabbed an opened box of saltines and sat down at the kitchen table. Three dry crackers took the edge off her hunger. She washed them down with another glass of water. What she really wanted was a big dish of ice cream—chocolate almond fudge. Or maybe butter pecan. She would treat herself on the way home.

The doorbell rang. Ruth opened the door to a tall woman with a prominent nose and a receding chin. She was dressed in a fashionably tailored short-sleeved blue suit and high-heeled navy pumps; she wore her steel-gray hair in a neat French twist. Ruth suddenly felt dowdy, shabby in her pink plaid house-dress. She should have worn her Sunday clothes, tried harder not to look like a hick.

"Must have the wrong address," the woman said, a puzzled expression on her face. "I got a call to write up a listing here, but this is the Warren house, isn't it? Name the office gave me was Persky."

"This is the right house. I'm Ruth Persky, Allison Warren's sister."

"Muriel Steiger. Wood Lake Realty." She offered her hand and Ruth shook it.

"Come on in."

Ruth led the real estate woman into the living room and offered her a seat on the beige velour sofa, then sat on one of the brown-and-beige striped chairs opposite. Ruth wouldn't have minded having furniture like this in her house, instead of the worn old junk Vern's family had bought who knew how many years ago. But with their financial problems, new furniture was a pipe dream. "Mrs. Steiger," she said, "what we'd like is to price this place right for a quick sale, but we don't want to sell too cheap. Allie thought it'd bring somewhere around eighty, eighty-five thousand. That sound about right?"

Muriel Steiger set her briefcase down on the floor. "I—I'm afraid I don't understand what's going on here. Where is Mrs. Warren?"

"She's not here. I'm taking care of this for her."

"I can't list her house for sale without her signa-ture . . . assuming she's the legal owner, that is. If the title's in Karl Warren's name, he's the one who'll have to sign."

"You know Karl Warren?"

"Everybody in Wood Lake knows Karl."

Ruth pulled a tissue from her skirt pocket and wiped her damp brow and cheeks. It was still far too hot in here. "This has nothing to do with that man. I've got a paper—" She searched through her purse. "Here it is. Allison got the house when they were divorced. Now she's turned it over to me, so it's legal for me to sign whatever papers it takes to sell. See here, where it's all notarized and everything?"

Muriel inspected the document. "This is a quit-claim deed all right. Looks to be in order." She folded it and handed it back to Ruth. "I'll have to check the county records to make sure the current title is in Allison Warren's name as sole owner." She gazed around the room. "I—I'm just not sure about the other problem . . ."

"What other problem?"

Muriel fidgeted, embarrassed. "Well, her leaving town the way she did, all that. This is a small town, Mrs. Persky. People talk. And word—well, rumor has it that your sister is in contempt of a court order, that she's guilty of—what do they call it?—I think it's parental kidnapping. So I just don't know if it's legal for her to sell her property under these circumstances."

"Let me get this straight," Ruth said, holding up the quitclaim deed. "Way I understand it, this piece of paper gives me title to this house, right?"

Muriel nodded.

"So I don't see where my sister's got anything to do with whether I sell *my* house or burn it to the ground. Right?"

"I—I see your point."

"If you sell this place, you get some kinda commission on the sale, right?"

"Seven percent."

"So where's the problem?"

Muriel shrugged her shoulders. "Guess there really isn't one, is there?" She pulled a sheaf of papers and a ballpoint pen from her briefcase. "It's just that I need to be sure. I can't afford to get in any trouble on this thing."

"Can't really see how that could happen, Mrs. Steiger."

Muriel forced a smile, which made her resemble a gopher. "Call me Muriel, please. Now you can start with filling out this section here. I'll need your name and address and the address of the property being listed for sale. I can take the legal description off that quitclaim deed; don't worry about that. While you're finishing this up, I'll just take a look around and see if you folks've got the price in the right ballpark. You happen to know how many square feet you got here?"

"Sorry."

"No problem. I can figure it out." Muriel pulled a hundred-foot-long steel tape measure from her briefcase, grabbed her notebook, and set off for the bedroom wing. "Nice place," she said when she returned. "Looks like about sixteen hundred square feet and this tract is built on quarter-acre lots. Shouldn't be a problem finding a buyer if we price it right. Gotta warn you, though—the market's been a bit soft lately. My suggestion is to list it at seventy-nine nine, be willing to accept an offer somewhere in the low seventies—if you really want a quick sale. Similar place on the next block went for seventy-seven nine-fifty a couple of weeks ago, but it had air conditioning and it was on the market for more than sixty days."

Ruth felt a headache coming on. Allison should have given her better instructions. When she said the place was worth eighty, eighty-five thousand, had she meant she wouldn't take less than that? Or merely that she was guessing about the price and Ruth should use her own best judgment? Hell, what Allison should have done was sell the place herself, keep Ruth out of it. Ruth knew nothing—less than nothing—about real estate. Didn't much want to learn, either. She took a deep breath. "I—I guess I'll have to accept your advice. Quicker I unload this place, the better I'll like it." She signed the papers and agreed to have the keys copied and to leave a duplicate at the Wood Lake Realty office on her way out of town.

"I'll have my sign in the yard by the end of the day," Muriel said as she headed for the front door. "By the way, I hope you and your sister checked with your tax men on this deal."

"What do you mean?" Ruth had never had a tax man; Vern had always taken care of that sort of thing for the farm and she'd never had a separate income of her own.

"Crossed my mind that there's gotta be tax implications here somewhere, your sister just giving you this place outright the way she did. Gift tax, income tax, I'm not sure exactly what. But I'd be surprised if Uncle Sam doesn't grab off a piece one way or another. Always seems to."

Ruth's hands clenched. "I—I'll keep that in mind."

"The mortgage payments are current, aren't they?"

"Far as I know."

"If you keep the payments up to date, the bank probably won't give you any trouble about keeping the loan, though they may want to change it into your name in view of the change of ownership. You wouldn't want the bank foreclosing while you're trying to sell."

The mortgage. Of course. Why hadn't Allison remembered it? "No," Ruth said, trying to keep her irritation out of her voice. "I certainly wouldn't want that."

Muriel flashed her gopher smile and left, firmly closing the screen door behind her.

Ruth listened as the saleswoman's footsteps clicked across the baking concrete sidewalk, the staccato rhythm of her heels pounding in her ears. Her head throbbed. She kicked at the leg of the coffee table, missed. This was just too much, she thought; Allison was asking too damn much of her. Now there were extra taxes and mortgage payments to think about. Well, she simply refused to worry about them. It was up to Allison to figure out how to pay them. They'd have to come from the money the house brought, and if there was nothing left, it wasn't going to be Ruth's problem.

Ruth told herself she needn't feel guilty. It was clear from looking around this place that Allison had far more than she did, always had. Ruth walked into the dining room, ran her hand over the oak trestle table, its oiled finish glowing. It was a stark contrast to the oilcloth-covered pine table she had at the farm. There was more than the house here to be sold; there were the furnishings and all of Allison's and Stephanie's personal effects as well. Maybe, she thought, she could take some of this furniture home with her; she certainly could use it. Still, it should bring some cash in, maybe enough to pay the mortgage or the taxes.

Ruth opened the china cabinet and examined the set of gold-rimmed dishes inside. Lenox, Eternal pattern, simple yet elegant. Her daughter Lucy would give her eyeteeth to have something like this in her trousseau. On the other hand, if Lucy really married that idiot farm boy she was sleeping with, she didn't deserve to have something this nice.

The cherry-wood box on the bottom shelf looked familiar. Ruth lifted the top and looked inside.

Grandmother Mitchell's sterling silver service, an old Wallace pattern with shells on the handles. So this was where it had ended up. Ruth had loved this set when she was a child; she could remember her own small hands gripping the spoons and forks at family holiday dinners. No way was Grandma Mitchell's silverware going to be part of any garage sale. If Allison had left it behind, it now belonged to Ruth. She carried the box out the front door and loaded it into her truck.

Maybe there were other things that belonged in the family, things that should never be sold. Ruth plowed through closets and drawers, fingering clothes nicer than any she'd ever owned, eyeing more toys than all her own children combined had ever possessed. If these were her own things, Ruth knew, she never could have left them all behind like Allison did. It just reinforced her opinion that Allison had always been spoiled, never even knew the value of what she had. Daddy had started it; it was his fault. From the time Allie was a baby, he had indulged her, given her whatever she wanted, while Ruth got the short end. Things never changed.

Before she left, Ruth helped herself to a few more of Allison's abandoned possessions. Three size-eight dresses that were just perfect for Lucy; they wouldn't bring more than a couple of dollars apiece at a garage sale anyway. A vase their mother had once owned. A china platter large enough to hold a Thanksgiving turkey. A barely used frying pan to replace the one with the cracked handle in Ruth's kitchen. The collection wasn't large and Ruth assuaged her conscience with the certainty that Allison owed her something for her trouble. Why, Allie hadn't even offered her gas money for the round trip to Wood Lake. Typical.

Ruth loaded her haul into the passenger side of the pickup truck and headed toward town to have the house keys duplicated. The sooner Muriel Steiger could start showing that house to potential buyers, and the sooner it was sold, the better Ruth would feel.

18

Karl pushed open the door of the Peterson Detective Agency's office with his leather attaché case, entered, then kicked it shut behind him. Pete, engaged in a phone call, held up his hand in greeting and motioned Karl into a chair.

Louise stopped her work at the computer keyboard and swiveled her chair around. "Hello, Karl. Didn't expect to see you this afternoon," she said, shoving aside a pile of papers on her desk.

"Got out of court early. My case was dismissed."

"—should've thought of that before you hired us, Mrs. Weitz." Pete was speaking angrily into the phone. "We put in three full days plus—"

"How about some coffee, Karl?" Louise asked.

"No thanks. I'm too hot as it is. Just came in to check on your progress, then I'm going home and get out of these clothes, get into something cooler." Karl ran his finger under the collar of his pale blue silk shirt; it came up damp. His eye fell on the rattling old window air conditioner. Why the hell didn't these people invest in an air conditioner that actually cooled the damn place? He certainly paid them enough that they should be able to afford one ... unless they'd been stupid enough to sink all their money into that new house they'd built. The place did look a bit rich for a couple of PI's. Karl found the way they kept their office even more irritating—papers strewn all over the place, wastebaskets overflowing, dirty coffee cups on the desks. It was a wonder they ever accomplished anything. Not wanting to risk soiling his pale camel suit jacket, he removed his elbows from the arms of the black vinyl upholstered chair. Lord knew how long it was since Louise had dusted around here. She'd better be more efficient at investigating than she was at housekeeping.

"—one good reason we should reduce that bill. We did exactly what you hired us to do and we expect full payment. Promptly." Pete listened for a moment. "You do that, ma'am, and I'll see you in court." He replaced the receiver, a surprised look on his face. "Jesus Christ! She actually hung up on me!"

Louise rolled her eyes. "Told you the old bat was as tight as they come."

Karl's annoyance showed. "Hope you two can find some time left over after you've collected your accounts receivable so you can get to work on finding my kid." His voice was heavy with sarcasm.

"Hey, buddy, we're workin' on it," Pete said, flipping a switch so the answering machine would pick up the incoming calls. "I was gonna give you a call tonight."

"Yeah? About what?"

"Got a preliminary report from Russ Quinn, our guy in San Diego. Looks like we may be onto something out there."

Karl leaned forward in his chair. "Let's hear it."

"Quinn says the father, Mitchell, is comin' off the sauce. Looks pretty shaky and sick, but he's sober as a deacon these days."

"Hmm. It's not the first time old Tim tried to dry out. Usually doesn't take for long."

"Don't know about that, but Quinn says the guy looks like he's on his last leg. Liver could well be Swiss cheese by now if he's been boozin' it up a long time."

"Tim's always been a drinker, far as I know. But what makes you says he's 'on his last leg'? He's had that hang-dog, dragged-out look old drunks get as long as I've known him."

Pete consulted his notes. "Lemme tell you what Quinn says. Reports that he picked up Mitchell's trail at his home. Green eighty-three Chevy four-door with three old guys in it pulls up to the curb and Mitchell gets out of the passenger seat. They have a conversation about an AA meetin' they just left and one o' the other old geezers asks Mitchell if he's comin' with 'em to the track at Del Mar that night. Mitchell says he's not feelin' up to it. Starts coughin' and spittin', all doubled over, and the other two guys have to help him into the house. He's leanin' on 'em pretty hard. They put him inside and they leave.

"Maybe an hour later, Mitchell comes out again, walkin' slow and careful like he's not sure he's gonna make it. He gets in his car and drives off. Quinn follows him and the guy makes a couple very interestin' stops."

"Yeah?"

"First he goes to his bank and withdraws close to three grand—in cash."

"Cash?" Karl's eyebrows rose.

Pete smiled. "That's right. Three grand in folding green stuff. Had to get the manager's approval to get the dough that way."

"And he's not heading for the track."

"Not accordin' to what he told the guys in the Chevy. And that's not all."

"Come on, come on, spit it out."

"Mitchell goes from the bank to the Honda dealership and has his car—it's an eighty-seven blue Civic—completely serviced, top to bottom. Pops for a new set of Michelins, too."

"Looks like old Tim may be planning a little trip."

"Or a big one. My theory is, if the guy thinks he's

about to check out anytime soon, he'll try to see his daughter and granddaughter . . . if he lives that long."

"He damn well better live long enough to tell us where Allison and Stephanie are. Assuming he knows. That all you got for me?"

Pete put down the notebook. "Well, yeah. For now."

"What about the tap on Mitchell's phone? Did Quinn get that set up?"

"He's been watchin' for an openin' where he can get a man inside to install a hot mike in the phone. Gotta wait until he's sure the old man's not comin' back for a few hours, though. Next time Mitchell goes to an AA meeting should do it. In the meantime, Quinn's got a real good parabolic mike setup he uses. He can pick up just about anything that's said inside the house with that gadget."

"Well, it had better work." Karl cast a disapproving glance around the cluttered office. "What else have you two been doing?"

"We're waitin' on those other things I told you about. But, hey, I thought you'd be pleased about this stuff we got on old man Mitchell. We keep our eye on him, looks like he may lead us right where we want to go."

"It's a start." Karl's tone was begrudging. "But I haven't exactly got my daughter back yet, have I?"

Pete took a breath before replying. "You knew it was gonna take time, Karl. I think we're makin' good progress, damn good progress, given the short time we been workin' on it."

Karl pushed himself to his feet. He towered over Pete and Louise, still seated at their desks. "My point is, I'd feel a lot better if I thought my job was getting your full attention."

"Look, buddy," Pete said, rising to his full height. He was a good three inches shorter than the lawyer, but more muscular. "We got a business to run here. You know that. We put as much on hold as we can get away with, but we got other clients. You gotta get some perspective on this thing, Karl, not let it eat at you this way. Truth is, I don't think we could do anything more for you if we had another six hours a day to put in on it. Which we don't."

Karl's mouth was a tight line. "I certainly hope you're right," he said, "because I want my kid back. And I want to be able to hold up my head in this town again, put a stop to all the goddamn wagging tongues. I'm sick and tired of the persecution I've been getting around here lately." He picked up his briefcase and started for the door. "Let me be real straight with you, Pete. If I don't get what I want, you won't have me for a client anymore. And, without my business, you and I both know your other clients combined couldn't even pay the rent on this dump. So how about *you* get some perspective." He turned and stalked out the door, leaving it standing open in his wake.

Louise crossed over to her husband and ran her fingers over the tense muscles at the back of his neck. "That son of a bitch!" she said under her breath. "That goddamn arrogant son of a bitch."

19

Allison followed the dusty Jeep up the road to the farm house and parked her station wagon in the gravel area Betsy indicated. There were six other cars already parked there, only one of them bearing a Montana license plate. The others were from states to the east and west as well as the south.

"You girls come on in now, make yourselves right to home," Betsy said, holding out a workworn hand for Stephanie's suitcase. "Bet you're both draggin' your tails with all that drivin'."

Following the directions of the helpline volunteer, Allison had telephoned when she reached Billings, then waited at the specified gas station until Betsy Madison arrived to lead them to the safe house. A tall, strapping woman in her late fifties, Betsy explained that this was her home. She and her husband, Harlow, were farmers, but their sideline, and Betsy's passion, was sheltering women and children who were traveling in the underground.

"Had a grandfather lived with us when I was a kid," Betsy explained. "My mother's dad. Never did work up the nerve to tell what he'd been doin' to me every time he got me alone 'til about three, four years ago. Held it in all that time, lettin' it fester, figurin' it was my fault, the way kids do. What finally burst my boil was one night Harlow and me was watchin' TV and they had on this story about little kids like yer Angel here. All them memories just come floodin' back on me. I started cryin' and couldn't stop. Scared Harlow half to death; I ain't much of a cryer as a rule. Poor man kept at me 'til I told 'im what set me off like that.

"Once it all came out, I found out Gramps'd started abusin' my little sister, Jeannie, soon as I got too big for him. Figure if I'd told like I should've all them years ago, maybe he'd never've bothered Jeannie. Ya know, sometimes I wonder if he did the same thing to my mother when she was a girl." Betsy would never know the truth; her mother was dead years before the family secret came out. "So you might say takin' in folks like you is sorta my way of payin' penance for not havin' the guts to tell about Gramps. My way of seein' that some other little kids don't live a nightmare like me 'n' Jeannie."

Allison expressed her gratitude. It felt good to be safe, and to be in a place where she didn't have to tell lies constantly. She had merely told Betsy to call her Ellie and her daughter Angel. No further information was solicited.

The Madisons' house was large, two and a half stories, with spacious rooms and a huge stone fireplace in the living room. An Irish setter sleeping on the multicolored braided rag rug in the living room immediately attracted Stephanie's attention.

"A doggie, Mommy," she shrieked. "Look at the doggie!"

Allison smiled. "I think that poor doggie is tired, Angel. Better let him have his nap."

"All these children sure do tire old Rusty," Betsy said. "Ain't as young as he used to be." The sounds of children at play drifted in the open windows. "Maybe Angel'd like to play outside a while with the other kids."

Stephanie ran to the window and looked out. "Can I, Mommy? Can I pu-leeze? I wanna slide."

Allison consented, accompanying Stephanie to the

backyard, where half a dozen girls and boys ranging in age from about two to eight or nine played on a set of swings and a jungle gym. "Do you have children?" Allison asked Betsy.

"Never had none of our own. Set up the playground for our little visitors. Folks in town must've thought me 'n' Harlow was in our second childhood, buyin' all this stuff." She laughed at the memory. "Finally told 'em we was gonna start up a dude ranch, needed this stuff for that. Angel'll be all right out here, Ellie, if ya wanna come on in the house, get yourself cleaned up."

Allison and Stephanie were assigned to sleep in what Betsy described as "the dorm." A room on the third level, it appeared to be a converted attic, with three sets of bunk beds along one wall and a single cot near the door. " 'Fraid we're pretty full up tonight," Betsy said. "Them bunks is taken. We got two moms up here. One's got three kids; the other just one little boy. But this single here's free and I'll have Harlow bring up an air mattress for Angel. She can bed down right here next to you."

Allison thanked Betsy, then set her two suitcases in the corner behind the cot. At the foot of each of the bunks were suitcases, each tightly closed. Although the room was large—about twenty-five feet by fifteen—there was no space for individual privacy. Not with three adults and five children sharing it. Allison wasn't certain she could trust her roommates not to help themselves to her belongings if she left them easily accessible, particularly her remaining cash. It seemed best either to keep her possessions locked away or to carry them with her.

When she came downstairs holding her purse, Betsy assigned Allison to kitchen duty, explaining that everyone shared chores at the farm. "This here's Beverly," she said. "She'll show ya what needs to be done to get supper on the table. I'll be in the barn, doin' the milkin', if ya need me."

Beverly was an extremely pretty woman in her middle thirties who wore her dark hair in soft curls around her face. She was busy pounding round steak with a meat hammer while, near her feet, a toddler girl patiently fitted bright yellow squares and triangles into a blue plastic puzzle ball. "Here, Ellie," Beverly said, "you can husk this sweet corn. Guess we'll need a couple dozen ears to feed this crowd."

"Sure." Allison peered through the kitchen window at the children playing outside.

Stephanie was climbing the ladder of the slide, determinedly gripping Flopsy in one hand and the railing with the other. When she reached the top, the child turned toward the house, spotted her mother, and called, "Look at me, Mommy! Look at me."

Allison smiled and waved, watching until Stephanie reached the bottom of the slide and ran around to climb the ladder again. Allison turned back to her assigned work and began pulling the pale green leaves from the corn and dropping them, along with the corn silk, into an empty paper grocery bag.

"Betsy'll want those husks for her compost heap," Beverly said, "so don't throw them out. That woman's got the most incredible garden. Grows everything you could imagine. Guess she needs it with the number of people she feeds around here." She filled a huge canning kettle with water at the sink and put it on the gas stove, then went back to her meat. "Have you driven far?"

"From Wisconsin. How about you?"

"California. Got as far as Great Falls when my car died. Didn't have the money to get it fixed. My daughter and I took a Greyhound here five months ago and we've been here ever since. Don't know when we'll move on. Or where we'll go." The child tossed the plastic ball aside and shrieked with glee as it rolled under the table. She pulled herself to her feet and staggered after it. "You stay in the kitchen with Mama now, Dolly," Beverly said. "It's so great to see her laugh again. Not that it's been easy."

"You sure it's safe to stay here so long?"

"As safe as it gets for somebody like me. I tell you, Ellie, if it weren't for Betsy and Harlow, I don't know what would've happened to us."

"They seem like good people."

"The best. Salt of the earth, good hearts. How long have you been on the road?"

Allison gave Beverly a short version of her story.

"You're new to this, then—this nomad's life. You'll get used to it, as much as any of us do. Did you have a job back in Wisconsin?"

"Clerked in a bookstore, just since my divorce. It wasn't anything much. I was a flight attendant for seven years before I got married. Then I met Ka— er, my husband. Thought I was going to be Suzy Homemaker, live happily ever after. Guess it just goes to show how dumb I was."

"Don't put yourself down. How were you to know?"

Allison started on another ear of corn. "I just can't get past that, you know. How could I fall in love with a man, marry him, live with him, and not have a clue that he could do something like he did . . . to his own daughter? I sometimes think I must have no ability to judge character whatsoever. Lord, I feel so stupid!"

"I know how you feel. I don't know how these guys can all look so damn normal on the outside. I mean, I thought I was a smart woman. I taught college back in California. I've got a Ph.D., for God's sake. Yet, 'til this happened, I actually thought child molesters were seedy-looking creeps who hung around playgrounds and jumped out of bushes at little kids. I didn't have a clue I was married to one, not 'til he started in on Dolly, anyway. God, Ellie, one woman staying here, her husband's a cop."

"My ex-husband is an attorney. Very wired into the court system, buddy-buddy with the cops."

Beverly gave the steak a last blow with the hammer. "You wouldn't have a chance with that kind of setup. Come back in here, Dolly." The child turned back from the dining room door and looked at her mother. "Come on, let's see if you can stack these boxes." Beverly placed a set of colorful plastic boxes in graduated sizes in front of the little girl.

"There, the corn's finished," Allison said. "Now what should I do?"

The two women talked while Allison peeled potatoes and Beverly browned the meat, then added onions and tomato sauce. Allison learned that Beverly had spent time in jail trying to protect her daughter. "I was fool enough to think I could just send Dolly to live with relatives and keep my job at the college," she said. "I thought that would keep her father away from her. But the judge hauled me into court and ordered me to tell where she was. When I refused, he threw me in jail. Then the college fired me. I didn't have tenure and I couldn't very well teach when I was locked up. My husband, on the other hand, did have tenure. He's still teaching."

"So what happened? How did you get out?"

Beverly sighed and an expression of agony distorted her features. "I finally gave in and told where Dolly was. They brought her back, then let me out."

"How long were you in jail?"

"Three months."

Allison wondered if she would have had the

strength to hold out under those circumstances. She hoped she'd never have to find out.

Beverly lifted the frying pan cover and checked the meat, then added half a cup of water. "When they brought Dolly back home, the judge awarded my ex full custody. I got visitation, but it was supervised visitation—a woman cop watching me every minute I was with my own daughter, like *I* was the molester. All this time Dolly had to go home with her father every night."

"How could you stand it?"

"Bottom line is, I couldn't. I waited until the cop got sloppy, began to trust me and let down her guard. Then I grabbed Dolly and ran. We had nothing but the clothes on our backs, the few dollars I had in my purse, and my car. Less than three weeks later, we were at the Madisons' ranch." Beverly lifted the frying pan cover again and added the peeled potatoes, placing them carefully around the edges of the simmering meat. "We've each got our own story," she said, "but it's amazing how much they all begin to sound alike. We all seem to end up in the same place—no money, no home, maybe no future. But in the meantime, at least our kids aren't being raped."

"What about the other women staying here, Beverly?"

"Want to wash those dishes over there? I'll dry." Beverly took a dish towel out of a drawer while Allison filled the sink. "Most of them are just traveling through, like you. Only one other woman besides me has been here very long. That's Wanda. She's from New Jersey, has a four-year-old son named Nicky. You want to talk about how blind the so-called authorities can be, talk to Wanda. Nicky actually got gonorrhea from his father."

"Jesus."

"Wanda went to the social service people and to

the cops, and nobody would believe her. The doctor who examined the boy was a friend of the father's, didn't report it like he should have. What Wanda got for her trouble was her ex filed a slander suit against her. I mean, do you believe the man's gall? I suppose that intimidated the authorities, but I don't think that's any excuse. What does it take to figure this out, anyway? All those people had to do was look at the medical records like Wanda told them to, or maybe test Nicky again. It shouldn't be so hard to add two and two. People just don't want to believe a nice-looking business type like Wanda's husband—particularly one with the chutzpah to file a slander suit—could do something like that to his little boy.

"So anyway, Wanda split. She's been staying here for about two months so Nicky can get the medical care he needs. It's ironic. Now she's the one who needs a doctor who can keep his lip buttoned. She can't afford to answer questions about how Nicky got gonorrhea because it might lead the New Jersey cops to her." Beverly laughed mirthlessly. "*Now* they're interested, now that it's a child-snatching case and the father's the supposedly injured party. Anyway, the Madisons found Nicky a cooperative doctor and the poor kid is doing okay."

Allison looked out the kitchen window again. "Is that Nicky next to my daughter on the swing?"

"Yeah, the little redhead in the green shorts. He and Wanda are staying in the same room you are."

"Oh. Who else is in there?"

"A woman named Larina and her three girls. They showed up a couple of days ago, drove up from Kansas City. Larina's the only one of us who isn't legally divorced. A battered wife. She's got a real mean scar on her forehead; says she got it when her husband hit her in the face with a broken beer bottle."

Allison winced.

"Nice guy, huh? He physically and sexually abused all three of the girls. They all went to court and told what had happened to them, too, but the wooden-headed judge accused Larina of poisoning the girls' minds against dear old dad."

Allison was beginning to feel pretty battered herself. "There's got to be some justice somewhere! I thought it was just me, that I was the only one who got screwed by the system."

"Hardly. There's thousands of us. Maybe hundreds of thousands."

Betsy kicked open the back door and entered, carrying a pail of milk in each hand. She was followed by a short woman carrying two more pails. "Looks like you girls're gettin' along just fine in here. My, but that smells good." She set the pails on the counter. "Ellie, this here's Melissa. Melissa, this's Ellie."

Allison and Melissa exchanged greetings. Melissa seemed tired, haggard. She was a thin dishwater blonde with dark circles under her eyes and deep frown lines around her mouth.

"Melissa, come on over here, hold these bottles fer me, willya?" With Melissa's help, Betsy began to pour the warm milk from the pails into a series of glass bottles.

The voices of quarreling boys drifted in from the yard. "Gimme that, you dumb jerk."

"I had it first. Let go, dickhead!"

A door slammed and the thumping of running feet was heard from the living room.

"Give it back, ya big shit. Give it back or I'll tear yer fuckin' eyes out."

"Ow! Ma! Ma!" There was a loud crash and Rusty began to bark excitedly.

Melissa set down the bottle she'd been holding and left the kitchen on a run. "Cut it out, both of you!"

she screamed. "Now look what you did, you stupid little shits." The women in the kitchen heard slapping sounds. Allison cringed, recalling similar words from her own childhood, on dark nights when her father would turn into a mean drunk.

"Ow! Cut it out!"

"I'll teach you to act like a couple o' damn assholes." Melissa's voice rose to a shriek. "Yer just like yer shit of an old man, both o' you."

"Stop it, Ma. I didn't do anything. *He* broke it. Ouch! Hey!"

Rusty's barking became more frenzied.

Betsy's face was grim. She set down her pail and stomped out of the kitchen. "Let go of that boy!" Her voice boomed. "Quiet, Rusty." The dog ceased his barking.

Allison crept through the dining room and stood at the archway that led to the living room. A surprised Melissa released the son whose arm she held. He looked about six. Another boy, perhaps a year older, cowered behind the sofa. His face bore the rapidly reddening imprint of a hand and tears threatened to spill from his eyes. On the floor were shards of glass.

"I'm really sorry," Melissa said. "My stupid kids broke your figurine. They're both so goddamn clumsy—"

"I can see somethin' broke." Betsy turned to the boys. "We don't allow no runnin' in the house, boys," she said. "No fightin' 'n' no foul mouths, either. Now you boys got the money to buy me another glass cat like the one you broke?"

The boys glanced at each other, then at Betsy. They shook their heads in unison.

"Well, ya can work it off. I'll figure out some chores ya can do around here. Now go outside and no more fightin', ya hear?"

The youngsters nodded solemnly and left the

room. When they had gone, Betsy turned to their mother. "Now, as for you," she said, her face dark. "I ever hear ya talk to yer boys like that again, I ever see ya slap either one of 'em, I'll see you're turned in for child abuse. Ya hear me?"

"You have no right—"

"I got every right. This here's a safe house for kids. Here nobody molests 'em, nobody hits 'em, nobody calls 'em names. Not in *my* house. Ya think the only way to abuse a kid is sex? Hell, gal, if ya do, ya got sagebrush between yer ears."

"The way I discipline my boys has—"

"I ain't done talkin' yet." Although perhaps three decades older, the muscular Betsy towered over Melissa. Her voice was low now, but commanding. "Ya want yer kids to respect ya, ya gotta show 'em respect. Where ya think they learnt them words? Huh? Words like shit 'n' dickhead 'n' worse. From you, gal. Prob'ly from their dad, too, but he ain't here. Whadya think yer teachin' 'em when ya hit 'em that way?"

Melissa did not reply. Her lower lip protruded slightly. She reminded Allison of a resentful, scolded adolescent.

"Those are the rules. Ya wanna stay here, ya follow 'em." Betsy turned on her heel and stalked back to the kitchen.

Melissa bent to pick up the pieces of shattered glass. Allison entered the living room and picked up an ashtray from the coffee table. "Here," she said, putting the ashtray on the floor next to the other woman. "We can put the broken glass in here." She began to help with the cleanup.

"She had no right to talk to me that way," Melissa said, her voice full of self-pity.

"But she's right," Allison said. "Yelling at your kids and hitting them like that just steals their self-esteem. If you teach them they're no good, that's all they'll learn."

"What makes you such an expert?" Melissa plopped a piece of broken glass into the ashtray.

"Personal experience. I was a kid like that. My mother died and my father drank. He'd come staggering home when he was on one of his benders. I used to hide under my bed, scared he'd find me and start in on me again." Allison shuddered as she recalled the terrified little girl she had been. "There was never any kind of sexual abuse, thank God for that. But my old man had a helluva nasty tongue on him and no compunction whatsoever about smacking me a good one in the face, hard enough to make my nose bleed. I thought he must hate me. And if my own father hated me, I figured I must be a terrible person. I kept trying to get him to love me, but no matter what I did, nothing ever seemed to change. You want your boys to feel like that?"

Melissa's eyes filled. "I don't hate my boys. It's just that they act so wild sometimes. I'm only trying to get them to behave."

"Look, Melissa, I know how frustrated you feel, but Betsy's right. Yelling at them like that, hitting them, that just makes things worse."

"So what am I supposed to do, tell 'em how thrilled I'd be if they acted like civilized human beings for once? I bet that'd really shape 'em up in a hurry. Wouldn't you say?"

"No," Allison said, rising to her feet. "I don't think sarcasm would work one bit better than what you've been doing. But I do have one wild idea. You might try telling them they're good boys and you love them. They could be so surprised that they'll be shocked into behaving." She walked out, leaving Melissa sitting on the floor, staring at the last few pieces of shattered glass.

"Nice speech," Beverly said, when Allison had returned to the kitchen.

"You heard me?"

"I've got good ears and you didn't exactly keep your voice down. Sounds like you had a pretty miserable childhood."

"It wouldn't win the *Good Housekeeping* seal of approval."

Beverly smiled. "Guess none of ours would. But you don't seem to have any scars from it."

"None you can see. But I spent a year in therapy after my marriage broke up. I thought that was the final proof that I was a horrible person, when I couldn't even make my marriage work. What I learned was that the reason I married a man like him, why I put up with his tearing me apart the way he did, was because it was so familiar. In a lot of ways, he was just like my dad, only as it turns out, a lot worse."

"So what did your husband do to you?"

Allison bit her lip. "I guess I should have seen the writing on the wall. Oh, he never hit me or anything like that. I'd like to think I'd have left him right away if he did that. He just . . . well, he knew just how to pick me apart, how to make me feel worthless. He used to say I was a terrible housekeeper, that I had horrible taste when it came to decorating the house, that my clothes were atrocious. And he—" She choked on the memory. "When I got pregnant, he said I'd turned into a fat slob, that he wasn't attracted to me anymore. He—he wouldn't even sleep with me anymore. After the baby was born, he got even worse. He kept calling me a ton of lard."

Beverly looked at her in amazement. "*Fat*? A ton of lard? You? Your figure's perfect."

"I gained nearly forty pounds when I was pregnant, kept twenty after my daughter was born. First time in my life anybody could tell I had breasts." Allison glanced down at her chest and smiled. "I've lost seven or eight pounds the past few weeks. Worried them off, I guess."

"God, Ellie, you must have been skin and bones before you got pregnant. I can't picture you weighing fifteen pounds less."

"I used to be real thin. My husband liked me that way."

"Let me guess. He didn't much like your getting pregnant, did he?"

"That's what my therapist thought. She said he probably wanted to keep me like a child he could control. Once I became a mother, it ... well, it changed things between us. I kept trying to do everything he said he wanted, trying to change, but he just kept on treating me like I was totally repulsive. I—I felt like the ugliest woman in the world."

"That's what he wanted, wasn't it? He wanted to control you completely. Control your very ego. Somehow all these guys seem to be control freaks." Beverly began to drop the ears of corn into the boiling water. "I guess that's why they go after little kids. Little kids are a lot easier to control than real adult women."

"I guess when he married me I was a lot like a little kid, even though I was almost thir—" Allison stopped herself. "Lord, Beverly, will you listen to me? This is embarrassing. I never even told my therapist half this stuff. I don't know what's gotten into me lately."

Beverly placed a consoling hand on Allison's shoulder. "It's okay, Ellie, honest. We've all got to get it out somehow, all the pain and frustration we've got inside us. Far better you talk to somebody like me, somebody who's been there, than do what Melissa's doing—taking it out on her kids."

* * *

The evening meal at the big dining room table was tense, with Melissa still pouting and shooting resentful glances at her hostess. The children seemed to sense the antagonism among the adults, which made them restless and quarrelsome. Allison was grateful when the meal was finished and she could retreat to the kitchen to help with the dishes. Organized as ever, Betsy assigned each of the women to a task: Larina bathed her girls; Melissa swept the dining room floor; Wanda and the older children took Rusty for his evening walk past the barn; Beverly and Allison drew kitchen duty. The only adult exempt from after-dinner work was Betsy's husband, Harlow, who had spent his day tending to the farm. Now he sat in the den enjoying an old movie on TV.

This time Allison dried while Beverly washed and Betsy stacked the clean dishes in the cupboards.

"Got some bad news today, Bev," Betsy announced. "Remember that tall, dark-haired woman, called herself Gertie, who stayed here two, three months ago? Came from somewhere back East—Maine, I think. Had a daughter named Cindy, about four, 'n' a boy called Sonny, about two?"

"I think so. They stayed in the blue room for a week or so, right? And the mother, Gertie, read all those romance novels?"

Betsy nodded. "That's them."

Beverly's face fell. "Did they get caught?"

"Not quite. Got a Federal Express with this story from the Portland paper in it. About this woman 'n' her two kids who come back there 'n' the woman admits all these things she's been sayin' her husband done to the kids was a lie. Name's Mary, somethin' like that, not Gertie, but it's her picture, it's the same woman. I knew 'er right off."

"But why?" Beverly asked. "Why would she do such a thing?"

"Said she just wanted to get him, that husband of hers. Seems he had another woman 'n' this Mary, or Gertie, or whatever ya wanna call 'er, was mad at him for that. One lie led to another 'n' the thing got outta hand. Next thing she knows she's gotta go on the run. She came home as soon as she ran outta money 'n' got tired of movin' around with the kids night after night."

Allison dried the dishes as she listened to the two women talk. Were women like Gertie common, she wondered? She couldn't fathom anyone's doing what she had done out of spite, yet Allison knew women who had tried to bankrupt their husbands during a divorce, and even one who'd tried to get her husband fired from his job. Still, a false accusation of child molestation had to victimize everyone, especially the children. Poor little Cindy and Sonny, yanked away from a dad who undoubtedly loved them, thrown into a nomad's life just because their mother was bitter and bent on taking revenge against their father.

"Lord, this kind of thing makes me steam," Beverly said, punching at the sudsy dishwater. "It just isn't fair. Women like her hurt all the rest of us and our kids. Every time something like Gertie's phony story comes to light, people are all the more willing to believe we mothers are *all* just a bunch of liars."

"Never thought I'd have to worry about somethin' like this," Betsy said. "Figured a certain number of my mothers might be honestly mistaken . . . ya know, meanin' well but makin' somethin' outta nothin'. But I never figured on out 'n' out lyin'."

"So what do you think, Betsy?" Beverly asked. "Did Gertie spill the beans about where she and the kids had been hiding?"

Betsy shrugged her broad shoulders. "Who can tell what a liar like that'll do?"

Allison's hands froze on the cup she was drying. "What are you talking about?"

Beverly pulled the plug and drained the dishwater. "If she gave the cops a list of the safe houses where she'd been, somebody could be watching this farm right now."

"Oh my God. I've got to get out of here." Allison put the cup and towel on the counter.

"Where ya gonna go, gal?" Betsy asked.

"I—I don't know, but I've got to go. They could be looking for me and Angel, they could have our pictures."

Betsy placed a restraining hand on Allison's shoulder. "Hey, hold yer horses a minute, Ellie. Ya gotta understand a couple things about us country folks. We don't move too fast. And we take care of each other. I 'spect the sheriff'd give me a call before he'd come all the way out here on somethin' like this. 'Specially if all he's got is a tip from somebody back East he don't even know. We been friends for years and this ain't exactly bank robbing we're talkin' about."

Lord, Allison thought, could she afford to rely on this woman's hunch? Yet it was already dark and she had nowhere else to go. Nowhere else to hide. Nowhere safe.

"Look, gal," Betsy continued. "At least stay the night with yer little one. You can move on in the morning if ya want."

"I—I guess that's best." Allison picked up the damp dish towel and hung it over the rack to dry. "What about you, Beverly? You going to stay?"

"For tonight, anyway." A deep crease appeared in Beverly's pretty forehead. "Tomorrow I'll have to take a look at my options."

Allison wondered whether she really had any.

*   *   *

Later, Allison lay awake on the hard cot in the dorm, listening to Larina's snores and the light breathing of the children dozing across the room. Stephanie lay on the air mattress next to the cot, her small body curled into the fetal position and her thumb stuck in her mouth. After the afternoon and evening of fresh air and physical activity, the little girl was exhausted and sleeping deeply.

Allison was exhausted, too, overtired. She lay tensely coiled in her bed, playing the day's events over and over in her churning mind. She couldn't stop thinking about that Gertie woman, who'd actually made up lies to accuse her husband. Allison could understand women who, in the trauma that accompanied divorce, might have misjudged things their children told them or things they thought they'd observed. But not ones who just plain lied.

As she lay sleepless, Allison ran the events of recent weeks through her mind. Stephanie's nightmares, her strange sexual behavior at the babysitter's house, the conclusions of the pediatrician and the child psychologist. Ninety-five percent certain, wasn't that what Dr. Gunderson had said? After a professional observation of Stephie using play therapy, the psychologist's opinion was that the child had indeed been sexually molested. And who else could have been responsible, if not Karl? Not Iris Brinker's husband; he was never home while the children Iris babysat were there. Some friend of Karl's? It was nearly impossible to believe Karl would have left his daughter in another man's care. And, if he had, he certainly would have revealed this in his own defense.

No, Allison told herself. She could not be mistaken. Stephanie was an incest victim and, as a mother, Allison had had no choice but to embark on this frustrating, tiring, often terrifying journey to protect her child from further abuse.

Still, if there were some other explanation for what had happened to Stephanie, Allison knew she would never be able to forgive herself. Unlike Gertie, she could never shrug off the guilt of having put her child through this kind of trauma.

Allison fell asleep trying to reassure herself that, of course, she had done the right thing for the right reasons. She almost succeeded.

20

"Hi, Ruthie. It's Dad." Tim was calling in the early afternoon. The higher long distance rates be damned; he might not live to see the bill anyway.

"Daddy. Everything okay? How're you feeling today?"

" 'Bout as well as a man dyin' of lung cancer oughta feel, I 'spose."

"Daddy! Cancer's nothing to joke about."

"Who's joking? Fact's fact. We both know I'm gonna cash it in one of these days. Might as well face it. I'm feeling about the same. You okay?"

"Sure, just still a little tired is all. Driving to Wood Lake and back in one day always takes the starch outta me."

"Wood Lake? Is—did Allie come back?"

Ruth made a clucking sound with her tongue. " 'Course not, Daddy. She's not comin' back to Wisconsin, not unless they drag her back. I told you about her wantin' me to sell the house for her, didn't I? I must have."

"Maybe, I don't recall. So you heard from Allie? How is she?" Feeling slightly dizzy, Tim leaned against the kitchen counter for support. When something so simple as talking on the phone could weaken him this way, he had to recognize that his days were numbered.

"Daddy, I haven't heard a word from Allison. You know I'll let you know right away if I do. This trip to Wood Lake was something we set up before, when Allie was here at the farm. She asked me to put her house on the market, try to get it sold and hold on to the money until she could figure some way to get it. So I drove up there and took care of the real estate listing, that's all. I'm real glad you called, though." Ruth's voice mellowed, took on almost a bashful quality. "Got some good news."

"Yeah? What's that?"

"The twins took a blue ribbon at the 4-H meet last night, for that lamb the two of 'em raised. First place in the whole county! How about that? Vern was so proud of 'em. Tony made the acceptance speech in front of about sixty people, then Dennis got up and said—"

"Good, Ruthie. You tell the boys their grandpa's real proud of 'em, too."

"I will, Dad. I tell you, you should've been there. That Denny can be such a love sometimes. Told that whole crowd that the credit really oughta go to his dad 'cause he—"

"About Allison, Ruthie." Didn't the woman realize this call was long distance? What did he care about some stupid farm contest, for God's sake? "When you hear from Allie, I got a message for you to give her. It's real important."

Tim heard only static on the line.

"Ruth? You still there?"

"I'm still here." Ruth's words were clipped.

"I want you to tell Allie I got everything all ready. Got my car serviced, my suitcase packed. Got plenty o' cash ready. She says the word, I'm on my way."

"On your way where?"

"Wherever they're hid, Allie and Stephie. They're in trouble, old Dad's gonna do what he can to help 'em out. They can count on that."

"Sure."

"When she left your place, she didn't happen to say how long 'til she might be callin'?"

"No, Dad, she didn't. But I can guarantee she'll call as soon as she starts running out of money. She was pretty darned anxious to get that house sold."

"Well, you be sure and tell her her old man's got some cash ready for her, and I can get more—plenty to tide her over 'til she can get what she needs outta that house."

"What about your medical bills, Dad? It's foolish for you to strap yourself to the wall just because—"

"I don't give a damn about me, Ruthie. I can always go to the VA hospital if I have to. One of my kids needs me, I figure it's about time I was there for 'em. Can't take it with me now, can I?"

Ruth sighed. "Okay, Dad, whatever you say."

"Better be goin' now, Ruthie. You give Tony and Denny my congratulations on that calf now, you hear?"

"Lamb, Dad."

"What?"

"They got the goddamn ribbon for raising a lamb, not a calf."

"Oh. Well, can't expect an old salt like me to know the difference . . . unless maybe they're on a menu." Ruth did not join in her father's laughter. "You take care now, Ruthie."

"Yeah. You, too, Dad. 'Bye." Tim heard a sharp click on the line and Ruth was gone.

Private investigator Russ Quinn stubbed out his cigarette, removed the tape cassette from the recorder, and marked it with the date and time of Tim Mitchell's call. Quinn was stationed in a Jiffy Home Cleaning Service van parked across the street from Mitchell's small bungalow. The street was a quiet one, lined by tiny thirty- to forty-year-old stucco boxes owned mainly by couples who were away at work during the day. Except for a few cars parked randomly, the street was empty. In the van, Quinn had use of the latest surveillance equipment. Most of it was illegal if used for eavesdropping, but he wasn't about to let that stop him. He figured Mitchell would never find the hot mike in his phone anyway. Poor jerk probably had no idea anybody'd even take an interest in him, his mind preoccupied the way it was with his health and his daughter. Even if he did happen to come across the mike, Mitchell'd have no way to figure out who put it there.

Quinn turned down the volume on the hot mike receiver now that Mitchell's call was completed and checked the position of the parabolic microphone. This was the boring part of the job, sitting here, waiting for a subject to take action. A guy could get awful tired of being cooped up in a van for hour after hour, nothing to do but eat junk food, smoke cigarettes, and piss in a bottle because he couldn't risk leaving the stakeout to find a bathroom. It could get downright depressing.

An ear-splitting wracking cough, followed by sounds of throat clearing, spitting, and labored breathing came through the receiver's speaker. His nose wrinkled in disgust, Quinn lowered the volume. He told himself he'd have to get used to these nauseating noises if he was going to sit on this stakeout, with the old man suffering from lung cancer and all. Tough break for the poor guy, but potentially great news for Pete Peterson's client. If Mitchell's daughter knew her dad was dying, chances are she'd risk seeing him just once more before the end . . . and she'd have to make it pretty soon. These lung cancer types didn't last long.

A whirring sound came through the speaker, then the tinkle of a liquid being poured into something metal. Quinn recognized the sound of an electric can opener. Mitchell was preparing his noontime meal, probably a can of soup. Quinn's stomach growled and he reached for the rumpled Winchell's sack. Only one jelly doughnut left. He poured the last of the coffee from his thermos and used it to wash down the doughnut, then lit another cigarette and inhaled deeply.

Quinn sat, listening to the sick man puttering around his kitchen until four o'clock, when Bernie Morello came to relieve him. He quickly filled Bernie in on Mitchell's phone call to his elder daughter, grabbed his empty thermos, and left.

All in all, Quinn hadn't put in a bad day's work. He had learned a couple of things he was anxious to pass on to Peterson: Mitchell was on his last legs and anxious to see his younger daughter and her kid, and Allison Warren was expecting her sister to sell the Wood Lake house and somehow send her a shitload of money. Clearly, the missing woman would be in contact with her family, probably sooner rather than later.

Quinn's confidence that they'd eventually locate Allison and Stephanie Warren began to grow. He'd been in this business long enough to know that the only skips who completely escaped a good trace effort were those with the means and the courage to cut all ties to their old lives. And it was becoming increasingly clear that that small elite group did not include Allison Warren.

21

Karl Warren stomped into the Wood Lake Realty office in a black fury. "What the hell're you trying to do to me, Muriel?" he demanded.

Startled, Muriel Steiger looked up from the multiple listing form she'd been completing. "Karl. What're you—"

"You know damn well what I'm doing here. I just drove by my old house, and you know precisely what I found—one of your 'for sale' signs stuck smack in the middle of the lawn." He leaned over and pounded his fist on Muriel's desktop. The desk shook. "I just can't believe you'd pull this kind of shit on me, Muriel. Here you are, working for the woman who stole my kid, and you don't even have the common decency to call and tell me where she is!"

Muriel pushed her desk chair back with shaky hands and rose to her full height. Her cheeks flushed pink and her heart raced. "Don't—don't you dare lecture me about common decency, Karl Warren," she sputtered, jutting out her weak chin as far as possible. "Who the hell do you think you are, coming in here talking to me like this?"

Karl was momentarily taken aback. Maybe overt intimidation wasn't the best way to get this broad's cooperation. He smoothed his brow and arranged a contrite expression on his features. "Hey, maybe I came on a little too strong," he said, opening his huge hands in supplication. "I didn't mean to insult you, Muriel. It's just that I'm a nervous wreck lately. I'm not sleeping much, I'm worried sick about Stephanie, my poor little baby. It's driving me crazy, not knowing is she eating, is she sleeping, is she even still alive? You don't know what it's like to have your only child stolen." Karl saw the tight line of Muriel's mouth begin to soften. "I—I even began to think you might actually *believe* the things that sick, vindictive woman has been saying about me." His voice and face registered complete astonishment that anyone could possibly believe he was guilty.

Flustered, Muriel quickly denied she'd ever had any doubts about Karl's essential character.

"Still, I'm sure you can see how I felt when I saw that 'for sale' sign. All this pressure I've been under, and then to be hit with what seemed to be . . . well, a betrayal of friendship is the only way I can think to put it. Hell, you and I've known each other since grade school."

Muriel nodded. "It has been a lot of years."

"Then you must be able to see how . . . well, how hurt I was to find out you were in contact with Allison—I mean under the circumstances—and you didn't even let me know."

"Karl," Muriel said, reclaiming her seat. "I haven't been in contact with Allison. I haven't seen her. I haven't talked with her. I have absolutely no idea where she and Stephanie are."

"Then how could you list the house for sale? Did she arrange the listing before she skipped town? That must be it. As an attorney, Muriel, I have to warn you—"

"Karl! Will you keep quiet for one minute and listen to me? I'm more than happy to tell you the whole story, but you're gonna have to shut up and give me a chance."

Karl lowered himself into a seat facing Muriel's

desk and kept silent as she described her meeting with Ruth Persky.

"A quitclaim deed, huh?" he said when she had finished her tale. "Wonder who advised Allison to pull that cute little trick."

"It all looked perfectly legal to me, properly filled out and notarized and everything. I suppose I could've turned down the listing, but I—"

"No, no. That wouldn't help. Ruth Persky'd just go to another broker."

"That's what I figured. I spelled out my concerns to her, about everything being legal and all, considering Allison's probably in contempt of court. At least that's how rumor has it." Karl nodded. "The last thing I want to do is get caught in the middle of anything messy. But it seemed above board. Now, if you can show me where I'm out of line on this thing legally, Karl, I'll cancel the listing."

Karl shook his head. "No, no, don't do that. There really wouldn't be any point." He was beginning to see how he could make the situation work for him, how it could be used to flush Allison out of her hiding place. "Listen, Muriel. I'm sorry I acted like . . . well, like a jerk. Honest, I can see I was way out of line."

"We won't mention it again."

"Good, and if that house is going to be sold, there's nobody else I'd rather see have the sales commission."

Muriel smiled bashfully. "Thanks, Karl. I really appreciate that."

"Just one favor, if I might ask?"

Muriel's eyebrows rose.

"A copy of the listing."

"Will this do?" She handed him a sales flyer describing the property and the asking price.

"Very nicely, thank you." Karl folded it precisely

in thirds and tucked it away in the inside breast pocket of his suitcoat.

Fifteen minutes later, he was at the office of the Peterson Detective Agency.

"You look like the cat that swallowed the canary," Pete said.

"This is your lucky day." Karl grinned broadly as he whipped the real estate flyer out of his pocket and, with a flourish, held it up to Pete's and Louise's view. "You two," he said, "are about to buy yourselves a house."

22

Louise could tell that Muriel Steiger was curious about why she'd asked to tour Allison Warren's house, but all Louise had said so far was that no, she and Pete were *not* planning to sell their new place south of town. Muriel probably thought the Petersons were about to be divorced and were seeking separate homes. But Muriel's thoughts about Louise's personal life weren't her biggest concern just now. Louise was far more worried that she'd let something slip and Muriel would realize she'd already been over every inch of this house. So she did her best to keep her mouth shut. Unfortunately, Louise's reticence seemed only to spur Muriel Steiger to work even harder in extolling the obviously incomparable virtues of Allison Warren's home.

As they moved on to inspect the kitchen, Muriel began to gush. "This place is positively immaculate, isn't it? There's no doubt Mrs. Clean lived here. You could eat right off that range top." Louise wasn't sure why anyone would want to. "It's all in move-in condition, and just *look* at this pantry cupboard!" Muriel whipped open the door. "Have you ever seen so much room for cans and packages? I tell you, if I had storage space like this at my house, I'd cut my grocery shopping trips down to once a month. Don't you just hate to shop supermarkets? Such a complete waste of valuable time."

149

Louise expressed polite interest and silently counted the minutes until she could make an offer to purchase this place and get the hell out of here. She doubted the sale would ever be consummated, anyway, and it bothered her conscience to lead the Steiger woman on.

Finally, the two women returned to the living room, Muriel having shown off every closet and cupboard in tedious detail and remarked on them with her apparently limitless array of superlatives. "Really scrumptious place, isn't it, Mrs. Peterson? I'm sure your husband will be crazy about it, too. There's even plenty of room to put a workshop down in that basement."

Louise almost laughed out loud at a sudden vision of Pete hovering over a workbench, trying to tell a chisel from a screwdriver. The man couldn't even change a tire. It had been Louise, not Pete, who'd managed to hang the drapery rods and the towel racks when they'd moved into their new home two years ago. She was the one who'd hooked up the office computer, too.

"Now, when would you like to bring Mr. Peterson to see the place?" Muriel asked. "Just name the time, any time at all. I'll work right around your schedule."

"That really won't be necessary." Louise opened her bag and began to search through it.

Muriel's face fell. "I see. Well, there are other houses available, of course. If you can just be a wee bit more explicit about what you're looking for . . . I have lots of other listings in the area and I'd be glad to—"

"No, please. You don't understand. I don't want to see any more houses."

"If this place isn't big enough or maybe you want a two-story, I—"

"This house will do." Louise pulled a checkbook

out of her bag and looked to make sure it was her personal account's, not the agency's. She waved it under Muriel's nose. "You said the seller's asking seventy-nine nine, right?"

"Oh." Muriel was taken aback. "You mean you want to *buy* this place? Just like that?"

Louise nodded.

"But won't your husband have to see it?"

"No need." Louise could see she would need to come up with a cover story after all. It was clear that a traditionalist like Muriel Steiger wouldn't be able to fathom a happily married woman's making her own decision to buy a house. "I—I inherited a little cash from a relative and I want to invest it," she said. "Anything I decide to do with my separate funds will be fine with my husband."

"How—how nice."

"Now, the asking price?"

"Uh, seventy-nine nine."

"I'll offer sixty-five even."

"Oh. But that's nearly fifteen thousand below what the seller wants."

"Fourteen nine under, to be exact."

"I don't think—"

"I'll give you a check for a thousand dollars earnest money now," Louise said, pulling a ballpoint pen from her bag. "You can assure the seller that I shouldn't have any trouble qualifying for a new mortgage with twenty to twenty-five percent down, although I'll want the sale contingent on my obtaining one at an acceptable interest rate. I'm sure you can help me find a lender."

"Of course, that's part of the service. But I don't know if the seller will take sixty-five thousand. That's awfully low, even in a soft market."

Louise shrugged. "Let me level with you, Ms. Steiger. I'm looking for a bargain—you know, for an investment to rent out to tenants, not to live in myself. I have to admit I know a little something about the background of this particular place, and I expect there's quite a bit of urgency about finding a buyer."

Muriel fidgeted. "I—I really can't discuss that. It just wouldn't be ethical. You understand. But you're sure you don't want to raise the offer just a teeny bit? Maybe seventy-two, seventy-three? I'm sure you'd have a much better chance of having your bid accepted."

"Sixty-five it is. At least that'll test the waters. The seller can always present a counteroffer. Now, how should I make out the check?"

Muriel wrote up the purchase offer and promised to do her best to obtain the seller's answer within twenty-four hours. She handed the pink copy to Louise and clipped the deposit check to the yellow copy.

"I'll wait to hear from you then," Louise said, holding out her hand. Muriel shook it with icy fingers, her face still registering her bewilderment.

Louise walked down the driveway, climbed into her car, and drove off. She never looked back.

23

Allison awoke first, her body cramped from the tense position in which she'd finally fallen into an uneasy slumber. She'd never liked sharing sleeping quarters. She'd had to do it plenty of times on flight layovers; the airline doubled up the stews' accommodations, refusing to provide them with private hotel rooms. But this was ridiculous—eight people sharing the dorm. Every time one of the children rolled over or moaned aloud in a dream, Allison bolted awake. And Larina was still snoring. Allison tried to be generous about it; the poor woman looked like she'd had her nose broken more than once and it had never healed quite straight. Larina probably couldn't help the fact that she snored any more than Allison could help the fact that the snoring interrupted her sleep.

She climbed off the cot and stretched. Lord, she was tired! Barefoot, she padded silently to the bathroom. At least she would have the place to herself for a few minutes until the others awakened. When she and Stephie were packed, they would hit the road again, the sooner the better. Particularly if there was any chance that the captured Gertie had spilled her guts to the Maine police about the Madisons' running a safe house on their farm.

By ten o'clock, Allison had loaded the suitcases into the Ford wagon and strapped Stephanie into her safety seat. She started the engine and began to

153

back out of the gravel parking area when the smell of burning chemicals assaulted her nostrils. Billowing smoke—or was it steam?—emerged from under the Ford's hood. Allison hit the brakes. "Oh, shit."

"Mommy said shit, Mommy said shit," Stephanie announced in a singsong voice, grinning impishly.

Damn right, Allison thought. She turned off the motor, released the hood latch, and climbed out of the car. A growing puddle of green liquid stained the ground under the engine.

"If yer lucky, it's jist one o' yer radiator hoses," Harlow Madison said a couple of minutes later. He was a man of few words; this speech was the longest Allison had heard him make. "Not so lucky, you'll have yerself a hole in yer radiator or maybe a leaky gasket."

Allison sighed, mentally tallying her dwindling cash. "What are we going to do?"

Harlow pulled on his chin. "Only thing to do. We'll clear yer stuff outta here, I'll get the pickup 'n' tow ya into town. Let Clyde take a look."

Harlow was as good as his word, but not until intricate arrangements had been made to take Beverly and her daughter Dolly along. It was decided that Beverly could do the weekly grocery shopping and Harlow could have his bimonthly haircut while they waited for Clyde, the town's mechanic, to render a verdict on Allison's car. The trip into town would have to serve multiple purposes.

Clyde's Car Repair was a filthy converted gas station a few blocks off the main highway. The asphalt in front had weeds growing skyward in its deep cracks, and the side yard was littered with the carcasses of old cars. A scruffy-looking mutt inside the garage eyed Allison suspiciously and growled. She wrinkled her nose as the mingled odors of oil and antifreeze drifted toward her. Allison hoped Clyde, a man whose fingernails she doubted had ever been really clean, knew what he was doing. His place of business was hardly designed to instill confidence in his customers. Still, Harlow had been quick to point out that Clyde's was the only game in town.

"You can't hang around this place with Angel," Beverly said, holding Dolly on her left hip and looking about her with distaste. "Tell you what. Angel can come down the street to the market with us. When you get this straightened out, you can catch up with us. It's just three or four blocks down Main Street."

Allison stooped down to Stephanie's height. "That's a good idea, isn't it, punkin? You go with Beverly and Dolly and I'll come as soon as I find out when the car's gonna be fixed."

"Can I buy some candy?"

"We'll see. Something special maybe, but not candy. How about an apple?"

"Apples're shit. I want candy." Stephanie stuck out her lower lip.

"You stop saying that word!" Allison closed her aching eyes for a moment and wondered why she allowed herself to get into these power struggles with a four-year-old child. She was the parent, she was the one who was supposed to be in charge here. Her own father would have ignored her childhood plea for candy and simply handed her the apple. Or, if he'd been drinking, he'd have clipped her across the mouth for sassing him. Which, Allison guessed, was why she tended to give in to her daughter's pleas. That and the almost unbearable load of guilt she was carrying. "Oh, all right, just one piece," she said, begrudgingly handing the child a quarter. "But you have to save it for after lunch."

Flashing a victorious grin, Stephanie stuffed the coin into her pocket.

*   *   *

Clyde rolled out from under the Ford, sat up on his wheeled platform, and wiped a greasy hand across his already-blackened forehead. "Got yerself a darned good hole in yer radiator," he announced, sounding pleased. "Prob'ly kicked up a rock."

"How much is it going to cost me to fix it?" Allison asked.

"Depends on how ya wanna have it done. I can prob'ly patch 'er up pretty good. Have to drain 'er first, do the patch, give 'er time to set, then fill 'er back up with antifreeze. Other way's replacin' the entire radiator. Yer gonna keep the car a while, that'd be the better way to go."

"But that'd be more expensive."

"Yup. Take three, four days to get the part, too . . . *if* the Ford dealer over in Billings's got one on hand." He didn't sound too hopeful.

Clyde estimated three hundred dollars for the patch, nearly double that for a new radiator. "That patch had better last," Allison said, approving the estimate. She had no real choice. If there were no unforeseen problems, the car would be ready tomorrow morning.

Allison headed down Main Street, feeling thoroughly depressed. She and Stephie would have to spend another night at the Madison ranch. And this car repair would leave her with well under a thousand dollars in her bag—which would have to last who knew how long. Allison's stomach clenched in fear. She'd simply have to find a way to get her hands on some real cash before long. If she didn't, she and Stephie would soon end up like Beverly and Dolly—or worse. She stopped off at a small branch bank and changed a twenty-dollar bill into quarters, then headed for a phone booth outside the Longhorn Cafe.

Ruth answered on the third ring. Allison wasted no time on chitchat. "Listen, Sis, I can't talk long.

I'm in a phone booth and I don't want to run out of change. Stephie and I are both doing okay, but my money's going a lot faster than I'd figured on. How're you doing on getting the house sold?"

"Glad you called, Allie. This is good timing. I just got off the phone with that real estate lady and she's already got an offer on the place. Not a great one, but it's something."

Allison's heart leaped. Maybe it wasn't going to be such a horrible day after all. "Oh, Ruthie. Thank God." She clenched the receiver and closed her eyes tightly, like a child making a birthday wish. "Go ahead, tell me about it."

Ruth related the whole story, beginning with Muriel Steiger's suggestion about pricing the house and ending with the sixty-five-thousand-dollar offer that had just been presented. "She says the market's soft, whatever that means. 'Fraid this financial stuff never was my strong point. So. What do you wanna do? Should I accept this deal or hold out for somethin' better?"

Allison thought it over. She had hoped to clear a good thirty thousand out of the house, but that would have meant selling for nearly eighty thousand, which looked like a pipe dream now. Still, sixty-five would net her only a bit more than fifteen thousand. Not much to start a whole new life. Still, it was a helluva lot more than the nine hundred plus change she'd have left after she paid Clyde.

"Allie? You still there?"

"Yeah. Sorry, Ruthie, I was thinking what to do."

Allison took a deep breath and plunged. "Okay, let's try this. Tell Muriel Steiger you want to counteroffer at seventy thousand. See what she comes back with. Maybe the buyer will take it, or maybe at least we can split the difference, come out with sixty-seven five or so. If not, we may as well take the sixty-five and get it over with. Lord knows when another buyer'll come along and I need money real bad."

The sisters agreed that Allison would call again in a day or two to learn what had happened. "Listen, Allie, before you go. I—I'm afraid I've gotta give you some bad news." Ruth's voice grew quiet and subdued.

A chill ran down Allison's spine. "What is it? What's the matter, Ruthie?"

"It's about Dad." Ruth explained about their father's terminal illness and his desire to hear from Allison as soon as possible.

"Lung cancer. Oh, my God."

"That's why he says he'd fallen off the wagon that day you called him. He'd just been told he was gonna die."

Allison felt a rush of guilt. "I—I was so mad at him for being drunk. I just slammed down the phone." Her eyes filled with tears. "Lord, how could I not have realized that there had to be something—" She choked up.

"Allie? Hey, Sis, don't blame yourself. How could you know? This kind of thing has happened a hundred times. How were you supposed to know this time was different?"

"It's just that—oh, hell, now there's no way I can make it up to him. I'll never even see him again."

"That might not be true." Ruth's tone was not convincing. "You can't ever give up hope."

"Sure," Allison said. Her joy about the pending house sale had evaporated. What the hell did it matter how much money she had when she couldn't even use it to see her father one more time before he died? "Listen, Ruth, I'd better try to give him a call before I run out of change. Thanks. Thanks for everything, you hear?"

"Sure, Allie. You take care, now."

Allison waited for the operator to ring her back

with the final charges, deposited more coins, then dialed her father's San Diego number.

"Hi, Dad, it's Allie." Her voice was small and unsteady.

"Allie! Baby, it's so good to hear from you. I been worryin' myself sick, not knowing where you were or what had—why didn't you let me know what was going on?"

"I—I tried to, Daddy, but at first I didn't want you to worry about me and Stephie and later . . . well, I guess I picked the wrong time to try and tell you."

"Hey, baby, I'm really sorry about that. If I'd've known what was happening, I'd never have touched that bottle, I swear. Wouldn't've mattered how depressed I was. I'm off the sauce for good now. Never gonna touch that poison again, I swear on my mother's grave."

"I know, Daddy. Ruth told me everything."

"She tell you about what's been ailing me, too?"

"Uh-huh. Oh, Daddy, I'm so sorry, I really am." Allison stifled a sob and wiped away a tear with the back of her hand. "I—I don't know what to say . . . except I love you and I really wish I could come see you. Oh, damn. It's just not fair!"

"Hey, don't worry, hon. We'll see each other. I'll come to you. Where're you two holed up, anyway?"

"I can't tell you that, Daddy. Besides, we're not staying. We're moving around all the time; we'll be someplace else tomorrow."

"I haven't got long, Allie. The doc says two, three months, maybe. Name a place and I'll meet you there while I still can."

"No! No, I just can't risk that, Daddy. Please, you've got to understand. I shouldn't even be making this call. They told me to cut all my ties to everybody I ever knew, particularly my family."

"Who's this 'they'? Who's telling you you can't see your own old man?"

"I can't tell—I mean, it's just some people who're helping us. Please understand. Stephie and I have to practically about disappear off the face of the earth if I'm ever going to be able to keep her away from Karl."

"*That* bastard! I'll throttle the son of a bitch, I ever get my hands on him. Man oughta be boiled in oil."

"I know, Daddy. You don't have to convince me. But I've got to look at my options, and the only realistic one seems to be to keep on running until nobody can ever find us. And that's going to take some doing. I know Karl. He's not going to sit still for my walking out with Stephie. He'll have every cop and every private detective he can find looking for us, even the FBI if he can get them. And the first place they're going to look is at you and Ruth. If you try to see us, Daddy, you'll just lead Karl right to us. You've got to realize that."

"Hey, the last thing I want to do is hurt you or Stephie, you know that. I just figured I'd be able to help. At least tell me where I can send you some money. You must need money."

Allison was sorely tempted. "Thanks, Daddy. I sure could use it, but it's taking too big a chance. What if somebody traced the package?"

"You really think that's going to happen?"

"It could. Look, I was told not to contact my family, no matter what. Sure, I think they could trace a package, a letter, a check, whatever. I don't know how, but Karl would find people who could do it. Hell, for all I know, your phone could be tapped. For all I know, if I give you an address, Karl could hear it."

"Hey, sweetheart, you're givin' the bastard too much credit. He's not *that* good."

Allison sighed. "Maybe I'm paranoid, but better that than careless."

"You're okay, though, you and Stephie? You still getting by?"

"Yeah, we've got people helping us. People we don't even know, letting us stay with them, feeding us. We're making it all right, Dad. I don't want you worrying about us. All I want is for you to take good care of yourself."

"I'm just fine."

"You eating like you should?"

"Sure."

Allison recognized that tone. She remembered when her father would go on a bender, wouldn't eat for days. She looked at her watch. "What did you have for lunch?"

"Shit, girl, it's not even lunchtime yet. It's only eleven-thirty."

"Oh, right, I forgot you're an hour earlier out there. So, what are you going to have for lunch? Something healthy, I hope, something that'll keep up your strength."

"Oh, for God's sake, Allie, I'm a grown man. I need somebody to nag me, I got Ruth. She's just like her mother. I always thought you were more like me, less one for the rules but a helluva lot more fun."

Allison smiled in spite of herself. "Okay, Daddy. I get the point. It's just that I'm worried and I'm scared and I really wish I could see you."

"I wish you could, too, baby."

"I've got to go now, Daddy. Stephie's waiting for me."

"One promise, Allie?"

"What's that?"

"If you need anything, anything at all—some money, a car, a place to stay, whatever—you call me. Collect if you have to. And . . . and just keep in touch, huh?"

"That sounds like two promises."

"Two, then. Who the hell cares?"

"Okay, Daddy. I'll do my best. I'll call you every once in a while."

"And you'll let me know if there's any way I can help you? I've got my car ready, I've got cash all set to go. You just name the time and place and I'll be there."

"Thanks, Dad."

"Take care, baby. I love you."

"I love you, too, Daddy. Be well." Allison replaced the receiver and leaned against the side of the phone booth, tears streaming down her face.

24

Russ Quinn flicked a bread crumb off the front of his shirt and lit a cigarette. As he watched the Mitchell bungalow from the street, he saw the sheer beige draperies at the living room window part slightly and Tim Mitchell's gray face appear in the crack. The old man's tired eyes surveyed the street. So he was checking out his daughter's warning that Karl Warren might have people watching him. Quinn smiled to himself. There Mitchell was, looking for the stereotypical gumshoe lurking in the shadows. Except that there were no shadows in the day's brilliant San Diego sunshine.

Quinn wasn't worried about being spotted. Today he sat in the back of the second of the agency's three vans, the yellow one with the Acme Construction Company lettering on the side. It was parked across the street from Mitchell's place, but three houses down the block. The most the old man would be able to observe from his living room window was an unoccupied construction van; Quinn, in the rear of the paneled vehicle, sitting in a reclining seat and peering through a specially built lens at the Mitchell house, would be completely invisible to his subject.

Mitchell looked up and down the quiet street, then shrugged and turned away from the window. The draperies fell back together.

Quinn laid his cigarette in the littered ashtray and grabbed the pen to label the latest audiocassette with the date and time of Allison Warren's phone call. He felt almost heady with success, even though Allison had told her father that she wouldn't see him. When a fugitive like the Warren woman risked calling her family members once, Quinn knew from experience that chances were excellent she'd do it again. And again. Until she was caught. And now he had confirmation that she knew about her father's terminal illness. He had heard the conflict in her voice—her desire to come to the aid of the sick old man competing with her better judgment. How long would it be before her loyalty to dear old dad won out?

Quinn had hoped that Allison Warren would simply set up a meeting with her father. But that would have been too much to ask. Besides, in a way it would have been too easy, trapping the woman that quickly, not enough of a challenge to satisfy Quinn's love of the chase. A filtertip in the ashtray caught fire, sending a stream of acrid smoke into the van. The PI quickly poured the dregs of his last cup of coffee on the small blaze. When it was extinguished, he dumped the soggy mess from the ashtray into the brown plastic wastebasket and opened the rear window a crack for ventilation.

Quinn could wait. Karl Warren had bucks and he was paying a generous per diem for this surveillance setup. As long as Quinn could keep on feeding bits of information back to Wisconsin, Warren would go right on paying.

The only thing Quinn could see that he might have to worry about was if Warren was able to interest the FBI in the case. If the FBI put a trace on Mitchell's phone, they might be able to pinpoint Allison's location the next time she called, then close in on her and the kid. Quinn didn't have the technology to do that, and he sure didn't want the government men finding that hot mike his operative had installed in Mitchell's telephone. But, hell, he couldn't lose sleep over that one. Chances were it would take months to get the Feds involved in a family snatch like this one. By that time, he figured he or the Petersons would have found Allison and her little girl. Or, at the very least, Tim Mitchell would be dead and there would be no more phone calls to San Diego for the FBI to trace. In the meantime, Quinn would be well paid for his bits of information.

And he was picking up some important fact, some part of the puzzle, each day. Today's piece really ought to be worth a bonus, the way he looked at it. Not only could he now document the fact that Allison was in contact with her old man, but Quinn now knew what direction she was traveling. "I forgot you're an hour earlier out there," he'd heard her say to her father. That meant she was in the Mountain time zone, obviously heading west from Wisconsin. Sure, she could be doubling back and forth to confuse her pursuers, but most of the fugitives he'd observed picked one direction and kept going, figuring that their best chance of escape was to put as much distance as possible between them and their old haunts.

If Allison Warren was heading west, and particularly if she was as strapped for cash as everyone indicated, it would be only a matter of time. Quinn's bet was that her resolve to avoid San Diego, her ailing father, and the money he had offered her wouldn't last another two weeks. When she made her mistake—and he knew she would—Russ Quinn would be the first to take full advantage of it.

25

"Okay, spit it out. What's buggin' you?" Pete Peterson asked his wife. They were in their kitchen preparing dinner, Pete slicing tomatoes for a salad and Louise dipping some walleyed pike fillets in beaten egg and coating them with bread crumbs.

"What do you mean?"

"You been quiet all day, Lou. I can tell when you got somethin' stuck in your craw. Now, what is it?"

Louise placed the last piece of fish on a plate and washed her hands at the sink. "Oh, I don't know. I guess it's just that this Warren case is getting to me."

"It's a case like any other case. That's the way you gotta think about it."

"But it's not, Pete. That's just it. It's *not* like any other case." She dropped onto a stool next to the counter. "I mean, here I am, making a phony offer to buy somebody's house, for God's sake. When was the last time we did something like that?"

"Never. Not exactly like that, anyway. But we've done similar, playacting a part to get some information or something like that, plenty of times. You never got upset about that. Want me to chop up some green pepper for this salad?"

"Okay. I bought some mushrooms, too." She rose and took the blue cardboard tray from the refrigerator, carried it to the sink, and began to wipe the mushrooms with a damp towel. "I don't know, Pete. Maybe it's not the house exactly . . ."

"Hell, Lou, it's not like you're involved in a fraud or anything. All you're doin' is fronting for Karl. People do that sort of thing all the time. Who knows? He may very well go through with this house deal, 'specially if he can get it that cheap. It'd be a damn good investment."

"It just doesn't feel right to me." Louise placed half a dozen cleaned mushrooms on the cutting board. "I suppose what's really bothering me is . . . well, I can't help thinking what if Karl really did molest Stephanie and we're the ones who bring her back here so he can do it again?" She bit her lip hard.

Pete flashed an indulgent smile. "You can't really believe that, Lou. Just look at the guy. Karl Warren's as straight as they come. He's downright boring he's so straight."

"But what if you can't tell by looking? I—I've heard stories about priests molesting little boys in the confessional, for God's sake. How can we be sure?"

"It's not our job to be sure. That was up to Judge Winston and he says Karl never hurt that kid. He had all the so-called evidence to look at and he didn't believe one thing Allison said."

Louise poured a layer of corn oil into a frying pan and put it on the stove to heat. "But what if Judge Winston was wrong? I'm not trying to beat a dead horse, hon, but I know if Stephanie was my little girl and anybody laid a hand on her, I'd—well, I'd probably kill the guy."

Pete put down his knife and put his arm around his wife's shoulders. "But what if. But what if. But what if. You're beginnin' to sound like a broken record. Hey, sweetheart, you gotta stop thinkin' like this is your kid and your problem."

Louise pushed Pete's arm away. "I *know* this isn't my kid, Pete. You don't have to keep reminding me."

Stung, Pete backed off. "You get your period, Lou?"

She reeled around, her face blazing. "Yeah, I got my period! What goddamn difference does that make?"

Pete held up his hand, as if to ward off a blow. "Hey, sorry. I didn't mean to get you upset, sweetheart, honest. I—I only meant I'm sorry. I'm sorry it didn't work out again this month. That's all." His voice became softer. "Hell, I thought that last round of tests Dr. Miller gave you would at least tell us what's wrong . . ."

Tears stung Louise's eyes. She was helpless to stop their tumbling over and running down her cheeks. Furiously, she swiped at them with the back of her hand. "I hate this! I just hate this!"

Pete moved toward her slowly, holding out his arms. "Me, too, baby. It tears me up to see you hurting this way." He folded her into his arms and let her cry against his chest. "There, there, it's okay," he said, gently stroking her hair. "Go ahead and cry. Just let it all out."

When her tears had subsided, Louise turned back to the dinner preparations. "Oh, shit," she exclaimed. "Look at that damn oil!" She grabbed the handle of the smoking frying pan and pulled it off the burner. "Now I'll have to start all over again."

Pete washed out the pan and handed it back to Louise, who heated a new batch of oil and quickly fried the fish while he tossed the salad. She loaded each plate with two fish fillets, a baked potato, and a Parkerhouse roll, then carried them into the small dining room.

"Way I see it," Pete said, wolfing down his fish and wiping his mouth on his napkin, "we got no choice but to find Karl's kid. We don't produce, he's gonna get himself some new PIs, and we just can't afford that. Know what we billed him last year?"

Louise shook her head.

"Sixty grand and change." Pete speared some salad with his fork. "We lose that account, Lou, we may as well fold our tent."

"You really think he'd pull his business, just like that?"

"Hell, yes. You heard him. He's already threatened us, right out in the open. Nothing subtle about Karl. And, one thing you gotta know about him, he doesn't make idle threats. He's a helluva lot like his old man."

"Well, you know him better than I do."

"Since we were kids. Can't say we were ever really friends, but we knew each other." Pete chewed his salad and swallowed. "Truth is, I was chicken to set foot on his place ever since the time his old man took after some of us with a shotgun."

"He what?"

Pete uttered a short humorless laugh. "The Warrens had an apple orchard on their place. Wealthies, if I remember right, and maybe a few greenings. Three of us boys sneaked in there one afternoon at the top of the harvest season and started helpin' ourselves to as much as we could eat or carry in our pockets. It was just a kids' prank. I think we were about ten, eleven years old. All of a sudden we hear this bang, louder'n thunder, and there's old man Warren, comin' after us with his shotgun smoking. Let me tell you, we dropped those apples and ran for our lives. I never felt that scared again 'til I hit Nam."

"You never told me about that. You mean the man actually tried to shoot three little boys?"

Pete shrugged. "Tell you the truth, I don't know. I 'spose he aimed over our heads, but we *thought* he was tryin' to shoot us. Found out later that he'd caught Billy Kaiser in the orchard once before. He'd warned him he'd shoot him if he ever caught him there again."

"Billy was one of the kids with you?"

"Yeah. Stealin' those apples was his bright idea. Guess he thought he could get away with it if there was three of us. Or else he didn't think Einar Warren was serious."

"Christ. The man must have been sick in the head." Suddenly envisioning her husband as the terrified ten-year-old he must have been, Louise was struck with a feeling of compassion.

"Maybe. At the very least, he was a stubborn old German who ruled his wife, his kids, and that farm with an iron hand. A real hardass. Nobody ever crossed Einar Warren and got away clean."

"He still alive?"

"Nope, been dead for years. So's the mother. There was a daughter, too ... Gretchen, that was her name. She was a year older than Karl, three years older than me."

"I never heard Karl mention he had a sister. What happened to her?"

"Ran off, eloped with some sailor, a guy from Great Lakes Naval Training Center. It was sort of a scandal around here for a while. Old man Warren didn't like Gretchen's sailor, ordered her not to see him. So after she ran off, the family acted like she died. Or, more to the point, like she never existed. Never mentioned her name again."

"What a fun group."

"Yeah, well. Reason I told you this stuff, Lou, is so you'll see where Karl's comin' from. He means what he says, just like his old man. Karl says he'll pull his business if we don't get his little girl back for him, you can bank on it. That's exactly what he'll do."

Louise pushed her food around on her plate. She didn't have much of an appetite. "So what you're telling me," she said, "is I'd better quit whining and feeling sorry for myself and just find the kid."

Pete flashed her a plaintive smile. "Only if you want us to keep on buying groceries and paying the mortgage on this place."

"Great choice."

"Yeah, well, one thing I've learned about life, Lou. It's full of shitty choices."

26

By ten o'clock, Allison was exhausted, but so tense and irritable that she knew she wouldn't be able to fall asleep quickly. The evening had been a trying one.

The low point had been when Melissa's two boys staged another scene. The older one tormented poor Rusty by pulling his tail and attempting to ride him like a pony, until the usually good-natured hound yelped in pain and nipped at the child in retaliation.

Stephanie became the younger boy's target. He grabbed Flopsy by her loose ear and tried to pull the bunny from Stephanie's desperate grip. Predictably, the ear was quickly ripped from the rabbit's head, sending the little girl into hysterics.

The poor child was panic-stricken as the boys played a cruel game of catch with the severed ear, throwing it back and forth between them, always just above her reach. Allison came running from the kitchen when she heard her daughter's cries. Livid at the boys' actions, she grabbed the older one by an arm and yanked the ear from his grasp. "Don't you ever come near my daughter again!" she screamed, shocked at the intensity of the anger she felt. She caught herself before she struck the boy; how easy it would be to turn into an abuser like Melissa . . . or like her own father so long ago. Just let the rage build until you lose control.

"There, there, punkin," Allison said as she hugged

Stephie close. "Mommy'll fix Flopsy's ear. Don't you cry, Angel." But Stephanie seemed unable to stop. Her wracking sobs tore at Allison's heart. The tattered bunny had represented security to the child; it was the one thing she never let out of her sight. The boys had sensed that, of course, had honed in on how best to torture the younger child. That they were acting out unexpressed anger at their own frequent mistreatment meant nothing to Allison. Her concern was solely with her own child.

It took over an hour to comfort Stephanie, borrow a needle and thread from Betsy, and repair Flopsy's ear. "There, you see? It's all fixed. Flopsy's just like new." Stephanie looked doubtful, her face still red and tear-stained. "Look, sweetie. Her ear isn't even loose anymore. It's even better than before."

Stephanie hugged the animal to her heaving chest. "If—if my ear gets pulled off, like Flopsy, can you fix it, Mommy?"

"What? Nobody's going to pull off your ear, sweetheart. You shouldn't worry about such things."

The child's voice was plaintive. "But can you, Mommy? Can you?"

"I—I don't know." What could she say to reassure the child, yet be truthful? "I guess maybe a doctor could sew back a person's ear if it got pulled off. It's harder to do with people than with stuffed animals, but I think it's possible. What makes you think about that?"

But Stephanie wouldn't answer; she simply buried her face in Flopsy's tummy. Allison wondered whether somebody had threatened to pull Stephie's ear off. Had Karl used that threat to get her to acquiesce to his perversions? Or perhaps to keep her quiet afterward? Could that be how Flopsy's ear originally had become loosened, as a warning that the same would happen to the child unless ... whatever. The terrible things Allison imagined overwhelmed her with feelings of anger and helplessness. And most of all, guilt. When was it she'd first noticed the bunny's ear was loose? Why hadn't she questioned Stephie about it at the time? Mercilessly, she flogged herself with self-doubt and self-reproach. Had she been blind to what was happening to her daughter? Could she have prevented it somehow? She bent down and kissed the top of Stephie's hair. "Nobody is going to hurt you ever again, Angel. Mommy will protect you." Allison would die before she broke that vow. She picked up the exhausted child and carried her upstairs to bed.

Finally, the children were asleep. Stephanie on the air mattress, little Nicky and Larina's three girls in the bunks. Allison waited patiently for the bathroom. Wanda had been in there for at least fifteen minutes. When she finally opened the door and emerged, the tiny room reeked of cigarette smoke.

"Damn it!" Allison snapped. "Why'd you have to stink the place up like this? The rest of us don't want to breathe this garbage."

Wanda's jaw slackened. "I—gee, I'm sorry. I just needed a cigarette and I thought—"

Instantly, Allison felt contrite. "Hey, sorry I snapped at you like that. It's been a bad day. It's just that . . . well, maybe you could smoke outside."

"Yeah, okay." Wanda turned on her heel and strode toward the dormitory.

Allison couldn't relax; sleep was out of the question. She got out of bed and put on her robe, then checked on the sleeping children. "I'll be downstairs for a little while in case Angel wakes up," she told Larina and Wanda. She had to have some space to herself, some room to think.

The front porch was cool and deserted. Allison lowered herself into a white wicker rocking chair and leaned back. The stars shone brilliantly in the sky, a canopy of diamonds sparkling overhead. By the light of the moon, she could just make out the mountaintops in the distance. This was beautiful country, yet she knew it wasn't where she belonged. It didn't feel like home. Would any place ever feel like home to her?

As she rocked silently, Allison let her mind stray over memories of her father, her life as a single career woman, her marriage. When had she ever felt at home? Even her career had been one of constant travel, one that precluded putting down roots. She'd tried to do that with Karl, but now she had to face the fact that there'd always been something wrong there, something vital missing. She'd been on edge since her first day with Karl, intuitively trying to live up to his expectations instead of feeling free to be herself.

The first time she'd ever felt completely comfortable, Allison realized, was when she held the infant Stephanie in her arms; when her baby's incredibly tiny fists had grasped her hair, as if holding on for dear life; when she bent to brush her lips across the top of her child's soft, fragrant head. Unconditional love and acceptance, that was what Stephanie had given her. Allison had never experienced it before, at least not that she could remember—she barely recalled her own mother. Her father's love had always depended upon whether he'd been drinking. Gram was more put out than loving after the child Allison was foisted upon her. Ruth? Her sister had always been more envious than affectionate. And Karl, of course, had had a long list of criteria for Allison to meet if she hoped to earn his love—a love she now knew he'd been incapable of giving. No, it was only Stephanie who'd ever made her feel needed and loved, completely and with no strings attached. It was Stephanie she could never bear to lose.

"Beautiful night, isn't it?"

Startled from her reverie, Allison jerked around

to see Beverly taking the chair next to hers. "Oh, it's you. Hi."

"I often come out here at night when I need some air. The dorm getting to you?"

Allison smiled. "That and a dozen other things. Guess I just needed to be alone for a while."

Beverly began to rise. "I'll go back inside if—"

"No! No, please don't do that. I've had some time to myself and I don't mind the company."

The two women chatted about the life in which they both found themselves. Allison was surprised to hear herself telling Beverly about her father's terminal illness and her growing fears about the future.

"I know what you mean. Dolly's only two. I won't be really able to go back to being me, whoever that is, until she's eighteen. Sometimes I don't know if I can take sixteen more years of this."

"But it's got to change, doesn't it? We can't spend all that time running away this way. We'll have to find a way to settle down somewhere, get jobs, send our kids to school, raise them like normal people."

Beverly shrugged. "Sure, that *sounds* great. But what can women like us do to earn enough money to live like normal people? We've got no resumés to sell ourselves and we sure can't go back to whatever we used to do. About all we're fit to do without a job history is work at McDonald's, and how are we going to live on what that pays?"

"I—I've got to admit I'm scared half to death."

"All of us are. You know, I used to think I would be a great actress someday, maybe even a movie star." Allison could believe it; Beverly was exceptionally pretty. "I did a few small roles in Hollywood, but I could see I was getting older and I wasn't going to make it. So I went back to college and got my degrees—a master's and then my doctorate—so I could teach other people to act."

"That's what you did at that college?"

"Uh-huh. I was an assistant professor of drama. Met my husband there. He was in the geology department, still is. But I can't ever go near the theater again, or a college, either, and that's all I know how to do. It's what I love. But those are the first places they'd look for me." Beverly sighed. "The truth is, I just don't know what other kind of work I can do to support Dolly and me." Suddenly she began to laugh.

"What's so funny?"

"I just thought of something. You ever see the play *A Streetcar Named Desire*? Tennessee Williams?"

"I saw the movie on TV. Marlon Brando was in it, right?"

Beverly nodded. "I was in the play once, played the part of Blanche DuBois, the older sister. It just struck me—I've gone from playing Blanche to *being* Blanche. How's that for irony? I've become a woman dependent on the kindness of strangers."

The women agreed that depending on charity could be a very expensive way to live. It might not cost much in terms of cash, but it required vast expenditures of privacy and individuality and a complete loss of personal control.

"I would never make my daughter sleep in a room with seven other people or expose her to little terrorists like those hellions of Melissa's if I weren't in this fix," Allison said. "But I guess I've got to take what I'm given, be grateful, and keep my mouth shut."

"Either that or move on, and I can't even do that without money and a car. I'm stuck here until somebody else—some other kind stranger—moves me." Beverly leaned back and gazed up at the sky. A rapidly moving cloud began to travel toward the moon. "At least we're protecting our kids from being molested," she said. "We've got to give ourselves points for that."

Allison was silent.

"Hey, you still awake?"

"Huh? Oh, yeah. I was just thinking. Know what? Last night when I was lying in bed upstairs I even began to doubt that. I started to wonder whether I'd made some terrible mistake. You know, maybe the way my daughter'd been acting wasn't caused by her father doing bad things to her after all. Maybe she'd seen some porno movies somewhere and that's what gave her nightmares and prompted her to take off her clothes in public. Or maybe it was somebody else who abused her, not her father."

Beverly leaned toward Allison. "And you figured maybe the physical evidence was just from rough underpants or some strong chemical that'd been used to clean the bathtub?"

Allison turned and stared. "Yeah. How did you know?"

"Ha! I've been there. We all have doubts like that. I had them so strong that I actually brought Dolly back from where I'd been hiding her. I talked myself into believing I had to be deluded about the facts, that her father had never really molested her."

"And what happened?"

"He started right in on her again. And this time he had her all to himself."

"But how come you changed your mind and went against your first instincts?"

Beverly grimaced. "The—the truth is I wanted out of jail so bad that I worked things around in my mind until . . . well, until black became white. I guess it's sort of like what happens to battered wives. When the bruises go away, they start telling themselves that the guy didn't mean it, that he's really a pussycat. Or that it wasn't really a beating they got; it was just a little shove and they must have done something to deserve it."

"You're telling me that all of us mothers feel this way?"

"I can't speak for everybody, but a lot of us do. Hell, look at the life we've got to live. Running all the time, looking over our shoulders, worrying about how we're going to feed our kids, where we're going to sleep tonight or tomorrow night. Wouldn't it be nice if all of a sudden things were different—just like magic? If somehow we could go back to our old lives but never have to worry again about our children being raped?"

"Sure, but—"

"So the easy way to make that happen is to convince ourselves that somehow we saw things all wrong, that maybe the courts were right and *we* were mistaken. The only problem is that black *isn't* white. And we *weren't* wrong. Take my word for it, Ellie. You go back home and it'll happen again and again and again. And maybe you won't be as lucky as I was. You may never be able to get Angel away from that man again."

She's right, Allison told herself. *This is the life I've chosen and it's the one I have to live from now on. Even if it means Stephanie and I will never live comfortably again, we can never ever go back.*

The cloud drifted across the moon. It seemed to Allison like a bad omen, like the shadow that had fallen across her life.

27

When the intercom buzzed, Karl Warren shoved the legal pad on which he'd been writing into his leather briefcase and told his secretary to send Peterson in. "Let's hear what you got, Pete," he demanded as the private investigator entered the office.

"Hello, Karl. I'm feelin' fine today, thanks. How're you?" Unbidden, Peterson took one of the chairs opposite Karl.

Karl frowned at the sarcasm. The man could be damned irritating at times. "Haven't got time for the polite preliminaries; I'm due in court in half an hour. What've you got?"

"Things're startin' to break our way on this one. We found her car." Pete paused as if expecting praise, but the attorney failed to oblige him.

"Where?"

"Minnesota DMV turned it up. She sold it last Monday at a place called—" Pete consulted his notes. "Stan Grann, the Used-Car Man. It's a used-car lot on Lake Street in Minneapolis."

"She buy a replacement?"

"Probably, but the DMV didn't have a record of any ownership transfer to an Allison Warren. Figure she'd buy her new one in another name anyway, unless she's dumber than I think she is."

"You check with the lot that bought the Buick, see if they sold her anything else?"

Pete ran his finger under his damp shirt collar,

pulling it away from his thick neck. "Here's my plan. I'll call this Stan Grann fellow, but I doubt he'd've risked his license by registering a car to her under a name he knows is a fake. Chances are she went some other place for the replacement. What I'd like to do is take that picture of Allison around to the other car lots in that same area, see if anybody recognizes her. Could help us find out what name she's using these days, maybe get a fresh physical description on her, too, in case she's done something to change her appearance."

"When do you figure on going to Minneapolis?"

"I'll leave this afternoon, if you approve the expenses."

Karl nodded. "Go ahead, move on it." He slid back the cuff of his pale yellow linen shirt and checked his Piaget wristwatch. "Anything else?"

"Couple of charge sales showed up on her credit card, but I'm inclined to think they're phonies."

"I'll judge that. What are they?"

"Both of 'em in Chicago. First one's four tickets to *Phantom of the Opera* at fifty-five bucks a crack. The other's from a jewelry store—five hundred ninety-seven dollars for a gold necklace. Hardly the kind of things a woman on the run is gonna buy."

"Card's been stolen."

"That'd be my guess. Unless Allison bought that stuff herself, hopin' we'd *think* her card had been ripped off."

"You're giving the bitch too much credit. I think we can forget about the credit card trail." Karl rose. "I've got to get to court. You finished?"

Pete flipped a page of his notebook. "Last thing is that eight hundred number we found on the memo pad by your wife's telephone."

"Yeah? You find out what it's for?"

"Shrink friend of mine says it's a hotline for women who're on the run with their kids. Puts them in touch with some kind of covert organization that helps them hide out."

"Shit."

Pete shrugged. "Hey, buddy, that doesn't mean the trail can't be followed."

Karl grimaced. He hated Peterson's habit of calling him buddy. The man was not his buddy; he was his employee . . . and he wouldn't even be that for long unless he hustled on finding Allison and Stephanie. "What've you got in mind?"

"Can't promise we'll get anywhere, but I'll have Louise call the number, say she's a woman with a kid she's tryin' to protect. See what she can find out."

Karl lifted his charcoal silk suit coat from the coatrack, smoothed an imaginary wrinkle from the lapel, and put it on. "Give it a try, but I wouldn't hold out much hope on that one. I think the Minneapolis car lots are your best bet." He picked up his briefcase and held the office door open for Peterson, then followed him out of the office. "Keep me posted," he said, pulling the door shut.

28

The station wagon, its repaired radiator guaranteed by Clyde's Car Repair for ninety days, was finally loaded and ready to go. Ninety days, Allison thought. Ninety days or until I leave town, whichever comes first. But she had to assume Clyde was honest and did good, professional work. If he didn't . . . well, she didn't even want to think about that. "Come on, Angel. Let's visit the potty one last time and hit the road."

As Allison packed the car with Beverly's help, Stephanie had sat on the grass nearby, patiently waiting. But now she had her own agenda. "I wanna see the baby kitties." She turned her clear, blue-eyed gaze on her mother. "Puh-leeze, Mommy?"

Allison was anxious to get on the road, to make some headway toward Helena. It was a clear, dry day, typical for August in Montana, but it could get hot toward midday and she was worried about putting too much stress on that radiator. "It's a long drive, punkin. We've really got to get going."

"But Betsy says they just got borned. I wanna see the baby kitties, Mommy." Her voice took on a pleading tone.

Allison smiled. "Born, sweetheart. The kittens were born, not borned. There's no such word as borned."

"Born. Puh-leeze, Mommy, can I see the baby kitties?"

"They're just over there in the barn," Beverly said, taking the child's part. "Betsy's out there doing the milking, so you can say good-bye to her at the same time."

Recognizing defeat, Allison laughed good-naturedly. "How can I say no? All right, but just long enough to take a quick look and say our good-byes. And you can't touch the kittens, Angel. You can only look at them."

The two mothers, Beverly toting Dolly on her hip and Allison holding Stephanie's hand, gazed at the wary gray and white cat as she licked her newborns' fur clean. The babies looked more like mice than kittens. "Look how tiny they are," Allison said in wonder. The birth of any creature always seemed such a miracle that it never ceased to fill her with awe.

Bidding farewell to the kittens, the women and children headed for the back of the barn, where Betsy sat on a small wooden stool, milking the first of the farm's three cows. As her strong hands pulled and squeezed, streams of warm milk hit the metal pail with a tinny, ringing sound. "Ever see somebody milk a cow before, Angel?" Betsy asked, smiling at her audience.

Stephanie stopped dead in her tracks and stared silently at the spectacle before her.

"Betcha didn't know this's where the milk on your cereal came from." Efficiently, Betsy continued her task.

The child began to whimper, obviously frightened. Allison dropped to her knees beside her. "What's the matter, sweetheart?" Stephanie didn't answer. "What is it? Tell Mommy."

A deep crease appeared between Stephie's eyebrows. "Penises."

"What?"

"That cow's got this many penises." She held up five fingers.

Allison had prided herself on teaching her daughter the proper names for parts of the human anatomy; no euphemisms for them. Yet it was clear that the child had gotten a few things mixed up. "Cows are girls, hon; they don't have a penis. That thing there is called an udder; it's where the milk comes from."

The child shook her head firmly. "No, Mommy, those are penises. See? Betsy pulls on them and yucky white stuff comes out . . . like when I pulled on Daddy's penis."

"Oh, my God." Allison's stomach lurched and bile rose in her throat. She clasped a hand over her mouth and swallowed hard.

Beverly's face froze. "I know how you feel," she said, placing a comforting hand on Allison's shoulder. She leaned over and whispered in her ear. "But look at it this way—now there isn't the least little doubt about what happened to your little girl. Or about who did it to her."

29

Ruth was washing the lunch dishes when the phone rang. She wedged a cracked blue plate into the dish drainer, quickly wiped her wet hands on her apron, and lifted the receiver off the hook. "Hello."

"Mrs. Persky? This is Muriel Steiger, up in Wood Lake."

The real estate lady. "Oh, hi, Mrs. Steiger. You got news about the house?"

"Sure do. Good news. I'm real happy to tell you that the buyer accepted your counteroffer."

"That's great!" Ruth said. She was almost as relieved as she knew her sister would be. She couldn't wait to put this unwelcome responsibility behind her. "How long 'til we can wrap this thing up and I get the money?"

"Shouldn't be too long. Mrs. Peterson has a solid credit history and, as I told you, she's prepared to put at least twenty-five percent down. The banks like that kind of buyer. I'd say it'll take three or four weeks to get a mortgage lined up, search the title, get all the paperwork ready. I'll mail you a copy of the signed counteroffer, unless you plan to be in town sometime in the next day or two."

Ruth wasn't going to Wood Lake if she could help it. "That's not necessary, is it? I mean for me to drive all the way up there again?"

"Well, not just yet. I'll let you know when we get mortgage approval. Then you can make whatever

186

arrangements you need to get the place cleared out before the closing. You want me to see if Mrs. Peterson wants to buy any of that furniture?"

Ruth's grip on the telephone tightened. Damn. She'd forgotten all about the furniture's having to be moved out, to say nothing of the clothes, dishes, books, and general bric-a-brac Allison had left behind. Even the refrigerator and the washer and dryer—were they supposed to go, too, or did they stay with the house? "I—I s'pose so. I guess I'll have to have some kind of garage sale to get rid of the rest of the stuff."

"That's a good idea, Mrs. Persky. Late summer like this, before school starts, is always a good time for a garage sale—unless you think you might want to put everything in storage."

"What does that cost?"

"Depends on how much space you need. Eighty to a hundred a month'd be my guess."

"I better go with the garage sale." Another waste of Ruth's valuable time. Well, she was entitled to compensation for that, she told herself, the pick of whatever her sister had left in the house. Ruth would sell what she could, keeping the money it brought in until Allison told her where to send it, then she would donate the rest of the stuff to charity. No way were the Perskys going to be stuck with a monthly storage bill for Allison's belongings.

"You want me to, I'll put an ad in the *Press* for you once you know what weekend you'll be holding your sale," Muriel offered.

Ruth accepted. The women agreed to talk again in a day or two and rang off. Ruth returned to her sink. As she washed the dishes, she tried to make a mental list of those items from Allison's house that she would bring back to the farm. She rinsed the soapsuds from an old china cup and saucer, a green and yellow flowered pattern, and placed them in the drainer. Dishes, that's where she'd start. Lord, she was sick of using these mismatched relics from the early days of her marriage—the days before kids and droughts and loan payments had usurped every last cent. It would be so nice to have enough dishes in one set to serve the whole family. In a few days, she promised herself, she would have just that.

30

"It's not going to work and I just plain won't do it." Louise leaned back in her desk chair and crossed her arms over her breasts. "These people aren't going to give me anything useful over the phone. And what am I supposed to do if they want me to meet somebody somewhere? How am I going to come up with this fictitious molested kid I'm supposed to be protecting?"

Louise and Pete had been quarreling about the hotline phone number for the past twenty minutes, ever since he'd returned to the Peterson Detective Agency office after his meeting with Karl Warren. Louise was adamant that the scheme Pete had concocted to get information from the hotline would not work.

"So what do you suggest?" Pete asked, pulling a Coke from the office refrigerator and unscrewing the bottle cap. "I hate to let that phone number go to waste. There's gotta be some way to find out if those people are hiding Allison and the kid."

Louise closed her eyes. This case was becoming more and more distasteful to her. Now, if she managed to infiltrate the underground network, she would risk exposing a lot of other little kids, in addition to Stephanie Warren, to their alleged abusers. She didn't like it one bit. Besides, her head was throbbing, she had cramps, and her back ached. All she wanted to do was go home to bed.

"Asked you a question, Lou."

"I'm thinking."

"Want one of these?" Pete held up his Coke.

"No, thanks. There any of that iced tea left?"

Pete rummaged in the refrigerator and brought out a tea-stained plastic pitcher. "Where's your glass?"

Louise held up a thermal plastic mug. "This'll do."

Pete filled it. "Need ice?"

"Uh-uh, it's cold enough." She took a bottle of aspirin from her desk drawer, removed two white tablets, and washed them down with a long drink of iced tea. "What do you think of this? How about when I call the hotline I say I'm a newspaper reporter or, better yet, a writer for some women's magazine? I can tell them I'm doing a story on this underground railroad thing, about what's happening to kids the courts have screwed over, no pun intended. You know the kind of story I'm talking about. If I come off as sympathetic to the cause, maybe I can get enough general information to at least give us a couple of leads."

"But if this thing is such a big secret, Lou, why would they agree to that kind of publicity?"

"Hell, they must need money to keep it all going. Women like Allison Warren haven't got much of anything. Look at what she had to leave behind. Those women and kids can't possibly be paying their own way. And who covers the phone bills for this hotline, the postage costs, whatever? Publicity can mean money, donations." Pete nodded his understanding. "We shouldn't forget, either, that these people are on a crusade. They want to convince the public that the mothers and children they hide didn't get a fair shake from the court system. Lord knows they're never going to change the courts if nobody knows there's anything wrong with them."

Pete drained the last of his Coke and tossed the bottle in the wastebasket. "Sounds okay."

"It's all I can think of."

"Think you can pull it off?"

"How the hell do I know?" Louise massaged her temples, wishing the aspirin would take effect.

Pete crossed over and stood by Louise's chair, then began to massage the back of her neck. "You'll do fine, Lou. You always do."

"That feels good," she said, feeling her neck muscles loosen. The headache began to subside. "All I can do is give it the old college try."

"Break a leg," Pete told her.

Louise sighed and reached for the telephone.

31

Karl drove his steel-gray Coupe de Ville out of the courthouse parking lot earlier than anticipated. The judge had postponed his case. Now he would have to go over the whole file again to prepare for the new date. It was just too hard to keep one auto accident case straight from another unless he prepared for each one right before he went to court. If he had known he was going to have the afternoon free, Karl thought, he could have set up that meeting with Allied Mutual. But it was too late now. Damned waste of time.

He turned the corner and drove toward the lake, then headed west on Main. He pulled the Cadillac into the street where he used to live with Allison and drove down the block slowly. The neighborhood appeared deserted, except for old man Henderson's dog napping in the middle of his driveway, flies circling its mangy ears. One of these days somebody was going to drive right over that old mutt.

Good. A SOLD banner now hung across the Wood Lake Realty sign on Allison's lawn. Louise Peterson had wrapped up her purchase offer. That ought to keep the gawkers away from this place and throw a monkey wrench at Allison at the same time. Karl would have about a month to put up or shut up on actually buying the house. With that inspection clause he'd had Louise write into the purchase agreement, he'd come away clean if he decided to back out, wouldn't even have to forfeit his deposit money. On the other hand, maybe he'd just go ahead and complete the sale, move back into the house. If Allison and Stephanie hadn't been found by then, he might come across some little clue, something he and Pete and Louise had all overlooked. If the house was sold to somebody else, that little clue would be lost forever.

Karl looked up and down the street. It was still deserted. Might as well take another look right now; he had the time. He pulled into the driveway, quickly got out and opened the garage door, then drove inside the garage. He glanced up and down the street again, then pushed the button that lowered the automatic door and hid his car from view.

Inside, the place looked no different than the last time Karl had been here, except for a stack of Muriel Steiger's listing notices on the living room coffee table and a light layer of dust that had settled everywhere. Good thing the place was sold or Muriel would have to become acquainted with a dustrag and vacuum cleaner to keep showing the place. Unless that bitch Ruth was willing to haul her ass up here to clean. Karl doubted that. Far as he could tell, Ruth had never demonstrated much concern for her kid sister.

It was hot and stuffy inside the house, but not as bad as the last time he'd been here. The weather had cooled down. Still, he dared not risk opening a window. If he did, Nosy Crowley would notice and come running to investigate. Karl removed his suitcoat, folded it, and laid it neatly across the back of a living room chair. Then he loosened his tie and began a room-by-room search.

An hour and a half later, he had found nothing to help him locate his daughter. Not a damned thing. He entered Allison's bedroom. There was nothing he or the Petersons had missed in the dresser drawers or the nightstands. Just the same tasteless collection Karl had seen last time. He opened the closet. There was something on the shelf he hadn't noticed before, underneath the hat box. He pulled it down. Another book about incest, another of the tools that bitch had used to try to crucify him in his own hometown.

Karl was certain now that Allison had tried to use what she found in these books to sell a bill of goods to Judge Winston. He'd known from the start that Stephie would never tell her mother the kind of things Allison claimed the child had said. And his little girl certainly wouldn't have told that self-righteous therapist a damned thing; Dr. Gunderson was a complete stranger. His baby would never tell; she'd never betray her very own daddy. No, it was Allison who'd blown the whole thing out of proportion. She'd turned a father's love for his only daughter into something shameful and sordid. First she'd dumped him, divorced him, then she had planned this whole charade to keep him from his rightful position with his daughter and ruin him in the process. As he skimmed through the book she'd tried to use against him, Karl's anger rose. When he found her, he would make her pay for it.

Shaking with a sense of outrage over the betrayal, Karl threw the offending book back on the closet shelf. It slid to the back of the shelf and hit the wall with a thud. His hand fell on one of the garments Allison had left behind, a low-cut salmon-colored negligée she'd had when they first married, back when she still had her slim, girlish figure. He yanked it from its hanger and held it up. He remembered the last time she'd worn it, her growing breasts straining the flimsy bodice; it had been the night she'd told him she was pregnant. He remembered her smiling up at him as though she expected praise, even gratitude. But Karl had felt nothing more than stunned, totally poleaxed. She hadn't even discussed it with him. She'd gone ahead and gotten herself knocked up without even talking to him about it. She'd never given a damn about what he wanted. He knew that now. All that had ever counted with her was what *she* wanted. That fucking cow! His big hands tore at the filmy pink fabric until it ripped, then tore at it again. He threw it to the floor and grabbed an emerald-green maternity smock. Livid with rage, Karl yanked at the garment until its buttons popped and it was completely shredded. Then he grabbed another. And another . . .

Panting in the hot, stagnant air, Karl looked around him. Half a dozen of his ex-wife's castoffs lay in tatters at his feet. He had to get out of this place before it drove him crazy. There was nothing to be gained here except further confirmation that he'd been used and discarded. He scooped up the pile of destroyed clothing, kicked the closet door shut, and headed for the garage. As he hurried out of the bedroom, his arms fully loaded, he never noticed the shredded red silk dress slipping from his grasp and falling silently to the bedroom floor.

32

The sky was rapidly growing dark by the time Allison spotted the roadside picnic area. If she kept on driving, they might reach Helena in another hour and a half, maybe two, but these mountain roads could be tricky in the dark. Besides, the dinner they'd eaten in the last town had further diminished their cash supply. The cost of a night in a motel would be a hardship. Allison pulled the station wagon off the highway and parked it near a picnic table. "We'll camp out here tonight, punkin," she said to Stephanie. "It'll be fun."

Although Allison had figured on reaching Helena with plenty of daylight to spare, things hadn't worked out that way. They had left the ranch late and the drive was slower than expected. After the incident in the barn, Allison had spent more than an hour questioning and comforting her daughter about the frightening sexual memory the milking scene had sparked. But the child remained tight-lipped, unwilling or unable to reveal many details about what had terrified her. Dr. Gunderson had explained about dissociation and repression—the tendency of molested children to disconnect themselves from their experiences and to forget what had happened to them while harboring extreme subconscious fears. Allison wasn't sure where the line should be drawn between helping to release Stephie from her buried terrors and further traumatizing her by badgering her to remember. Finally, all she was able to do was try to reassure the little girl that Mommy would never let Daddy scare her or hurt her again.

Allison was pleased to see that Stephie finished her glass of milk at dinner without complaint. At least milk seemed not to have taken on a negative association. Allison was learning to be grateful for any small sign of progress.

The picnic area was deserted. They climbed out of the car and walked across the parking lot to the public restroom, and found it unlocked. "We can wash up in here, Angel," Allison said, pushing open the door to the women's side. "Then you can put on your J's and go to sleep in the back of the car."

"You gonna sleep with me, Mommy?" The little girl's brow was deeply furrowed.

"Of course, sweetie. Mommy'll be right there with you, all night. I wouldn't leave you alone."

After they were ready for bed, Allison lowered the backseat and moved the suitcase and cooler into the front to make room for them to lie down in the rear of the station wagon. Betsy had given them an old blanket and Allison had brought pillows from Wood Lake, so they could be relatively comfortable. Stephanie snuggled in behind the passenger's seat, hugging Flopsy to her chest, while Allison locked the car doors and lay down beside her. The carpeted makeshift bed was hard, but at least it was flat and there was just enough room for Allison to stretch out. As the night progressed, she listened to the wind in the treetops and watched as stars sparkled through the feathery branches overhead. Finally, lulled by the sound of her daughter's soft, regular breathing, she grew drowsy and dropped off to sleep.

Allison stood at her father's bedside as he lay dying. A sturdy oak casket waited nearby, ready to receive his body. She reached out and grasped her father's limp hand. "Allie," he gasped, "I can't get air. I can't breathe. Help me!"

She wanted to help him, she wanted to so very badly, but the young doctor in the white coat explained that there was nothing anyone could do. It was too late. Tears rolling down her cheeks, she stood by helplessly as her father's tortured breathing finally ceased. The doctor picked up the old man's wasted body as if it weighed nothing at all, then gently laid it in the satin-lined box and closed the cover.

Allison sat on the empty hospital bed and wept, knowing now that she would never see her father alive again. She felt compelled to do something for him, to give him some last sign of her love. At least she could offer flowers. Wiping her tears away, she searched the hospital room for some blossoms to place atop his coffin. She spotted a golden mum plant but, as she began to pick its fuzzy blooms for a bouquet, she was startled by an eerie knocking sound. She dropped the flowers and listened. *Knock, knock. Knock, knock. Knock, knock.* She looked around the room, but she was the only one there. *Knock, knock. Knock, knock. Knock, knock.* The sounds had to be coming from inside the closed coffin. Her father was still alive!

Frantically, Allison's fingers tugged and pulled at the heavy brass latches on the side of the wooden box, but she could not release them. She pulled harder. Her fingertips bled, but still the casket would not open. There was so little air inside; she knew that if she didn't hurry, her father would suffocate. He would die, and this time it would be her fault.

Allison jolted awake, her heart beating wildly and her breaths coming in short, quick bursts. The nightmare had ceased, but she could still hear the knocking. She bolted upright in the back of the car, her hands clasping the blanket to her chest like a shield, and stared out at the black night. *Knock, knock.* Suddenly a light shone into her face, blinding her. She blinked and her heart skipped a beat. Were they about to be robbed? Or even raped? Please, God, no! *Knock, knock.* Her body began to tremble. The light moved away from her face and fell across Stephanie's sleeping figure. Instinctively, Allison moved to protect her child, throwing herself between Stephanie and the intruder with the flashlight. She held her breath. As her eyes adjusted to the changing illumination, she recognized the source of the knocking—a man's bare knuckles rapping rhythmically against the car window. The noise stopped and the hand pressed a shiny badge against the glass.

The intruder was a cop. Allison released her breath, unsure whether to be reassured or even more frightened. The policeman motioned for her to roll down the window. He couldn't possibly know who they were ... could he? Allison tried to tell herself there was no way this cop, out here in the middle of Montana, could be looking for Allison and Stephanie Warren.

Allison leaned forward. Her hands shaking, she managed to crank down the glass about three inches. "What's the problem, officer?" It was a struggle to keep her voice steady.

"You can't sleep here, ma'am. Park closes at dusk."

"Oh. Sorry, I—I didn't know."

"Had a girl raped out here a few weeks back. Place isn't safe for a woman and a child alone."

"I didn't realize. Th—thanks for letting me know, officer." Allison dropped the blanket, grateful she'd chosen to sleep in her jeans and a turtleneck shirt. "It's just that it was getting dark and my daughter was so tired, I—I thought—" Now she was chattering too much, from nerves. Shut up, she told herself, shut up before you arouse his curiosity.

"Have to ask you to move on outta here, ma'am. By rights, I should cite you, but seein' as you're from outta state, I'll let it go this once."

"Thank you, officer. I really appreciate it."

Scrambling toward the front of the car, Allison was relieved that the policeman had not asked to see her driver's license. All she had was the forged document that identified her as Elyse Michaels, and she wasn't sure it would pass inspection. She didn't want to be forced to test it. It was risky enough that the officer had noted the Minnesota plate on the car.

She rolled up the window, pulled on her shoes, and climbed awkwardly into the front seat. The clock on the illuminated dashboard read two-ten. She needed the restroom again, badly, but she didn't dare delay their escape and she wasn't about to leave Stephanie alone here in the car. Maybe there would be a gas station open somewhere along the road. Turning the key in the ignition, Allison prayed that her daughter would remain soundly asleep in the back, unaware of the intrusion. She glanced quickly over her shoulder at the still-peaceful child, then jerked the car into gear and pressed down slowly on the accelerator.

The squad car waited with its lights on as Allison, her hands still trembling on the steering wheel, headed the station wagon out of the picnic area and north toward Helena.

33

Allison and Stephanie were waiting on the granite steps of the Montana statehouse when a uniformed guard unlocked the door precisely at eight in the morning.

"I gotta go potty, Mommy," Stephie begged for the dozenth time. They found the women's room first, just in time for the little girl to avoid having an accident. When they emerged, Allison asked directions to the department that issued birth certificates.

"Take one of those forms at the back of the room, fill it out completely, and don't forget to sign at the X," the clerk said, not bothering to make eye contact. She was a dour woman with gray hair pulled back severely into a bun at the nape of her neck. "Five dollars for a certified copy, three for an uncertified, cash or check."

"I guess I'd better have a certified copy," Allison said. "I'll need to have a certified copy for a passport, right?" She felt compelled to offer the clerk an explanation for why she wanted the birth certificate.

"Have to ask the State Department about that, lady. We don't issue passports here. Don't get back in line until you've got your paperwork completed. And signed." The clerk pushed a button and a bell rang. "Next!"

Allison wondered why the woman had spoken so sharply. It wasn't as if she and Stephanie were holding up a crowd; the "line" consisted of only one other person, a man in a business suit carrying a black leather briefcase. He smiled and raised a palm in mock apology; not all Montanans are so ill-tempered, he seemed to be saying. Exhausted and feeling pretty testy herself after last night's ordeal, Allison managed to return the businessman's smile. She was grateful for his small gesture of kindness.

Sitting cross-legged on the hard floor, Stephanie grasped a pencil in her chubby hand and drew pictures on the back of one application form while Allison stood at the counter, filling out another in ink. She listed her name as Katherine Mary Andrews, her date of birth as September 10, 1955, and her birthplace as right here in Helena. Surreptitiously consulting the notes she'd made at the Wyoming library, she added the names of the Andrews child's mother and father and signed the form with the name Katherine Mary Andrews. After checking her new signature, she carried the completed paperwork, along with a five-dollar bill, back to the clerk.

"Takes about fifteen minutes. You can wait over there." The unsmiling civil servant gestured toward a row of green vinyl chairs against the wall.

"Thanks. Come on, Angel, let's sit down."

Stephanie followed behind, holding out her artwork. "Look, Mommy, I drawed a cow," she said proudly.

"Why, so you did, sweetheart. It's a very nice cow, too." The child beamed.

"Morgan!" the clerk bellowed. The man in the suit approached the counter, took the document the clerk handed him, and placed it in his briefcase. He smiled and waved good-bye to Allison as he left the room.

"Andrews!"

"Wait here, Angel. I'll be right back." Allison collected the birth certificate, checking to see that it was properly certified. As she walked back to where Stephanie sat, her spirits began to lift. "Come on, sweetheart, let's go get some breakfast." Maybe they'd splurge and have pancakes. Or French toast with cinnamon. Allison felt like celebrating. The legal document she held represented the vital first link in the process of assuming a new identity. Now that she had a genuine birth certificate, she could get a new Social Security number, a valid driver's license, a voter's registration card—all the legal identification she would ever need to leave Allison Mitchell Warren behind forever.

34

Tim Mitchell tried to comprehend the loan documents spread out before him, but the legalese was so thick he was having serious trouble. His eyes blurred each time he tried to concentrate and he felt his energy rapidly diminishing. He'd arranged this second mortgage on his house by telephone, but the loan agent from E-Z Finance had told him he'd have to come into the office to sign the loan documents. Worried that, when she saw him, the agent would decide he looked too ill to be a good credit risk, he'd taken extra care with his appearance this morning. He'd showered, washed his hair, shaved, dressed in clean clothes—niceties he often ignored these days. But truth was, he knew he still looked like hell. By the time he was finished with his personal grooming, he'd had to sit and rest awhile. Still, he'd managed to make it downtown to E-Z Finance by eleven. And so far he'd managed not to cough all over the desk. Not too bad, he reassured himself, for an old man on his way out.

Luckily, Tim thought, his fear that Mrs. Sanchez would take one look at him and require a medical report before funding his loan seemed to be unwarranted. The pretty black-haired young loan agent apparently was concerned only with making certain that he signed all the forms in the proper places.

If only he could be sure he wasn't being conned. This kind of deal made him anxious as hell. Christ, he'd give anything for a cigarette to calm his nerves, just one last smoke. But he'd made himself a promise to quit and he wasn't going to break it now. Tim didn't know a damned thing about E-Z Finance except what he'd learned from the company's TV commercials, the ones offering quick cash for any purpose if you owned your own home. He had a purpose all right, one he didn't care to discuss, and he definitely needed cash quick. "Tell me again why I can't get my check today," he said.

"State of California requires a seventy-two-hour waiting period. It's to give consumers a chance to cancel their loans if they change their mind." Mrs. Sanchez flashed him a winning smile. "I'm sure that won't happen in your case, Mr. Mitchell, but I'm afraid we have to follow the regulations just the same. Three days from today, we'll record the deed with the county and your check will be all ready for you to pick up. Or we can mail it to you if you'd rather not bother coming in again."

"No, no, I'll come in for it." No sense delaying the money any longer than necessary. Besides, Tim would have to take the check to his bank and convert it to cash, so he might as well figure on making a morning of it. He pointed to a column of numbers. "These figures here—" He could feel a tickle in his throat; he swallowed hard.

"Those are the loan costs we discussed."

"Right, but how much is actually gonna end up in my pocket by the time you take off—" The cough refused to be suppressed. It erupted in full force and Tim doubled over, hacking loudly and struggling for air. Shaking visibly by the time the coughing spell subsided, Tim gasped, "Picked up a helluva cold somewhere."

"Sorry to hear it." Wiping a look of distaste from her face, Mrs. Sanchez leaned forward and pointed out individual sums on the document, her full breasts straining against her pink flowered blouse as she spoke. She was a good-looking woman, but nowadays Tim hardly cared about that sort of thing. When he bothered to notice the opposite sex, he didn't even have the energy necessary for a good fantasy, so there didn't seem to be much point.

"The initial loan amount, this figure right here, is thirty-five thousand," Mrs. Sanchez said. "Since you elected to deduct the loan costs from the funded amount instead of paying them separately, we'll deduct the loan origination fee, the county tax stamps, the title insurance policy, the agent's commission . . ."

As she continued itemizing the seemingly endless column of fees he was being charged, Tim found his attention wandering. He tuned back in as she said, "The funded total comes to thirty-three thousand, one hundred twelve dollars and thirteen cents."

"So it's costing me near two grand just to get this loan?"

She circled a number. "Eighteen hundred eighty-seven dollars and eighty-seven cents, to be exact."

"Seems awful high."

The woman smiled again, refusing to be offended by Tim's implied accusation. "The difference between E-Z Finance and a bank or savings and loan is that we can give you your money in a hurry. And, as you know, you don't have to meet such stringent income requirements to qualify for a loan with us, Mr. Mitchell. It can be very difficult for retired people like you to show sufficient income for a new loan . . . but I'm sure you already know that. Consider, too, that your initial costs may be a little higher with us, but you can pay off your loan at any time with no prepayment penalty."

Such a deal. She sounded like she gave this speech a dozen times a day, but Tim knew he might as well sign the damned papers. The fees were highway robbery, and the annual interest rate was a good three percentage points higher than most banks were charging, but the woman was right. He was in a hurry and, with only his military pension for income, no responsible mainstream lender would touch him. "Where do I sign?" he asked.

Mrs. Sanchez put red Xs in five spots. Tim wrote his name in each place, noticing that his signature was becoming nearly illegible. But Mrs. Sanchez didn't seem to mind. She notarized the documents, ripped off a yellow carbon copy of each, and put the remaining copies in a manila file folder.

"These are your copies, Mr. Mitchell," she said, putting the yellow forms into an envelope and handing it to him. "I'll see you in three days."

Drawing as deep a breath as he could manage, Tim summoned enough strength to push himself slowly to his feet. He teetered slightly as he headed toward the door, pushed it open, and emerged into the relentless San Diego sunshine.

35

Louise Peterson sat cross-legged on her living room floor, staring at the illustrated instructions for assembling a gas barbeque grill. "Using tool M, connect part eleven to part fourteen," she read aloud. Parts eleven and fourteen lay on the carpet before her, but where the hell was the right-angled gismo called tool M? She searched among the dozens of parts that might, with a good deal of luck, be assembled to create the appliance illustrated on the carton. Louise had put together the bicycles she'd given her nieces and nephews last Christmas, and she'd laid the vinyl tile squares on the laundry room floor, but those projects were child's play compared to this. She pulled out a sealed plastic bag that appeared to contain gaskets, washers, a gas connection, a shut-off valve, and—dared she hope?—something that looked suspiciously like tool M. The phone rang.

Louise got to her feet and hurried to the kitchen table, which she'd converted into her desk for the day. She lifted the receiver on the third ring. "Hello."

"Is this Louise Peterson?"

"Right."

"I was told to call this number? To talk to you about the underground? The hotline said you're writing a story for *Woman's Life*?" The caller's anxiety was betrayed by her tendency to make each statement into a question.

"I'm freelance. If my article isn't in *Woman's Life*, it'll be in something similar. I appreciate your calling. I hope you don't mind answering a few questions for me. I'll try not to take too long." Louise's contact with the hotline had resulted in an agreement that several underground volunteers and mothers on the run would call her today, provided that she agreed not to ask for any details that could identify them. Because she dared not give the detective agency's phone number, Louise had spent the day at home—something she didn't really mind doing. She'd been putting off assembling that gas grill for over a month. This call was the fifth she'd received.

"I—I guess I don't mind," the caller said. "They told me you don't need to know who I am? 'Cause my husband'll kill me if he ever finds—"

"No, no, don't worry about that. I'd just like to hear some of your story, mainly about what it's been like for you to live in hiding, how you keep from being found, that sort of thing. I think my readers should know how other women have to live in order to protect their children."

Like the others, this woman was quite open about her own situation—as open as she could be without revealing either her name or her hometown. Her slight southern accent told Louise she was probably from Virginia, or maybe the Carolinas. The caller said she had an eleven-year-old daughter and they'd been in hiding for almost three years now.

"How do you manage to send your daughter to school?" Louise asked.

"Sometimes, if we stay long enough in one place, I send her to whatever local school there is, 'til they get too curious about where her previous school records are, anyway. I always tell the new school that I've written the old one to send the records. Then I stall 'em as long as I can, tell 'em the letter must have got lost in the mail, that I'll have to write another one, that sort of thing. When push comes to shove, we just pack up and move on." Louise made a noise of encouragement. "Then, when my girl's not in regular school somewhere, I pretty much tutor her on my own. It's not too hard at this age, but I don't know what I'm going to do when she gets into high school—you know, she'll need to know algebra, world history, that sort of thing. I'm not too strong on that stuff anymore. Been too long since I was in school myself."

A life lived in other people's homes was difficult at best, the woman told Louise. "You're always in somebody else's way, invading their privacy—at least that's how I feel about it," she said. "But without all the people who've helped us, my daughter and I— well, we'd be sleeping in the street. I know we would." Louise heard the catch in the other woman's voice.

"Why do you think these people in the underground have helped you and the other families like they do?"

"Lots of different reasons, I guess. One lady was real religious, claimed God told her to help the poor. Guess we're *that* all right—poor, I mean."

"What was it like living at her house?"

There was a pause on the line. "I don't . . . well, it's not that I'm not plenty grateful, because I am, but it was sorta hard on me and my little girl. I'm not a real religious person and this lady was always quoting Bible passages at us. Made me feel like some kinda heathen she was trying to convert. But don't get me wrong, they're not all like that."

"No, I suppose not."

"Like there was this couple we stayed with in Ala— I mean, down south. They were real nice. We even had our own bathroom, all to ourselves." The woman's voice was filled with wonder and gratitude. It made Louise feel guilty that she and Pete had two and a half baths for just the two of them. "The husband was a lawyer and he felt bad 'cause he had lost a case like mine. He was representing the mother in court, and the father ended up getting full custody of the kids. So this lawyer and his wife started taking in women like me and their children whenever they could, sorta trying to make up for that. We were only there a couple of weeks, though, and we had to move on. Can't stay in one place too long. It's too easy for somebody to find you if you do."

By the time Louise completed this fifth interview call, she'd learned a great deal about the stressfulness of the lives these shattered families had chosen to lead. Or, in their opinions, the lives they'd been forced to lead by the perversion of both the children's fathers' sexual desires and the American court system. Much as she wished she weren't, Louise was convinced that these people were sincere. These mothers truly believed they had sacrificed every aspect of their past lives to protect their children in the present. And the volunteers she'd talked with seemed to be good people willing to take a risk for somebody else. From where Louise sat, people like that were unfortunately rare these days.

According to the network spokeswoman who had called earlier, there were hundreds of these safe houses around the country and thousands of women and children had enjoyed their protection. Hundreds more people donated money to pay motel bills or transportation costs or to buy food for the fugitives when no safe houses were available. Others lent their "skills," not all of which were technically legal. Louise assumed that this included helping the fugitives create new identities, probably with forged documents. The representative had been understandably reticent to offer many details about that aspect of the cause.

Still, with her new, wider perspective, Louise realized she had discovered precious little that would be helpful in tracking down a woman like Allison Warren, who'd disappeared into the underground with her child. Apparently these families kept moving around from house to house, often passed off to curious neighbors as distant relatives or friends come for a visit. A few days to a few weeks in one place, then they were off to the next. Their names had been changed, of course, probably more than once. Their physical appearances were altered. They carried false identification. And they were thoroughly coached on how to avoid being found. One of the volunteers, Louise was told, was a female cop, a mother herself. She had instructed several other volunteers on the fine points of disappearing without a trace, and her advice had been passed around in a typed and Xeroxed manual that had become the Bible of the movement.

Louise shuddered involuntarily; it was a lifestyle she was grateful she would never have to endure. It also was one that she found herself increasingly reluctant to expose. She felt sorry for the poor souls caught up in it. Truth was, she also felt guilty as hell that she wasn't really writing that magazine article. She felt like someone who'd conned her way into an orphanage and now was in the process of robbing the orphans.

Shit! Louise pushed away her notes and returned to the barbeque grill. Here, at least, was a project where she had a decent chance of succeeding. One where her fitting all the parts together correctly had no predictable chance of hurting anyone.

36

"Look, fella, I got a weak memory, all right? Might be the same woman, might not." Stan Grann, the Used-Car Man, barely glanced at the photographs Pete Peterson held in his hand. "And I know I never saw any kid."

Pete peeled a twenty-dollar bill off the roll in his pocket. "This refresh your memory any?"

Grann waved it away. "What kinda jerk you take me for? I said I don't remember this Allison whatshername—"

"Warren."

"—the broad who sold me the car, and I don't remember any woman with a kid. I do a lot of business here. I can't remember everybody."

Pete forced a smile. "Hey, no offense, buddy." He put the twenty back into his pocket. Pete had begun his Minneapolis search with the car dealership that the Minnesota DMV said had purchased Allison's car. But the owner was uncooperative. The Buick still stood on Grann's used-car lot, a price of fifty-five hundred dollars written across its windshield in large, white figures, but Grann claimed to have no memory of Allison Warren. "You have any employees who might remember her?"

Grann's jaw was rigid and his eyes were cold. "I bought that car myself. I remember that much. I was alone here on the lot that day. But my mind's a blank about the woman who sold it to me."

Pete had a hunch that this guy remembered her quite well. "A cash purchase like that one is routine for you, huh?"

"Who says it was cash?"

"Like I told you, the woman's a fugitive, Grann. She's wanted by the cops. She's not exactly gonna take your check to the local bank and haul out her ID to cash it, is she?" The salesman remained mute. "Look, buddy, I'm sure you don't want the local gendarmes to get the idea you're aiding and abetting fugitives here, right?"

Grann thrust his large belly closer to Pete and glowered at him. "I bought that car strictly legal. I don't remember the woman who sold it to me, and it'd be none of your fucking business if I did. That clear enough for you . . . *buddy?*" The salesman's last word erupted in Pete's face, showering him with spittle.

Pete backed up a step. This was pointless. He shoved the photographs back in his folder, turned abruptly, and stalked back to the agency car.

Three hours later, Pete struck paydirt. He'd shown Allison's and Stephanie's photographs to half a dozen used-car dealerships up and down Lake Street. He'd given each the approximate date Allison Warren would have replaced the Buick, the maximum amount she could have paid, and the fact that it had been a cash transaction. He'd practically depleted his roll of twenties, offering enticements for each dealer to open his books and search for sales that fit the criteria. But he'd bombed out. Here at Bargain Used Auto, however, he got lucky.

The cashier, a chubby gray-haired woman in her mid-sixties, cheerfully checked her records for Pete. "Al sold somebody a Taurus on that day," she reported. "Cash sale. Remember it myself. Not that often somebody shows up carrying better'n four grand in small bills. Always makes me worry it might be drug money. Could be that's the one you're lookin' for."

Pete brought out the photos. "This the woman who bought the car?"

"Never saw her myself. Have to ask Al." The cashier directed him out to the lot where a wiry middle-aged man in a blue shirt was giving the hard sell to a teenage kid shopping with his father. Pete waited patiently until the father said he'd have to think about it and led the youth off the lot.

"You Al?"

"You bet."

Pete explained his quest and showed the salesman the photographs. "This the woman who bought that Ford from you?" He pointed to the photo of Allison in a bathing suit. "Probably had this kid with her." He held Stephanie's photograph next to her mother's.

Al's eyes rested on the first picture. "Kinda skinny, ain't she?"

"She's put on a little weight since then—in all the right places." He flashed Al a just-between-us-boys kind of look.

"Whaddya want with her?"

"Woman's got serious mental problems, ran off with the kid. Her husband wants his kid back."

"That right?"

Pete pulled the remaining wad of bills from his pocket. "If you can be sure this is the woman who bought that car from you, tell us what name she used, any other details—" He peeled off a twenty, folded it lengthwise between his index and second fingers, and held it out. Al's hand darted forward and the bill disappeared into his shirt pocket, the one below the plastic nametag that said "Al."

"Have to search my memory, but I think I remember her. Problem is she didn't look quite like this . . ."

Pete tensed with anticipation. He stuffed a second

twenty into Al's shirt pocket. "Think hard. How was she dressed? What was different about her appearance? What about the kid?"

"Never saw the kid." Al was positive about that. "No, she came in here with another broad. Brunette in short-shorts. Kind of legs that wouldn't quit. Nice little ass. That's the one did most of the talkin'."

"But you're sure that this was the other woman? The one who actually bought the car?" Pete asked, indicating Allison's picture.

"Ninety percent. There's something that bothers me about her, though, something besides the extra weight." The salesman held the photo close to his face and contemplated. "Got it! It's the hair. Her hair's all wrong. The broad that bought that Taurus wagon, the one carryin' all that cash, she wasn't a blonde. She had bushy red hair."

"Take a good look at her face. If you put red hair on this woman, gave her a permanent wave, added a few years to her age and a few pounds to her figure, would it be the same person?"

Al nodded decisively.

Half an hour and another forty bucks later, Pete left Bargain Used Auto feeling like a king. He now knew that Allison Warren had used the name Elyse Michaels to buy a replacement car. She had used a California driver's license with that name and her photo on it—red hair and all—as her ID. The driver's license clearly was forged, but that didn't matter to Pete. If she'd gone to the trouble of obtaining the phony document, she'd probably keep on using it. Best of all, Pete now had a description of the car Allison was driving, including its serial number and the number on its Minnesota license plates.

The net he had cast finally was tightening.

37

"Want some honey on your peanut-butter sandwich?" Allison asked. Stephanie nodded. Using a disposable plastic knife, Allison spread two pieces of bread with peanut butter and two others with honey, then assembled the parts into two sandwiches. The top of a battered dressing table, draped with a paper napkin, served as her makeshift kitchen.

Allison had driven hard all day, putting two states between them and Montana. When dusk fell, she'd turned the station wagon into the parking lot of a cheap motel outside of Spokane. The hotline had no place available to put them up tonight, but tomorrow a couple of beds were scheduled to open up in town. Afraid to risk sleeping outdoors a second time, Allison opted to spend thirty dollars on the motel and forage makings for a simple dinner from a convenience store across the street.

She placed each sandwich on a paper napkin, and handed one to Stephie. "Can you hold on to that okay?" The child's small hands tried to lift the sandwich to her mouth, but it bent and the top slice of bread threatened to slide off onto the floor. "Here, I'd better cut it for you." Allison took the sandwich back and half-cut, half-tore it with the serrated edge of the plastic knife. She handed one section to her daughter, took a bite of her own sandwich, then opened a small carton of milk, into which she thrust a straw. There weren't even a table and chairs to eat at in this dump. They had a choice between standing while they ate or sitting on the sagging double bed. Fearful of having to sleep with crumbs in the bed, Allison chose the former. Besides, they'd been sitting all day; standing for a few minutes felt good.

"Ummm. This is *good*, Mommy." Stephanie smiled through the peanut butter that now was smeared across her face. "I was starved!"

"Here, have some milk, Angel." Allison held the milk carton while Stephanie sucked noisily on the straw. Thank goodness kids were so easy to please with simple food. Unlike a typical adult, Stephanie didn't consider having to make dinner out of a peanut butter sandwich, a carton of milk, and a banana any particular hardship. In fact, Allison mused, the child probably preferred this meal to steak or lobster. She chewed on her own sandwich and thought longingly of gourmet meals she'd enjoyed in some of the major cities of the world during her airline career. "Maxim's probably couldn't make a better peanut butter and honey sandwich," she said wistfully.

"Who's Max—Max—what you said?" Stephanie asked.

Allison laughed. "Maxim's is a famous restaurant in Paris, sweetie," she said. "They serve snails, but they call them escargots. Someday we'll go there."

"Oooh, yucky!" Stephanie stuck out her peanut butter–coated tongue. "I'm not gonna eat *snails*." Allison winked. "You're teasing me, huh, Mommy?" The two finished their sandwiches, agreeing that they undoubtedly tasted a lot better than the snails they'd seen in Grandpa's garden in San Diego when they'd visited there last year.

Allison rewrapped the remaining bread and capped the peanut butter and honey. They ate their bananas in front of the flickering TV. Only three channels were available, but luckily one offered a sitcom that quickly captured Stephanie's attention.

After cleaning up the remains of their meal, Allison plopped herself down next to her daughter on the bed. She spread out the collection of blank ID cards she'd carried from St. Paul in front of her on the worn chenille bedspread. These cards didn't offer any official kind of identification, but they were the type of thing people carry in their wallets. Not to have several of them in her own would seem suspect. Allison picked up one that certified that the bearer had completed an American Red Cross course in Senior Lifesaving. With a black pen, she carefully printed the name Katherine M. Andrews in the center of the card, then flipped it over and signed the same name in blue ink where a signature was called for. When the ink had dried, she rubbed the card across the sole of her shoe, then bent its corners, admiring the used effect she'd achieved. She picked up the next card, which identified the holder as a member of the National Audubon Society, and repeated the process.

Tomorrow they would move into another safe house, one where Allison planned to stay until Katherine Mary Andrews had an official Washington driver's license to accompany these less-important documents.

But for tonight, even this swaybacked bed in this humble motel looked awfully good. Allison was so tired she was bleary eyed. And this place had one attribute she craved but knew she would have to live without for the foreseeable future—it offered complete, wonderful, delicious privacy.

38

"Sergeant Buck Linn on line two," Karl's secretary announced over the office intercom.

Karl shoved aside the deposition transcript he'd been marking up in preparation for his afternoon meeting and leaned across his desk. "I'll take it." He punched the lighted button on the telephone and picked up the receiver. "Buck, what's up?"

"Got some news I think you're gonna like." Buck paused for effect before making his announcement. "We got Allison charged with felony child stealing this morning. Official help is on the way, pal. If we can show she took Stephanie across the state line, we can request FBI assistance on this thing."

"Hell, it's about time." Karl's tone was less than grateful. "That bitch was out of Wisconsin with my daughter inside twenty-four hours; I'll stake my life on it. By now they could be on Mars."

"Hey, lighten up. This is record fast action and you know it. Without a friend or two over here greasin' the gears for you, you'd be chewin' your nails for at least another month."

Karl's grip on the receiver tightened and he stifled an angry retort. He knew that antagonizing Buck Linn wouldn't help get Stephie back. But he loathed having to kiss ass for what he ought to have coming to him. "Don't think I'm not grateful for your help, Buck. I just wish we could've gone after the two of them the minute I realized they'd cleared out of

220

Wood Lake. Would've been a helluva lot easier to find them then."

"Thought you were gonna get Pete 'n' Louise workin' for you."

"I did, but they're no FBI."

"Don't be so quick to piss on 'em. I don't want you to start kiddin' yourself about this, Karl—the Feds aren't gonna give your case the kinda priority you got in mind. This's small potatoes for them and, with all of us gettin' hit with budget cuts, you're gonna be a low priority. You ask me, the best way to handle this is to keep on usin' the Petersons, dig up as much as you can on your own, then ask for official help where and when you need it."

You wouldn't think that was such a hot idea if you were paying the bills, Karl thought, but he kept it to himself. "So you'd keep them on the case?"

"You bet. I'll do what I can from over here, but hittin' it from both directions is gonna find your kid that much faster. What've you been able to turn up?"

Karl chose his facts carefully. Quinn's illegal eavesdropping on Tim Mitchell would have to remain private. But the information that had been turned over last night could be very useful. "Pete got some good stuff in Minneapolis yesterday," he said.

"Let's hear it."

Karl pulled his notes from the top desk drawer. "Allison sold the Buick in Minneapolis and bought herself a silver Ford Taurus wagon. It's got body damage on the passenger side." He gave Buck the Ford's serial and license plate numbers.

"I'll put 'em in the computer right away. Won't be able to get you an APB on her, but if she gets picked up for speeding, or breaks down on the road, we could get lucky."

"We're pretty sure she's heading west, maybe on the way to see her old man in San Diego. Word is he's got terminal cancer. Pete turned up an alias and a new description for Allison, too. She's using a phony California driver's license under the name Elyse Michaels, and the salesman who sold her the car says she had curly red hair when he saw her. Might be a wig, or maybe she's dyed hers." That baby-blond hair was the last thing about Allison that Karl had found attractive. It sounded as though even her hair looked like hell now.

"All *right*. This is real good stuff. Can you send over some photos of both Stephie and Allison?"

"Yeah, but the only one I've got of Allison is pretty old, and her hair's not going to look right if she's changed it like that salesman said."

"Send it on over anyhow. I'll give it to Swede Johnson—he's the artist does our composites. Have him age her a few years, change the hair, run off a stack of duplicates."

"Thanks, Buck. I really do appreciate your help."

"Just keep your chin up and your blood pressure down, old pal. You're gonna get your kid back. Now that the paperwork's outta the way, things're gonna start goin' your way."

39

"How do you handle forwarding the mail if a customer moves?" Allison asked. "I'm probably going to be leaving the state before too long, so having my mail sent on is going to be important." With a whiny Stephanie almost hanging on her left arm, Allison was attempting to interview the owner of a mail-receiving service on Third Avenue, near downtown Spokane. She had written down the addresses of four such services listed in the phone directory's Yellow Pages; this was the third they had visited this morning. The novelty long ago had worn off for Stephanie and the little girl was demonstrating her boredom. "Stop pulling on me," Allison snapped at her. "That hurts."

The owner of the service, who introduced herself as Meredith Cray, was a tiny brassy blonde about Allison's age. Standing behind a waist-high counter, she wore a slim navy skirt and a crisp white blouse with a bow at the neck—the perfect efficient-secretary get-up, Allison thought.

"We can forward your mail any way you want—to another address, even to another name," Meredith Cray told her.

"When I've moved and gotten settled, could I send you a supply of big envelopes with my new address and some money for postage and have you repackage my mail before you send it on?"

"Sure, if that's the way you want to do it. Just so

you include a signed authorization when you mail me the envelopes and money."

Stephanie yanked on her mother's denim skirt. "Mommy, I'm tired. I wanna go to the park and play. You *prom*ised."

"Stop pulling on me, Angel. I'll be done here in a minute."

"But *Mom*-my—"

Allison turned, skewered her daughter with a stern look, and spoke sharply. "I said stop it and I mean stop it *now*!" Stephanie stuck out her lower lip in response, but she released her grip on her mother and remained silent.

Meredith Cray pretended not to notice the confrontation between mother and daughter. "All our services are completely confidential, of course," she added brightly. "Our customers really appreciate that."

Allison turned her attention back to the task at hand. This service seemed to have everything she might need in a mail drop. She could use the business's street address as her own, instead of a post office box number, and the place was open twenty-four hours a day. "How much for three months' box rental?"

"Forty-five dollars. That includes the forwarding service, but any postage costs will be extra, of course."

"And if I send you my change of address, you'll make sure it's kept private? You won't give it out to anybody?" Allison bent across the counter and whispered, "You know how is it—boyfriend trouble."

The other woman smiled conspiratorially. "Like I said, everything here is absolutely confidential. Nobody gets any information about you unless you personally approve their having it."

Allison pulled out her wallet, removed two twenties and a five, and handed them across the counter, then signed the signature card with the name Katherine M. Andrews.

Meredith Cray made a notation on the card and handed Allison a key with the number "202" stamped on it. "If you prefer, Ms. Andrews, you can use apartment number two-oh-two or suite number two-oh-two for your correspondence instead of the box number. Your mail will all end up in box two-oh-two just the same."

"Great." Allison stuffed the key and her cash receipt into her purse and grabbed Stephanie's hand. "Come on, kiddo, let's go to the park and work off some of that excess energy before we both go crazy."

Three hours later, Allison sat in the parking lot outside the Washington Motor Vehicles Department building in Spokane. Stephanie, now smeared with dust and grime from the playground, napped with her beloved Flopsy in the back of the station wagon while Allison studied the Washington driver's manual. It seemed silly, having to take and pass a driver's test all over again. She'd been driving without an accident since she was sixteen, had even managed to drive on the left side of the road in Australia and England. But Katherine M. Andrews had never held a driver's license, and if she intended to become Katherine Andrews, she would have to start all over again.

"I've been living in New York City since high school," she'd told the teenage clerk when she applied to take the written test. "You've got to be crazy to own a car there, so I never had to learn to drive. Guess it's about time I did, huh?" She received a smile, a shrug, and the driver's manual in response, but no particular curiosity about why a woman her age had no prior license to exchange. The birth certificate Allison had obtained in Helena served as adequate proof that she was indeed Katherine Andrews.

And the address of the mail drop on Third Avenue now became the place she listed as her home address.

The Washington rules and regulations were not significantly different from Wisconsin's and, when Allison went back inside and took the written exam, she scored ninety-one percent.

A second clerk, this one a portly woman with lacquered gray hair, handed her a yellow receipt with her new name, address, and physical description typed on it. "This is your driver's permit," she explained. "You can drive with it only when you're accompanied by a licensed driver."

"How soon can I take my behind-the-wheel test?" Allison asked.

"Practice driving and as soon as you think you can pass the test, call this number and schedule an appointment." The woman wrote a telephone number on the back of the receipt.

On her way out of the building, Allison stopped at the bank of pay phones near the exit and dialed the phone number the clerk had written down. Still another clerk answered and efficiently made an appointment for Katherine Andrews to take a behind-the-wheel driving test the next afternoon.

As she walked back to the car, Allison felt a surge of confidence. It was all working out just the way the underground volunteers had promised her it would. In just a few days, she had found a new name and a new address, and she was well on her way to having a new picture ID to bolster both. Good-bye Allison Warren; hello Katherine Andrews.

40

It was a typical hot, dry late-summer afternoon in Spokane as Allison shooed Stephanie toward the bathtub. The child had been playing outdoors all day, creating a miniature town in the loose dirt beneath the tall pine trees in the backyard. Every visible inch of her small body was filthy. "Come on, toots, give Mommy your clothes so I can throw them in the washer," Allison said. "I've got to get that last load done before Tamara gets home from work."

Tamara Watson owned the small house where they had been staying for the last five days. A secretary at a local lumber firm, Tamara was a divorced mother with two teenage sons. Allison and her daughter were the fifth fugitive family that the Watsons had hosted this year. The accommodations here were spartan—two beds in the unfinished walkout basement of Tamara's small suburban Spokane house—but the Watsons were a warm, generous lot and Allison was grateful for the taste of privacy they'd been given here.

Today, with Tamara and her boys all out at their jobs, Allison saw a chance to do her laundry and to make use of the house's sole bathroom before the usual evening rush. She'd promised to cook dinner for everyone and time was running short.

Stephanie stepped out of her green sunsuit and pink cotton panties, leaving them in a heap on the floor, and pulled off her dingy white socks. She climbed into the bathtub and sank down into the tepid water, which quickly turned gray. "Flopsy needs a bath, too, Mommy. I tried to hold onto her, but she falled down and got all dirty."

"Flopsy *fell* down, punkin, not falled down." Holding the stuffed bunny by its ears, Allison swatted it briskly, creating a cloud of dust that tickled her nose. She removed the creature's dress and said, "I'll wash Flopsy's clothes with our stuff, but I'm not sure what to do about her fur. "I'll see what I can do with it after I get this load in the machine." She laid Flopsy on top of the toilet tank and scooped up the soiled clothing from the floor. "I'll be back in a minute and help you shampoo your hair."

When Allison returned, Stephie was cheerfully washing the bunny in her bathwater. The worn gray fur was thoroughly soaked and Stephanie was energetically rubbing the bar of soap against it, creating a thick coating of white suds. "See, Mommy? Flopsy *loves* baths."

"Oh, Jesus." Allison didn't know whether to laugh or scold. She dropped to her knees beside the tub and grabbed the stuffed animal out of Stephanie's hands. "Sweetheart, Flopsy can't have a bath like real people. Her stuffing might never get dry again." Using a face cloth, Allison quickly attempted to wash off the soap without further soaking the bunny.

"I'm sorry, Mommy. I didn't mean to hurt Flopsy." Stephanie's blue eyes widened and filled. "Honest, I didn't."

"I know you didn't mean to hurt her, Angel, and I'm sure Flopsy knows it, too." Allison wrapped the bunny tightly in a towel and squeezed out as much water as she could. Flopsy emerged looking sodden and a bit misshapen, but definitely cleaner than a few minutes earlier. "There, we'll hang her up outside and hope she'll dry."

An hour later, clothespins in Flopsy's ears held

her to the backyard clothesline and Allison was maneuvering a shopping cart down the aisles of the neighborhood supermarket, with a newly scrubbed and shampooed Stephanie tagging along. Tamara Watson was far from affluent and Allison felt guilty about accepting her charity. Their compromise was that Allison would buy groceries and do the cooking every second night for the rest of their stay at the Watson house. That should be only a few days longer, just until Katherine Andrews's new driver's license arrived at the mail drop on Third Avenue. With the license as her photo ID and the Montana birth certificate, Allison then could apply for a new Social Security number in the Andrews name. That task accomplished, it would be time to head west once again.

"Want peas or green beans tonight?" Allison asked, leaning over the frozen food case. The blast of frigid air it emitted was a soothing contrast to the dry heat outside the store.

"I wanna popsicle, Mommy."

"That wasn't the choice I gave you, was it?"

"Noooo, but . . . I want peas. *And* a popsicle." The child grinned impishly. "A cherry popsicle. Puhleeze?"

"Oh, all right, one cherry popsicle, but you have to save it for dessert." And eat it over the sink, Allison decided; no more baths for you today, miss. She put two boxes of frozen peas into the cart and searched for the popsicles. There they were, but it looked as though they were sold in packages of six. Damn. Allison wished she hadn't already promised.

"Goody, goody," Stephanie shrieked, jumping up and down, when she saw the box of frozen treats go into the shopping cart.

"Think you put one over on Mommy, don't you?" Allison laughed good-naturedly.

"Allison?" asked a male voice somewhere behind her.

Allison was momentarily startled, then decided someone else must share her name. She checked her shopping list. "Let's see, we need to find the meat section. Let's go buy some hamburger, Angel. We'll make meatloaf tonight. Think Tamara and the boys will like that?"

"Uh-huh. *I* like meatloaf. It's my very most favorite food, 'cept for pizza, and pis-getti, and hot dogs, and fried chicken, and birthday cake, and—"

"Allison," the voice repeated.

"And popsicles," Allison said with a smile. "Meatloaf is one of my very most favorite foods, too. That's why I decided to make it, because it's a very most favorite for both of us."

Allison was turning her cart away from the frozen food section when a hand fell on her shoulder. She jumped, caught her breath, and jerked around.

"Allison, Allison Mitchell. It *is* you. I almost didn't recognize you. Your hair—you look so different."

Her mind racing wildly, searching for some means of denial, of escape, Allison's eyes finally focused on the man standing next to her. She recognized a familiar face from her past—Blair Connors, a pilot from the old days at Northwest Orient. They'd flown together between Minneapolis-St. Paul International and the West Coast dozens of times.

Blair pulled back his hand. "Hey, Allie, sorry. Didn't mean to scare you. It's me, Blair Connors, remember? What are you doing in these parts?"

"I—I—" Allison had trouble finding her voice. Her thoughts spun out of control. What should she say to him? What *could* she say? Who might Blair tell that he'd seen her here? Should she lie to him or tell the truth and hope he'd keep her secret?

"Hey, relax. You look like you've seen a ghost."

Blair kneeled down next to Stephanie. "Hi, there, little lady. Who're you?"

Shy, Stephie slid behind her mother's legs and hid her face.

"She—she's my daughter," Allison managed to say.

"Going to be as gorgeous as her mom someday," Blair said, rising. "How old is she, about four?"

"Right, just four."

"Christ, Allie, how long has it been? If your daughter's already four years old, it has to be—what?—five, six years since we've seen each other?"

"Almost six, I guess."

Blair pulled at his chin. He was a tall man, about six foot two, with a slim build, sandy hair, and electric blue eyes. "So you got married, had a baby. Is your husband here with you?"

Allison chewed on her lip, feeling awkward and self-conscious. "No, no . . . he's not. I—I mean we're divorced."

The ghost of a smile played across Blair Connors's lips. "Is that right?" He did not sound disappointed. "Me, too. Divorced, I mean. Been living here in Spokane since my wife and I split up two years ago. She's still got the house on the Sound, but I was flying out of Spokane so much it seemed sensible to take an apartment here. Found out I liked the climate better. Not so much rain on this side of the state."

Allison didn't know what to say. Her eyes darted from side to side, as though searching for a way out. The truth was that she remembered Blair Connors very well, and with almost embarrassing affection. She recalled a time when she'd devoutly wished he were divorced. Nothing serious had ever happened between her and the handsome pilot, but she had always felt a current of electricity between them, a certain magnetism whenever their eyes met. If he hadn't been a married man ... but he was. Until now.

"Hey, how about dinner one of these nights?" Blair asked, his eyes crinkling around the edges. "I could show you the sights—such as they are here in Spokane. Where're you staying?"

"I—I don't think that would work out," Allison said, clearly flustered. "We're just—I mean, my little girl and I are leaving real soon. Tomorrow, I think. Maybe tonight." Christ, she wished she knew how to handle this without looking so suspicious, so guilty ... of something. She thrust her shaking hands into the pockets of her shorts.

"Allie." Blair's voice softened. "Are you in any kind of trouble? Maybe I could help if you—"

Allison felt her eyes fill and her lower lip began to tremble. He *had* noticed her distress. Well, why wouldn't he? The man had eyes. "No! No, you can't—" she stammered. "I mean, there's nothing, nothing wrong. It's only that—I'm—I'm just late, that's all." She made a show of looking at her watch, being shocked at the late hour. "Nice to see you again, Blair, but I've really got to run. Sorry." She grabbed Stephanie by an arm, turned, and nearly ran as she propelled her cart down the aisle, pulling her child behind her.

Blair Connors stared after her, a puzzled expression etched around his blue eyes.

"Mommy, who's that?" Stephanie's voice echoed her mother's own fear.

"Just a man Mommy used to know a long time ago."

"How come he scared you, Mommy?"

"Mommy wasn't scared, punkin. I was just trying to hurry." Lord, Allison thought, even a four-year-old hadn't been fooled by the pitiful way she'd handled that encounter.

Allison rushed frantically as she searched for the

remaining items on her shopping list, furtively looking over her shoulder every few seconds to see if Blair Connors had reappeared. Or if any other ghosts from her past had suddenly materialized.

"Mommy, that man . . . he scared me."

That night, for the first time in nearly a week, Stephanie awoke in terror, screaming hysterically that the snakes were coming to get her.

41

Ruth Persky pulled the pickup truck in to the curb across the street from her sister's house in Wood Lake, climbed out, and stretched. She was glad to have the long drive behind her—the first half, anyway.

She glanced up at the sky. It was beginning to cloud over. Ruth had been praying for rain all summer; the farm crop this year had been seriously stunted by the drought. But it would be just her luck, she thought, to have her prayers answered on the one Saturday she planned to hold a yard sale of the things Allison had left behind. Well, she couldn't drive up here again next weekend. She already was wasting most of this one. She'd been awake since four today, on the road since five, to allow time to set out the sales goods before noon, when the customers would start arriving. If the sale were rained out, it would be just too bad. She'd done her part. After today, that real estate woman could worry about getting rid of whatever was left in the house.

Ruth pulled the house key out of her purse and opened the front door. She cranked open the living room windows to let in some fresh air, then opened windows in the kitchen as well. The cross-draft began to cool the house nicely. But it did nothing to allay the uneasiness she always seemed to feel whenever she was alone here. She knew there was no logical basis for her feeling. What was it she really feared? That Karl Warren would barge in on her, that he would accost her as he had his own daughter? That was ridiculous. Ruth was a middle-aged woman and she had every right to be here. Ironically, until the sale of the house was completed, she actually owned the place. Karl Warren had no legal right to come near it or near her, and there was no real reason for Ruth to fear he would try. She shrugged off her discomfort, chalking it up to fatigue.

Where to start? At home, Ruth had made up a hand-printed sign listing the furniture to be sold, with what she thought was a fair price following each item. She certainly couldn't be expected to haul the furniture onto the front lawn, but she also didn't want too many people wandering through the house unattended. She would carry enough of the kitchenware, clothing, and toys out to the garage and driveway to create attention. Any shoppers interested in buying furniture could check the list and wait until she could usher them inside individually to inspect it.

But first Ruth would pick and choose among Allison's leavings for her own family's benefit. She'd already decided to take home the two sets of dishes—the casual pottery in the kitchen cupboards and the good china in the dining room buffet. And her daughter Lucy had been thrilled with the dresses Ruth had brought back from her last trip to Wood Lake. Anything youthful enough for a teenager in a size six or eight would be set aside for her.

Ruth packed the dishes she selected for her family into three cardboard cartons and set them by the front door. Now to find some clothing for Lucy. Ruth discovered a perfectly good camel-hair coat in the front closet and laid it on top of the cartons, then headed toward the master bedroom in the back of the house. As she walked down the hallway, a splash of brilliant red caught her eye. From a distance, it looked like someone had spilled fresh blood on the pale bedroom carpet. But that was silly, Ruth told herself. She was letting her imagination run away with her.

Fighting a stubborn sense of foreboding, Ruth crept closer to the stain. But it wasn't blood at all; it wasn't even a stain. It was only one of Allison's dresses—or it once had been one of Allie's dresses. With two fingers, Ruth lifted the brilliant red fabric from the carpet and held it out in front of her, as if it were something dead, something revolting. The delicate silk dress had been slashed to shreds, destroyed with a frightening maliciousness. Ruth's spine tightened and she looked around fearfully. This was a clear act of rage; whoever did this had been bursting with fury. Had vandals intruded here? Could they still be in the house? But the place was clearly silent, deserted.

The ruined scarlet silk gripped tightly in her hand, Ruth quickly examined the closet, then Stephanie's room. But there were no other visible signs of trespass or damage. Vandals would never have invaded this place to destroy one dress and then depart, locking the doors behind them. With chilling certainty, Ruth knew exactly who had been here, who had searched her sister's personal belongings and left behind this evidence of his hatred for her. It could only have been Karl Warren. Picturing the venomous rage he must have vented here, Ruth shivered involuntarily, then dropped the bright silk garment into the bedroom wastebasket.

By the end of the afternoon, Ruth was exhausted, but feeling pleased with herself. The humidity hung heavy in the air and the sky was gray, but the rain had held off and the day's sales receipts totaled nearly eight hundred dollars. Allison should be happy with that. The bulk of the money had resulted from a soon-to-be-married couple's purchase of the bedroom and dining room furniture, but smaller purchases of Stephanie's toys and clothing, pots and pans, even some of Allison's castoff shoes, helped swell the total.

Shortly before five, the last of more than twenty shoppers loaded his bargain—a forty-dollar pair of Stiffel lamps—into the trunk of his car and drove away. Ruth began carrying the remainder of the unsold pieces back into the house. If she could clear the driveway quickly enough, she figured, she could be back at the farm before midnight, allowing time for a dinner break. She was bone-tired and she disliked driving the country roads in the dark, but the idea of spending the night alone here was even less appealing than the long, solitary drive.

As she grabbed an armload of unsold blankets, a dark Cadillac pulled into the driveway and Karl Warren emerged. Ruth froze, unsure what to do. Her former brother-in-law was the last person she wanted to see. She held the blankets across her chest, almost as protection against him, and stood her ground. "You've got no business here," she said, lifting her chin.

Karl kept walking toward her. "I came to find out where my child is," he demanded. He seemed immense, towering over Ruth.

"I haven't the slightest idea where she is. And you've no right to ask me." Ruth saw Karl's huge hand clench into a fist; she flinched reflexively. She stole a look down the deserted street. Where were the neighbors? Would anyone come to her defense if Karl threatened her, if he became violent?

"You know that aiding and abetting a fugitive is a crime, don't you, Ruth? That's what you're doing here."

"I'm doing nothing of the sort."

"The FBI is looking for them now, you know. That'll mean federal prison for you when they're found. Even if they're never found, you could end up behind bars. That'd be ironic, you in prison just because you wouldn't tell where your bitch of a sister took my daughter."

Ruth backed toward the open front door, feeling for the concrete steps with her foot. She stumbled, then caught herself. Karl followed her closely.

"Know what they do to women in prison?" he asked, an oily smile on his lips. "I guarantee you won't like it, Ruth. You won't like it one little bit."

"I don't *know* where they are. I don't know, damn it!"

"Is that a fact? Well, fuck that, Sis. I don't believe a word of it."

"Don't you call me Sis. I'm not your sister."

The smile disappeared. "No loss to me. You never were much of a sister to Allison, either, if memory serves me." Karl's tone grew equally confidential and sinister. "What I can't figure out, Ruth, is why you're doing this. I'd've bet my last nickel you didn't even *like* Allison much." Ruth's mouth fell open. "Hit a nerve there, didn't I? Thought nobody noticed? Hell, you were so jealous of your kid sister you wore your resentment like a neon sign."

Ruth began to shake visibly, from outrage now as much as from fear. Karl Warren had no right to invade her life this way, to expose her innermost secrets, her hidden guilts. He had no goddamned right! "Get the hell out of here." She spat out the words.

"You don't want to go to prison, Ruth, believe me. Not for that bitch. She's not worth it. You and I both know that. Come on, give it up before—"

"You! Who are you to preach to me about the law, about prison. I—I could call the police, I could have you arrested right now, right here."

Karl began to laugh.

"You think I'm bluffing? I'll show you, you son of a bitch. This is *my* house now. You broke into my house and I've got proof. You came in here, destroyed Allie's things. I've got that red dress you tore up—"

Karl's face darkened and his voice thundered. "Shut up. Shut up, you fucking whore!" His white-knuckled fist extended, he stepped forward. Stunned by the intensity of his sudden rage, Ruth tossed the armload of blankets into his path, rushed through the front door, and slammed it shut in his face. She shot the deadbolt home and, breathing heavily, braced herself against the door.

This was the final straw. It was all too goddamned much. Ruth closed her eyes against tears of fear and frustration and vowed never to set foot in Wood Lake or this house again.

42

Allison sighed with relief as the Portland skyline came into view over the crest of the highway. Right now, she wouldn't wish nine long hours in the car with a fidgety four-year-old on her worst enemy.

"Won't be long now, Angel," she said. "We're almost there."

"I wanna eat, Mommy. Flopsy, too." Stephanie shoved the stuffed rabbit, its worn fur now matted and stiff from its recent bath, toward her mother's face. "See, Mommy? Flopsy's starved."

"Don't push that bunny in my face. I can't see where I'm driving." Allison shoved the stuffed animal away. "You'll make me have an accident. I know you're hungry, kiddo, but you'll just have to be patient a little while longer. Let's sing one hundred bottles of pop on the wall one more time." Anything to stop the whining and wiggling, Allison thought, although she couldn't blame poor Stephanie. She felt like whining herself.

The last three days at Tamara Watson's house had been terribly difficult, filled with almost unbearable tension, and the nights had been interrupted time and time again by Stephanie's recurrent nightmares. Undoubtedly, it was all Allison's fault, but she'd been so frightened by her chance encounter with Blair Connors that she literally couldn't think straight. Poor little Stephanie had sensed her mother's anxiety and mirrored it. For the last few days, it had been clear that the poor child feared her last remaining safety net was falling apart.

Allison fretted constantly. If she could run into one old friend, she told herself, she certainly could run into others. She chided herself for having been stupid enough to spend more than a week in a city on Northwest Airlines's route structure. She should have known she would encounter somebody she knew, sooner or later. Truth was, she was lucky it had been Blair Connors. He was a decent man and Allison knew he genuinely liked her. She suspected she could have told Blair the truth and trusted him to keep her secret. But she hadn't dared take that chance. And there were other people from her airline days with whom Allison had had far cooler relationships. What if she'd come across one of them, one who might even know through the grapevine or from the news back in the Midwest that she was on the run? Clearly, she had to get out of Spokane. Yet she couldn't afford to leave without the all-important new driver's license in her wallet. She drove in Spokane, using the receipt she'd received when she passed her behind-the-wheel test, but it was good for only thirty days and it wasn't a photo ID. She had to have the real thing before she could move on.

Each day, as Allison drove to Third Avenue to check her post office box, she was terrified that she would run across Blair a second time, that this time she wouldn't be able to escape without offering him a plausible explanation for her admittedly strange behavior. But she hadn't seen the tall man with the sandy hair again.

Finally, it arrived—the driver's license with her photo, complete with the bushy red hair she thought made her look hideous, and Katherine Mary Andrews's name and birthdate. All completely legal and worth solid gold to a mother on the run. Allison nearly cried with relief.

The afternoon she received the driver's license, she went to the Spokane office of the Social Security Administration and filled out papers for a Social Security card. Allison knew she could try getting a job using a false Social Security number, or using someone else's, but either of those solutions would risk sparking an official investigation if an account were found to be receiving contributions from two different employers. This way was far safer.

Still, it was nowhere as easy as getting the driver's license had been. The Social Security clerk, a tall woman with dark brown hair pulled into a severe bun on top of her head, wanted to know why a woman over thirty had never before had her own Social Security number. In her view, Allison's situation was clearly suspect.

Forewarned by the network volunteers, Allison had what she thought was a logical answer prepared. "I—I've been living in a commune," she explained, wondering if she sounded as nervous as she felt. "Ever since I was sixteen. We were pretty much self-sufficient on our land. Raised our own food and all, you know. I've never had a real paying job before, so I didn't figure I needed a Social Security number."

"A commune." The woman's eyebrows rose skeptically.

"Uh-huh, right. I lived there until just a few weeks ago. It—I mean, I thought it was time for us to move on."

"And you've never filed an income tax return before?" The woman's tone was incredulous.

Allison squirmed in her chair. "I never earned any money. You don't have to pay taxes if you don't have any income." She tried to sound sure of herself, even a bit indignant about being questioned.

"What about your husband?" the clerk asked, her disapproving eye falling on Stephanie. "Didn't he earn a living? Didn't you ever file a joint tax return?"

Allison bit her lip, wishing she'd had somewhere, anywhere, to leave Stephie while she told these blatant lies to a public official. "I—" She leaned closer to her clerk and half-whispered her answer. "I was never actually married."

"I see." The woman drew back as if she feared contamination. "And where, may I ask, was this, uh, this commune?"

"In northern California, near—uh, near Eureka, in Humboldt County."

"Oh, California." Her tone implied that the commune's location explained this craziness. Washingtonians apparently were willing to believe that Californians were capable of any manner of aberrant behavior. "Well, sign your application at the X, *Miss* Andrews. When the paperwork's been processed, your card will be mailed to your local address."

"Thank you," Allison said, scratching the signature onto the line that was indicated. She grabbed her receipt and shooed Stephanie toward the exit. Allison wouldn't wait for the Social Security card to show up at the mail drop. She'd have to find a place to locate permanently before she could get a job anyway. The service could forward the card to her new location when it arrived.

Early the next morning, Allison and Stephanie started for Portland, relieved to leave Spokane behind.

Allison drove across the city before pulling into a southside motel advertising single rooms at $29.95 a night, doubles for $32.95. She wanted to be as far as possible from the Portland Airport. One night here, two at the most, and they'd move on farther south. Like Spokane, Portland was a frequent stop for Northwest Orient flights, and it was possible that Allison would encounter someone she knew here. But it was time to get rid of the Ford, to exchange it for another set of wheels, one officially owned by Katherine Andrews. And for that she needed a city large enough to have a good selection of used-car dealers. Her only other choice in this part of the country was Seattle, and going there would be taking an even bigger chance; Seattle was an actual NWA base city.

Once she had the new car, Allison planned to head toward northern California as quickly as she could. A town somewhere between the Oregon-California border and Santa Rosa might be a good place for her and Stephanie to settle down and live a normal life. It was nowhere near any of Allison's relatives, so she figured Karl and his henchmen would be less likely to look for her in that part of the country. There were no Northwest Airlines stops there, and no large cities with their crime and filth. Yet the atmosphere was as live-and-let-live as it gets in any American small town. The Social Security clerk in Spokane was right; if somebody wanted to live an alternative lifestyle, California was definitely the place to do it. For a woman like Allison, who of necessity had to disappear and reinvent herself, it seemed the best possible choice.

In the morning, Stephanie helped her mother unload everything from the Taurus wagon into their cramped motel room. "What kinda new car are we gonna buy, Mommy?" she inquired.

"I don't know, hon. Depends on what's the best deal. I just hope we can find an honest salesman, 'cause Mommy doesn't know beans about cars."

"*I* know beans about cars," Stephie declared. "Red ones are best. They're my very most favorite of all."

Allison smiled to herself. "I can't promise we'll buy a red one, but we'll look."

Their first stop was to find a mail-receiving service here in Portland. Allison located an acceptable one on Southwest Salmon Street, near downtown, and paid cash for three months' box rental. Now, when Ruth obtained the cash from the house sale, she could mail it to Katherine Andrews's Spokane mail drop, where it would be forwarded to her Portland mail drop, where it would be forwarded again, to wherever Allison ultimately settled. She figured that trail should be convoluted enough to keep her final destination secret.

The best price Allison could get for the Ford was thirty-five hundred. She realized she was on the selling end of the deal now, not the buying end, but a full thousand less than she'd paid for the vehicle less than a month ago in Minnesota seemed unfair. "Four thousand," she said.

The salesman shook his head. "Thirty-five's my top offer, lady. Got ourselves a recession in these parts. I'll be lucky to make a couple hundred on 'er myself."

Maybe she could make it up on the other end, Allison told herself. Hell, she'd have to. Her cash supply was getting terrifyingly low. "All right, thirty-five. Cash," she agreed. She signed the transfer papers as Elyse Michaels, stuffed the bills in her purse, and called a cab.

The cab dropped Allison and Stephanie on a block where three used-car dealers competed for business. If they weren't all owned by the same person, Allison concluded, she ought to be able to get a decent deal here. Tightly gripping her purse, which now held more than four thousand dollars, in one hand and her daughter in the other, Allison worked up her courage and approached the first dealership.

"I like *this* one!" shrieked Stephanie, darting

toward a refurbished Volkswagen bug painted psychedelic pink with red lightning stripes on its sides. It wore a five-thousand-dollar price tag.

Allison rolled her eyes. "I don't think it's quite big enough for us, sweetie. And besides, it's out of our price range."

The salesman, who introduced himself as Ralph, smiled. "She's got good taste," he said with a laugh. "It's a classic."

"Maybe, but a classic what? Listen, mister, what I'm looking for is a car that won't cost me more than three thousand dollars, preferably a station wagon. I don't much care what it looks like, but I want something so reliable that you could sell it to your own sister without getting heartburn. I'm assuming you get along with your sister . . ."

He held up his hands. "Hey, my sister's a swell kid."

"Can you find me what I'm looking for?"

"Got just the thing for you." Ralph's recommendation was a decade-old pale yellow Volvo station wagon with a price tag of thirty-two ninety-five. "Now, you gotta understand about Volvos," he said, launching into his sales pitch. "They're built to go two hundred thousand miles easy. Not like American cars, where you gotta start worryin' the minute you're outta warranty. This little honey's got about a hundred and a quarter on her, but she'll give you another seventy-five, no problem."

With Stephanie in the backseat and Ralph in the passenger's, Allison took the vehicle for a test drive around the neighborhood. The engine sounded smooth enough, although the ride was a lot bumpier than the Ford wagon or Allison's old Buick had offered. "Feels closer to the road," was Ralph's term for it. "All European cars have that feel." Hell, she didn't know what to do.

"Ralph," Allison said, looking him in the eye. "I've

got three thousand dollars to spend and I've got to have a car right away. I can't afford to spend three thousand and then have to put one more dime into getting anything fixed. Maybe this car really is reliable, but ... well, ten years old, over a hundred thousand miles ... I—I just don't know."

"Look, what did you say your name was?"

"Katherine."

"Katherine, I've got a friend lives near Eugene. Drives a sixty-eight Volvo sedan with better'n three hundred thousand on her. Body's rustin' out pretty bad, but that old engine just keeps right on tickin'." He scratched his left ear. "I can sell you something else if you want me to. A Chevy, a Ford, you name it. Something newer, with lower mileage. But you ask my opinion, you're not gonna get this kind of quality."

Allison hesitated. Ralph *looked* honest—as honest as any used-car salesman ever looked, anyway. She got out and circled the yellow wagon. Its body had a few small dents, but no visible rust. She kicked the tires, although she wasn't quite sure why you were supposed to kick the tires on a used car. Maybe it was to see whether they collapsed on impact. They didn't. "Oh, all right," she said. "But if this thing breaks down on me, I promise I'm going to come back and haunt you."

"I wouldn't want that!" Ralph said with mock horror. "But seriously, Katherine, there's no percentage in it for me to cheat my customers. This machine ain't very sexy, but she'll get you where you're goin'."

Allison bought the car, filling out the registration papers as Katherine M. Andrews and listing the Salmon Street mail drop as her home address.

"How do you like our new car, Angel?" she asked as they drove off the lot.

"It's not red," Stephanie said, disappointed.

"But the man says it will get us there."

"Get us where, Mommy?"

That's the question, Allison thought. She just wished she had the correct answer.

43

Allison and Stephanie spent a second night in the Portland motel. In the morning, Allison loaded their belongings into the yellow Volvo station wagon, then paid the motel bill in cash. She was down to just under five hundred dollars and fighting a feeling of rising panic. No more motels. Even the cheap ones were just too expensive and she needed to conserve her remaining cash for gas and food. Tonight they would find a safe house, she assured herself. California had to have plenty of them, and she was determined to cross the Oregon–California border before nightfall.

When the last item was in the car, Stephanie balked, acting particularly whiny this morning. She held onto Flopsy as though the bunny were an appendage, and she sucked her thumb whenever she wasn't making demands that Allison had long ago tired of countering: "I don't wanna ride in the car anymore, Mommy. I'm tired. I wanna go home. I wanna play with my friends. I wanna go see Iris. I wanna watch telebishun." *I wanna I wanna I wanna.*

Allison sighed and patiently explained—for what seemed to her the thousandth time—why it was impossible for them to return to Wood Lake, now or ever. Soon they would find a new home and make new friends. They would live near the ocean, which looked a lot like Lake Superior, except the water was salty and it was lots bigger. Allison was rather pleased that she managed to hold her temper in check by telling herself that Stephanie, like any young child, was bound to forget. More important, the little girl had no real way of comprehending the dangers that lay in wait for them back home. Some things simply could not be explained adequately to a four-year-old.

"You can color in your book while I drive, punkin," Allison said. "And don't forget the tape player in the new car. We can play the tapes we bought yesterday and sing along." Was it possible that the three audiocassettes Allison had bought on sale for ninety-nine cents each might help save her sanity? "I'll bet you'd like to hear 'Puff the Magic Dragon' again, wouldn't you?"

Stephanie stared at the ground listlessly, scraping the toe of her sneaker on the cracked asphalt parking lot. "I s'pose," she mumbled without enthusiasm.

"Come on, kiddo. In you go." Allison lifted her daughter into the safety seat and belted her in securely. It promised to be a long drive, in more ways than one.

By the time they turned west off Interstate 5 onto Highway 199, Allison didn't care if she never heard "Puff the Magic Dragon" again as long as she lived. "Songs for the Nursery" had become even more irritating. And the only stations the old car radio could pick up featured country-and-western music, which she could not abide. She'd been driving in a light rain for the past two hours, her neck and shoulder muscles taut as she pushed the unfamiliar vehicle on the slickened highway, and she craved nothing as much as a hot bath, a glass of wine, and some quiet solitude. Dream on, she told herself.

"I don't feel good, Mommy," Stephanie announced, sniffling and wiping her nose on the sleeve of her red sweatshirt. "I wanna go home."

"Don't use your sleeve, punkin! Here, use a Kleenex and blow your nose like a big girl." Allison reached back, felt for the box of tissues behind the passenger seat, and handed one to Stephanie. "I sure hope you didn't pick up a cold." Tamara Watson's younger son had begun sniffling and sneezing the day before Allison and Stephanie left the Watson house in Spokane. Allison had assured herself that the boy's problem was just hay fever; now she wasn't so sure.

Stephanie held the tissue to her nose and obediently blew into it.

"Just another couple of hours and we can see the ocean, sweetheart. Just like at Grandpa's." Allison tried to sound upbeat. There was nowhere to stop before they reached Crescent City anyway. They would have to keep driving.

She pulled off the road into a gas station and pumped another fifteen dollars into the Volvo's seemingly insatiable tank, then helped Stephanie use the station's dirty bathroom.

"I'm cold, Mommy." Stephanie hugged herself and shivered.

Allison placed her hand on the child's forehead; she felt a bit warm to the touch. Damn. Had she remembered to pack the baby Tylenol? "I think you've got a touch of fever, punkin," she said. It took fifteen minutes of rummaging in the back of the car for Allison to locate the baby Tylenol. The bottle was in her cosmetic bag inside the big suitcase, but there were only two tablets left. "Here, chew these up and swallow them, sweetie," she said, handing the tiny pills to Stephanie. "They'll help you feel better. I'll find you a glass of water to wash them down." Allison wrapped the child in a blanket and strapped her back into her safety seat. Within a half hour, the four-year-old was sleeping soundly.

Periodically, Allison reached over and lightly touched

Stephie's brow, finding it still warm to the touch. Why in the hell hadn't she packed up the medicine cabinet back in Wood Lake and brought its contents along? Now she had no thermometer, no more children's Tylenol, no more than a couple of Band-Aids. She'd left in such a hurry, she hadn't even thought of bringing such mundane supplies. Now she would have to spend her precious dollars to replace them.

The rain had disappeared and the sun was beginning to set by the time they reached Crescent City. Stephanie was still sleeping. Allison doubted she would sleep much tonight after such a long nap, but she hated to wake her. She pulled into a public parking area at the beach and gazed out at a sea quickly being turned to liquid fire as it reflected the brilliant red and orange cloud-streaked sky. Stephanie stirred and awakened. "Look, sweetie—the ocean. We made it!"

The child rubbed her eyes and squinted through the windshield. "Birdies, Mommy."

A pair of pelicans flew by, skimming the surface of the sea. Suddenly one seemed to halt in midflight to dive straight down into the water. "Those are pelicans, Angel. I bet that's a mommy pelican and she's looking for a fish to bring home to her baby."

They watched the sky and water turn from red to purple, then drove to a public telephone in a Union 76 parking lot. Allison left her daughter in the car while she stepped outside to call the hotline.

She was hit with bitter disappointment. "Sorry, Allison, but the closest safe house we have to where you are is in Mendocino," the volunteer on the line told her.

"How far is that from here?"

"Just a minute. I'll check." The line crackled as Allison waited. She should have checked before she left Portland, yet she'd known she wanted to come here, to see the sea that always refreshed her psyche, regardless. She hadn't wanted to know if there was no help available here, so she simply hadn't bothered to call. It was clearly her own fault. The voice came back on the line. "Looks to be the best part of a day's drive south of where you are. But there's a campground near you. One of our families traveling north used it last month."

A campground. There went the hot bath. "I haven't got any camping equipment, just my car."

"Hold on a minute, let me check the computer listing." The line crackled again briefly. "Okay, here it is. It's called Shoreline Campground and it's on the south edge of town. The other lady and her kids slept in her car. Could you do that?"

"Is it safe?" Allison hadn't forgotten her experience with the highway patrolman in Montana.

"Safer than a tent would be in one of these camps, and people sleep in them all the time."

"I—I guess I could. Lord knows I'm too broke for a motel."

"This'll cost you only a couple of dollars a night, four or five at the most. It has showers and toilets and picnic tables, and you can even cook a little if you pick up some charcoal."

"Guess it'll do for one night." Allison didn't bother to say she thought she might have a sick kid on her hands. What would be the point? The volunteer couldn't help that.

"Oh-oh," the woman said.

"What?"

"Looks like I gave you the wrong story on that other thing. Our place in Mendocino—there's a note in the computer that says the people there are out of town all this month. Looks like you're going to have to make Marin County or San Francisco before we can be much help to you."

Allison wrote down the address of a safe house in

San Rafael, north of San Francisco, but it would take two days' driving time to get there.

"Don't worry," the volunteer said, sounding cheery. "Just ask at the campground. They'll tell you where to find another camping spot on the way to San Rafael. They've got some pretty nice places out there in California. From what I've been told, anyway."

You don't have to live in one of them, Allison thought ungratefully. But she thanked the hotline volunteer, adding that she expected to be at the San Rafael house in a couple of days.

It looked like staying in the car at the campground wasn't going to be as bad as Allison had feared. At least she wouldn't have to worry about the police rousting them in the middle of the night. Her campsite, from which she could see the rocky shoreline, included a picnic table and an electrical hookup. She fashioned a bed in the back of the old Volvo, then draped extra clothing and a blanket over its windows to afford some privacy from the other campers.

The family staying in the next campsite let Allison heat a can of soup on their propane-fueled camp stove and insisted that she accept a glass of their apple juice for Stephanie, who ate little and continued to complain of feeling cold and achy. Allison opened the bottle of children's Tylenol she'd bought at a nearby superette and gave the little girl two more.

The wife next door, a small woman in her late forties with a long salt-and-pepper braid, confessed to Allison that her family had been living in public campsites like this one for the past six months, moving on each time they had stayed the maximum number of days the state allowed. "Thank the Lord we still got our camper," she said of the white-paneled vehicle in which the family of four slept. "Ever since my Hugo lost his job and we got evicted from our place down in Santa Rosa, we ain't been able to find another place to live. Nowheres near work he can do, anyhow."

"There must be something available," Allison said, skeptical.

"Available ain't the problem. First 'n' last 'n' a security deposit's the problem. To get a decent two-bedroom place down there'll run you two grand just to get moved in. Anything cheaper, you wouldn't want to live in the neighborhood, 'specially not with kids. Whole area's turning into commuter housing for San Francisco yuppies, you want my opinion."

"Oh." Allison felt ashamed that she had accepted charity from these people. Why was it always the poorest folks who were most generous with what little they had?

Allison drifted up from the depths of slumber slowly, then jerked awake as she recognized Stephanie's cry of pain. The child was curled into a tight ball, her head buried beneath the blanket. "What's the matter, sweetie? Did you have a bad dream?" Patting her daughter through the blanket, Allison looked around and saw the first light of day peeking in at the edges of the covered windows. Her watch said it was almost seven o'clock.

Pulling the blanket back, she could see that Stephie's dark hair was soaked. Wet curls clung to the child's scalp and her small hand pulled hard at her left ear. Allison laid her palm on her daughter's forehead. The problem was no dream. "You're burning up, Angel!"

"Owie, Mommy. I hurt."

"What hurts, baby? Tell Mommy what hurts."

"My head. Owieeee. Owie owie owie." Stephanie pulled harder at her ear and tears spilled from her eyes.

An ear infection, Allison guessed. Shit. Stephanie

would need an antibiotic, at the very least. And if it wasn't taken care of, the eardrum could rupture, or worse. Sleeping virtually outdoors like this probably hadn't done the poor kid a bit of good. "Don't pull on your ear, punkin, and try not to cry. It'll make your head stuffier and it'll hurt even more." She picked up the little girl and cradled her in her arms, pressing her lips against the damp curls. Allison could feel the heat from Stephie's small body radiating through the layers of clothing. Feeling as helpless as only a mother of a sick child could, she desperately wished for a magic cure. But her wish went unanswered.

The third doctor Allison called agreed to see Stephanie that morning. The first pediatrician listed in the Yellow Pages was on vacation and the second was booked solid until late afternoon. Increasingly desperate, Allison didn't think she could stand to see her child in pain for that long.

"This ear's infected." Dr. Minerva Pedroza held a black, funnel-shaped medical instrument to Stephanie's left ear, pressed a button to turn on a light, and peered through it. "Please try not to move, Angel. I need to see inside your ear so I can decide how to make it all better." Her voice was gentle, and despite her apparent youth—Allison estimated the other woman to be no older than her late twenties—Dr. Pedroza radiated confidence and competence.

"We stayed at the Shoreline Campground last night," Allison confessed. "Is that why—"

"You have a camper?"

Allison looked at her lap. "No, we—we slept in the car. I kept the windows closed, though." She ached for absolution.

"It does get pretty damp at night around here, but dampness alone wouldn't give Angel an ear infection any more than not wearing a sweater would give her a cold. That stuff's nonsense. No, your little one picked up some germs somewhere. Sleeping in the damp might've made her worse ... but that doesn't really matter now, does it?"

The doctor listened to Stephanie's breathing and charted her temperature at 103 degrees. "She's not going to feel much better until that ear starts to drain and we get her fever down."

"She doesn't need to be hospitalized, does she?" Allison held her breath.

Dr. Pedroza smiled. "No, don't worry about that. Not yet, anyway. A few days on antibiotics ought to take care of this." She scratched out a prescription. "You say you're just traveling through Crescent City?"

Allison nodded.

"I'd like to see Angel again tomorrow. And I'd like to suggest you stay in a motel for the next couple of nights. Think you can manage that?" The pediatrician's eyes radiated sympathy.

"I—I guess I'll have to."

"The Shorebird on Highway 101 is not too expensive. And they let you cook a little in the rooms there. I think each room has a tiny refrigerator and a microwave. It's not much, but it'll get you by."

"Thanks."

"And don't worry about being charged for the return visit." She handed Allison the signed prescription. "Give her one teaspoonful three times a day for the next ten days, and be sure to use up all of the medication, even if she looks and feels better. Otherwise, the infection might return. And give her one children's Tylenol tablet every four to six hours until tomorrow to control the fever." The doctor lifted Stephanie down from the examining table and flashed her a friendly smile. "You'll feel a lot better once we get that nasty old fever down, little lady. I promise you that."

In the outer office, Allison paid the doctor's bill in cash. On the bill, the doctor had crossed out her usual charge of sixty dollars for an initial visit; the sum of forty-five dollars was written in its place. Even the reduced rate hurt.

While the prescription was being filled, Allison used the pay phone in the pharmacy to call Wisconsin. "Ruthie? Hi, it's me."

"Allie."

"Yeah. Listen, Sis, I haven't got much time, but I had to call and find out what you've heard about the house sale. I'm running out of money fast."

"I was wondering when I'd hear from you. I gotta tell you, Allie, this thing's starting to get to me. I'm not going back up there again—"

"What do you mean?"

Ruth explained about her encounter with Karl.

"Shit, Ruth, just don't let him intimidate you like that." Allison sounded more confident than she felt. In truth, Ruth's tale of Karl breaking into her house and destroying her clothes made her feel almost like she'd been raped. Her stomach clenched. What would he do to her, and more important, to Stephie, if he ever found them?

"Easy for you to say off . . . off wherever you are. I'm the one's gotta look the SOB in the eye. No, Allie, I don't care if you get down on your knees and beg me, I'm not going up there again. That Steiger woman can just send the papers down here when time comes to sign them. My life's too short."

Allison sighed. She recognized that tone in Ruth's voice—the stubborn streak that meant she wasn't going to budge and the resentment she obviously still harbored. "Okay. I'm sure you can arrange to sign those papers on Mars if you want to. Muriel Steiger's not going to want her commission held up. She'll probably drive the papers to you personally if that's what it takes to get them signed. My question is, how much longer is it going to be? I'm just about scraping bottom here."

"Talked with her just . . . guess it was day before yesterday. She says the Peterson woman's applied for a loan at two different banks. It'll take—"

"Peterson? What Peterson woman?" Allison stiffened.

"The buyer, of course, Mrs. Peterson."

Allison willed herself not to panic. Peterson was a common name. "What's this Mrs. Peterson's first name?"

"Don't recall. Linda, maybe, or Laura. Something starts with an *L*, I think."

"Louise?"

"Maybe."

"Look it up, will you? I'll hold on." Gripping her extra coins for the phone so tightly that they bit deeply into her palm, Allison was nearly overcome by a feeling of sheer and utter defeat.

"Yeah, it's Louise all right," Ruth said when she came back on the line. "You know her?"

"Not well," Allison replied. Shit! She explained that Louise Peterson was a private investigator Karl employed. Why hadn't she thought to ask Ruth for the buyer's name when this first came up? At least she wouldn't have gotten her hopes up this way. Truth was, she'd been so greedy for a quick sale, so anxious to get her money out of that house, that she hadn't thought to ask the right questions. "The son of a bitch has duped me again," she said, her voice breaking. "That goddamned bastard!" What was she going to do now? What could she do? A tear rolled down her cheek; she wiped it away furiously.

"Allie?"

"Yeah?"

Ruth spoke quietly. "I got eight hundred dollars I can send you. From the garage sale. That'll help out, won't it?"

"Yeah, yeah, sure it will. Thanks." Allison directed Ruth to mail the cash in four separate installments—to guard against theft—to Katherine Andrews at the Spokane address. "Don't put my name on the envelopes at all. Katherine's a friend and she'll forward them to me when I get settled somewhere," she added. "Just make sure nobody sees you mailing the money, Ruthie. It'd be best if you could go into town and mail it right from the post office."

"Sure, okay. Soon's I get a chance to drive into town. I'll send you one envelope each time I go in, okay?" Allison made a noise of agreement. "There's always Daddy, remember. If you get really desperate." The resentment had crept back into Ruth's voice.

"How is Daddy? Have you talked to him?"

"He calls every couple of days. Seems to be holding up pretty good, or so he says." Allison could hear Ruth's throat tighten. "He wants to hear from you, Allie."

"I—I'll try to call him. If I can. It's just that I—well, I'm afraid Karl may have people watching Dad, trying to see if I'll get in touch with him." Allison did not add that talking with her father was just too depressing for her; she was already overloaded with reasons for feeling blue.

"Dad says he's borrowed against his house to get some cash for you. Guess he figures you need it more than—I mean, I guess he figures you're gonna need it."

Now Allison realized the reason for Ruth's renewed envy. Dad had forced her to convey his offer of money to Allison, but he hadn't offered any to Ruth herself or to her family. Allison knew she'd probably be bent out of shape, too, if the reverse had taken place. She felt a pang of compassion for her older sister. "Hey, Ruthie?"

"Yeah?"

"Listen, I want to tell you I'm sorry if I haven't made it clear how much I appreciate what you've been doing for me . . . for Stephie and me both. I just want to say thanks. I honestly don't know what I'd have done without your help." Even if the house sale had been done with smoke and mirrors. But that wasn't Ruth's fault.

"It doesn't ma—I mean, just forget it. We—we're sisters, right?"

"Yeah, sure. But that doesn't mean I shouldn't tell you how grateful I am. Got to go for now, Sis. I'll be watching for that mail." Allison hung up the receiver and waited for the operator to ring her back with the extra charges. Then she plunked the last of her loose change into the telephone's coin slots.

Stephanie's prescription was ready when Allison returned to the pharmacy counter. She counted out twenty-nine dollars and stuffed the bottle of pinkish liquid into her purse. "Come on, Angel," she said, taking her daughter by the hand and heading for the exit. In a few days, Allison knew, this bottle of synthetic penicillin would cure Stephanie's ear infection. If only, she thought wistfully, she could buy a tonic to cure the disease that had infected the rest of their lives.

44

When Karl entered Morrisey's Bar, he saw Buck Linn waiting for him in his favorite booth at the back. Karl wished his old pal had just spat out whatever news he had on the telephone. He couldn't see the point of all this intrigue—waiting until Buck was off duty, meeting in a downtown bar. But he dared not let his irritation show; he plastered a broad grin on his face and thrust out his hand. "How're you doing, Buck?" He slid onto the brown leatherette seat opposite the big policeman.

"Beer, Karl?" Karl nodded. Buck waved at the bartender. "Couple o' Hamm's on draft over here, Morrisey."

"So what's your news?" Karl asked after they'd taken the requisite first gulp.

"Your hunch about the West Coast was right on the money. Tracked Allison to Portland. We're getting close, Karly, we're gettin' damned close." The grin on Buck's face widened and he fidgeted with as much excitement as a small boy about to meet his favorite ballplayer.

"All right, Buck. Way to go! So she's in Portland, huh?"

"Can't say if she's still there, but we do know Allison sold that Ford wagon in Portland, the one she bought in Minneapolis. Got a call from Portland PD this afternoon. They checked with the Oregon DMV and struck gold. Elyse Michaels sold that buggy for cash in Portland four days ago. How the hell's that for fast work?"

Karl reached for a pretzel. "Good, Buck, damned good. Really got to hand it to you guys. But I'm confused here. Why would the bitch want to sell the Ford? She only had it a few weeks."

Buck drained his glass and signaled for another beer. Karl opted to nurse his first. "My guess is she wanted to get herself another car in case we found out about that switch she pulled in Minneapolis," the big cop said. "Which, of course, we did."

"Know what she's driving now?"

Buck shoved a fistful of pretzels into his mouth and chewed them loudly. Crumbs tumbled onto his chin. Karl averted his eyes and tried to hide his repulsion. "Let's not get too greedy, old man," Buck told him, washing the mangled pretzels down with a gulp of beer. "Portland PD's workin' on it. We faxed 'em the photos—the one of Stephie and that computer-enhancement one Swede Johnsson did of Allison. They'll take 'em around to the Portland used-car dealerships soon's they can free up somebody to do it."

"Fucking bitch." Karl made a fist and pounded the table. "What're chances she's using another phony name?"

Buck shrugged. "I sure as hell would be if I was her. But, on the other hand, she went to a helluva lot of trouble to get that fake driver's license for Elyse Michaels. She might figure new wheels'll be enough to do the trick. It's a hard call."

Karl drained his beer and looked at his watch. He took his wallet from his back pocket and slipped out a ten-dollar bill, then a five. "This one's on me, pal." He tossed the cash on the table and slid out of the booth.

"Hey, why the hurry?"

"Sorry, but I want to run this by Peterson right away. I can still catch him if I get a move on."

"You still got him on the case?"

Karl nodded. "You bet. Pete's man is running that surveillance on Allison's father. The direction she's heading, I wouldn't be surprised if she turns up at his place in San Diego one of these days." Karl offered his hand again and the men shook. "You're doing real good work here, buddy. I won't forget it. You let me know what's happening on the Oregon end and I'll see what Pete's guy has got in San Diego."

"Sure thing."

"We got her in a real vice now," Karl said, his dark eyes narrowing. "All we've got to do is keep on cranking it closed."

45

It was five days before Allison and Stephanie reached San Rafael. They had stayed three nights in the Crescent City motel—eating microwaved TV dinners, canned soup, and oranges—before Allison could be satisfied that Stephie was well enough to camp out on their way south. She dared not place her daughter in the kind of close contact with other children that a safe house would require, either, not as long as she still had that infected ear.

Although she begrudged the money the motel had cost her, Allison appreciated the privacy and relative comfort it offered. It even had given her what might well be her last chance for a while to dye her blond roots Copper Penny red without an audience.

After leaving Crescent City, mother and daughter stopped one night at a mountain campground nestled among the huge redwoods, and the next at a place near Sea Ranch. The coastline at Sea Ranch was rugged and unspoiled and Allison longed to stay. But the town was nothing more than a wealthy resort community of houses built to blend into their hillside sites. With the exception of the hotel and restaurant, there were no local businesses near Sea Ranch that might offer employment. Allison would have no way of earning a living there, unless perhaps she was willing to clean houses; even that kind of work would be largely seasonal. In addition, the only rental housing in the area started at a hundred dollars a night, and there was no day-care center within a hundred miles. Settling in Sea Ranch was an impossible dream. Reluctantly, Allison bade the place farewell and prodded the old Volvo toward San Rafael.

With the loss of the money from the house sale as well as the unexpected expenses in Crescent City, Allison now realized she would have to find a safe house where she and her daughter could stay until she had a secure job. It was a lot to ask of anyone, but she prayed that some charitable soul would agree to let them stay indefinitely. Perhaps, as Beverly was doing at the Montana ranch, Allison could offer housework or cooking in return for room and board while she searched for work.

It was growing dark by the time they reached San Rafael. Hungry for adult conversation, Allison had been listening to a talk show on KGO radio while Stephanie slept. Allison spotted the stoplight noted in the hotline volunteer's directions; the safe house should be right around the next corner. She turned off the radio. "Angel, wake up," she said, as she rounded the turn. "We're almost there."

Stephanie rubbed her eyes and blinked.

Fourteen twenty-one was the number of the safe house. There was fourteen ten . . . fourteen fifteen . . . fourteen twenty . . . fourteen—Allison caught her breath. Parked in front of the pale green rambler numbered fourteen twenty-one were two black and white police cars, their shortwave radios squawking loudly. Her knuckles white against the steering wheel, she drove slowly past the house, then turned back toward the main highway at the next corner.

"Where are we, Mommy?" Stephanie asked.

"I—I thought I found the right house, sweetie, but I guess I was wrong." Allison heard the quaver in her own voice. "I guess we better find a phone. Mommy'll have to call and get new directions."

Allison stopped at a Shell station and used its public phone to dial the toll-free number. She identified herself and explained her problem.

"Thank goodness you called in time. We were worried sick about how to warn you," the voice on the line told her. "One of the women staying at the San Rafael house got picked up by the cops this afternoon and she apparently told them where she and her kids had been staying. That place is pure poison now."

Realizing how close she had come to getting caught, Allison began to shake all over. Yet she still had to depend on the network. There was no real alternative. "What—where can we go? I'm just about broke. There's no way I can afford a motel around here."

"Whoa. We do have another place in San Francisco I'm pretty sure we can wedge you into. Can you hold on while I check?" Allison pulled her sweater tighter. Several minutes later, the voice came back on the line. "The San Francisco place is packed. The owner took in a couple of other families from San Rafael, and one from another place in San Francisco, but she's willing to keep you and your daughter at least for tonight. You may have to sleep on the floor, but the price'll be right."

Allison breathed a sigh of relief. "Just so it's safe." She took down the address. Checking the gas gauge and finding it still registering half full, she turned the car toward the Golden Gate Bridge and the city beyond.

". . . and this is my daughter, Angel," Allison said, coaxing Stephanie through the doorway of the house on Kirkham Street, south of Golden Gate Park. Built townhouse style, the place had a tucked-under garage and three narrow floors of living quarters above.

"Sylvia's my name," their hostess said, smiling warmly. She was a short, white-haired woman in her sixties; her rotund figure added to her appearance of jocularity. "Sorry it's so crowded around here tonight, but we'll make do."

"I guess you're getting the overflow from San Rafael," Allison said. "We were supposed to stay there tonight, too."

Sylvia's dimpled hands flew to her face. "The San Rafael house is only the start. Another place in Noe Valley closed up today, too. The family there heard about what happened in San Rafael and got scared. Next thing you know, they're out of the business of sheltering folks like you and I've got four more houseguests here."

"Oh, Lord, I really am sorry to barge—"

"Don't even mention it, my dear," Sylvia said, taking Allison gently by the arm and leading her upstairs. "At my age, I sometimes think it takes an emergency like this to get my blood flowing. I always said I was at my best in a crisis; it's just the dull everyday things I can't cope with." The little round woman roared with laughter at her own joke. "Come on upstairs, girls. I'll warm up some of that casserole we had for supper. I bet you're famished, and I wouldn't mind having another little taste myself."

Staying at Sylvia's house made Allison nervous. Its close proximity to its neighbors seemed to offer little privacy from prying eyes. And, after her experience in Spokane, she was almost irrationally worried about being in a city where so many Northwest Airlines crew members lived and worked. She was too frightened to walk down the block to the drugstore or to take Stephie to the park in the morning;

she didn't want to risk running across anyone she knew.

The number of other families staying here made her uncomfortable, too. Sylvia explained that the house had three bedrooms, one of which was hers. Four families had arrived to fill the remaining two bedrooms plus the living room. Although Allison was grateful for a free place to sleep, she couldn't help but see that this was worse than the Montana ranch with its crowded dormitory. At least there she had had a real bed to sleep in. Here there was only the floor.

As they walked through the living room toward the kitchen at the back of the house, a girl about six years old ran up to Sylvia, grabbed her arm, and pointed frantically at Allison and Stephanie. "Are they going to take me away? Are they going to take me away?" she asked, over and over. The child's terrified eyes were disturbingly odd; no hair surrounded them.

Allison was stunned and ashamed that her presence had somehow frightened the little girl, no matter how innocently. "Of course we're not going to take you away," Allison reassured the child. "We're not going to hurt you."

"Everything's all right, Candy," Sylvia said, gently stroking the girl's head. "Don't you worry about a thing, sweetheart." Candy slumped to the floor and huddled against the wall, hugging her knees to her chest. Her small fingers quickly entwined themselves in her dark brown hair as the others passed by her into the kitchen.

"What's the matter with that child?" Allison asked in a low voice after the kitchen door had closed behind them.

"Candy's real bad off. She needs psychological counseling something terrible. Poor little thing has pulled out all her eyelashes and eyebrows and now she's starting in on the hair on her head. Dawn—that's the girl's mother—she's worried half to death about Candy's self-destructiveness, but there's not much she can do about it while they're hiding out this way." Sylvia placed a covered glass casserole in the oven and set the temperature at 350 degrees.

Allison's gaze fell on Stephanie. Her own daughter's clear blue eyes were fringed with lashes so long and dark they almost seemed false. If she stayed in hiding for months, maybe years, could Stephie become disturbed enough to pull out her own lashes and brows? Or worse? Allison wondered whether it was stress that made a child compulsively attack herself that way. Or had Candy somehow turned her anger—over being molested and over being chased from place to place like a fleeing criminal—inward against herself? Allison simply didn't know the answer. All she knew was that she would do anything, anything at all, to prevent something like this from happening to Stephanie. She was determined to create a normal life for her child—and soon—no matter what it cost her.

As the last family to arrive at Sylvia's house, Allison and Stephanie were assigned to sleep on the living room floor. Mitzi, a red-nosed brunette nearly six feet tall, and her two-year-old daughter had claimed the Hide-A-Bed sofa there, but Sylvia positioned the sofa cushions on the floor to form a mattress for the newcomers.

Allison brought their blankets and pillows up from the Volvo. "This'll be fine. Don't worry about us," she reassured Sylvia. At least they were safe here and out of the fog that was rapidly soaking the street outside.

Allison and Mitzi tucked their children in for the night, then moved into the kitchen for a last cup of decaf. Mitzi folded her long legs under the kitchen table, pulled a tissue from her pocket and blew her nose. "Don't worry," she told Allison. "It's just a sinus infection. You can't catch it." Allison was relieved; she didn't need any more doctor's bills.

As they sipped their coffee, Allison learned that the other woman had been on the run for about two months and now planned to head east. "I hear there's a good place to stay near Sacramento," Mitzi said. "I figure I'll leave here tomorrow and give it a try. I thought I might like to live in San Francisco, but there's no way I could afford to rent anything around here. The prices are un*real*."

"I want to settle down somewhere so bad I can taste it," Allison confessed. "This constant moving around, looking over my shoulder, is getting to me."

"Gets to the kids, too. Maybe even worse than the women."

"Like that poor little Candy, with no eyelashes."

Mitzi nodded. "And I saw one even worse off when we stayed near Bakersfield. This girl about nine years old, she's got what they call multiple personalities—you know, like Sybil in that TV movie. Kid like that should probably be in some sort of mental hospital. In intensive therapy, anyway. But how's her mom going to get it for her when they're living on the run like this? Even if they could stop hiding, I don't see how they could afford that kind of psychiatric help with no job and no health insurance."

This conversation was becoming too depressing for Allison's taste. She finished her coffee, washed out the coffee pot, and loaded their cups and saucers into the dishwasher.

"Where're you heading?" Mitzi asked as she wiped off the table with a damp sponge.

"Wish I knew." Allison described the kind of place

she had fantasized about, a small city near the ocean where she and her daughter could rent an apartment or house. Somewhere her child could go to school and take ballet lessons and do all the things normal little girls do. "But all the towns I've seen so far are too crowded, too expensive, or don't seem to have anyplace I could find work."

"You look at Monterey?"

"No, have you?" Allison knew the Monterey peninsula was a little over a hundred miles south of San Francisco, but she'd been there only once, years ago. That had been a brief visit to the gingerbread town of Carmel.

"We stayed there for a couple of nights last week. Maybe you'd like it ... if you're sure you want to live by the water. There's a pretty good safe house there, too, if you can get in."

"How come you left?"

Mitzi shivered and hugged herself. "Truth is, I can't wait to get out of this goddamned fog. I haven't been able to kick this sinus infection since we've been staying near the coast. Maybe it's some sort of allergy or something, but I feel sick all the time. Guess I'll just have to live in a drier climate."

Allison didn't mind fog at all; it was an inevitable part of living near the water she loved. And Monterey was beginning to sound intriguing. "You think I could find work in Monterey?" Allison asked.

"What can you do?"

"Without a real resumé, who knows? I can type a little, I guess. I can cook and clean. Maybe I could sell something. Actually, I think I can do a lot of things. The real question is, who'd hire a woman without a past?"

"You're going to have to deal with that anywhere you go."

Allison switched off the light over the sink. What

the hell, she thought as she headed for her make-shift bed on the living room floor. From where she stood, Monterey sounded like the best idea she'd heard in weeks. In the morning, she would fill the Volvo's tank and head south. With an early start, they could be there before noon.

46

Karl dialed the next phone number on the list. He had set aside this morning to follow up with the organizations dedicated to assisting parents in finding their missing children. Louise Peterson had sent each of these groups photographs of both Stephanie and Allison, along with their physical descriptions and information about the court case. But the response had been lukewarm by Karl's standards. Stephanie's photo was not yet receiving any publicity and Karl was well aware that his child's picture on national television, or even printed on a milk carton or grocery bag distributed in the right part of the country, could do more than a team of private detectives to locate her.

"I know we've already sent you a photo and a description of my little girl," he told the woman who answered this latest call. "But certainly you can understand how completely desperate I am. My little girl's mother is—well, she's mentally unstable; that's the kindest way I can think to put it. Allison is an extremely vindictive woman and I know that she's systematically brainwashing my daughter against me. She's actually threatened to harm Stephie rather than give her up, too. You don't know how that terrifies me. The truth is, I lie awake nights worrying . . ." Karl painted a verbal portrait of an innocent and loving father prostrate with grief ever since the moment his adoring daughter was snatched from his arms.

"This has been the hardest thing I've ever had to face," he continued, orchestrating a catch in his voice. "My poor baby . . . I miss her so—"

"I understand, really I do." By now, the woman on the phone sounded near tears herself. "But there's only so much we can do for you, Mr. Warren. There are so *many* children like your little Stephanie, some of them abducted by strangers. Our list of names is so long. You have to understand our limitations."

Karl sensed it was time for his finale. "I know I'm not alone in my grief, ma'am. If I were, there wouldn't be a wonderful organization like yours to turn to, would there?"

"No, there wouldn't. So you can see why—"

"Ma'am, please, just hear me out a minute longer. What I'm trying to say to you in my awkward way is that—well, I guess it's best to just say it flat out. I'm a fairly wealthy man, financially speaking, yet this thing has taught me a hard lesson. I now realize that the only possession that ever really mattered to me is the one that was taken from me so cruelly, my daughter Stephanie. I don't expect your charity. I'm willing—more than willing—to finance any help you can give me. I'd be happy to make a generous donation to your organization—totally confidentially, of course—if you could only cut a few corners to help me find my daughter."

Karl went on to describe just what he would consider corner cutting worthy of his proposed "generous donation." He wanted Stephanie moved to the top of the list of children who would be highlighted in the charity's publicity efforts, and he wanted those efforts to be broadcast as widely as possible. Like the representatives of all but one of the groups he'd already approached, this one agreed to see what she could do and get back to him.

"Bless you for your understanding," he said. "I knew I could count on you and your wonderful resources."

"Our prayers are with every one of our grieving parents," the woman said.

Smiling to himself, Karl rang off; certainly he'd hooked another live one. He jotted down a few notes about the call, picked up the receiver, and dialed the next number on his list.

47

Tim Mitchell put down the rag and the can of oil and leaned back against the sofa cushions to catch his breath. Today, even a fairly sedentary task like cleaning his small collection of handguns was enough to exhaust him. Still, he'd managed to finish the job. The three guns, now immaculate, lay on the coffee table in front of him, loaded and ready for war. And, in Tim's mind, this was nothing less than war. It was Tim Mitchell and his daughter and granddaughter against the bastards of the world, against the kind of filthy scum that would let a grown man rape a little child and get away with it. Tim aimed to be well armed for this, his last good fight.

The reliable old .38 revolver was his favorite; although it was nothing next to the firearms he'd handled during his Navy days, it had always been his choice for target practice. Nowadays, the NRA boys on the firing range all tried to show they were macho enough to handle the mule kick of a Colt or Smith & Wesson .44 magnum, but they didn't impress an old warhorse like Tim. Give him a trusty .38 any day—a little less punch, maybe, but a helluva lot more control. Besides, Allie'd never be able to handle a .44 magnum. She'd squeeze off one round and the kick would land her flat on her behind. Probably wouldn't be able to hit the side of a barn with the damned thing, either.

Tim knew he'd have to teach Allie to shoot. She wouldn't like the idea much, but by the time there was a showdown he couldn't count on being around himself, much as he longed to be. On a day like today, he couldn't even depend on having the strength to raise the gun, aim, and squeeze the trigger. And somebody had to keep that fucking pervert away from Stephanie, no matter what it took to do it.

The .22 was a nice little piece. That'd be easiest for a skinny little girl like Tim's Allie to control. Trouble was, a .22 wasn't much better than a toy when it came to a real war. Allie'd have to be a damned good shot to do any permanent damage with one of those things and, if she ever had to shoot that bastard she'd been married to, she might as well finish him off once and for all.

The third weapon in Tim's small arsenal was a slim little automatic, easier to aim and shoot than the others, but prone to jamming, like all automatics. He would pack all three handguns, but it was the .38 in which he placed his confidence.

Tim lay back against the cushions and dozed for a while, letting his mind take him back to his days in World War II. That was a real war, nothing like these pissy little contests the United States kept getting itself into nowadays. Grenada . . . Panama . . . what kind of sorry contests were they? Tim had been just a kid himself during WWII, even younger than Allie was today, but he'd done the job right and he'd done it with pride. No question about being on the side of the justice in that one. And Tim knew he still had one good fight left in him . . . provided that it presented itself pretty damned soon.

A bell clanged. Tim tried to summon the strength to move his legs toward the ship's bridge, but something was weighing them down. The bell jangled again, jolting him awake. It was the telephone. Still fuzzy-headed, Tim leaned forward and grabbed the receiver off the coffee table.

"Daddy, hi."

"Allie. Is that you?"

"Uh-huh. How are you getting along, Dad? How're you feeling?"

Tim dismissed his health problems, demanding to know all about his daughter and granddaughter.

"I can't tell you where we are, Daddy. We can't be sure there's nobody listening—"

"That's gotta be bull, sweetheart. Who'd want to listen in on an old salt like me? I'm too damned dull."

Allison chuckled to herself. "Glad to see you've still got a sense of humor, Daddy, but I'm dead serious. I just wanted to call and let you know we're okay. We're staying in a real nice place now—we've even got our own bedroom—and I'm looking for a job."

"What kind of job?"

"Anything I can get, to be honest. Waitress, sales clerk, you name it. I just hope to get something that'll pay enough so Stephie and I can live decently on our own and stop depending on charity."

"I knew you were gonna need money, Allie. You didn't forget about the cash I got for you, did you?"

"You mean from your house?"

"I've got it all set and I'm ready to bring it to you, Allie, anytime . . . plenty of money, and a couple other things you might find some use for, too."

"Dad, don't be silly. You need that money. You've got medical bills to pay."

"The hell with that! Let the V.A. pay 'em. The only way I'm gonna rest easy in my grave is if I know you and Stephie are set. Please, Allie." Tim's voice broke. "Please—I got—I gotta see you, just once more before—"

"*Don't*. Please don't do that to me, Daddy. You're

making me choose between you and my child. If I risk seeing you, I'm risking the rest of her life. Can't you see that?"

Tim could hear his daughter's anguish. He couldn't reply.

"Daddy? Daddy, you still there?"

"Yeah. Yeah, I'm still here." Tim's gaze fell on the handguns. Helluva lotta good they'd do her sittin' here. "I—I can just send you the money, Allie. You don't havta see me."

"Keep your money, Dad, at least for now. I'll have a job in a few days and then we'll be okay. I know we will. We—we *have* to be okay."

"Sure, but just in case—"

"Just in case . . . well, then I'll call you. I promise, Daddy."

"I love you, Allie. Always did love you. Sorry I never got around to tellin' you that much."

Now it was Allison's turn to choke up. "It—it's all right, Daddy. I always loved you, too. Please take care of yourself." The line went dead.

In the van down the street, Russ Quinn smiled to himself as he marked the time and date on the cassette recording of Tim Mitchell's phone call. For the past week, Quinn had been worried that the old man would die before the Warren woman contacted him again. But now she not only had resumed her calls to San Diego, she and the kid apparently were settling down somewhere as well.

Lucky for Quinn, the silly broad didn't seem to realize how much easier it was for a hunter to hit a bird that was fool enough to light somewhere and rest.

48

It was near midnight and Allison could hear the fog-horn at the tip of the Peninsula braying. She sat on one of the twin beds in the Monterey safe house adding the column of figures she'd written on a pad of paper. Stephie was sleeping in the other bed, but Allison was still too tense to sleep, and her attempt to budget their living expenses was doing nothing to relax her.

Housing, even a studio or small one-bedroom apartment, would be the largest cost. After an examination of the rental ads in the Monterey *Herald*, Allison estimated they would need at least five hundred dollars a month for rent, plus another three hundred for food, seventy-five for gasoline (she prayed that the car wouldn't need any repairs), twenty-five for clothes for Stephanie (Allison's own wardrobe would have to make do). . . .

The numbers already added up to nine hundred dollars a month and Allison hadn't yet figured in babysitting costs, car insurance, health insurance, or a dozen other likely expenses. At a minimum, she figured she and Stephie would need twelve hundred a month to live even a spartan existence here, and expenses at that level would require her to earn about three hundred dollars a week net pay. She chewed her pencil and stared hard at the numbers. They didn't change. If she worked forty hours a week, she'd have to net seven-fifty an hour, probably gross something over nine dollars. Ouch!

The two jobs Allison had been offered during the week they'd been in Monterey would pay her just about half as much as she would have to earn. The Seaview Lodge wanted her to work as a hotel maid for five dollars an hour, and a local fast-food franchise had offered her four-fifty an hour to wait on customers and cook whenever extra kitchen help was needed. She would have to work both jobs full time to earn enough for minimal living expenses, an impossible feat for the mother of a four-year-old.

There had to be something else. Maybe, Allison thought, she could find waitress work at a place where the tips were good; nine dollars an hour didn't seem an impossible sum for a good waitress to earn. She'd applied for two such jobs so far, but both had required experience and Allison had none, at least none she could cite.

Ironically, Allison couldn't even start one of the low-paying jobs she'd been offered until she had a new address and could get a California drivers license. Employers were jittery now that the law covering the employment of illegal aliens had changed. They all demanded that job applicants provide proof of their American citizenship, such as birth certificate or Social Security card, plus a photo ID, before they would be added to the payroll. Katherine Andrews's driver's license did not have her current address.

Allison had arranged with the Spokane mail drop to forward mail addressed to Katherine Andrews to the Portland address. Then the Portland mail drop would send it on to general delivery here in Monterey. But receiving mail sent on that convoluted route took time—too much time.

Stephanie stirred and moaned in her sleep, kicking at the blankets, but she did not wake. Allison pulled the blankets back over the sleeping child and gently kissed the top of her head.

Shoving aside her list of figures, Allison began to pace the room. This experience had given her a renewed appreciation for the poor. How did they survive in an economy where the wages paid for unskilled work wouldn't even cover their rent? She recalled the family she'd met in Crescent City—husband, wife, and two kids—who'd been reduced to living in their Winnebago in a public campground. Perhaps the hardest thing to accept was that she and Stephie were poor now, too; they didn't even have a camper.

There had to be an answer. Allison wouldn't give up until she'd found it. She grabbed the *Herald* again and started over with the Help Wanted columns. She'd tried for an apartment manager's position, which would have been ideal, but she couldn't supply the required references. How about advertising sales? No—the job called for experience. She had no skills as an educator or engineer or hotel manager. Housekeeper. That was a possibility. There were three ads for housekeepers. One was a live-in position, caring for an invalid. "Excellent references required." Scratch that one. The second was a part-time job, three days a week. It wouldn't pay enough. But the third had definite possibilities. Allison read:

Housekeeper, English speaking, live-in, for Big Sur seniors. Good simple cooking required. Must drive. Non-smoker. Good attitude. Room/ board, small salary. 555-2395.

She was certainly qualified. She could cook and clean as well as anyone and there was nothing short of a road grader that Allison couldn't drive. She didn't smoke, and she was determined to show "Big Sur seniors" the best damned attitude they'd ever seen.

If she could get a job that offered room and board, she and Stephanie could make do with a small salary, provided it wasn't too small. The biggest problem, she well knew, would be whether the old folks would accept Stephanie. But what the hell, it was worth a try. All they could do was say no, and Allison was getting used to hearing that word. She would call first thing in the morning.

"Can you cook pea soup? I mean the old-fashioned way, clear from scratch, none of this canned slop like the last girl tried to pass off on us." The old woman sat in a flowered wing chair in the living room, her walking cane propped against it. She was small, no more than ninety pounds, with wisps of unkempt white hair escaping from the old-fashioned flowered turban she wore. She'd hit Allison with a barrage of pointed questions—did she know the proper way to make a bed, did she know how to set a table correctly, could she iron Chester's cotton shirts without scorching them the way the last "girl" had?

"My grandmother used to make pea soup starting with a ham bone. Cooked it all day long. Is that the kind you like?"

Odette Lampley almost smiled. "It's got to be pale green, with just a hint of ham, not too salty," she said. "Chester's off salt—got high blood pressure."

Chester sat silently next to his wife, a short round man with twinkling blue eyes. Both were in their eighties and seemingly frail. Chester seemed to be more physically mobile than his wife, but it seemed clear to Allison that Odette Lampley called the shots in this household.

Allison felt the interview was going fairly well, given Odette's apparent conviction that the relationship between a potential employer and a job applicant ought to be an adversary one. Allison had driven the Volvo the thirty miles south along scenic but treacherous Highway 1 early in the morning, arriving in this favorite youth hangout of the sixties an hour ahead of time. She and Stephanie had taken a walk among the giant redwoods in the state park to kill time until Allison's appointment with the Lampleys.

The morning fog burned off early and the sky was clear and sunny by the time Allison located the two-lane dirt road that led downhill to the Lampley home. As she drove toward the restless sea, she counted thirteen houses, each set off in its own clump of trees. "Look, Mommy, a doggie!" Stephanie declared excitedly as they encountered a barking Irish setter tethered to a front porch. They spotted a mother quail and her brood of chicks walking in the tall grass at the side of the road, too.

As she pulled into the Lampley's driveway, Allison could hear the waves crashing against the rocks below, a sound she'd always found soothing. The main house was a compact modern structure set on a cliff overlooking the Pacific. In the side yard stood a tiny old redwood cabin—undoubtedly the original structure built on this land—its front door painted a brilliant yellow. Allison wondered whether this dollhouse might be the "room" mentioned in the ad? It was old, but private. It would be perfect. She caught herself up short; she couldn't afford to want this job too much. It was a long shot at best that the Lampleys would hire a mother with a four-year-old child in tow. Particularly one with no documentable work experience and no references.

"You stay here in the car, Angel, until Mommy comes back to get you. I have to go inside that house over there and see if I can get the people who live here to give me a job. But they don't know I have a little girl, so you wait here until I have a chance to tell them about you, okay?"

Stephanie nodded seriously. "We need a job, huh, Mommy?"

"We sure do. Here, sweetie, you can color while Mommy's gone." Allison pulled a pad of paper and a well-used package of crayons from the glove compartment and handed them to the little girl. "I'm gonna draw the birdies, Mommy."

"That's a great idea, punkin. You draw the mommy quail and her babies and you can show them to me when I get back."

Half an hour later, Odette Lampley had finished quizzing Allison on her domestic skills and had begun on some of the others the job would require. "Are you a good driver?"

"I've never had an accident and I've been driving since I was sixteen."

"Yes, well. The roads around here are dark at night. Tuesday nights I'd need you to drive me to my meeting at the library. And you'd have to drive into Carmel every week to do the shopping. Groceries cost a fortune here in Big Sur; Chester and I'd go broke if we had to depend on what we can buy locally."

"I enjoy driving," Allison said, hoping she was displaying the "good attitude" the Lampleys' ad had specified.

"Then there's the mail," Odette went on. "It's delivered at the mailboxes at the top of—" The old woman's face froze as she stared past Allison's shoulder.

A small voice rang out from the direction of Odette's gaze. "Mommy, I gotta go potty."

Allison swallowed, turned, and said, "I'd like you to meet my daughter, Angel."

The silence from the old couple was deafening.

"I drawed the birdies." Her lower lip quivering, Stephanie held out her masterpiece.

Odette Lampley straightened in her chair. "The

bathroom is down that hall." She pointed imperiously to the right of the kitchen. "And see to it that you leave it in the immaculate condition in which you will find it."

Feeling unfairly chastised and completely defeated, Allison rose from her chair. She would take Stephie to the bathroom, then they would head back to Monterey. She should never have come on this fool's errand. She should have known an old couple like the Lampleys would have no room in either their house or their hearts for a little child.

"May I look at your drawing while you're using the facilities, Miss Angel?" Chester finally came to life. He held out his speckled hand and smiled warmly at the child. She walked shyly toward the old man, handed him the piece of paper, and darted back toward her mother. "Thank you very much," Chester said. Odette glowered at him.

From the bathroom, Allison could hear angry, muffled voices in the other room. You'd think she'd committed some kind of crime, she thought. That nasty old woman didn't deserve to live in a beautiful place like this; she didn't deserve someone like Allison working for her; and she didn't deserve a sweet old man like Chester, either.

After they had used the bathroom, Allison took special care to wipe the sink dry and fold the hand towel carefully. She wouldn't give that old witch the satisfaction of finding anything to complain about. She would simply thank the Lampleys for the interview and leave.

The old couple were quiet by the time Allison and Stephanie returned. Before Allison could take her leave, the old woman spoke. "We'd expect you to do the same amount of work as if there was just you alone," she said.

Allison was stunned. Did Mrs. Lampley mean that

the job was still available? "I—of course," she muttered.

"We paid the last girl a hundred dollars a week, plus room and board, but she didn't have an extra mouth to feed. We'd have to deduct for that. For you, it would be eighty dollars a week."

Allison tried to calculate quickly in her head. With food and rent taken care of, eighty a week—three hundred twenty a month—might be just enough to get by. In any case, she'd be far better off than if she took one of the Monterey jobs. "That will be fine."

"Then we'll give it a try," Odette said. "But if it gets too noisy around here, or if you don't do enough work, or if toys are left around . . ."

"Oh, you don't need to worry about that," Allison said, stretching a point. "Angel's a very well-behaved child." She willed it to be true. "You won't even know she's around."

"Well, then. How soon can you start?"

Allison made arrangements to begin work the next afternoon, as soon as she could move their things down from Monterey.

"Chester will show you the cabin," Odette said, dismissing all three of the others with a wave of her bony hand.

"You've drawn some delightful birds, young lady," the old man said as he struggled to his feet. "Are they quail?" Stephanie nodded. "I think I've seen those very same quail along the road myself." He grinned at the child and held out the drawing to her.

"You can have it," she said shyly. "I drawed it for my mommy, but I can draw another one."

"If your mommy doesn't mind, I'd be most honored to have this." Chester affected a slight bow from the waist. Stephanie giggled. "Follow me, ladies," he said, leading them outside.

As they reached the door, Allison was certain she heard Odette say, "Hrmph!"

The cabin was fairly primitive—two rooms plus an old-fashioned bathroom with a claw-footed tub. The living room, furnished in a combination of ruffled chintz upholstery and Goodwill Industries rejects, had a wall kitchen with a tiny old gas stove and a bar-sized refrigerator. A second wall featured a blackened stone fireplace with wrought iron implements, and a third held a bank of windows that badly needed washing. There was no ocean view from here, but the wave action against the rocks was still refreshingly audible.

The cabin's tiny bedroom held a double bed and a rickety chest of drawers. The quilt on the bed was an old wedding band pattern patchwork that had been mended many times, but it was clean, and there was a pole with hangers in the corner that served as a closet. The ancient small house was a far cry from the modern rambler Allison had called home back in Wood Lake, but this place represented a safe port in a devastating storm. As such, Allison found it indescribably beautiful.

"The accommodations here aren't exactly plush," Chester admitted. "But I hope you'll find them comfortable enough. Odette and I always feel that the scenery and quiet here in Big Sur can make up for certain, uh, physical challenges."

"This will be just fine." Allison felt her eyes begin to sting.

"We have a rollaway bed in the garage that you could bring over if you wish. It might be more comfortable for the little girl." Chester pointed to a spot next to the swaybacked sofa. "I think it would just fit in that corner over there."

Blinking rapidly to retain her composure, Allison said she would see to it first thing tomorrow.

"There's one more thing I wanted to talk to you about while we've got a moment alone," Chester said. He glanced back toward the main house, as if he feared Odette would hear what he had to say. "I want to explain, uh, Katherine—is it all right if I call you Katherine?"

"Of course." Allison glanced at Stephanie and silently ordered her not to volunteer that Katherine was not her mommy's right name. The child remained obediently silent.

"What I'm trying to say, Katherine, is that we've had a bit of turnover in this job in the past couple of years. Our housekeepers tend to become impatient with Odette's, uh, comments and they quit on a moment's notice. I—I know that my wife sometimes seems caustic, maybe even cruel, in what she says to people, that she tends to bark orders instead of asking politely but, you see . . . well, it's not really her fault."

Allison shot Chester a quizzical look. "I'm afraid I don't understand." How could Odette Lampley's abject rudeness not be her own fault?

"Odette has had a few small strokes. Nothing major, thank God. Not yet. Just enough to make her use a cane to walk, but these strokes have affected her brain a bit, what you might call her sense of judgment, of propriety. The truth is, whatever Odette thinks just pops out of her mouth as soon as she thinks it, with no thought whatsoever about how it might affect other people. Then she honestly can't understand what she's done to offend." Chester's gaze fell on Stephanie. "Like a typical young child, Odette is blunt, insatiably curious, completely lacking in guile."

"I see."

"Let me be frank with you, Katherine. Odette was not enthusiastic about hiring a mother with a small child for this job, but I—well, I had a feeling. I thought that it just might work out all right, that maybe you could understand my wife's problem, that you might be a bit more tolerant because of—" he smiled at Stephanie, who was now beginning to explore her surroundings—"well, just because."

Allison smiled. "I do understand. I hope we all can try to be tolerant of one another."

Chester flashed a crooked grin, revealing a full set of yellowed teeth. "Maybe you could just think of it as having two children instead of one? One a bit older than the other . . ."

"I think I can manage that just fine," Allison told him, feeling certain her luck had finally changed for the better. She could withstand a few insults to work here, to keep a roof over her head and her daughter's, to put food on their table. If keeping Stephanie safe from harm required nothing more than putting up with an old woman's sharp tongue, Allison silently vowed that she would thank her lucky stars each and every day of her life.

49

Louise Peterson had been reading at the Wood Lake Public Library for the past two hours, her mood gradually becoming blacker. She made a final notation on her pad of paper and closed the last of the books on incest and child molestation.

Louise had come to the library in a seemingly futile effort to reassure herself that Karl Warren was innocent of molesting his daughter. Her phone conversations with the mothers on the run had taught her a bit about the victims of these crimes, but very little about the kind of men who were guilty of perpetrating them. She knew, of course, that they came from all walks of life—that they could be factory workers or priests, sharecroppers or police officers. But there had to be something essential that these men shared or maybe that they lacked—common personality traits or childhood experiences—that turned them into sexual outlaws. Something that made them noticeably different from normal fathers. Louise had hoped to learn what that something was by reading these treatises on the subject; she'd hoped even more that this exercise would convince her Karl Warren had been falsely accused.

She checked her watch. One-twenty. She'd better hurry. Pete would be wondering why she'd taken so long for lunch, and she didn't plan to tell him. In the past few weeks they'd had far too many arguments about her reluctance to work on the Warren

292

case. Pete would simply accuse her once more of looking for trouble where none existed, of ruining their investigation business with another of her foolish hunches.

Yet, reading over her notes, Louise felt even more strongly that there could well be truth to Allison Warren's accusations about her ex-husband. Of course, there was no irrefutable proof in the brief profile Louise had compiled as she read study after study in the psychology books and journals piled in front of her. But neither had she come across even one good reason to believe that Karl couldn't possibly be guilty. What had she been looking for, anyway—some solid proof that all child molesters were under six feet tall or had been raised by divorced mothers? Something, anything that would disqualify Karl. She hadn't found it.

Until today, Louise had always thought that child molesters had to be victims of sex abuse themselves when they were children. And somehow she couldn't quite see Karl in that category. But from what she had read here today, she learned that childhood sex abuse was *not* always found in these men's backgrounds. Most were indeed abused children, but many molesters had been victims of their parents' verbal or physical—not their sexual—abuse.

From the once or twice she'd met him, Louise had not been able to picture old Einar Warren as a child molester—she'd found him to be so, well, almost sexless—though she chided herself that she had no way of knowing the truth. Incest was not something most people brought up in polite conversation, certainly not thirty or forty years ago. And by now the truth was long buried. Still, from what Pete had told her, all of Wood Lake had been aware that cantankerous old Einar had believed in and practiced harsh corporal punishment as a way of disciplining children. Louise couldn't erase the thought of young Pete and his friends fleeing Einar's shotgun so many years ago. Surely there was no excuse for a grown man's shooting at boys stealing a few apples.

And the Warren girl—what was her name? Gretchen. As a teenager, Gretchen had run off with her sailor and, as far as Louise could determine from the discreet inquiries she'd made around town, the girl had never returned, not even for her parents' funerals. What could make a daughter hate her family that much? Louise knew she'd probably never find out, but it was obvious that the Einar Warren household had sorely lacked an atmosphere of healthy parental love.

Louise chewed her pencil as she reread another of the disturbing notes she'd made: *Men who are sexually attracted to young girls tend to be uncomfortable around grown women.* She herself frequently had been annoyed by Karl's tendency to ignore her; did he snub her because he actually feared women? Or maybe his discomfort went beyond that; did the man harbor an irrational hatred for the opposite sex?

Louise also noted that men guilty of incest were often attracted to very childlike women, and she recalled that the one photo of Allison Karl had kept was the revealing bikini shot. In it, Allison's baby-blond hair and slim, flat-chested figure were clearly displayed. Allison might have been close to thirty when Karl Warren married her, but in Louise's opinion, she'd had the face of a sixteen-year-old and the body of a twelve-year-old.

The list of character traits that Louise had gleaned from the books and articles continued on to a second page. *Becoming a father is typically a difficult time of life for men who later force their daughters into incestuous sexual relationships,* she read. She knew little about the reasons for the Warrens' divorce, but if she recalled correctly, things had started to sour between Karl and Allison around the time of little Stephanie's birth. And hadn't Pete mentioned something about Karl's not having paid much attention to his daughter during her infancy? A failure to bond with a daughter as a normal father would was another of the traits Louise's sources had mentioned.

Depressed, Louise ripped her pages of notes from the lined pad, crumpled them, and tossed them into the wastebasket. No sense having Pete come across them, and she certainly wouldn't need these jottings to remember what she had learned today. The information already was engraved on her mind . . . and on her conscience. Now the question was, what would she—or could she—do about it?

50

Odette Lampley squinted at the Safeway cash register receipt she had plucked from the grocery bag. "Eighty-five seventy-six. Hrmph! Almost ten dollars more than last week," she said, frowning. "Sure you didn't put any of your own stuff on here?"

Unpacking the groceries in the Lampleys' kitchen, Allison struggled to keep her voice calm. "Anything I bought for myself, or for Angel, was rung up separately, Odette, just like we agreed."

"A person has to watch to make sure things are on the up and up. Some of the girls we had cheated us." She poked a bony finger at a plastic bag filled with green beans. "These things look pretty sorry to me. These the best they had?"

No, I purposely chose the worst ones I could find, Allison wanted to say. But she held her temper. "I checked both Safeway and Lucky and none of the beans looked good today. But I knew you wanted green beans for supper tonight, so I compromised and bought a small bag. We can have zucchini along with the beans. I know Chester likes it."

"Well, all right then." The old woman limped out of the kitchen. Allison exhaled slowly and began stacking cans of tuna, tomatoes, and applesauce on the pantry shelves.

"How come 'Dette's so mean, Mommy?" Stephanie sat on a high stool at the counter, plucking dry

Cheerios from a cup and popping them into her mouth.

"She doesn't intend to be mean, hon. She's just old," Allison whispered. "She doesn't mean any harm. And you should call her Mrs. Lampley, not Odette."

"I don't like her."

Allison could understand her daughter's judgment all too well. Although Stephanie was mainly ignored by Odette, Allison had been nearly overwhelmed by the old woman's rudeness over the past few days. Whenever Chester wasn't around to run interference—and he took frequent, forgivable walks—Odette blurted out crude comments and embarrassing questions: "Why did you dye your hair that godawful color? It's garish, if you ask me." "What kind of name for a child is Angel? She should have a proper little girl's name, like Sarah or Jane." "Where's your husband? I'll bet he left you. It's not going to be easy to catch another one when you've got a child the poor soul would have to put up with." Allison frequently longed to tell the old bitch to shut up, but instead she held her tongue and gave bland answers or simply pretended she didn't hear the barrage. Anything to keep the peace. Truth was, she'd had some practice in handling verbal abuse during her marriage to Karl. If she lasted in this job, she'd be a certified expert.

Allison closed the pantry door. "I know you don't like her, Angel, but Mr. and Mrs. Lampley have been very good to us. They've given us a place to live here and a job and we have to be grateful."

"I wanna watch telebishun. How come they don't have any telebishun?"

"Because the TV signal doesn't reach into Big Sur, kiddo. You have to have a signal that travels through the air close by to get television."

"Jeffrey has telebishun." Jeffrey was a six-year-old

who lived up the road, the only playmate Stephanie had found in the days they had lived at the Lampleys'.

"Jeffrey's family has a satellite dish that catches TV signals from high up in the sky and brings them down to earth. The Lampleys don't."

"Can I go to Jeffrey's and watch telebishun?"

"Not this afternoon, punkin. It's already getting late and Mommy has to start dinner. Why don't you read one of your books? Or play outside awhile?" Please.

"I don't wanna. I wanna watch telebishun."

Between Stephanie and Odette, Allison often felt she was running some sort of bizarre day-care center here. Still, after more than a week on the job, she was beginning to feel at home, almost safe. Today she and Stephie had made the weekly run to the Monterey Peninsula to do the Lampleys' grocery shopping, a chore she didn't mind at all. It took her away from the sometimes-claustrophobic closeness of this rural life and gave her a chance to check the Monterey post office for mail deliveries as well. Katherine Andrews's Social Security card was waiting there for her, but there was no money from Ruth.

Most of Allison's original cash stake was now gone and her first paycheck from the Lampleys had turned out to be almost laughably small. After her employers had withheld for Social Security and federal and state taxes, Allison had only a little over sixty dollars left, and most of that had gone to pay for gasoline, a few essentials like bath soap and deodorant, and new sneakers for Stephanie, who had outgrown her last pair. Allison was continually thankful that their room and board was included, tax-free, but the worry that some emergency might send her and Stephie back on the road kept her awake nights. She had to have that eight hundred from Ruth. It was the only safety net she had.

"God damn it!" Odette screeched from her bedroom. "Kit, come in here, *now*." Her employer had insisted upon calling Allison Kit. As a child Odette had had a good friend named Katherine, she explained, and she'd always called her friend Kit. So, from now on, Allison would answer to Kit.

"I'll be right back, Angel." Allison fled the kitchen, expecting to find Odette lying on the floor, or to discover, at least, that she had broken something valuable. But as she entered the master bedroom, all she found was the old woman sitting at her vanity table, her shoulders slumping and her eyes filled with tears.

"Will you look at this mess?" she asked, stroking her thin, white hair with a gnarled hand. "My library meeting is tonight. I can't go looking like this."

The wisps of white were indeed disheveled, and far from stylish. "Why don't you just wear your turban?" Allison suggested.

"I wanted to look good, damn it. I've been trying to fix my hair like I used to, but my hands just won't do what I want them to. There's no curl left, anyway. I barely managed to get this horrible mess washed this morning. Just wait 'til you're old like me, then you'll see. Oh, I *hate* this!" She pounded the glass surface of the vanity as a tear slid down one withered cheek.

"Maybe I can help." Allison felt a surge of pity for the old woman. It must be terrible to be locked inside a body that no longer worked. "I've got some electric rollers out in the cabin. I'd be happy to see what I can do with your hair just as soon as I get the chicken in the oven."

"Oh, would you? I'd so love to be pretty again, to turn heads the way I did when I was a girl." The naked desire on Odette's face was pathetic.

"Give me half an hour," Allison said, patting the old woman's bony shoulder. "We'll do your hair, and maybe put on a little makeup, too. When we get through with you, you'll knock 'em dead at that library meeting."

Odette smiled crookedly, the right side of her wrinkled face sagging. Yet it was the first sign of pleasure that Allison had seen her display. It warmed her heart.

51

He'd had a long, hard day in court and Karl Warren was beat. He came home, downed a quick martini, hit the shower, and was just stepping out when the phone rang. Damn. It was tempting to let it ring, but it could be important; he was expecting several calls. He grabbed a towel, wrapped it around a waist that was becoming middle-aged flabby, and ran, dripping, toward the den.

"Yeah?"

"Karl, glad I caught you home. News just came in from Portland PD. They found the place that sold Allison the replacement car." Buck Linn paused for effect. "And we got lucky. She used a new name."

"Holy shit. Good work, Buck. Let's hear it." Karl grabbed a pencil and stood, naked and shivering on the rapidly dampening beige carpeting, as he took down the information.

"Fellow at the car dealership remembered her real good, thought she was cute. Said she didn't know shit about cars, wanted all kinds of advice about what kind to buy. He figured she was plannin' some kinda trip. She had Stephie with her, too, so there's no doubt we're talkin' about the same woman."

"Good. What kind of car did she buy?"

"Fella sold her a yellow Volvo wagon, nineteen seventy-nine model." The police sergeant recited the Volvo's serial number and the number of its Oregon license plate. "Name she used for the deal was Katherine M. Andrews. Showed a Washington driver's license issued in that name for ID, too. All-cash deal. Everything fits, Karly—no question we got the right broad."

"What did he say about the photos? He notice anything new about the way Allison looked? Or Stephie?"

"Nope. Said Allison looked just like that enhancement we did on that old photo, where we aged her and made her a redhead. Stephie looked just like her picture, too. Only difference is she's got shorter hair now."

"Hey, thanks, pal. I'll call this in to my contacts at the stolen child groups first thing in the morning, and how about you lean on the FBI to put out a bulletin? I'd sure as hell hate not to follow up on this information as quick as possible. We don't want to give Allison a chance to ditch this car like she did the Ford, or to get still another fake ID. Not when we're so close I can taste it."

"Do what I can. Like I told you before, the brass ain't gonna buy an APB on a parental kidnap, but I think I can get 'em to fax a flyer with this info and the photos to all the major PD's in the Pacific Coast states. Be surprised how often that sorta thing pays off. You get some hotshot flatfoot lookin' for a promotion, and he keeps his eye out, spots the car. 'Specially if she leaves Oregon and ends up back in Washington or maybe California, where that yellow license plate's gonna stand out."

"I owe you one."

"Yeah, and I plan to collect, too. Pitcher at Morrisey's after my shift on Friday, okay?"

"You're on." Feeling rejuvenated, Karl hung up the receiver and stared at his notes. It wouldn't be long now.

52

It was a glorious day, with the sky brilliantly blue and the noontime sun shining warm overhead. Allison and Stephanie sat at the edge of Nepenthe's patio, overlooking the Big Sur coastline. It was Allison's day off and she planned to enjoy every minute of it. The view was indescribably beautiful here—sheer cliffs dropping sharply into the churning surf, a green meadow that was home to a pampered herd of cows, and the endless sea, bright turquoise gradually fading to bluish gray, as far as the eye could see. Allison had read about this restaurant, which once had been the vacation home of Orson Welles. If she'd had Welles's money, she thought, she'd never have left this place.

Allison forced her attention to the menu. "Do you want a tuna sandwich or a hamburger?" she asked. The prices were high here, but the portions looked large. She and Stephie could order one meal and split it. The first cash installment from Ruth—ten twenty-dollar bills—had been waiting at the Monterey post office this morning, and Allison felt like indulging in a minor splurge.

"I want french fries like they got."

Stephanie, her bare legs dangling from her white plastic chair, pointed at a couple seated nearby. The two tourists flashed the child a friendly smile in response.

303

"Okay, punkin, but you have to have a sandwich, too, and drink all your milk."

"I wanna hamburger and french fries and milk."

"Sold."

Allison ordered one ambrosia burger special, a basket of fries, a glass of milk, and an iced tea. They ate their meal as they listened to the tinkling sounds of the wind chimes on the gift shop patio below them. When they had finished eating, mother and daughter piled back into the Volvo and headed for Pfeiffer State Beach.

The beach, like Nepenthe, was described in a book about Big Sur that Chester Lampley had lent to Allison, and she was looking forward to having a chance to sit at the water's edge and relax. She checked her odometer carefully to locate the unmarked entrance to the steep two-mile-long drive down the single lane road to the beach. Most of the narrow road was dark, shaded by eucalyptus, pine, and scrub oaks. As it wound around sharp curves, portions bordered what had once been a creek but, now, during California's extended drought, had been reduced to a trickle of water in a deep gorge. Suddenly the steep descent ended and they emerged into sunlight. Here, on this flatter ground, were four or five narrow roads leading off the main one, each posted with a sign warning: PRIVATE PROPERTY, NO TRESPASSING. Then the end of the road, and the state property came into view. Allison parked the Volvo in a half-filled circular parking lot. From here, it was only a short hike over a slight pine-crested rise to the sea.

"Lord," Allison exclaimed as the panorama hit her eye. Nothing in Chester's book had prepared her for this raw, natural beauty.

"Look, Mommy," Stephanie shrieked with pleasure, "I see waves!"

Waves were only the beginning. The rugged, unspoiled shoreline featured mammoth rocks perched in the surf just off shore. As Allison and Stephanie crossed the loose sand toward the water, they spied giant blowholes—vast tunnels in the rocks through which huge waves crashed, forming a shower of water that appeared to burst from the rock itself.

"Can I go swimming, Mommy? Can I? Can I? Puh-leeze?"

"I think the water here might be too cold and rough to swim, hon, but we can try a little wading if you like."

Allison greased herself and Stephanie with suntan lotion and they spent the next three hours enjoying the surrounding area. Stephie built sand castles, kicked them down, and then poked her fingers at sea anemones she found in the tide pools. She pointed and stared in disbelief at a nude couple sun-bathing unobtrusively behind a rock. "Mommy, that man and that lady are naked!" And she frolicked on the damp sand at the water's edge, retreating quickly with a gleeful yelp as each wave approached her bare toes.

Watching from a nearby seat on the dry sand, Allison felt for the first time in months like the normal mother of a normal four-year-old. Brushing away a tear, she prayed that somehow it would last.

By four o'clock, Stephanie was clearly ready for a nap. They dressed, gathered up their towels, and headed back to the car. The drive uphill was slow; the old Volvo handled the curves well, but the winding one-lane road required vehicles heading uphill to pull into turnoffs whenever they met a car heading down. But, luckily, as there was no State Parks Department sign marking the road's entrance off Highway 1, few tourists ventured there.

At the crest of the hill, they once again were drenched with sunlight. Allison blinked and turned right onto the main highway. They would be back at the Lampleys' house well before dinnertime. She had left a pot of homemade vegetable beef soup for the old folks to reheat for their dinner. Tonight, Allison and Stephanie would eat in their cabin, gloriously alone.

"I gotta go potty, Mommy." Exhausted now by the day's outing, Stephie's tone revealed that she was quickly growing irritable.

"We'll be home in ten minutes. Just hang on, sweetie." Allison pressed down hard on the accelerator and was immediately greeted by a thumping sound. Suddenly the thumping became louder and the Volvo's front end began to vibrate wildly. Damn. A blowout. Holding the steering wheel steady and pressing down gradually on the brake pedal, Allison controlled the big car until it came to a safe stop at the side of the road.

"What's the matter, Mommy? How come the car got all shaky?"

"We've got a flat tire," Allison said, resting her forehead briefly against the steering wheel. Shit. Just what they needed. She hadn't changed a tire since high school, and her sole experience with that chore back then had convinced her to join the auto club. Well, she was on her own now. She turned on the emergency flashers, pushed open the car door, and climbed out.

The right front tire was ruptured, clearly a total loss. Luckily, the spare looked all right, if a bit worn, and the car still had its jack. The question was how she was going to get the damned tire onto the car. Allison examined the jack. To her, it seemed little more than twisted pieces of steel, nothing at all like a jack for an American car. Apparently there was some specific slot on the underside of the Volvo where the contraption was supposed to fit, but Lord knew where the hell it was. Allison circled the car once more, got down on her knees, looked beneath the car, and ran her hand along the underside of the chassis. Her fingers quickly turned black, but she still had no idea how the jack was meant to work.

"Need some help?"

Allison jerked upward, knocking her head against the car. "Ouch, damn it." She struggled to her feet, but almost lost her balance a second time as she recognized the source of the inquiry. A Monterey County sheriff's vehicle had pulled in behind hers, and a smiling young deputy was watching her with barely concealed amusement. "What?" Allison felt herself begin to shake.

"Looks like you could use a little help, ma'am. Why don't you give me that thing?"

"I—I guess so." Allison looked down at her hand, embarrassed to realize that she was holding the jack like a weapon, primed and ready to swing at the deputy if he tried to arrest her. She forced a smile and held the jack out toward him. "I can't figure out how you're supposed to use this thing."

"It's not hard once you know what to do." Fifteen minutes later, the deputy had the tire changed. He got to his feet and began to brush the tan dust from his uniform.

"I'm really sorry. You got all dirty." *Act normal*, Allison told herself for the hundredth time. This cop had no reason to suspect her of anything if she didn't hand him one.

"All in a day's work, ma'am. Glad I was able to help you out."

"Me, too."

The deputy pointed at the Volvo's Oregon license plate. "Just traveling through, are you?"

"Uh, we're planning to stay awhile. It's such pretty country around here." She had to keep her answers general.

"Mommy, puh-leeze. I gotta go potty *real bad*."

For once, Allison was grateful for Stephie's small

bladder and frequent need of a bathroom. "I—we better get going before she has an accident," she told the deputy.

"Sure. Wouldn't drive too long on that spare, if I were you. You might try Stinson's garage, across from the library. He carries tires." The deputy grinned. "He's got rest rooms, too."

"Thanks, officer, I really appreciate it." Allison climbed back into the driver's seat and gripped the steering wheel firmly until her hands stopped shaking. She waited until the sheriff's car pulled out into traffic and disappeared, then turned the Volvo around and drove toward Stinson's.

Half an hour later, Allison was still so grateful the young sheriff's deputy had not recognized and arrested her that she almost didn't mind paying a hundred and sixty dollars, plus tax, for a new set of front tires.

53

Pushing her cart down the aisle at the Carmel Safeway, Allison checked her shopping list. She had the fresh vegetables and fruit, the Sara Lee frozen coffee cake Odette craved, a dozen eggs, ten pounds of flour, oatmeal . . . At the meat counter, she selected two frying chickens, three pounds of hamburger, and a package of pork chops. They could have the chops tonight, with a pineapple glaze. She would simmer them slowly to make sure they were extra tender. Odette's teeth had been bothering her lately and she was having trouble chewing meat, particularly if it was the least little bit tough.

"Mommy, I wanna box of popsicles. Cherry. Puhleeze. You promised."

"That's not true, Angel, I did not promise. I said you could have one treat this afternoon and you already had a frozen yogurt cone. Besides, popsicles would just melt before we got home."

Stephanie scurried away to the cereal aisle. "Can I have Sugar Snax, Mommy? I won't eat 'em all now, I promise."

Allison sighed. "No, you may not have Sugar Snax. They're expensive and they're not on the Lampleys' list, so we'd have to pay for them ourselves. I already told you, we're broke." During today's shopping trip to the Monterey peninsula, Allison had made a trip to the post office, but this time there had been no cash-filled envelope from

Ruth waiting to be picked up. "Come on, Angel, stop begging. I want to get the last few things on Odette's list and get out of here before it gets any later."

The errand list had been lengthy today, requiring half a dozen stops at area stores. Allison had picked up a set of sheets from Macy's, a book for Chester from the Thunderbird Bookshop, three bottles of sauvignon blanc from Liquor Barn, a prescription from Long's Drug, and Chester's navy suit from the dry cleaner's. Now she was tired; she couldn't wait to pay for this cartload of groceries and head back to Big Sur. "Come on, kiddo. If you don't stay right next to Mommy the way I told you to, you'll have to ride in the cart."

"I don't wanna ride in the cart. Only babies ride in the cart. I'll be good, I promise."

Allison checked off the meat purchases. Now only milk and cheddar cheese remained on the list. She reached into the milk case and pulled a half gallon of lowfat off the shelf. As she bent to put it in the cart, her eye fell on the back of the carton. Involuntarily, her grip loosened and she dropped the heavy container as if it had exploded; it landed on a ripe tomato, spattering blood-red pulp everywhere. "No!" she cried aloud. Her stomach clenched and she doubled over, unable to breathe. *No! This could not be!* Her imagination was playing tricks. She grasped the slime-covered milk carton and picked it up again. Dear God, it was no trick. There, for all the world to see, was Stephanie's picture printed in black and white. Above her daughter's image were the words, "Stolen . . . Have You Seen This Child?"

Allison quickly scanned the printed words beneath the picture.

Stephanie Suzannah Warren, stolen from her home in Wood Lake, Wisconsin, August 1990. Age four, 39 inches tall, 37 pounds, dark brown hair, blue eyes. Believed to be traveling with Allison Mitchell Warren, also known as Elyse Michaels.

Elyse Michaels! How in hell had they found that name? If they knew about Elyse Michaels, what else did they know? At the bottom was a phone number for something called the Stolen Child Rescue League, along with a plea for anyone knowing anything about Stephanie's whereabouts to call collect, twenty-four hours a day.

Allison felt assaulted, stripped naked in public. The other shoppers' eyes seemed pinned on her. Her hands shaking uncontrollably, she somehow managed to thrust the milk carton back onto the shelf and turn it so the photograph was once again hidden at the back. She grabbed Stephie by the hand and propelled both the child and the loaded grocery cart toward the checkout counter.

"Owie, Mommy, you're pulling too hard. That hurts."

"We've got to get out of here, right now." Allison's mind raced. Which would be less noticeable—if she tried to check out these groceries quickly and unobtrusively, or if she just left the loaded cart here in the aisle and ran? Damn it. There was a long line at the checkout stand. What if the next shopper in line had a carton of that milk? If someone noticed Stephanie was the child in the picture? Allison couldn't take that chance. The hell with the groceries. She pushed the cart down a side aisle, left it, and yanked Stephie toward the door. "Come on, punkin, quick. We have to hurry!"

In the car, Allison willed herself to calm down. She couldn't afford to have an accident, and this section of Highway 1 was treacherous. She was near panic, and she couldn't risk indulging in it. If she fell apart, they would have no chance at all. Take a deep breath, she told herself, exhale slowly, force yourself to let up on the accelerator. Don't attract attention.

The old Volvo soon was caught behind a slow driver. There was no place to pass on the curves along the cliffs, so Allison had no choice but to slow down, to proceed cautiously. She had to think what to do next. She and Stephie had to leave this area. With Stephie's face plastered on all those milk cartons, there was no way they could stick around here—why, her new playmate Jeffrey could be drinking from one of those milk cartons at this very minute! And Allison had no way of knowing how widely that brand of milk was distributed. It could be all over the whole damned state.

Yet how could they manage to escape? Allison had less than a hundred dollars in cash left, and if they—the Stolen Child Rescue League, the police, Karl, maybe even the FBI—knew about Elyse Michaels, did they also know about Katherine Andrews? About the Volvo? The police might already have Allison's description and her car's license number.

Was there nowhere they could turn for help? The Monterey safe house would be of no use now, not with this local publicity. And Allison wasn't about to confide in the Lampleys; she wasn't even sure they'd be willing to help if they knew about the trouble she and Stephie were in. Using the underground network would mean driving as far as they could on whatever gasoline their few remaining dollars would buy, and hoping the car wasn't spotted and stopped. And then what? How far could they get on their meager cash supply? Where could they hide?

Much as she hated to ask him, Allison knew there was only one person who could possibly save them—her father. She would just have to risk calling and asking him to get some money to her somehow. Then maybe she and Stephie could fly somewhere far, far away, maybe to Canada or Mexico. No, that wouldn't work; Allison wouldn't be able to get a work permit and, sooner or later, the money would run out. Some distant part of the United States would be best. Maybe Hawaii. That could work. They could ditch the Volvo and fly to the Islands. You didn't need a passport to go there, or a work permit to get a job, yet it was almost like being in a foreign country—far enough away that Karl and his henchmen would never think to look there, at least not yet.

Allison pulled the car into the parking lot of the River Inn in Big Sur village and searched her purse for coins to use the pay phone outside the small grocery store. "You stay right here, Angel. I've got to make a phone call."

Tim Mitchell answered on the third ring with a breathless, raspy "Hello."

"Daddy, hi, it's me."

"Allie baby, how are you?"

"I'm in trouble, Daddy, bad trouble. I need your help. I need that money you said you had for me."

As she explained the situation as briefly as she could, Allison obsessively watched the cars that passed by on the highway, terrified that each and every one was driven by someone who'd seen those milk cartons. She felt certain that anyone peering inside the Volvo and seeing Stephanie would immediately call the police. *The police.* Oh, Lord, she'd forgotten about that cop who changed her tire the other day. He'd gotten a good hard look at Stephie, and he knew exactly which car they were driving.

"Allie, you still there?"

"Sure, sure, I'm here, Daddy. I'm just scared to death, that's all."

"Well, calm down and think straight. The sailor that panics in a storm ends up drowned; you know that. Just tell me where to meet you and I'll bring you the cash. I'm ready to leave soon's I can put a few things together."

"I—I don't know what to do, Daddy. You shouldn't try to drive all this way, and I'm afraid to try and come to you. I don't even know if I have enough money to get us down to San Diego. Besides, I'm so goddamned scared somebody'll recognize Stephie I can't think straight. I'm even scared to be talking to you on the phone like this."

"You can't even think about coming here, Allie. I'll come to you. I can make it. We'll meet somewhere not too public and I'll give you the money. Now calm down and think. Where's a good private place, somewhere close to where you are, so you don't have to be out on the road any more than necessary?"

"Daddy, isn't there someplace else I can call you? A friend's or a neighbor's? I just have this bad feeling about your phone. What if it's tapped?"

"Okay, okay, if it bothers you that much." There was a pause as Tim considered his options. He came back on the line. "Okay, I've got something. Looks like Terry Perkins across the street is home; I can see his car. Give me ten minutes, then call me over at his place." He gave Allison the phone number.

Ten minutes later, Tim, sounding weaker and more out of breath, answered Terry Perkins's phone. "Now, tell me where to bring the, uh, stuff you wanted," he said.

Allison quickly rejected the idea of having her father come to the Lampleys' house. It was too risky and she didn't want to involve the old couple in her problems. Pfeiffer State Beach—that would do. "We can meet in the parking lot, Daddy. It shouldn't be too crowded and it's far enough from the highway that we can stay out of sight if you're late."

"I'm not gonna be late."

Allison gave Tim precise directions about where to find the turnoff from Highway 1.

"I want to make sure I got this all straight now," he said. "You said this place is not too far south of Big Sur village, right? I'm to look for the Ventana Inn sign on the right hand side of Highway 1, then I drive north exactly one mile ..." Tim repeated Allison's directions just as she had given them.

"You've got it down right, Daddy. How soon do you think you can make it?"

"Give me twenty-four hours, Allie. I can be there by four o'clock tomorrow afternoon."

"You sure you're really up to this?"

"Count on me, sweetheart. I'm gonna get there if it's the last thing I do."

Hanging up the phone, Allison was overwhelmed with a feeling of sadness, with an intuition that, indeed, this trip might very well be the last thing her father ever did.

54

Russ Quinn could hardly contain his excitement. The chase was winding down and he was riding the winning nag. He steered the agency van around the corner, tires screeching, and came to a stop in the Shell station's parking lot. He punched Pete Peterson's number into the phone, followed by the agency's credit card number, and listened to the distant rings.

"We got her, Pete," he said when the other private investigator came on the line. "The Warren woman's meeting her old man and a shitload of cash tomorrow at four o'clock." Quinn related the conversation he'd just overheard. "Hell, I just about shitted my pants when the broad insisted they talk on a different phone. Thought we were gonna lose 'em. But, hell, that parabolic mike of mine picked up the whole thing like old Mitchell was sittin' next to me in my van. Couldn't get the woman's side of the second conversation, but Mitchell couldn't've been more obliging. The old fool repeated her directions word for word."

"Nice going, Russ. Couldn't've done better myself."

"So, how do you think your man's gonna want to handle this? Want me to tail Mitchell and set up some guys at the other end to snatch the kid, or do you guys want to head on out yourselves? You can just hand it over to the cops, too, if you want, but you're gonna hafta come up with a cover story about how you got the time and place."

"Don't worry about that. Nobody here's gonna say shit about your bug ... or your mike. In fact, why don't you send one of your guys back into Mitchell's house as soon as he splits and get that little sucker outta there? No sense borrowing trouble."

"Sure thing. I've got somebody can do it tonight. Listen, Pete, I gotta get back to my watch, make sure the old man doesn't slip out on us. If he takes off before I hear from you, I'll try to tail him. You figure out what you want to do, call my office. I'll be in touch."

Quinn rang off. He plunked four quarters into the cold drink machine beside the telephone, collected a can of Coke, ripped off the flip top and tossed it aside. He raised the can in a one-man toast: "Here's to Russ Quinn, best damned private eye in the whole fucking business." Heading back to the van, Quinn drank deeply, savoring the sweet, tingling coldness on his tongue ... and his pending victory over the foolish Allison Mitchell Warren.

55

Louise gripped the back of the seat in front of hers and looked around nervously. Didn't they carry barf bags in these little planes? She couldn't spot one. Her stomach rolled again. She closed her eyes until the spasm passed. If only she could make it until this goddamned motorized kite landed in Chicago, she'd be okay. She could tolerate flying in big jets; it was just the constantly bumpy ride of these toy-size planes that got to her.

She hadn't wanted to come on this trip anyway, but Karl had insisted. Stephanie might feel reassured if another woman was with her after Allison was taken off to jail, he said. The lurching small plane ride wasn't the only reason Louise was feeling sick. The thought of that poor little kid's being snatched away from her mother nauseated her, too. She didn't want any part of this mad dash—by private plane to Chicago, then a six o'clock United Airlines flight to Los Angeles and Monterey—or any part of its anticipated finale in Big Sur tomorrow.

"You're lookin' a little green around the gills, Lou," Pete said, rubbing the back of her neck. "Anything I can do to help?"

She shook her head.

"She'll be all right," Karl volunteered from the front of the cockpit. He was seated next to the pilot, a former client of Karl's who was paying back a favor. "We'll land at O'Hare in another fifteen minutes. Air sickness is all in your head, anyway. If you don't give in to it, it goes away."

How the hell would you know, you arrogant son of a bitch? Louise wanted to say. Mr. Sympathy there in the front seat probably had never been airsick in his life, and he sure as hell wouldn't know empathy if it crawled up and bit him.

Pete took his hand off his wife's neck and patted her clenched fist in a silent gesture of support. Louise wished he'd find the guts to tell Karl to keep his opinions and advice to himself, but these days Pete was too worried about keeping the agency together to stand up for anybody.

"What did you tell Buck Linn about where we got the information about tomorrow?" Pete asked Karl.

"Told him we got an anonymous tip from a good Samaritan who saw Stephie's picture."

"Just so we all stick with that. Russ Quinn expects us to keep his ass covered."

"No problem. I'll be checking back in with Buck tonight. By then he'll have the Monterey County sheriff lined up to help us on the other end."

"Good. Keep things all nice and legal from here on out."

The plane lurched again and started its descent. "Everybody buckled up?" the pilot asked.

Karl and Pete answered affirmatively. Louise clapped a hand over her mouth and tried not to breathe.

56

"We've been talking it over and we want to tell you not to feel you need to quit your job here, Katherine. Odette and I will hold it open until you come back from your father's place." It was after dinner and Chester Lampley was pacing the living room floor, his hands folded over his rounded belly. The ritual cup of coffee he enjoyed each evening was quickly growing cold on the lamp table.

Allison was ashamed, lying this way to her elderly employers, but she dared not tell them the truth. When she and Stephanie had returned from the Peninsula without the groceries, she'd told them she'd just learned of an emergency in her family, that she'd had to rush home without finishing her list of errands. She was terribly sorry not to give them proper notice, but she and her daughter would have to leave here tomorrow. Her father was dying of lung cancer and she had to go to him right away.

"Chester's right, Kit. Go see your father, stay a week, two if you like. We can manage for a little while . . . somehow. Then come back here, to us."

Allison bit down on her quivering lower lip. "I wish I could. But I don't know if my dad has a week left or a month or, if we're lucky, maybe even longer. He—he hasn't got anybody to take care of him but us, Angel and me." This story was close enough to the truth to bring natural tears to Allison's eyes.

Seated in her rocking chair near the window overlooking the rocky Pacific shore, Odette raised her cane and began using it to punctuate her thoughts. "But Kit, Chester and I need you here," she whined. "We haven't got anybody else, either."

"You folks aren't going to have any trouble finding another housekeeper."

Odette's cane flew in an arc, coming dangerously close to the bone china coffee service on the table in front of her. Allison deftly moved it out of harm's way. "We won't find anybody to fix my hair for my library meetings!" the old woman complained. "Or make the pea soup the way I like it." Odette was like a young child, oblivious to anyone's needs but her own. Yet Allison wasn't really annoyed. After the initial hostility Odette had displayed, she had begun to show signs of genuine affection for her new employee—little thank-yous and uncharacteristic words of praise. Now, having gained her employer's trust, Allison was about to desert her, to throw her back into the self-pitying depression from which she was only just beginning to emerge.

Stephanie is your first—your only—responsibility, Allison told herself. Guilt over the Lampleys, even over her own father, would only get in the way of what she had to do to save her daughter. She could never forget that. "I—I'm sorry," she said. "Really I am, but there's nothing I can do. My family has to be my top priority." She turned to go. "I'll go clean up the dinner dishes. Then I have to get started packing up the cabin."

"It's just not fair," Odette called after her. "You're not being one bit fair!"

57

It was well after midnight by the time Karl and the Petersons had checked into their rooms at the Monterey Hyatt. Their plane had been an hour late getting in to Monterey Airport, and Karl had insisted upon picking up the rental car as well as checking tomorrow's routing on the county road map before he dismissed the private detectives for the evening.

Louise was exhausted. "Jesus Christ, I thought we'd never get rid of him," she complained when Pete had closed and locked the door to their room. "What a horse's ass that guy is!"

"I don't want to hear any more of that, Lou. The man's keeping us alive. You ought to show more respect, make at least some attempt to participate in a conversation with him."

"Well, hallelujah for him and his goddamned checkbook. He's still a horse's ass. And you aren't doing so well in that department yourself, my friend. Every time our exalted employer took one of his nasty snipes at me, you just sat there and let him do it."

Pete turned away and snapped open the larger of the two black suitcases. "You put my shaving kit in here?"

"I'm still talking to you, Pete." Louise yanked at her husband's shirt sleeve.

Pete brushed her hand away. "What the hell do

you want me to say, Lou? You think it makes me feel good to listen to him talk like that?"

"Sure looks like it from where I'm sitting."

"Okay, okay. I'm sorry. I'm fucking sorry I don't have the guts to throw over the whole goddamned business I've spent my life building up just to defend your honor. But I don't. Satisfied?"

"How could any girl not be thrilled by your priorities, you son of a bitch. Make a buck, that's your thing, your only thing . . . even if it means pimping your own wife. Or selling out helpless little girls." She stalked into the bathroom, slammed the door behind her, and turned the shower taps on full blast. The roar of rushing water drowned out the harsh sounds of her bitter sobs.

58

It took Tim Mitchell three trips to unload his car at the Santa Barbara motel where he would sleep a few hours before getting back on the road to Big Sur. He had so little strength left these days that everything he did seemed to be in excruciatingly slow motion. Each little task took an extra effort. But he had to get everything out of the Honda before he could rest. He would need his small overnight bag, and he certainly couldn't chance leaving either the box of cash or the duffel bag filled with guns and ammunition outside in the car.

When he had piled his belongings on the brown Formica-topped dresser and double-locked the door, Tim popped open the small brown bottle of painkillers the doc had given him last week. Knowing he had to stay alert in traffic, he'd gone without his codeine during the drive up from San Diego. Now he felt as if he'd been brutally tortured. Every cell in his body throbbed in agony.

Two of the little round tablets wouldn't kill him. He would need to get some sleep if he was going to make the rest of this trip tomorrow. And who knew what would happen once he found Allie and Stephie? The cash and guns he was carrying weren't worth shit if the cops were tailing the two of them already. Tim might well have to figure out a way to keep his daughter and granddaughter hidden for a time.

One, two, down the hatch. Tim followed the tablets with a glass of water, then crawled onto the bed, fully clothed, and waited for the numbing effect of the codeine to overtake him.

59

"I'm just not going and there's nothing you can do to change my mind." Louise sat on the edge of the hotel bed, still in her nightgown, watching her husband dress for the morning meeting with Karl Warren and the local authorities. Her arms were rigidly crossed over her nearly bare breasts. "I refuse to take part in that ambush."

Pete shoved an arm into the sleeve of his yellow shirt. His square jaw was set. "I'm tellin' you, Lou, you're making a big mistake."

"You're the one making the mistake. How're you going to live with yourself if that son of a bitch abuses that little girl again? And he will, you know. His kind always do."

Exhaling loudly, Pete buttoned his shirt. "We've been over and over this and I'm getting fuckin' tired of it, Lou. Sometimes I just don't know where your head is these days."

"My head is where yours ought to be . . . if you'd get your eyes off the goddamned bottom line for two seconds. I'm concerned about what's *right*." She vaulted off the bed, grabbed her hairbrush from the dresser top, and began to stroke her hair angrily.

"Who're you to decide what's right? Karl's got a court decision on his side, and you haven't got enough evidence to convict him of spitting on the sidewalk."

Louise thrust the hairbrush toward her husband,

using it to punctuate her words. "Some things you just know, you just *feel* them, and I can feel who's telling the truth here. I've got to believe Allison and Stephanie, not that son of a bitch you sold out to."

Pete pulled on his shoes and tied them. This was pointless. He'd been married to Louise long enough to know she wasn't going to change her mind. She'd agreed to help bring Stephanie back to Wisconsin on the airplane, but she simply would not come along to Big Sur to recover the child. Christ, she could be bullheaded! He simply couldn't convince her that it was none of their business whether Karl Warren was guilty; that was Judge Winston's responsibility and the judge had ruled Karl innocent. If the judge had been wrong, Pete much preferred not to know. "Have it your own way. I've got to get a move on. What do you want me to tell Karl about why you're not there?"

"What the hell do I care what you tell him? Why don't you tell him the truth—tell him I think he's a goddamned baby rapist?" She threw the hairbrush across the room, where it landed with a thud against the wall, leaving a sharp dent in the plasterboard.

Pete stared at her, his lips a thin line. "I'll tell Karl you're sick, that you've got female trouble."

"You do that, coward."

Pete turned his back on his wife's tantrum, stalked out of the room, and pulled the door shut behind him.

60

Allison wedged the Igloo cooler into the backseat next to the suitcase, then tossed the pillows and blankets on top. "Where did you put your coloring books, Angel? And your crayons? You want to bring them along, don't you?" Allison had spent the morning clearing out the cabin and now she had nearly finished packing the Volvo.

Stephanie sat on the cabin steps hugging Flopsy, her face solemn and tear-streaked. She pulled her wet thumb out of her mouth. "I don't wanna go away, Mommy. I'll be good. I promise."

Allison's heart somersaulted. "Oh, precious, we're not going away because you were bad. It's not a punishment. You've been so good—the best little girl any mommy could ever have." She crouched down onto the steps, hugged her daughter, and gently kissed her dark curls. How could she make Stephie understand? She was so little and so many terrible things had happened in her short lifetime. The poor kid had had nightmares again last night, undoubtedly brought on by Allison's own badly disguised fear. Now they were both exhausted—not a very good way to start off on what promised to be a grueling trip.

Was it better to be bluntly honest and risk increasing Stephie's fears, or to try to hide the truth from her? Allison opted for an abbreviated version of reality. "We have to leave here because first we're going to see Grandpa and after that he's going to help us get away from some bad people."

"What bad people?"

"People who want to take you away from me and send you to live with your Daddy."

Stephanie's blue eyes widened and filled. "I wanna live with you, Mommy. I don't wanna live with Daddy."

"Please don't cry, punkin. I know you want to stay with me. That's what I want, too, more than anything in the world. And I'm doing everything I can to make sure you and I can stay together . . . forever and ever."

"But how come we can't stay *here*, with Chesser and 'Dette? Do *they* wanna send me back to my daddy?"

"No, honey. Mr. and Mrs. Lampley don't even know about your daddy. But I'm pretty sure he's got some other people around here looking for us, and if they catch us, they'll take you away from me. So we have to get away real quick and hide before they can find us. You can understand that, can't you?"

"Uh-huh, I guess so." Stephie's thumb found its way back into her mouth. Her tears ceased, but Allison couldn't help but think of this as a severe setback. For a short while, Stephanie had relaxed, she'd become almost a normal four-year-old, she'd been happy.

Allison, too, had been happy here at the Lampleys' home, in this incomparably beautiful setting—despite Odette's demands and the cabin's shabbiness. It just didn't seem fair that they had to move on so soon, but it couldn't be helped. If this whole ordeal had taught Allison anything, it was that life wasn't necessarily fair. Now all she could do was pray they got away in time.

She rose to her feet and held her hand out to Stephie. "Come on, Angel. Let's go have some lunch and then we'll go say good-bye to Chester and Odette."

61

Louise piloted her rented tan Chevrolet south along Highway 1. She'd waited until Pete and Karl had left the hotel for the day, then put her plan into action. The rental agency delivered the car to the hotel, along with detailed road maps of the area Louise had specified. By the time she reached the village of Big Sur, it was still only shortly after noon. There was plenty of time left.

Louise spotted the entrance to Big Sur State Park on her left and checked her odometer. According to the map, the turnoff for Pfeiffer Beach should be exactly one mile farther up the hill. Applying the gas, she clocked off the mile, a tenth at a time.

62

"Looks like your warrant's valid, all right, sir," said Mott, the taller of the two deputies. He handed the legal papers back to Karl. "You guys want to follow us down there in your car? Won't be room in the squad car for everybody."

"We'll follow you," Karl said.

As had been prearranged, he and Pete had met the two young Monterey County sheriff's deputies outside the Big Sur post office. The parking lot that served it and the small grocery store next door was crowded. Featuring an outdoor bulletin board that advertised everything from local psychics to stud bulls, the place was clearly a popular community gathering spot.

"Okay, then," Deputy Mott said. "Now, all we ask of you is, let us take the woman into custody ourselves. She gives us any trouble, just keep out of our way. We'll take care of it. Understand?" Karl and Pete nodded obediently. "We'll get your daughter back, Mr. Warren. Just don't do anything dumb. All you have to do is point out your ex-wife as soon as you spot her and we'll take over from there."

63

Tim's arms and back were stiff and achy; he'd been gripping the Honda's steering wheel and piloting the little car along these often-treacherous roads for nearly six hours now. He'd stopped for lunch and a brief rest at Lucia an hour or so ago, then got back on the road. He wished he could have stayed awhile on the restaurant's weathered deck hanging over Big Sur's steep cliffs, maybe doze a bit in the sunshine. But he couldn't afford to waste time; he'd promised Allie he wouldn't be late.

But now his endurance was nearly gone, and pain was beginning to overwhelm him once more. He pressed down on the accelerator. If he could just find the spot Allie had specified a little ahead of schedule, he'd have time for another rest before she and Stephie showed up. Maybe he'd even risk taking his first codeine pill of the afternoon, just enough medication to take the edge off his physical agony. He was beginning to need relief badly.

For the first time in days, Tim's thoughts turned to the bottle and he longed for the pain-free oblivion a few shots of whiskey could bring him. But he wouldn't let himself give in to his craving. Not now, not when he was this close. He was determined to do at least one thing right during his piss-poor excuse for a life . . . even if it killed him.

The turnoff was exactly where Allie'd said it would be. Tim struggled to guide his car the two miles downhill on the winding narrow road. Parts of the route were so darkly shaded here it almost seemed nighttime, and he had to strain to make out the roadbed in the rapidly shifting light patterns.

But he made it. He approached the loop at the end of the road, entering the circular parking lot his daughter had described. He backed into a space where he could keep an eye out for her arrival, turned off the engine, and checked the clock. It would be another half hour before Allie and Stephie got there; Tim figured he had plenty of time to use the public men's room over there, and gulp down a pain pill.

He swallowed the pill, then surveyed the parking lot as he made his way slowly and painfully back to the car. There was a camper truck with Indiana plates on the opposite side, along with three beat-up older cars and a shiny red Toyota pickup, all of which appeared to be local. They were all unoccupied. But as he unlocked the driver's door of the Honda, Tim heard the crunch of approaching tires on the gravel. He turned and stared. The newcomer wasn't Allie; it was a Monterey County sheriff's vehicle carrying two uniformed men. It drove most of the way around the circle toward the exit, then backed into a parking space.

Close on the squad car's tail was a dark green Ford sedan. The Ford parked next to the squad car and, as he watched, Tim saw two big men climb out and transfer to the backseat of the county vehicle. He couldn't get a good look at any of the men's faces, but he didn't like the smell of this. He didn't like it one damned bit. From where he stood, it looked an awful lot like somebody'd sold Allie out. In another fifteen or twenty minutes, she and Stephie would come barreling down that hill, right into a trap.

Keeping a careful eye on the sheriff's vehicle, Tim climbed back into the Honda and surreptitiously opened one of the cardboard boxes resting on the passenger's seat. He pulled out his .38 revolver and, with trembling hands, checked to see that it was fully loaded.

64

Taking no chances that her target would elude her, Louise had been watching the road to Pfeiffer Beach for well over an hour. She'd backed the rented Chevy into a nearby unpaved driveway off Highway 1 and left the motor idling. The road she had chosen was clearly marked PRIVATE, NO TRESPASSING, but so far no one had challenged her right to park there.

During her surveillance, Louise had seen several vehicles turn off the highway onto the unmarked beach access road. Two beat-up old cars—a seventy-eight Dodge and a seventy-five Buick—carrying groups of aging hippies had been first. Then a few minutes later, a Honda Civic driven by an old man. Louise suspected the man in the Honda was Timothy Mitchell, but she'd never seen Allison Warren's father, so she couldn't be certain. The latest visitors were the Monterey County sheriff's deputies, followed by Karl and Pete in the rented Ford. Predictably, Karl was driving the Ford; the man never could stand not to be the one in control. Spotting the Ford, Louise ducked low to avoid being seen. It wouldn't help Allison Warren if Karl and Pete realized that Louise had become a traitor to their cause.

The minor players were all in place now. The only thing that remained was for Allison and Stephanie Warren to show up. Louise was virtually certain the mother and daughter were not already at the rendezvous point. At two-thirty, she had made a quick trip downhill to look for them, and Allison's yellow Volvo station wagon had not been at the beach parking area. Louise could only hope that her quarry had not been hidden away on one of the posted side roads near the beach.

While Louise waited, no Volvos turned off the highway onto the beach road. In fact, she saw only two of the Swedish vehicles on the highway itself, both of them sedans.

Several other vehicles passed by, going in both directions: a gray Mercedes, two Winnebagos, a truck carrying propane fuel, a speeding blue Corvette. Finally, Louise spotted it. Stuck behind a slow-moving camper that was having trouble making it up the hill was a yellow Volvo station wagon with yellow license plates. A woman with red hair was behind the wheel.

Louise saw the Volvo's right-turn signal begin to flash. Throwing her rented Chevy into gear, she gave it gas, pushing it to the limit in an effort to overtake Allison.

The Chevrolet and the Volvo took the right turn into the narrow downhill road almost simultaneously. Louise applied more gas, then jerked her steering wheel quickly to the left, catching the station wagon's right rear corner with the Chevy's left front fender. The grinding sound of metal against metal pierced the air and both cars braked to a halt. The drivers' doors flew open.

Allison Warren, her left leg half out of the Volvo, was angry. "What in the hell kind of stunt—"

Louise rushed around her car toward the other driver. "Allison, stop! Wait!" she called.

"You! I know you! Oh, my God." Allison pulled her leg back inside, slammed her door shut, and looked around in a panic. She couldn't turn back toward the highway; the Chevrolet was blocking the road. She was trapped. There was nowhere to go but downhill. She threw the car into gear and accelerated toward the beach.

"Don't go! I'm only trying to warn you!" Louise's shouts went unheeded. She climbed back into the Chevy and sped off in pursuit of Allison and her child. Damn! Now she'd really blown it. There had to be some way to warn them, some way to save Allison and Stephanie from the trap that awaited them below.

65

Her heart racing, Allison barely managed to navigate the sharp twists and turns as she sped toward the beach. In the passenger seat, Stephanie held Flopsy tight against her chest and whimpered. The Peterson woman was sticking close on their tail, honking her horn as the two cars raced downhill in tandem.

Karl's investigator must be crazy. Had Louise Peterson actually thought Allison would turn herself in, hand over her daughter, without a fight? If she could just make it to the bottom of the hill without skidding off the road or hitting an uphill-bound vehicle, Allison thought, her father could help her either elude or confront Louise. It was the only chance they had. Please let Daddy be on time, she prayed, please let him be there waiting for us.

The Volvo bumped over the dip that became a drainage ditch whenever it rained, a signal that the end of the road was near. Allison accelerated as she reached the parking circle. Thank God! There was Daddy's Honda and he was at the wheel. He was even wearing the red plaid shirt Allison had given him last Christmas. She honked the horn and waved frantically, signaling him to follow her back uphill. With Louise so close on her tail, she dared not stop here. From the corner of her eye, Allison saw her father start his car and begin to pull out. She continued around the circle and back onto the road in the uphill direction. As she rushed ahead, everything became a blur, everything except the road ahead and her pursuer's Chevrolet in her rear-view mirror.

As Allison escaped the parking circle and headed back uphill, Louise kept the Chevy close behind. But as soon as the investigator saw the sheriff's vehicle cut off the Honda and fall into line behind her Chevrolet, she slowed down, allowing Allison to increase her lead.

In her rear-view mirror, Louise saw the deputy in the passenger seat motioning to her to pull over into one of the turnoffs and let the squad car pass, but she pretended not to see him. Each time she neared a wide spot in the road, she increased her speed to prevent the squad car's getting past her. Whenever the road was too narrow for two cars, she slowed down. If she could effectively keep the road blocked this way, Louise hoped, Allison and Stephanie might have at least some chance of escape.

A siren squealed. In the mirror, Louise saw the squad car's lights flash. She could no longer ignore the authorities, unless she was willing to risk jail. Braking to a halt in the narrowest part of the road, she turned off her engine, pulled the key from the ignition, and waited.

Aware only that the road behind her was momentarily deserted, Allison turned the Volvo sharply to the left and skidded into an unpaved private drive. Pulling behind a stand of eucalyptus trees, she stopped the car and shut off the engine. If she and Stephie were to have any chance of escape, she knew they couldn't hope to do it in the Volvo. It was clear now that Karl and his people knew about it. The only possible escape route she could see was to find a way to team up with her father and try to get out of Big Sur in his car.

"Mommy, I'm scared. Where's Grandpa?" Tears slid down Stephanie's cheeks.

"Don't cry, sweetie. Try to be brave, and stay real quiet, and we'll hide here for a while so they can't find us." Allison rolled down her window and listened for the noise of passing traffic beyond the trees. It seemed best to wait here, to let the private investigator think they'd made it back to Highway 1. Allison would have to find a way to reconnect with her father later.

Suddenly a siren pierced the air. Police! Were they looking for her now, too? She looked around frantically, but could see no way out of here.

Deputy Mott climbed out of the official vehicle and rushed toward Louise, who lowered her window obediently. "What's the matter, Officer?" she asked.

"Get out of the way, lady. You're blocking the road."

"Oh, gee, I'm sorry. When I heard the siren and saw your lights, I thought you wanted me to stop. I couldn't figure out what I could've done wrong, though. I always try to be such a careful—"

"Just move out of the way. *Now!*"

"Sure, no problem. Be happy to, Officer." Louise inserted the key in the ignition, then bent it hard to the right, exerting as much force as she could muster. The key snapped in two. "Oh dear, look at that," she said, holding up a section of the broken key for the deputy's inspection. "I don't know how that happened. My key just broke right off in the ignition. Now how am I going to get my car started?"

The three other men exited the sheriff's car and surrounded Louise.

"What the fuck are you doing here?" Karl Warren demanded.

"I—I was just trying to help," Louise replied. "I'm sorry. Looks like I just made a mess of things." Playing stupid was a new role for Louise, an uncomfortable one she wasn't sure she could pull off successfully. She saw Pete glowering at her, but he kept his mouth shut. He had nothing to gain by exposing his wife's defection.

From his Honda, Tim saw the two big men emerge from the back of the squad car in front of him and head toward the Chevy blocking the road. He didn't know the sandy-haired guy, but he certainly recognized the dark-haired one. Tim now had a clear view of the goddamned bastard who had molested Stephie and was now trying to steal her away from Allie. There was no way Tim Mitchell was going to let that happen, not while he still drew breath. He couldn't see where Allie and Stephie were now, but with this crew on their tails, it didn't look like they had much chance of making a clean getaway. At least not without help.

Tim emerged from the Honda, his right hand wrapped firmly around the .38. Adrenaline flowing, he no longer felt shaky. He grabbed his dark blue windbreaker off the seat and tossed it over his right arm to conceal the gun from view, then marched determinedly toward his former son-in-law.

"Pervert!" he shouted.

Karl whirled and faced the frail old man.

Tim's voice was strong. "You're nothin' but a fuckin' pervert, a filthy, useless piece of shit!"

Karl's face turned purple. "Don't push me, old man. You know what's good for you, you'll shut your lying mouth."

Tim continued to advance on the larger man until they stood only inches apart. "You don't deserve to live, you son of a bitch. You'll never get my grandchild. I'm gonna see to that."

"Why you—" Karl lunged at him, but Tim managed to drop into a crouch, avoiding the blow. Tim squeezed the trigger, and the jacket over the revolver exploded. The first bullet hit Karl square in the stomach. Before he could double over, Tim fired a second round point blank into his chest. Karl was dead by the time he hit the ground.

The explosions reverberated loudly against the hills. Allison caught her breath. Gunshots! There was no mistaking their thunder, not for anyone who'd ever lived on a military base. Her father was down there, near the gunfire. She threw open the car door and stood, hands clenched, temples pounding. Had somebody—the police, or maybe that woman PI Karl had sent—had somebody shot Daddy?

"What banged, Mommy?" Stephanie's blue eyes were wide, but she was no longer crying. She sat buckled into her car safety seat, clutching Flopsy.

"I—I don't know, sweetie." Allison squinted through the woods, but the road wasn't visible from here; the bushes were too dense. "I think maybe I better go and try to see if Grandpa's all right. Can you stay here like a big girl and be real quiet until Mommy gets back?"

"I—I guess so."

"Just hang on tight to Flopsy and be quiet like a little bunny. I'll be back in a few minutes." Allison leaned into the car and planted a wet kiss on her daughter's cheek, then set out in the direction of the beach road.

Allison crept along quietly, doing her best to keep out of sight. She rounded the last curve, then made her way slowly to the top of a small rise. From here she could see three vehicles stopped on the road below—the Chevrolet Louise Peterson had been driving, the county sheriff's car, and her father's Civic. Daddy was down there ... somewhere. But where? Crouching low behind the bushes, she moved closer.

A police radio crackled. A deputy spoke into it. Allison could pick up only a few of his words. "—dead man—suspect's an old—got—custody—"

Oh, Lord, somebody's been shot, shot dead. Where was her father? She had to see him, to make sure he was all right. What was going on down there?

Moving on her hands and knees, Allison crept through the bushes, closer to the police action. The branches tore at her flesh, but she barely noticed. She saw Louise Peterson standing by the side of the road, a hand clapped over her mouth. And a big, blond man. Wasn't that Karl's other detective, Pete?

Closer, just a little closer. Now Allison could see a bundle—no, not a bundle, a person—on the ground. A flash of red plaid— Oh, God, no! It was Daddy. Something had gone horribly wrong and the police had shot Daddy. Thrusting the sharp branches aside, Allison sprang to her feet.

Startled, Deputy Mott turned and spotted Allison. "There she is! That's the woman."

Allison tried to run, but the bushes tripped her and she fell. She got up and tried to move, flailing at the branches. Brambles cut her skin.

The deputy sprinted up the rise. "Stop!" he ordered, closing in fast.

"No, no! Please," Allison cried as the deputy's hand closed tight around her bleeding arm. "Let me go. *Please* let me go. My daughter—my poor baby—"

66

Stephanie sat dutifully in her carseat, just like Mommy had told her to, but Mommy had been gone a long time now. In the terrified child's mind, it seemed hours had passed, although it had been far less. As she hugged Flopsy close to her chest and listened to the wind whistling through the tops of the eucalyptus trees, her fear grew. Why didn't Mommy come back? Had the bad people who wanted to make her live with Daddy caught Mommy? Grandpa, too? Maybe now the bad people would come after her and Flopsy.

She had to find Mommy. She pushed on the seat belt release button with all her strength. It snapped open. She unlocked the Volvo's door and pushed against it. As she jumped to the ground, the dry grass crackled beneath the soles of her red sneakers. Clutching Flopsy tightly in her left hand, the child headed in the direction she thought she'd seen her mother go.

She emerged from the grove of trees into a field and looked around, but Mommy was nowhere in sight. There was a big white house and a red barn off to the right, with a dog sleeping in the yard. Had Mommy gone there?

Stephanie started toward the house, but as she walked, she saw a man come out of the barn. He was a very big man, as big as Daddy. But it wasn't Daddy. This big man had yellow hair, like Mommy's used to be, and a bushy beard. The dog lurched to its feet and scurried to the man, who smiled and pulled its ears. The child turned away and hurried in the opposite direction, toward a high hill. "Come on, Flopsy," she said. "We gotta get away fast." The man could be one of the bad people.

The long grasses and weeds on the hillside tickled Stephanie's short bare legs and made them itch as she climbed, putting distance between herself and the big bad man. But she didn't stop to scratch. She climbed higher and higher, falling once and skinning her knee. It bled a little and she felt like crying, but she didn't want the bad man to hear and come after her. So she buried her face in Flopsy's worn fur and whimpered. Then she got to her feet and trudged ahead.

A lone seagull soared above. Now Stephanie could hear the ocean's distant roar. The wind blew harder and she shivered in her yellow tank top and shorts. Was Mommy at the beach? If she got to the top of the hill, maybe she could see Mommy and call to her. Hugging herself for warmth, the child journeyed upward.

Deputy Mott located the Volvo in the grove of trees, where the Warren woman had said it would be, but it was empty. The passenger door stood ajar and the little girl was nowhere in sight. He used his walkie-talkie to communicate with his partner, who was waiting for backup at the crime scene. "Kid's not here. Looks like she got out of the car and wandered off. I'll look around for her. Out."

He headed toward the white farmhouse.

Stephanie reached the top of the hill. She could see the beach and the huge waves from here, the one where she and Mommy had built a sand castle. She knew it was the same beach because she could see the big black rocks and the sea caves down below. Mommy had shown her how waves came right through the holes in the caves.

There were lots of people walking and sitting on the beach, but they were a long way away and the child couldn't tell if Mommy was down there. She could see a woman with curly red hair like Mommy's was now, but she wasn't with Grandpa. She was with another lady and a small black dog. Stephanie aimed Flopsy's drooping head in the direction of the red-haired woman. "Is that Mommy, Flopsy?" Flopsy didn't answer. "Mommy! Mommy!" Stephanie called. But her small voice was lost in the wind and no one heard her.

Stephanie wanted to climb down to the beach and find Mommy, but while the route she had taken uphill from the car was a gradual one, the ocean side of the hill was much steeper—a virtual cliff. As she moved along the edge of the precipice, searching for a route down, her small sneakers dislodged lumps of pale brown dirt. The dirt clods tumbled down the hill, gradually at first, then with rapidly increasing speed. When they hit bottom, they splattered into dozens of small pieces.

The farmer said he had not seen a little girl, but he offered to help Deputy Mott look for her. The two men started their search by heading uphill, away from the farmhouse.

"Grass is trampled here," the farmer pointed out. "Little kid could've come through here easy."

The elevation increased and the men rounded a bend. Mott spotted a flash of yellow at the crest of the hill. He shaded his eyes from the sun and squinted. It looked like the Warren kid, all right. He picked up speed and shouted. "Stephanie. Stephanie! Wait there! We're coming to get you."

Stephanie heard a voice calling her name, a man's

voice. She spun around and saw two big men heading uphill toward her. One of them knew her name. The other one looked a lot like the man who had pulled the dog's ears. Terrified, she hesitated a moment, then bolted in the other direction. The bad people had found her! She had to get away. She had to find Mommy. She darted along the edge of the cliff, but there was nowhere to hide. The men were advancing along the route she had taken uphill, so she couldn't double back, and it was too steep here to climb safely down to the water. As the men closed in on her, she perched at the cliff's edge, frozen in fear. The dirt beneath her feet began to crumble.

"Them cliffs ain't too stable," the farmer said. "Ain't safe for her to be that close to the edge."

"Stephanie, get back," Mott called to her, panting now with the exertion of the climb. "Get back or you'll fall."

Her small brow furrowed, the child clutched her stuffed rabbit and edged away from her pursuers. "I want my Mommy!" she shrieked. "I want my Mommy!" The dirt slipped from beneath her feet and she fell, landing face down. She slid over the edge.

The deputy's heart leapt as the child sank from his view. "Holy shit! The kid's gone over." He and the farmer sprinted the remaining distance.

Near the brink of the cliff, Mott fell to his knees, then stretched out on his stomach. "Stay back," he ordered the farmer. "Dirt here won't support the two of us." He wriggled his prone body closer to the brink, careful not to dislodge more of the unstable cliffside. Peering over the precipice, he spotted her. About a dozen feet below, clinging precariously to a narrow ledge and whimpering, was the little girl. Her face and clothing were smeared with dirt, but she still clutched a filthy stuffed animal. "Stay still,

Stephanie, honey," he called to her. "Stay real still and we'll get you out."

"No!" Stephanie shouted. "Go 'way! I want my Mommy!" Her eyes wide, she wriggled her bottom along the narrow ledge, trying to increase the distance between herself and her would-be rescuer.

Mott bit down hard on his lower lip. Son of a bitch! The kid was obviously afraid of him. And if she moved around anymore on that ledge, it was likely to disintegrate, sending her flying downward to her death. It wouldn't do a damned bit of good for Mott to try to climb down after her. That ledge sure as hell wasn't going to hold his weight. "I'm not going to hurt you," he called. "Just stay real still so you don't fall and we'll get more help." He inched his way backward.

Allison sat in the grass at the side of the squad car, her wrists handcuffed behind her back, and looked around. Karl's body lay sprawled on the ground, awaiting the medical examiner's team. As she looked at him, she felt nothing. Not anger, not relief, not regret, just nothing. All her emotions now were being consumed in other directions.

Louise and Pete Peterson sat in the rented Chevrolet, both gesturing animatedly. Allison could not hear what they were saying, but she could tell they were engaged in a heated argument.

She wanted to cry as she saw her father sitting handcuffed in the backseat of the sheriff's car, his gray head bowed. From where she sat, she could hear his labored breathing, but the deputy wouldn't let her talk to him, even to offer him comfort. The cop insisted he wasn't about to "let the two of you concoct some kind of story." That was a joke. As though Tim Mitchell had enough energy left to concoct anything. Allison could see that her father wouldn't even be alive much longer unless he got medical help soon.

She could not tell how much time had passed since the taller deputy had spotted and grabbed her at the side of the road. Surely he would be back with Stephanie any minute now. Allison both craved and dreaded her daughter's arrival. She wanted to see her, to reassure her, before they took her away to . . . to what? A foster home, probably. Yet she didn't want the poor child to be hit by this gruesome scene—her father lying dead in the road, her mother and grandfather arrested and handcuffed like common criminals. *Oh,baby*, she thought, her eyes brimming, *I tried so hard, but all I've managed to do is fail you miserably.*

The police radio crackled and the deputy crawled back inside the squad car. Allison could hear only bits and pieces of the conversation. "—kid fell—steep cliff—chopper might be—"

Slowly it dawned on her. They were talking about Stephanie. Something terrible had happened to Stephanie! Allison pushed herself awkwardly to her feet. "What have you done to my child?" she demanded. "Where is my baby? I want my baby!" She ran toward the squad car.

"Hold it, lady." The deputy told her what had happened, adding that he had called for a rescue helicopter. "They'll get your daughter back safe. Don't you worry, now." His heavy-lidded brown eyes betrayed his own doubts.

"No, no. Don't you see? Stephie's terrified of men. He—he made her afraid." Allison thrust her head toward Karl. "Let me help. Please." Tears rolled down her face. She couldn't stand here, bound and helpless, while Stephanie fell to her death. She just couldn't. "*Please!*"

"There's nothin' I can do about it, lady. I've got

to stay here and I can't just let you go running off by yourself."

Sirens sounded in the distance.

"They're coming. Help is coming. Please, when the others get here, let me go to Stephie. Come with me if you want to, but I've got to go to her. Before it's too late."

Stephanie huddled on the ledge, her chin resting on her knees, and looked out at the churning sea. She shivered in the harsh wind. Most of the people on the beach below were leaving now, heading back to their cars with their children and their dogs. She still couldn't see where Mommy was, and she was afraid to look above her. She was scared that the bad people would still be there, trying to get her. Her lower lip quivered and she wept.

"What you need's this here rope," the farmer said. He had gone to his barn and returned with a thick coil of jute. "Lower a man over the edge and grab the kid before she falls."

Deputy Mott shook his head. "Take a good look at that ridge she's on. Add a man's weight to it and it's going to crumble just like that." He snapped his fingers. "Even ease a man over the edge there and chances are the falling dirt he'll dislodge will knock the kid off her perch. Hills around here are nothing but packed sand. Put pressure on them and they fall apart." He turned and looked behind him. His partner was approaching with the Warren woman. She was no longer handcuffed, but Mott didn't think she'd run for it, not with her kid in danger. He actually was glad the mother was coming. She could help keep the child calmed down until the chopper arrived.

"I'm going after her," Allison said when she'd assessed the situation. "Tie that rope around me and lower me down to her."

Deputy Mott repeated his argument about the instability of the cliff.

"Damn it, Stephie could fall any minute if somebody doesn't get her off of there. I weigh a good hundred pounds less than any of you do. I can make it. I know I can."

Mott looked at Allison. She was a small woman, all right, didn't really weigh much. And the helicopter rescue presented a big risk, too. The wind generated by the chopper's rotors might dislodge as much dirt as lowering somebody over the side to rescue the little girl, maybe more.

"*Please*. She's my daughter. I can't just let her sit there."

Mott nodded. Two minutes later, the deputies had tied the rope securely around Allison's chest, under her armpits. "Stay as still as you can, Angel," she called to Stephanie. "Mommy's coming to get you."

Stephanie looked up. She could see a pair of legs coming down over the side of the cliff above her and she could hear her mother's voice.

"Don't move, sweetheart. Mommy's coming." Allison's armpits burned as the rope cut into them. Yet the pain was nothing next to her fear. A clod of dirt tumbled down, hitting the ledge where Stephanie was huddled. It split into pieces and rolled downhill. Let me reach her in time, Allison prayed. Just let me reach her in time. She angled her feet against the wall of the cliff, as she'd seen mountain climbers do, but each place she touched dislodged more dirt the instant her foot made contact.

"Mommy! Mommy, I'm scared."

Me, too, Allison thought, but she said, "It's all right, Steph. I'm coming. Just stay right there." It wasn't much farther now, she told herself, not really much farther. Just a few more feet. The trick was to reach Stephanie quickly and get her out of there, before the hillside turned into an avalanche. The rope slackened a bit and, holding her breath, Allison slid the remaining distance.

Stephanie was only three or four feet to her left now, clutching Flopsy in desperation. Allison inched her way nearer. "When I get close enough to you, put your arms around my neck and hold on real tight," she said. "We'll go back up the hill together, but I need you to hold onto me just as tight as you can."

"Now!" Allison reached for her daughter and half lifted her off the crumbling ledge. The movement dislodged the remaining clumps of dirt. Allison could hear a whooshing sound as the clods rolled down the hillside, and then a series of thuds as they hit and broke apart.

With the child's added weight, the rope cut unmercifully into Allison's underarms. "I've got her," she yelled. "Pull us back up." Pain shot through her back and shoulders. "Hold on tight around my neck." Stephanie clung to her mother. Allison loosened her grip on the child, holding her tightly with her left hand while she grabbed the rope overhead with her right to release some of the pressure on her armpits.

Suddenly Stephanie let go of her mother's neck. "Flopsy!" she screamed. "Flopsy falled!" She jerked her head to watch as the bunny catapulted downward.

Allison released her hold on the rope and grabbed her daughter. The two spun around, dangling precariously. Gritting her teeth against the shooting pains above her breasts, the mother kicked out at the side of the cliff to halt their spin.

Half a dozen more sharp tugs on the rope brought them to safety. Allison stumbled over the edge. Clinging to Stephanie, she fell to the grass.

Both mother and daughter lay sobbing with pain, relief, and fear as Deputy Mott cut the rope away.

67

"I'm not finding anything important in this desk," Louise said, as she poked through legal pads, phone messages, pens, and pencils. "Could Karl have set aside one of those file drawers for his personal papers?"

Two days after Karl Warren's death, the private investigator was trying to fulfill promises she'd made to Allison. First, Louise had spent over an hour below the cliffs at Pfeiffer Beach in search of Stephanie's cherished stuffed rabbit and had managed to return it to the terrified child. Now, she was engaged in a legal task. Assisted by Karl's longtime personal secretary, Thea Mueller, Louise was searching the dead attorney's office for his will and life insurance policies.

Allison remained in the Monterey County jail, awaiting extradition to Wisconsin. Judge Royall Winston, who had ruled in Karl's favor in the custody case, was enraged over the attorney's murder. Rumor had it that the judge planned to deal harshly with Allison after she was returned to his jurisdiction.

Allison's main concern, of course, was Stephanie, who was being cared for temporarily at a Monterey foster home. Allison was frantic with worry over what would happen to her child if she ended up in prison. Louise promised she would do whatever she could to see that Stephanie was well taken care of—

perhaps by Allison's sister, Ruth—if Allison did indeed go to prison.

The first item on Louise's agenda was to determine whether Karl's estate would go to his only child. Money couldn't substitute for two loving parents, but in Louise's opinion, having it could only help Stephanie. In addition to the basic necessities of life, this little girl was going to need intensive psychotherapy, maybe for years to come. And psychotherapy cost money. It seemed only right that Karl Warren should be the one to pay for it—dead or alive.

"I don't remember ever seeing any special files like that," Thea said, opening a file cabinet. A matronly, gray-haired woman, her eyes were red from weeping. Karl Warren might not have been the world's greatest employer, but having your boss murdered—that was too much for any secretary to handle. "Only thing in here is case records."

"Shit." Thea shot Louise a disapproving look, which the PI ignored. "What about a safety deposit box? You ever see a numbered key around here?"

Thea shook her head.

"Try the bookcase, then, will you? Maybe he stashed something there. I'll just finish up on the desk." Louise pulled open the lower right-hand drawer. Like the others, it was filled to the brim. Here she saw telephone books for Wood Lake, Superior, and Duluth. Nothing of use there. But the drawer seemed quite deep. Maybe there was something underneath the phone books. She lifted them out. That was strange. The phone books were only five, maybe six inches deep, yet they seemed to fill this big drawer completely.

Louise stared at the empty bin. There was definitely something wrong here. She reached underneath and felt along the guides. There seemed a good four inches between her hand and what appeared to be the bottom of the drawer. Was it a false bottom?

"Thea, come here a minute. Help me get this thing all the way out."

The two women jiggled and pulled the heavy drawer until they got it out of the desk. They laid it on the floor and Louise rapped her knuckles on the interior; the bottom portion sounded hollow. At the very back was a small round hole. She crooked her index finger inside it and, bracing herself, pulled sharply upward. The false bottom opened.

"Holy Christ!" Louise said.

Both women gasped and stared. Inside were pages ripped from magazines, photographs, videotapes— every form of child pornography imaginable. Children alone, children with adults, children with other children, children with animals. Louise's stomach turned. What kind of people could look at this filth and find it sexually stimulating? She answered her own question—men like Karl Warren.

She sifted through the contents of the drawer, feeling increasingly contaminated, as though she were dipping her hands in raw sewage. Yet she felt compelled to find out what was here, to learn how deep Karl's infection had run. At the very bottom was an unmarked manila envelope, held shut by a well-worn brass clasp. Louise opened it and pulled out a stack of Polaroid pictures. It took a moment for their subject to register. "My God! How could he? How could the bastard do this?" The photos fell from her hands to the floor.

Louise and Thea stared open-mouthed at the pictures. They were all poses of little Stephanie Warren—naked—from the time she was a toddler until only a few months ago. Home studio shots, these were in many ways tame compared with the professional material hidden in the desk. Yet they were somehow more shocking; these had been taken by the child's own father.

"I just don't understand it," Thea said, gnawing on her plump knuckles. "Mr. Warren wasn't a stupid man; he was an attorney. If—if he did this, if he took these pictures, why on earth didn't he get rid of them before Mrs. Warren took him to court?"

Louise thought she knew the answer. "For the same reason he molested his daughter," she said. "Because he thought he was entitled. He kept these pictures because he thought he could do any damned thing he wanted to . . . and get away with it."

68

"Allison Warren!" the jail matron shouted. Allison's head turned at the sound of her name. "Get your things together. You're leaving."

So, Allison thought, she was being sent back to Wisconsin this quickly. She had expected the extradition proceedings to take a lot longer. She'd been here only four days, though it felt more like a century. Since she was booked and locked in this cell, the hours had passed with excruciating slowness. She had been unable to eat and she'd slept only a handful of hours since the nightmare at Pfeiffer Beach. Her body ached. Her back and chest were still deeply bruised and rope-burned from her rescue of Stephanie, and her arms and legs were full of scratches. Yet her many wakeful hours were haunted more by her anguish over the fates of her daughter and her father, and by the constant din of noise in this cage for humans. She felt she was going mad. How did people manage to survive here? Human beings were supposed to be able to get used to almost anything, but Allison couldn't yet understand how.

Listlessly, she gathered up the few possessions she'd been allowed to keep in her cell—a toothbrush, a comb, a bottle of shampoo, deodorant. Everything else had been confiscated before she was booked. But she probably wouldn't need much where she was going. One thing about prison—you didn't need much. They gave you clothes, food, the basics. Anything beyond that, you had to do without. Without choices, without privacy, without your family . . . But she couldn't let her thoughts get started along that track again. If she kept thinking about never seeing her father alive again, and about how long it might be before she could be with Stephie, she wouldn't be able to stand it. She'd slowly and surely lose her mind.

The matron, a muscular woman with permed black hair, opened the cell door and ushered Allison out. "You don't look all that happy about leaving," she said. "You gonna miss us? Ha! That'd be a first."

"Happy?"

"Most of the girls can't wait to see the last of this place. But you look like you'd just as soon stay."

Allison shrugged. "I figure it's all the same to me. No reason the Wisconsin jail's going to be any improvement."

"Wisconsin?"

"I'm being extradited, right?"

A smile crept across the matron's tanned face and she began to laugh. "Hey, girl, didn't they give you that message from your PD? This damn place! Nothin' ever gets done right. You're getting out and, far as I know, it's for good. The charges against you have been dropped."

Louise Peterson was waiting as Allison signed the release papers. Louise was tired, too, but she felt better than she had in days. She'd taken the red-eye from Chicago to San Francisco, then rented a car and driven two hours south to the county jail in Salinas. But she wasn't about to miss being present when Allison got the good news.

"Did you do this?" Allison asked, her lined face betraying her tension.

Louise smiled and nodded. "I had a hand in it."

Allison bit her lip. "Whatever you did, thank God. I—I was so scared. I thought Judge Winston was going to put me away for life. I thought I'd never see my baby—" She burst into tears.

Louise placed an arm around Allison's thin shoulders. "Come on now, it's all over. Everything's going to be okay." When Allison had dried her tears, Louise explained: "You might say the judge saw the light—the light of negative publicity, that is." She told about finding Karl's cache of child pornography, including the pictures he'd taken of Stephanie. "So I went to see Judge Winston and showed him this stuff. At first he gave me some bull about how maybe his custody decision had been off base, but that wasn't *his* fault—he'd had to rule on the evidence presented and this garbage wasn't in it. Besides, he said a man had been murdered and he couldn't just forget about that."

"Sounds like him. Covering his backside."

"Yeah, well, I pointed out that he was leaving plenty of his ass open to view, the way I saw it. That he'd better rethink his stand if he wanted to stay on the bench. After all, a case like this one could get national publicity. You know—Oprah, Phil, Geraldo, maybe even a spot on 'Sixty Minutes.' Especially if there was a high-profile court trial and the mother ended up serving prison time for nothing more than rightfully trying to protect her kid. I thought it ought to make pretty interesting viewing.

"So Judge Winston thought it all over in context of next fall's election and decided to change his tune. He realized it might be prudent to avoid playing the bad guy in this thing . . . any more than he already has, of course."

"So he dropped the contempt charge."

"And he leaned on the Feds to forget about the parental kidnapping rap. The murder accessory charge was never any good in the first place; they never could've made it stick. So you're free and clear, Allison. You and Stephanie can live a normal life again."

"A normal life." Allison's chin began to quiver once more, but she swallowed hard and held onto her composure. "I'm not even sure I know what a normal life is anymore."

"Maybe it's like riding a bicycle—it all just comes back to you." Louise led the way to her car. "At least now you can afford a psychologist to help Stephanie put all this behind her. As soon as Karl's will is probated, she'll be a pretty wealthy little girl."

Allison smiled. "Can I go pick her up now? Where is she?"

"Ah, bureaucrats, you can never hurry them. She's supposed to be at the county welfare office in Monterey at noon. There was something about how they had to send a social worker to the foster home to pick her up and no one was available until then. We've got a couple of hours. I thought you might like to see your dad."

"I—I was just tryin' to help, Allie." Tim Mitchell lay in the jail ward of the county hospital, a clear plastic oxygen mask covering his nose and mouth and an intravenous tube in his left arm. He was skeleton thin and his skin was gray. The wrinkled hand Allison held in hers was icy cold. She leaned closer to hear his faint words. "I was tryin' to help, but they told me you got put in jail."

"It's okay, Daddy. They let me out now and I'm going to go get Stephie in just a little while. Everything's going to be okay."

"Where's Ruthie?"

"I just talked to her. She says Vern's going to drive her to Minneapolis to catch a plane. She'll be here late tonight."

The old man's eyes closed and he seemed to doze

off. The doctor said he was heavily sedated, in no pain, but he didn't have much time left. It was time to call in the family.

Allison looked around her at the spartan room. There were three other beds in this long narrow chamber, two of them occupied by other ill prisoners. There was no privacy; jail wards didn't offer privacy. If her father weren't near death, he wouldn't even be allowed visitors. This was not where she wanted her father to die. "Daddy? Daddy, can you hear me?"

Tim's eyelids fluttered open. "I hear you, Allie."

"I just—I feel so bad. If it weren't for me, you wouldn't be here, in this awful place. I just want you to know how sorry I am."

"You didn't put me in here, girl. Not your fault. I got cancer."

"I mean *here*, in a jail ward. At least you could be in a regular hospital."

"I pulled the trigger, not you."

"But I should've been able to handle things myself, Daddy. It wasn't your responsibility. I should've known what would happen . . . somehow. I should've been able to take care of it myself."

Tim's grasp on his daughter's hand tightened. "You got a bum deal, Allie," he whispered, "and I owed you . . . plenty. This was—this was my chance to pay off a little. I know I was a lousy dad. But it wasn't 'cause I didn't love you." Out of breath, he gulped in oxygen with a wrenching guttural sound.

"You all right, Daddy? Want me to call the doctor?"

"Not—not used to talkin'."

"You don't have to talk. Just rest."

Tim's eyes closed once more and he slept.

Allison held his hand gently, feeling the increasingly faint throbbing of his pulse. She leaned over and whispered into his ear, "I always loved you, too,

Daddy." Gently, she kissed his withered cheek, then moved quietly away.

Allison was at the county welfare office in Monterey half an hour early. She wanted to meet Stephie alone, so she'd asked Louise to drop her off in front of the building. Now, unable to sit still, she paced the floor in the waiting room, checking the big wall clock every few minutes. What was taking so long? She approached the receptionist for the third time. "Excuse me. I was supposed to pick up my daughter here at noon and it's already almost quarter after." She pointed at the clock. "Is there any message for me?"

"No, Mrs. Warren. If I had a message, I'd let you know. They're just late. Now please take a seat and I'll call you as soon as—"

"Mommy!"

Allison's heart leapt and she turned. A woman pushed open the double doors behind her and Stephanie shot through them.

"Mommy!"

Her vision blurred with tears, Allison dropped to her knees. Stephie flung herself into her arms and held on for dear life.

Allison buried her nose in her daughter's neck and breathed in her little-girl scent. "Oh, sweetheart, I missed you so much. I missed you so much I could hardly stand it."

Stephanie loosened her grip and tilted back her head. "Me and Flopsy knowed you'd come," she said. "We knowed you'd come and get us."

"Me, too," Allison said. Then she could no longer speak. She could only hold her daughter close and make a silent vow that she'd never, ever let her go again.

ON THE EDGE OF YOUR SEAT!

☐ **SEE MOMMY RUN by Nancy Baker Jacobs.** She became a fugitive from the law and her husband—in order to save her child from unspeakable abuse. (172299—$4.99)

☐ **PRESSURE DROP by Peter Abrahams.** Nina Kitchener has no idea what lay behind the disappearance of her baby from a New York hospital. And nothing will stop her terror-filled quest for the donor who fathered her child . . . nothing—not even murder. (402359—$4.95)

☐ **SOUL/MATE by Rosamond Smith.** A psychopathic serial killer with a lover's face . . . "Headlong suspense . . . What if a well-meaning, intelligent woman should encounter a demonic twin?"—*The Atlanta Journal and Constitution.* "Taut, relentless, chilling!"—*Chicago Tribune.* (401905—$4.95)

☐ **NEMSIS by Rosamond Smith.** "A terror-invoking psychothriller brimming with atmosphere."—*Cleveland Plain Dealer.* "Extraordinary . . . a murder mystery with a literary twist . . . rich in social observation and psychological insight . . . well-written . . . the dialogue has rhythm, pitch, melody and mood"—*Boston Globe* (402952—$5.50)

Prices slightly higher in Canada.

Buy them at your local bookstore or use this convenient coupon for ordering.

NEW AMERICAN LIBRARY
P.O. Box 999, Bergenfield, New Jersey 07621

Please send me the books I have checked above.
I am enclosing $_____ (please add $2.00 to cover postage and handling). Send check or money order (no cash or C.O.D.'s) or charge by Mastercard or VISA (with a $15.00 minimum). Prices and numbers are subject to change without notice.

Card #_____ Exp. Date _____
Signature_____
Name_____
Address_____
City _____ State _____ Zip Code _____

For faster service when ordering by credit card call **1-800-253-6476**
Allow a minimum of 4-6 weeks for delivery. This offer is subject to change without notice.

⊘ SIGNET BOOKS

Exciting Fiction
From Joy Fielding

(0451

☐ **KISS MOMMY GOODBYE.** He kidnapped the children! An ex husband's ultimate revenge. This handsome, twisted man woul lead Donna on a terror-filled quest to find her little boy and girl tha would take her across the country and beyond the law . . . " knockout!"—*The New York Times* (155068—$4.50

☐ **THE DEEP END.** A novel of domestic terror. The stranger's call let no room for doubt. "You've been a bad girl," he said. "I'm goin to take down your panties and spank you . . . and then I'm goin to kill you . . ." She was in trouble. "Heartstopping!"— *Richmon Times Dispatch* (148029—$4.50

☐ **THE OTHER WOMAN.** "Hello, I'm Nicole Clark. I'm going to marr your husband." The message was clear, but what wasn't clear wa what Jill could do to save her perfect marriage and her attractiv husband from the sexy and clever Nicole. Jill knew what it meant t be David's mistress, she knew everything that could happen. Bu she didn't know what to do about it . . . (125509—$4.95

☐ **LIFE PENALTY.** Her child is murdered—and when the police fail i their investigation, a mother's grief turns into a searing quest fo revenge. Daring him to strike again, she embarks upon a spine chilling search through a dark and dangerous underworld . . where only one of them can come out alive. . . .

(138481—$3.95

There's an epidemic with 27 million victims. And no visible symptoms.

It's an epidemic of people who can't read.

Believe it or not, 27 million Americans are functionally illiterate, about one adult in five.

The solution to this problem is you... when you join the fight against illiteracy. So call the Coalition for Literacy at toll-free 1-800-228-8813 and volunteer.

Volunteer Against Illiteracy. The only degree you need is a degree of caring.